BET AGAINST ME

Praise for Fiona Riley

Not Since You

"Riley strikes an impressive balance between steamy sex scenes and sweeping romance in this tender second-chance-at-love story...Riley endearingly captures the growth of Charlotte and Lexi's relationship from when they were in high school to when they are reunited as adults. Readers will root for this well-matched couple."— *Publishers Weekly*

Not Since You "is well written and hot. So hot."—*Jude in the Stars*

"This book has all the elements of a perfect romance—beautiful characters seeking to rekindle a lost love with heat and passion under sunny skies and starry nights on a cruise ship traveling to a tropical paradise."—*The Lesbian Book Blog*

"[A]n entertaining story with a lot of sexy scenes. Not surprisingly, this would be a good beach vacation read. I recommend to those who are interested in romance, second chances, vacationing, cruises, bartending, friends who collude, dirty talk, sexual tension, and packing (not luggage)."—*Bookvark*

"This book is exceptional lesbian fiction, and the characters (especially Charlotte) were swoon-worthy...honestly, I think I hugged my Kindle at one point...This is to date the sexiest book Fiona Riley has ever written and let me tell you, she has written some of the sexiest lesbian fiction scenes to date."—*Les Rêveur*

Media Darling

"What an extraordinary story that I wanted to start all over again when it was finished. WOW!...Once again Fiona Riley has blown me away in the bedroom department...or you know, the floor, kitchen or anywhere Emerson and Haley could get their hands on each other. I reckon her sex scenes are getting hotter and hotter with every book. Five Stars."—*Les Reveur*

"A great mix of characters, some great laughs, and a good romance. A great well written read that was emotional and fun."—*Kat Adams, Bookseller (QBD Books, Australia)*

"{A] sweet romance with the addition of a critique of the media role in their portrayal of celebrities. Both main characters are multi-layered with their personalities well defined. Their chemistry is absolutely off the charts…an entertaining, poignant and romantic story with a side of social critique to celebrity culture and the media. Five stars."
—*Lez Review Books*

"I really dig the way Fiona Riley writes contemporary romances because they're sexy and flirty with a whole lot of feelings, and *Media Darling* is no exception."—*The Lesbian Review*

Media Darling "was well-executed and the sex was well-written. I liked both of the characters and the plot held my interest."—*Katie Pierce, Librarian, Hennepin County Library (Minnesota)*

Room Service

"The sexual tension between Olivia and Savannah is combustible and I was hoping with every flirtious moment they would jump each other… [A] sexy summer read."—*Les Rêveur*

"*Room Service* is a slow-burn romance written from the point of view of both main characters. Ms. Riley excels at building their chemistry that slowly grows to sizzling hot."—*Lez Review Books*

"Riley is a natural when it comes to delivering the heat between characters and undeniable chemistry."—*Book-A-Mania*

"*Room Service* by Fiona Riley is a steamy workplace romance that is all kinds of fabulous…Fiona Riley is so good at writing characters who are extremely likeable, even as they have issues to work through. I was happy to see that the leading ladies in *Room Service* are no exception! They're both fun, sweet, funny, and smart, which is a brilliant combo. They also have chemistry that sizzles almost from the get-go, making it especially fun to watch them grow in ways that are good for them as individuals and as a couple."—*The Lesbian Review*

Strike a Match

"Riley balances romance, wit, and story complexity in this contemporary charmer…Readers of all stripes will enjoy this lyrically phrased, deftly plotted work about opposites attracting."—*Publishers Weekly*

"[A] quick-burning romance, with plenty of sex scenes hot enough to set off the alarms."—*RT Book Reviews*

"*Strike a Match* is probably one of the hottest and sexiest books I've read this year…Fiona Riley is one to watch and I will continue to get extremely excited every time I get one of her books to read."
—*Les Rêveur*

"While I recommend all of the books in the Perfect Match series, I especially recommend *Strike a Match*, and definitely in audio if you're at all inclined towards listening to books. Fans of the other two installments will be happy to see their leads again, but you don't have to have read them to pick this one up. It's sweet, hot, and funny, making it a great way to spend a day when you just want to hide away from the world and immerse yourself in a lovely story."—*Smart Bitches, Trashy Books*

"*Strike a Match* is Fiona Riley's best book yet. Whether you're a fan of the other books in the series or you've never read anything by her before, I recommend checking this one out. It's the perfect remedy to a bad day and a great way to relax on a weekend!"—*The Lesbian Review*

"I love this series and Sasha is by far my favourite character yet. I absolutely loved the gritty firefighter details. The romance between Abby and Sasha is perfectly paced and full of wonderful grand gestures, magical dates, and tender, intimate moments."—*Wicked Reads*

"Fiona Riley does a nice job of creating thorny internal and external conflicts for each heroine…I was rooting for Abby and Sasha, not only to be together, but also that both of them would grow and change enough to find a true HEA. The supporting cast of family members, friends, and colleagues is charming and well-portrayed. I'm looking forward to more from Fiona Riley."—*TBQ's Book Palace*

Unlikely Match

"The leads have great chemistry and the author's writing style is very engaging."—*Melina Bickard, Librarian, Waterloo Library (UK)*

"Two strong women that make their way towards each other with a tiny little nudge from some friends, what's not to like?"—*The Reading Penguin's Reviews*

"*Unlikely Match* is super easy to read with its great pacing, character work, and dialogue that's fun and engaging…Whether you've read *Miss Match* or not, *Unlikely Match* is worth picking up. It was the perfect romance to balance out a tough week at work and I'm looking forward to seeing what Fiona Riley has in store for us next."
—*The Lesbian Review*

Miss Match

"In this sweet, sensual debut, Riley brings together likable characters, setting them against a colorful supporting cast and exploring their relationship through charming interactions and red-hot erotic scenes… Rich in characterization and emotional appeal, this one is sure to please."—*Publishers Weekly*

"*Miss Match* by Fiona Riley is an adorable romance with a lot of amazing chemistry, steamy sex scenes, and fun dialogue. I can't believe it's the author's first book, even though she assured me on Twitter that it is."—*The Lesbian Review*

"This was a beautiful love story, chock full of love and emotion, and I felt I had a big grin on my face the whole time I was reading it. I adored both main characters as they were strong, independent women with good hearts and were just waiting for the right person to come along and make them whole. I felt I smiled for days after reading this wonderful book."—*Inked Rainbow Reads*

By the Author

Miss Match

Unlikely Match

Strike a Match

Room Service

Media Darling

Not Since You

Visit us at www.boldstrokesbooks.com

BET AGAINST ME

by
Fiona Riley

2020

THIS TRADE PAPERBACK ORIGINAL IS PUBLISHED BY
BOLD STROKES BOOKS, INC.
P.O. BOX 249
VALLEY FALLS, NY 12185

FIRST EDITION: SEPTEMBER 2020

CREDITS
EDITOR: RUTH STERNGLANTZ
PRODUCTION DESIGN: STACIA SEAMAN
COVER DESIGN BY TAMMY SEIDICK

Acknowledgments

Thank you to all of my BSB family and all of the amazing readers out there. Embarking on a new series is always a scary endeavor, but I've had the best support and encouragement along the way. Thank you so much.

To Dean Poritzky: thank you for all the help and the inside scoop into the world of luxury real estate. You were an invaluable resource and I am so grateful you took the time to meet and chat with me.

To Jeanne Press: thank you for introducing me to Dean! You're the best :)

To Kim Tran Dobrowski: Thank you for all your help with the Zhua Zhou. And thank Baby Brian for me, too.

To Ruth Sternglantz: I'd be lost without you, your grammar skills, and your infinite patience. Thanks for reworking every calendar you have to make this book come to fruition. You're too good to me.

And finally to Kris Bryant: Thank you for the long phone calls, the late night word sprints, and the endless encouragement. You're my writing rock and I love you. Now stop getting so distracted and catch up to my word count, you slacker.

For Jenn.

Thank you for taking a gamble on me.
You are my luckiest charm, my deepest love,
and having a family with you remains my greatest accomplishment.

You are my everything.

CHAPTER ONE

Trina Lee stood in front of her desk and looked to her right at the shelf lined with awards. She had sacrificed more than a few dates, more than a few girlfriends, and most of her weekends over the last five years to fill that shelf with an array of glittering, glistening, gleaming plaques and accolades that led her to this day, the day she'd be named Realtor of the Year. And honestly, she couldn't freaking wait.

"That's an impressive trophy shelf you've got there," Ellison Gamble, her boss and the owner of her realty office, Gamble and Associates, said from the doorway of Trina's corner office.

"There's always room for more," Trina replied, waving at the shelf as she looked at her boss. Ellison was leaning against the doorframe with that elegant, confident ease that she always seemed to embody. Nothing ever riled Ellison—she was calm and collected in the most intense of situations. That was one of the things that made her such a ferocious businesswoman. She was unshakable. And her success was legendary. At only forty-one, Ellison was the youngest owner of any luxury real estate office in Boston. Not to mention the most successful, at least in Trina's opinion. Ellison had it all, and Trina wanted to make Ellison proud, because she admired Ellison, and not just because of her amazing wardrobe. Luxury real estate was not for the weak or thin-skinned, and Ellison had helped Trina become who she was today. She owed her life to Ellison, or, at least, her trophy shelf. "Or, worst case scenario, I'll ask my boss for another shelf."

"I'm sure she'd be agreeable to that," Ellison replied. "You had an amazing year, Trina. You've had an amazing few years. Make sure that you enjoy yourself tonight, no matter the outcome."

Trina beamed at the compliment before a moment of insecurity crept in. "You'll be there, though, right?"

Ellison stood. "Of course. I wouldn't miss it." She held up her phone and pointed to it. "I have a conference call with Charles Langley, and then I'm meeting Talia at my place to get dressed."

"Oh, tell Talia I said thanks again for the dress recommendation," Trina said. Talia was Ellison's personal stylist, a contact Ellison had shared with her when they'd started working together. Brand representation and image were important to Ellison's business model, and that was fine by Trina since she had a weakness for shopping and designer clothes. She had a closet full of commission checks spent on Talia's clothing recommendations. She wouldn't change a single thing though—Talia had never steered her wrong. And that red dress she was going to slay in tonight was no exception.

"Will do." Ellison turned to leave.

A thought occurred to Trina. "Did you say Charles Langley? As in the new Harborside project in the Seaport, that Charles Langley?"

Ellison looked back over her shoulder and gave Trina a broad grin. "You're finally reading those emails I've been sending, huh?"

Trina made a face. "No. Well, *yes*, boss. But no, not really." She really should get better about those interoffice memos. The truth was she knew Charles Langley's name because he was quickly becoming the most sought-after luxury developer in the city. Everyone knew about the Harborside project. That luxury condominium complex had been under construction on the water's edge for over a year and a half. You couldn't drive through the Seaport without seeing Langley's construction vehicles and cranes littered everywhere. He was practically a fixture in the landscape there.

Ellison shook her head. "Suddenly I'm not so sure you're getting that extra award shelf."

"Just tell me—it's about the Harborside, right? Did you secure the contract? Tell me you did. Then tell me it's mine." Trina was practically salivating at the thought. If the preliminary mock-ups were any indication, Langley had spared no expense on those condos. And though they were still under construction, Trina was positive they would sell faster than he could finish them. And that was a very good thing for everyone involved.

"We're just having a friendly conversation," Ellison said with a wink. "But never say never."

Trina barely contained the squeal of excitement. "See you tonight, Ellison."

"Save me a seat at the table," Ellison said as she walked out of view.

Trina let her gaze settle on the framed magazine article featuring her photographed wearing her favorite crimson power suit. The picture was stunning and one she used for most of her social media and marketing, and the article was…well, it was kind of a dream come true. She had been named as one of Boston's 30 Under 30, and though it was considered a superfluous title by some, it had come at a time in Trina's life when she'd needed the professional acknowledgment to feel like she was doing some good in the world. While making buckets of money, that was. That list helped kick-start her best sales year to date, last year, the one she was nominated for tonight. In some ways, that magazine article had been the motivational kick in the pants she hadn't realized she needed.

"Are you done gloating to the boss about your awesomeness, and are you ready to go? We have hair, champagne, makeup, champagne, clothing, champagne…you know, all the essentials to get to before you take home the big prize tonight. Time's a-wasting, Lee." Lauren Calloway slipped through Trina's door and broke her from her reverie.

"Jeez, when you put it that way, it almost sounds like we're late. Which is preposterous because I'm never late. Which makes it even more unbelievable that you, Lauren Calloway, are my best friend and most trusted colleague, because you've never been on time for anything in your life," Trina teased. "You know, come to think of it, why are we even friends again?"

"You wound me." Lauren feigned offense and placed her hand over her heart. "We're friends because without me, your overly cocky, insufferable trophy-collecting ego would suck all the air out of the room and we'd all be as dead as"—she pointed to the graveyard of plants that lined one of Trina's windows—"those orchids you keep killing."

Trina sighed. She certainly lacked the green thumb her mother had. She liked to think she also lacked her mother's overly judgmental existence as well, seeing as she was able to maintain plenty of friendships. Granted, none of them were romantic, but still. Her mother was challenging to be around, but the woman had a way with plants. She made a mental note to bring the dead ones to her next time they crossed paths, which was as infrequently as Trina could make it these days. There was a collection of dead plants in her guest room at home that attested to this fact.

"It's true—I can't be trusted with flora or fauna," Trina acquiesced. "There you go again, talking about all the hot women you've conquered in your wake. Brag, brag, brag. Poor Flora and Fauna didn't stand a chance." Lauren bumped her hip as she joined her in leaning against the front of her desk.

"It was rather rude of me to date family members, wasn't it?" Trina rested her head on her best friend's shoulder. She was grateful to have a coworker and best friend in the same person. It made the occasional absurdity of this job easier to handle.

"Are we talking about the Patterson twins now? Or the fictional Flora and Fauna sisters I just made up?" Lauren paused before shifting away from Trina to gawk at her. "Wait, do you have something to tell me?"

Trina laughed. "No. We both know I'm married to this job, Lau. Who wants to date someone who's always working, never free on weekends, and constantly scanning social media for listing opportunities?"

"Another Realtor?" Lauren joked. "Just kidding, we both know that you could never handle that kind of competition outside of the bedroom."

"As if there would be any competition," Trina scoffed.

"And there's the ego I know and love," Lauren said. "You really should go on a date, though, Trina. I mean, you're the total package once you get past all that bravado and annoying successfulness."

"Are you hitting on me?" Trina pulled her friend into a hug and swayed them both side to side. Lauren being gay was an added bonus to their friendship. She'd spent many a night on Lauren's couch commiserating over women and how hard dating had become. Neither of them had been successful at it, but at least they were failing together.

"Alas, no. I could never live up to your punctuality standards," Lauren said before adding, "and you're way too short for me."

"Hey." Trina slapped her shoulder as Lauren wriggled away. "Five three is a perfectly acceptable height. Plus, in heels I'm the same height as you."

"Until *I* put on shoes, that is," Lauren said as she grabbed Trina's purse from her chair and handed it to her. "Let's just admit your affinity for the tallest possible heels is so you can be more like me, your best friend and most loyal confidant."

"I hate you." Trina took the purse and followed Lauren toward her office door.

"Lies, all lies," Lauren said as she linked arms with her. "So, are you ready for tonight?"

"Yes," Trina said without hesitation. She'd gone over the numbers and sales again and again, and the fact was her competition didn't hold a candle to her successes. Except for that mysterious Kendall Yates. She didn't know much about her, but her sales had been impressive, especially since she'd done them, it appeared, exclusively alone. Trina prided herself on her solo accomplishments, but she had a great team at Gamble and Associates, and she would often buddy-up on properties. She'd learned long ago that luxury real estate was more of a community job than a solitary one. With the support of Lauren and the other agents at Gamble, and the help of junior agent Jax, whom she was more than a little indebted to, she was able to take big risks and know that she had backup if she needed it. She had a support system of people who trusted her to make the right decision and lead the charge if need be, but who would also be there to help her if she needed them. Like, if she locked herself out of her office, or if she'd ordered too much Thai food when she was sleep deprived and blindly using her food delivery app during an office meeting. They were good people and she was glad to be around them.

"Good. Because Ellison is going to have a bronze bust of your head made when you close this deal tonight," Lauren deadpanned. "I heard she plans to put it at the entrance to the bathrooms. Like a greeter of sorts."

"That's a terrifying notion." Trina thought of people rubbing the head for good luck after their bathroom trip when they probably didn't wash their hands, and she shuddered. "And gross. Totally gross."

She thought about Lauren's teasing for a moment. She would be lying if she didn't admit that a large part of her wanted to make Ellison proud. Because it was Ellison who had helped her realize that though success came from hard work, it also came from teamwork. Which is why she was so proud to be nominated this year—she'd done her homework, she'd put in her hours, she'd worked hard alone and as a team member. And she'd damn well earned this award. She deserved it. And that sense of accomplishment was something she had been chasing for longer than she'd like to admit.

As she turned to close her office door and flick off the light, she let her gaze settle on the orchid graveyard. She wasn't the best at everything, but she knew she was the best at selling properties. She'd had a gift for it since she'd first stumbled onto the career while in college. Her parents had balked when she took her psychology degree to the Real Estate Board, but her schooling had served her well. She was great with people, she was patient and understanding, and she knew how to gauge just the right amount of pressure to apply or space to give a client. But she was damn competitive, too. And even though her mother never approved of her career path, she'd silenced her father with that first big luxury home sale commission check. She'd chosen a path that her family didn't understand, but she was excelling in it, and she had no plans to stop anytime soon.

She shut off the light and closed the door. The promise of tonight's outcome made her vibrate with excitement. Because even though a career in horticulture probably wasn't in her future, there was one full of fast cash, expensive price tags, and the *rush* of closing a deal. And that part, well, that was something that never seemed to get old. She let herself bask in that as Lauren talked animatedly next to her in the elevator ride down to the lobby. She smiled because life was good. She'd done well for herself, and she was proud of that. Nothing could bring her down from this high she felt right now. Not one thing.

CHAPTER TWO

K endall Yates hated waiting. Like, really hated it. To say being forced to wait for something, or worse, someone, was a pet peeve of hers was the understatement of the century. And as she waited for her boss, Whitaker Sharkney, to stop schmoozing with every single human being who came through the door, she had visions of strangling him with that goofy bow tie he always wore.

"You look tense. You need a drink," Whitaker said as he waved over one of the waiters. He handed a champagne flute to Kendall as he guided her toward the balcony. "Relax. Drink up."

"Thanks," Kendall said as she accepted the glass so as not to be rude, though she had no intention of drinking tonight. She wanted to have her wits about her since this day seemed to only get worse, not better, as it went on.

The morning had started off with an awesome spin class with her bestie, Margo Channing, leading the exercise session. She'd had an all-star performance in class, but the success high quickly plummeted when she reached her office. She did not even have her coat off before news came in that a multi-million-dollar single home sale she'd effectively secured had suddenly fallen through. But the news about her father that followed shortly after was what made her feel like the world's largest stone was sitting in her stomach. And try as she might to focus on anything else, she couldn't. Because how did you ignore news that the man you hated more than anyone in the world had been released from prison? The uncertainty of what that meant for her was making her feel jittery.

So no champagne tonight, not even the celebratory kind, because the last thing she needed was to be uninhibited at a formal social event like the Northeast Real Estate Awards for fear that she might let the truth slip: Kendall was scared, for the first time in a long time. Because the walls that had kept him in had kept her safe, but with no walls, nothing would stop him from interfering with her life again. No amount of distance. No attempt at a new life. Nothing. Dick Yates took what he wanted when he wanted it, and if he wanted to take what little joy she had scrounged up since starting over these past few years, she knew he had the power and connections to do it.

"Ah, look at all those gleefully ignorant hopefuls out there," Whitaker said as they looked down at the ballroom below. "A roomful of hardworking agents waiting to accept their awards and not anticipating having to be gracious losers. But there's always a winner and a loser, right? And I can't wait for you to win tonight." He clinked his now near empty glass with her full one.

"We'll see," Kendall said as she gave him a small smile. His confidence was refreshing, but she knew that more than just numbers and sales went into this award. Realtor of the Year came with a long checklist of items that needed to be fulfilled before a candidate would even be considered. Aside from individual and team sales volume, considerable weight was given to community contribution, charitable work and service commitments completed in the calendar year, and the candidate's perceived integrity and adherence to the Code of Ethics of the industry. Oh, and no one with less than fifteen years' experience had ever been a contender. But times were changing, and of the four finalists this year, two were young rising stars in the industry, and Kendall was one of them.

She flipped open the program for tonight and scanned the faces of the finalists. The other superstar she was up against was Trina Lee, Gamble and Associates' lead agent, who had a reputation for being practically ruthless when closing a deal. And though Kendall had never met her in person, she'd traveled in her wake and seen the stats: Trina was the gold standard, a mirror of her mentor and boss, Ellison Gamble, who'd had a similar rocket-like start to her career. Ellison was an all-star in her own right—well, depending on who you talked to, Kendall thought.

Almost as if on cue, Whitaker tapped Trina's photograph and snorted. "I can't wait to see the look on Ellison's face when her prize pupil falls to the new kid in town." He patted her on the shoulder as he added, "They're not going to know what hit them."

"Why do you hate her so much?" Kendall blurted out before thinking better of it.

Whitaker paused. "Trina? She's too cocky."

"No." Kendall could sort of understand that opinion, assuming all those rumors she'd heard about Trina were true. "Ellison. Why do you hate Ellison?"

Whitaker appeared uncomfortable, adjusting his bow tie and pulling at his collar as he answered, "I don't *hate* her. I just think it's time that she realizes that there are other stars in this town besides the ones in her office. It's a testament to my faith in you, Kendall. That's all."

Kendall didn't believe that for a minute. She'd heard rumblings over the year and a half that she'd worked at Sharkney Realty that Ellison had been a protégé of Whitaker's, way back when. Kendall assumed he now resented her professionally because she'd been so successful on her own. Kendall could see how that would be frustrating for anyone. Seeing someone succeed in spite of you must be annoying as hell. She was damn sure that's how her father felt about her walking out on the family business three years ago.

Oh, what she would give to see his face if she won tonight. He'd sworn to her that she'd be ruined if she left his real estate empire back in Connecticut. But his controlling ways and ethically and legally questionable business dealings left a bad taste in her mouth. She was sick of being under his thumb and influence, of being tainted by association. No success she ever had was considered her own, as long as he had anything to say about it. He was convinced he'd made her, in every way possible. She'd long grown tired of that narrative, so when the opportunity for a fresh start in Boston presented itself, she took it. And she hadn't looked back once.

"Look, you joining our team was a breath of fresh air, I'll admit that," Whitaker said as he handed his empty glass off to a passing waiter. "I wasn't sure what I was getting into when you walked through that door, but you were so confident and sure of yourself, I would have been a fool to ignore that fire and let you slip away."

"I was more than a little sure of myself." Kendall remembered that first day well. She'd come in guns blazing, mustering up all her confidence and prep school charm training to woo Whitaker into hiring her. She had an impressive sales record back in Connecticut, but she'd be basically starting from scratch in Boston. It was a risk to take her on, but one that she knew had paid off exponentially. That's what made tonight so wonderful—in no time at all, she'd succeeded where her father promised she'd fail. And she knew without a doubt in her mind that she'd been fueled by her hatred for her father the entire time. She never seemed to tire; she never ran out of fight. She felt like she had something to prove, and she'd fucking done it. She did this all on her own and she deserved this. All of it. "Turns out you made the right choice."

"You could say that again," Whitaker said as he grabbed another passing glass and drained half of it. "Of course, I did my due diligence and looked into your past. You being a Yates from Connecticut and all—it seemed too convenient and coincidental for you to be the phenome that you were without some connection to the famed Dick Yates. That was an added bonus. Clearly your entire family has a talent for making money. Cheers to that."

Kendall froze. Whitaker had never mentioned that he'd made the connection. He'd also never told her he'd looked into her. And she sure as hell never talked about her father, ever. "You did what?"

Whitaker waved his hand and motioned around them. "You can't be surprised, Kendall. I mean, look at the caliber of people we're up against here. This is a cutthroat business. One sale could net an agent fifty to eighty thousand dollars or more in commission. We're in the business of selling luxury to the highest bidder. I wasn't about to put my neck out for someone who showed up with lots of confidence but a sales sheet from anywhere but here. You talked a good game, Kendall, but your name is what got you through the door."

Kendall felt the color drain from her face. "You can't be fucking serious."

"I don't get it. You're mad? Why?" Whitaker looked confused. "You clearly have proven yourself capable and deserving of this nomination. You absolutely slaughtered the competition and did it entirely alone. Your numbers are all individual—not even Ellison's pet can say that. She's got team volume contributions on her dance card. You don't need a team. You've been a one-woman wrecking crew and moneymaker from the get-go. The flair for sales in your family line is incredible."

"I need to use the ladies' room. I'll see you at the table." Kendall didn't wait for his reply. She was seeing red, and she needed to get away from him as fast as possible before the other part of her father that she inherited besides his *talent*—his anger—reared its ugly head. That was not a trait she was proud of, and it was something her mother often commented about, how similar she and her father were in the rage department. But she wasn't her father. She didn't fly off the handle and verbally abuse anything with a pulse that crossed her path. But, admittedly, she had to work hard to keep her temper at bay once she was triggered. And suddenly her faith in her control was failing her. Today had been a day of too many bombshells for her to handle. She was feeling *very* triggered, and she needed some air. Now.

She let the cool water from the faucet trickle down her fingers before watching it slowly swirl down the drain. Whitaker's revelation shouldn't have surprised her or angered her like it did. It was more that this whole fucking day had been one load of shit piled on another. This was supposed to be an exciting day for her, a celebration of her successes, regardless of who won Realtor of the Year. She was up for an armful of achievements, and even if she didn't take home the top prize, she knew she should be proud of the fact that she was even short-listed at all. She'd fought so hard for this, and yet, right now, it felt empty. She felt empty.

She shut off the faucet and looked at herself in the mirror. Her bloodline was all over her face, which annoyed her in this instance. She had her father's green eyes. But hers were kinder and so much brighter. Her mother's thick, wavy blond hair sat atop her head in an elaborate updo she'd definitely overpaid for on Newbury Street earlier. Her features had served her well over the years, but tonight they were a painful reminder of where she came from. There didn't seem to be enough distance from that past for her, especially not today.

She reapplied her lipstick even though her makeup was flawless. Years of being one of the faces of the Yates real estate empire had taught her the tricks of the trade, and she was as good as any Hollywood makeup artist for sure. Image was everything in this business, and the more beautiful you were on the outside, the easier it was to sell something, anything. Especially luxury real estate, which was the business of extravagant living and beautiful people. And Kendall knew she had a pedigree in both. She'd thought by coming to Boston to start over that she could leave some of that behind. She'd erased her social media presence, fudged a few details on her résumé that wouldn't draw too much attention and didn't impact her sales numbers, and basically became reborn here. She'd started from scratch, and it had been damn hard.

She brushed an errant hair off her forehead and tucked it into the ornate antique clip she'd found at that little boutique in Brookline. She looked beautiful, but that empty feeling from before was there and it was palpable. She'd wanted to pave her own way, and she'd thought that she had. Suddenly she wasn't so sure of that. How many clients had Whitaker floated her way that he'd already tainted with mention of her father? Or worse, had other people made that connection and assumed she was just an extension of Dick Yates in another city? No one had said anything to her, but she didn't trust herself right now.

She started doing a mental tally of all the transactions she'd closed. Her banner year had come to its peak with a last-minute, end-of-year sale that narrowly made it through before the close of business on New Year's Eve. The sale had seemed like great fortune at the time, lucky even. But was it more than that? Had that sale, like all the others, been influenced by her father? Had she just overlooked something? Had she ignored the signs? Did everyone know she was Dick's daughter?

Two laughing agents came into the bathroom, and Kendall looked at them, feeling as insecure as her thoughts were chaotic. Tonight was supposed to be a night of celebration, but it certainly didn't feel like one. And on top of feeling empty, she had never felt so alone.

CHAPTER THREE

Trina swore she must be dreaming. But this wasn't a dream—it was very obviously a nightmare. Just moments before, her picture was on the screen behind the podium on the stage, and her accomplishments were being lauded to a room full of applause, and it was announced that she was...the runner-up. The runner-up? Impossible. This was impossible.

Last year's winner, Carter Something Unremarkable, rambled on, and Trina felt numb. "This was the closest race we've ever had in the history of this award, and what a wonderful problem it is to have—two incredible salespeople working toward the same goal, upholding the highest of standards in the industry. It's a proud day for us and for our industry as a whole. Congratulations to this year's winner, Kendall Yates."

Trina was vaguely aware of her hands clapping, but the rest was sort of a blur. Kendall gave a short speech—too short a speech, if you asked her. One that didn't seem worthy of a winner. Who the fuck was this Kendall Yates anyway?

"You okay?" Lauren leaned over her shoulder, breaking her trance.

"What?" Trina did not feel okay. She felt...blindsided.

"You have this creepy plastic grin on your face, and your hands are getting red from clapping." Lauren reached out to still her robotic movement. "Look at me."

Trina turned to look at Lauren but caught Ellison's gaze from across the table. Ellison was expressionless, save for one raised eyebrow. An almost contemplative one. Trina was not feeling contemplative. She was feeling sick.

"Let's take a walk." Lauren didn't wait for her to answer, instead pulling her to her feet. Trina did her best to walk as casually as possible with her friend, but a part of her felt like it was still sitting at that table, locked in position by disbelief.

Lauren smiled and thanked some people on Trina's behalf as they wove between the tables toward the stairs leading to the outdoor balcony. Trina managed a few tight grins, but words failed her. *She* had failed her. She'd lost. How had she lost?

The cool night air on her face caused her to blink back tears, the sudden temperature change making her eyes water. Or maybe she was just crying. She wasn't sure.

"Okay. It's okay," Lauren said as she rubbed her hands up and down Trina's arms, but Trina shivered all the same. This dress was not meant for a cold evening like this. This dress was made for an over the top, pretentious celebration. This was not a loser's dress, and yet, it apparently was that, too.

"How did I miss this?" Trina asked, still unbelieving of what transpired. "I watched the numbers. I scrutinized the sales data on MLS and followed the buzz around every Realtor in Boston for an entire fucking year. And yes, Kendall Yates's name was thrown around here or there, but there was no way she was going to hit the numbers by the close of the year. She never works with other agents, her community contributions are the bare minimum, and no one knows a thing about her. She's like a ghost. Who the fuck even is she? Where did she even come from?"

"Connecticut." Ellison's voice was soft. Trina hadn't realized she'd followed them out there. The previously empty balcony suddenly felt crowded.

Trina turned to face her, wiping her last tear away as she tried to quiet the white noise in her ears. "Connecticut?"

Ellison nodded, her expression bleak. "She's Dick Yates's daughter. She came to town quietly but evidently didn't stay that way."

"You're joking." Trina frowned.

"Whoa, whoa. Slow down." Lauren shook her head and put her hands up. "The white-collar crook with the pretty sizeable real estate empire who went to jail for real estate fraud? That guy?"

"If by sizeable you mean the rumored thirty million dollar plus real estate empire and monopoly in all of Connecticut," Trina said. Everyone in the business knew about Dick Yates and his jail sentence, but she didn't know the details except that he was rumored to be a bully and someone who drove all his competitors out of town through force and other means. He was also believed to be aligned with enough shady politicians to have gotten deal after deal approved by any city he'd stepped into within Connecticut's borders, though she'd not seen any solid proof of that. But she had heard enough to let her know she never wanted to meet the man. And she certainly never wanted to be beaten by his daughter.

Ellison sighed. "Yes, that guy."

Trina took in the information and something broke inside her. "I busted my ass for God knows how long, and some nepotistic newb just waltzed in here with Daddy's contacts and stole it from me?"

Lauren looked horrified but Trina couldn't stop herself. The chill from before was gone, her rage about the newly revealed information making her feel like she was on fire. "This is ridiculous. Who did she have to pay off on that judging board to make this the closest race in history? I'd like to see some receipts to support this fucking fake news."

"Ellison." Whitaker Sharkney's tone was gloating as he stepped onto the ever more crowded balcony. "Such a shame about Ms. Lee." He turned, seeming to feign surprise at noticing Trina three feet away. "Oh, my apologies, Trina. I didn't see you there."

"I bet." Trina's lip curled and her instinct told her to lunge at him until she felt Lauren's hand on her wrist, steadying her.

Ellison turned to face him, her expression cold. "Whitaker, it's always a pleasure. How's business? Good? You lost every single category you had an agent in tonight, so maybe not so much."

"Except the category that mattered, you mean." Whitaker grinned like a Cheshire cat, and Trina scowled.

"Well now, I saw the numbers, Whitaker. It seems to me you owe Ms. Yates a piece of the business. Since she's the only one generating any of it. Not unlike when I was doing all the work for you all those years ago, right? What was it you called me when I asked for my fair share? *Ungrateful*, I believe." Ellison had an edge to her voice that Trina hadn't heard before.

Whitaker snarled. "You were too big for your britches then—and now, it seems. Kendall took a fifth of the time it took your shooting star to achieve her success. It's just too bad you put all your chips on a losing agent. Guess you gambled and lost, huh?"

Ellison's laugh was chilly. "A gambling reference? Really? I suppose I should expect nothing less from a *shark* like you." Her smile had ice in it. "You always were a cheat, Whitaker. Seems like that hasn't changed."

Whitaker glared at Ellison, and Trina wasn't sure what to do, until she noticed Kendall approaching over his shoulder, and then her mouth jumped out in front of her brain.

"Were you in on this twisted little fuck-you game Sharkney over here is playing?" Trina called out, and Kendall stopped short of Whitaker's side, her expression one of surprise.

"Excuse me?" Kendall replied. With her this close, Trina was able to see the emerald glow of her eyes and the way that necklace she wore complemented them so nicely. The combo of the white Chanel pantsuit and no shirt on the strikingly beautiful woman would have normally caused Trina's heart to skip a beat, but in this case, Kendall's statuesque beauty only fueled her rage. She was beautiful and well-dressed on top of being unjustly awarded Trina's title? No. Fucking. Way.

"That depends, do you need excusing?" Trina replied. "Like, should we excuse your win tonight because your father's name did all the work? Or should we excuse the fact that you certainly leveraged that little bloodline nugget to get some numbers on your side to secure the win? Are we excusing cheating? Because that's what this feels like. Nepotism. Plain and simple." Trina spit the last bit out as bile rose in her throat. She hated to lose, but she hated losing due to favoritism more than anything.

Kendall cocked her head to the side and seemed to survey Trina before answering. Her voice was low, and her words were fast when she said, "I came over here to tell Whitaker I was leaving because I have better things to do than exchange small talk with losers like you. But since you've decided to drag me into whatever death spiral of shame you feel for being the first-place loser to my win, then you'd better brace yourself. Because I'm not going anywhere. And you can say all you want about my family's name and how you think it might have influenced tonight's award, but I can assure you, I did this all on my own. And I'll do it again and again." The smile she gave Trina was as fake as the blond hair on her head. "Get used to the feeling of coming up short."

"And I suppose that threat is meant to make me shake in my Louboutins, is it?" Trina laughed. "What a heavy burden that legacy must be for you. I can't imagine what all those open doors and windows must be like. Drafty, I bet. One long, clear hallway of Daddy's favors and money helping you reach your goals. You probably haven't had to work for anything in your entire life, have you? What a gift."

Kendall's nostrils flared and Trina knew she'd hit her target. "Listen, bitch—"

"That's enough." Ellison stepped forward, her hands raised between them. "Let's settle this, shall we?"

"Settle what? Your sore loser is verbally attacking my star agent." Whitaker's arms were crossed in what appeared to be boredom. "It's been settled. You lost. Kendall's right—you ought to get used to that."

Kendall shot her boss a look and Trina would have cared except all she could think about was how much she hated Kendall even though she knew next to nothing about her.

Ellison turned to Kendall and addressed her. "You're insisting you did this all on your own. All I'm saying is—prove it."

"I don't need to prove anything to any of you." Kendall's gaze on hers remained unwavering as she spoke. Trina wanted to punch her.

"You don't," Ellison replied. "But there is no way that your award will ever carry anything but doubt and rumors. Unless you can replicate your success. Without a shadow of a doubt, prove that you earned the title."

"I'm over this," Kendall said in a huff as she turned to leave.

"So Trina's right then." Kendall stopped when Ellison spoke. "That legacy burden is too much for you. I understand, I know Whitaker does. He built his entire career using his uncle's connections. You aren't that different, I guess. I'm glad you found each other," she said.

"We're done here." Whitaker reached for Kendall, but Kendall pulled away from his grasp.

"You don't know anything about me." Kendall's voice rose.

Trina scoffed. "Oh, I'd bet Wikipedia will tell me all I need to know, but I'm sure that doesn't mesh with your fictional underdog narrative, so please, continue with your vague, sweeping declarations."

Lauren chuckled and Trina almost forgot she was out there with them.

"Oh, c'mon, Whitaker," Ellison taunted. "Are you too afraid to be proven for the fraud that you are? You're the one who said I gambled and lost. What do you say to a friendly wager, one that will prove which of these ladies is the true Realtor of the Year?" Ellison's question was provoking.

"I'm listening," Whitaker said as he leaned in, his beady eyes darting back and forth. He looked like a rat. With a bow tie. What grown man wore a bow tie?

"I had a long chat with Charles Langley today. The Harborside is nearly ready for the showing of some select units while the rest are being finished. He hasn't signed with a realty firm to represent him yet, but the buzz on that property is plenty loud. It's expected to sell out long before the construction finishes." Ellison leaned against the railing behind her and motioned toward Whitaker. "Charles mentioned you were in the hunt for that opportunity. I mean, you'd be foolish not to be, since it's guaranteed profit with next to no heavy lifting. You know how new builds go: fast sales, clean paper trails, high payouts."

"What's the point of this monologue, Ellison?" Whitaker snapped. "Charles hasn't made his decision yet, so this is a useless discussion."

Ellison gave him a small smile, and she looked at Kendall as she spoke. "Charles did make his decision. He chose Gamble and Associates to represent him. I made him an offer he couldn't refuse. So he didn't."

"Booyah." Trina felt her rage ebb with the revelation that Ellison had secured the contract. This was an opportunity she had been dying for, and it was hers now. Things suddenly seemed less shitty.

"You're lying," Whitaker sputtered, looking significantly less arrogant.

"I'm not." Ellison kept her gaze on Kendall. "I'll make you a similar offer, Ms. Yates. Prove yourself worthy of that title you just won by taking on the friendly wager. I'll agree to co-represent the Harborside with Whitaker's group, and you and Trina fight to outsell each other."

"What?" Trina couldn't believe this. Ellison must be drunk, right? "You're joking."

"No, thanks." Kendall waved Ellison off and turned to leave again.

"Tell me more," Whitaker said as he leaned in again, the look of greed in his face unmistakable. He was disgusting.

"I said no, Whitaker," Kendall barked at him, and he surveyed her briefly before turning his attention back to Ellison.

"There's no reason to be rude, Kendall," he shot back. "Ellison has something she'd like to propose." Whitaker dismissed her, and Trina cringed. Even though she had no idea what alien had invaded Ellison's brain and taken over her physical form at this exact moment, she had never once felt dismissed by Ellison. Not ever. Not that Trina had any real idea what the fuck was going on right now, but still, Whitaker Sharkney was an ass.

"We'll both represent Langley. We'll iron out the details, but we'll work as a partnership. The office that contracts the highest sales total in the building wins. There are eight floors and five units on each, two penthouses, and a commercial space for rent on the first floor, rear of the building. Langley already has buyers lined up for some of the spaces. We'll just have to fill the rest," Ellison said.

Trina looked over at Lauren's gaping expression and felt exactly the same way. Why was Ellison offering to give up part of the profits? And why would she offer that to Whitaker, of all people?

"But it doesn't seem like it's something you're interested in." Ellison shrugged as she added, "If Kendall's too afraid she can't perform without outside help, then there's no point in discussing this further. I don't need the partnership. This was just a way to determine the real all-star here. It's really too bad for you, Whitaker. The remaining units are collectively projected to sell for over eighty million dollars."

"We're in." Whitaker nodded and stuck out his hand. "Let's talk specifics tomorrow."

"Like hell," Kendall replied, looking furious. "Who's the *we* here, Whitaker? Because it sure as hell isn't me. You two want to play some sick fuck millionaire's chess game, you can do it on your own time. Leave me out of it."

"Sounds like they gave that trophy to the wrong person tonight then," Trina said. "Because there's no way I'd pass up a guaranteed payday, even for pride. Guess you can, since you're on Daddy's payroll no matter whether you close a sale or not, right? Man, you got it rough, girl." Trina heard the words leaving her mouth. Was she actually goading Kendall into taking her money now? What was in that champagne tonight?

Kendall's eyes flashed with anger and she stepped toward Trina. "You *are* as cocky as people say, aren't you? Even in the face of such an embarrassing loss, you're like an angry chihuahua nipping at ankles. It's pathetic."

"Did you just make a short joke?" Trina laughed and loved that Kendall looked even more mad than before. "Because that's twice now. You'll have to do better than that, Blondie. I do my best work when I'm antagonized."

Kendall hissed. "You would never win this competition. I beat you once and I'll do it again."

"Bet against me," Trina challenged as she smiled her first genuine smile since before the awards started tonight. Fuck that stupid award— this was where the excitement was. She'd make it her goddamn life's mission to beat Kendall Yates. It was decided. Whatever Ellison's motives were didn't matter. That Harborside top seller title was hers. "Give me all the fuel I need to light your ass up."

"Great," Whitaker said as he clapped. "It's been decided then."

Kendall looked at him like he'd lost his mind but said nothing. Trina took this as a win since Kendall was visibly shaking with anger, and Trina preferred they not progress beyond verbally sparring to physical altercation. She was plenty scrappy and had no concerns about her ability to quite literally kick Kendall's ass, but this dress was rather form-fitting and it might slow her down a bit.

"Send me the details of your proposal tomorrow, and let's see if we can agree to the terms," Whitaker said, his expression a child's on Christmas morning. "This will be fun, Ellison. How exciting."

Ellison gave him a brief nod as he walked away but said nothing to Trina and Lauren, which Trina found to be more than a little maddening.

Trina watched him leave with Kendall near his side, speaking angrily, her voice raised but her words inaudible.

"Does anyone want to talk about what just happened? Or what the hell is going on?" Lauren sounded as confused as Trina felt.

"Trina's going to get that title, like she deserves. And we're all going to make a boatload of money in the process," Ellison said as she placed a hand on each of their backs and ushered them back inside. "It's cold out here. Let's celebrate the fact that we swept every category we were in—"

"Except Realtor of the Year." Trina hated admitting that.

"Except that," Ellison agreed, but she didn't look upset in the least. On the contrary, she looked charged. Trina felt like Ellison's mood was contagious. "Tonight is for playing. Tomorrow we'll figure out the big stuff."

"Why do I feel like there's something you aren't telling us?" Trina asked, and Lauren nodded beside her.

"Because there is," Ellison said with a smile. "There's always more."

Lauren slapped her forehead. "I feel hungover. Did all that just happen?"

"Enjoy the night. Bill everything to me. I'll leave a card at the bar," Ellison said as she patted Lauren on the arm. "I have to make a quick call. I'll be back in a bit."

As Ellison walked away, Trina blurted out what she'd been stifling since Ellison proposed her ludicrous plan, "Why do I get the feeling I just got myself into a world of trouble?"

Lauren waved over the bartender and ordered two doubles. "Oh, because you certainly did."

"She called me short. Twice," Trina argued.

"True." Lauren nodded. "But you called her a spoiled rotten rich girl whose only achievement in life was leveraging nepotism to get ahead."

"Which is all true," Trina pointed out as she stirred the drink the bartender handed her.

"Maybe so." Lauren took a long, slow sip of her glass. "But it was kinda harsh."

"Seriously?" Trina was offended. "You're defending her?"

"Oh no." Lauren shook her head. "Absolutely not. I hope you annihilate her. I'm just saying, I get why you might be a little nervous."

"I'm not nervous." That was a lie. Something told Trina that she was in over her head. But she couldn't take back what she'd said. She wouldn't.

"Okay." Lauren didn't argue, but Trina had known her long enough to know that was her way of claiming victory.

After a pause, Lauren asked, "So, are we going to talk about how she's super-hot, or is that off the table?"

"Off the table."

Trina needed to stay focused on the task at hand: reclaiming the title that was rightfully hers. She couldn't get hung up on the way she had let her eyes linger on Kendall's retreating form a few minutes ago. She wasn't checking her out or anything—she was just making sure she was leaving. Which was totally fine, right?

"So that means we're also not going to talk about how she's, like, totally your type, too, right?" Lauren's subtlety needed work.

"Right." Trina hated that in any other universe, under any other circumstances, she would have pursued Kendall. She would have flirted her way into a few drinks, and if she played her cards right, probably into Kendall's bed. But this wasn't another universe, and the circumstances were what they were. Kendall was the enemy. Her beauty was just a distraction.

"Then it's decided. We hate her and we're taking her down," Lauren said as she raised her glass. "Let's drink to a new adventure."

"To kicking Kendall Yates's coattail-riding ass," Trina replied, and Lauren clinked her glass in response. She wasn't sure what tomorrow would bring, but she was sure that whatever happened, at least she'd have Lauren by her side. And for tonight, that was enough.

CHAPTER FOUR

Kendall replayed last night's events over and over in her head. The whole thing felt like some surreal dream. She'd won the award she'd been hoping for, but Gamble and Associates had taken every other award that night. Had Kendall not won, Whitaker's group would have limped home, again. That had been the pattern of the last few years. His company had been *just* outearned by Ellison's at every turn. She was more than sure that was the reason Whitaker had been so elated that she'd snagged the top prize. She knew this award was more for him than her. And that enraged her. But not as much as his agreeing to Ellison's proposal. How dare he?

"We're getting coffee to celebrate your big win last night," Margo said, "and yet, you're holding that cup so tightly you might break it." Margo nudged her hand. "For someone who just won, you aren't nearly as relaxed or elated as you should be."

"Sorry." Kendall relaxed her hands, and they ached as the blood rushed back into them. She had no idea she'd been clutching the almost too hot cup so tightly. She surveyed her bright red palms and sighed. "Last night didn't exactly go as planned."

"You mean you didn't expect to win?" Margo scratched her head. "I'm confused. I thought you had this in the bag. Just yesterday you were practically floating out of spin class with anticipation."

Kendall nodded—Margo was right. Yesterday morning she had been on top of the world. There'd been no news about her father for so long, she'd almost thought she was through with him, and the award felt like it was in the bag. There was so much awesome to be excited about. That all changed, quite literally, with one phone call. "Yesterday was just a really tough day. It started off on the wrong foot and ended up shoeless by the end of the night."

"This sounds like the day had no sole at all." Margo's dad joke landed with a thud, and Kendall couldn't help but laugh.

"I'm not even going to comment." She leaned back and took in Margo's appearance. She was wearing a shirt with the Cyclebar logo on it, and Kendall had noticed her bright purple exercise leggings when she'd walked in—Margo'd come right from work. Spin class was how they met two years ago. She had no friends when she'd moved to town, and her schedule kept her working pretty much every waking hour, so when the boutique stationary cycle bar opened next to her office, she was thrilled. She'd be able to keep in shape without wandering too far, and that was a game changer. What she hadn't expected was just how enjoyable cycling would be. She'd never tried it before, and truthfully, she'd never exercised before without feeling like it was punishment. But Margo's classes never felt like punishment, and the added bonus of being able to compete with the other cyclists to achieve the top rank in the class helped stoke that fire of hers. She liked data, and she liked seeing her number rise and those of her peers fall. Cyclebar had given her an outlet to release some of the tension from life and work, while also giving her a place to let her competitive nature run unchecked. But most of all, it had brought Margo into her life, and that was the greatest surprise of all. She thought about that now. She knew Margo had squeezed this coffee in between her classes today, and Kendall was grateful, even if her current demeanor didn't express that fact.

"I'm sorry I'm not much company."

Margo reached across the table and patted the back of her hand. "Let's start at the beginning. What happened between our spin class and today? Besides the big win. Which seems to have made things worse, somehow."

"Okay, so, class was good—"

"*Great.* Class was great because your instructor is amazing, and it was also a class of personal bests for you. You destroyed the other cyclists. They weren't even close to your number one ranking," Margo pointed out.

That was true. Kendall had been feeling it that day. She'd pedaled harder and faster than she could remember ever having done in the past. It helped that Margo was the instructor, too. She did her best to line up her workouts with Margo's schedule, but it wasn't always possible. The truth was, she always did her best when Margo was cheering her on from the front of the class. Margo had the best energy—she was so positive it was infectious. Kendall had not found that trait in another person without also finding their endless positivity to be annoying. But Margo was different. Her positive outlook was genuine and refreshing. She always brought a unique perspective to things. Kendall could really use that perspective now.

"First off, a major deal I was banking on fell through, and that was a total downer."

"That sucks," Margo said with a frown. After a long moment, Margo asked, "Is there a second off? Is that even a thing?"

"Right after the lost deal call, I got a call informing me my father was released from prison." Kendall swallowed hard. That physically hurt to say aloud.

"Whoa." Margo's eyes widened. "Really? I know you said your dad was out of your life, but prison? You never talk about your family."

"There's not much to talk about," Kendall replied. That wasn't true, though. She'd spent years talking about her family in therapy. She didn't want to expend the effort anymore. That was what had changed. They never would, so she decided to.

"I mean, *prison*, Kendall," Margo pointed out.

"You know how I told you my dad was in real estate, too? Well, that was kind of an understatement. He had a big company that I used to work for, which has since folded. Because he committed real estate fraud, among other heinous things, and then he went to jail for it. But now he's out. And I'm trying not to freak out because I just found some semblance of balance and normalcy here, and I just…I don't know, knowing that he could potentially reenter my life in some way makes me feel panicked." Just talking about it was making her heart race.

"I could see that." Margo's response was soothing. She wasn't the judgmental type—that was another thing about her that Kendall loved. She just existed and expected others to exist. No preconceived notions, no unnecessary baggage, just Margo in the world with seemingly infinite patience and understanding. Kendall was amazed by it.

"Maybe it won't change anything and I'm just overreacting. Maybe he won't try to find me or meddle in my life. Maybe he's moved on." She heard herself say the words she didn't believe. Her gut told her that the call was just the tip of the iceberg. But she could lie to herself, she supposed. It wouldn't be the first time.

"Maybe." Margo humored her and she loved her for it. "And the award last night?"

Kendall frowned. That was another story entirely. Her father's situation brought her a mix of pain, fear, and sadness—and anger, too—

but that was sort of secondary to the other feelings. Last night, though, last night brought her rage. "Last night my boss made a bet that I would outsell an entire rival real estate office on a shared project."

"What?" Margo's hand stopped in midair, her coffee cup hovering by her lips. "Say what now?"

Kendall felt that familiar bubbling of anger from last night. She pressed her palms to the table and felt the coolness of the wooden surface as she spoke. "All right, so, you know how a few weeks ago we were going over the competition and chatting about them?"

"Yes." Margo had humored her and stopped by her apartment for dinner a few weeks back. They'd been catching up about life when she'd noticed all the real estate magazines on Kendall's counter. She'd teased her about oppo research, as she called it, but Kendall had been a bit bashful, because that's exactly what she had been doing. "Right, a couple of old white guys and the hot Asian woman."

Kendall scowled because that was something she had thought, too, before she'd actually met her. Now her impression of her was very, very different. "Trina Lee. Her name is Trina."

"Duly noted," Margo replied. "Continue."

"Anyway, I'd had the award about five minutes before Trina came at me and accused me of winning by virtue of my last name and not my hard work. Which is total bullshit because you of all people know how hard I've been busting my ass this past year," she said.

"In spin class and in life." Margo nodded, sipping her coffee. "Except you have no dating life whatsoever. But I digress. Continue."

Kendall shot her a look. "Success comes from sacrifices. What's one less date that ends up going nowhere if I end up crushing Trina and her smug expression?"

"Back up. Tell me more about this Trina person. What happened?" Margo made a rewinding motion with her hands.

"She basically called me a spoiled little rich kid and accused me of only succeeding through nepotism. In response to which I might have lost my cool and called her a sore loser, among other things," Kendall said as she pressed her palm to her forehead, embarrassed. "I might have also called her a bitch."

Margo placed her cup back down and leaned forward. "Is there a catfight at the end of this story? Because you don't have any visible scratches. So that means you won, right?"

Kendall shook her head and laughed. "No. But if there had been, I totally would have won." Though Trina was shorter than her, she didn't come across as meek or petite, that was for sure. Especially when she was slinging insults. Which Kendall normally would have found kind of hot—she liked a confident woman after all, just not one so confidently coming at her. Though she'd be lying if she said she didn't notice the way Trina's dress fit her like it was painted on. The dress was gorgeous and the woman in it was much more attractive than her picture, which annoyed Kendall even more.

She shook her head to regain focus. "That's not the point. The point is she came at me with a fierceness that was totally unnecessary. And then the bet happened."

"What bet? You lost me." Margo looked confused.

"Whitaker has some fierce rivalry with the owner of Gamble and Associates. They're our primary competition in this market. He obsesses about their successes ad nauseam, but I didn't realize how deep his hatred of Ellison Gamble went until last night. When Trina started accusing me of cheating—"

"Which is totally rude, by the way. She loses hot points for that," Margo added.

Kendall rolled her eyes at that as she continued, "Trina accused me of cheating to beat her and Ellison warned that once news got out about my family, gossip would spread, and people would assume I'd won unjustly. Which is so fucking wrong, but whatever. Haters are gonna hate, right?"

"Right," Margo replied.

"Anyway, Ellison proposed a bet to Whitaker, that whichever one of us could outsell the other on a joint project would prove they were the best Realtor. And before I could even argue that I had no interest in their stupid rivalry, Whitaker agreed to it."

Margo held up her hand. "There's a lot of stream of consciousness happening here, and I'm just a lowly Cyclebar instructor and occasional yogi. You need to break this down for me so I can cheer you on and make the appropriate signage for the next awards event."

Kendall smiled at her friend's enthusiasm. "There's this massive luxury condo going up in the Seaport. The Harborside. Have you heard of it?"

"Duh. They have ads all over the city. The owner of my franchise location wants a spot in the commercial section over there," Margo replied nonchalantly.

"Really? That could be useful intel. I want you to introduce us." Kendall's mind went right into work mode.

"Yeah, sure." Margo waved her on. "You were saying?"

"Right. The Harborside is almost ready for showings. Ellison Gamble says she secured the representation of the building, but she's offering a partnership to Whitaker as a way to see who can outsell the other, me or Trina," Kendall replied.

"Why would she do that?" Margo asked.

Kendall had been wondering the same thing. It seemed foolish to give up a share of potential profits. "I don't know. But I'm hoping I'll know on Monday. We're all meeting as a group to go over the specifics."

"You and Trina? In the same room together?" Margo's eyes widened. "I'll call in sick. You might need me. Who am I kidding? I just want to see what goes down. I'll bring popcorn."

"Kettle corn or movie theater, buttered?" Kendall was hungry, and both flavors sounded good about now.

"Buttered, duh." Margo finished her cup and leaned back with a stretch. "So, all jokes aside, why did you agree to this?"

"Well, I didn't." Kendall had practically quit when Whitaker stopped her from storming off after the balcony interaction. "But after I thought about it, I wanted vindication. Screw Trina and her accusations. I earned that title, and I've got the talent to prove it. I'm not afraid of Trina or Ellison Gamble. If they want to set me up for a home run, I'm going to take it. And the Harborside is a definite home run. I'll win no matter what happens—this is the holy grail of property sales. I'll make Whitaker make me an offer I can't refuse, and then I'll crush this silly competition. Let them scramble around and try to beat me. Hell, I already have a renter for the commercial space, and we haven't even gotten started." She winked at Margo.

"Oh damn. I see what you did there." Margo gave her a fist bump from across the table. "Let me know when you wanna meet with Sandra. I'll start putting in a good word now."

"And this is why you're my best friend."

"Ditto, sales superstar." Margo checked her cell phone and wiped her mouth with a napkin. "Speaking of which, it's back to work for me."

Kendall stood to embrace Margo when she got up to leave. "Thanks for listening to me vent. I really needed it."

"Always." Margo gave her a quick kiss on the cheek and a brief shoulder squeeze. "You're gonna kick Trina's ass. I just know it. You got this."

Kendall felt like the stress and anger from earlier had finally subsided. She knew she could do this. She'd done it before, and she could do it again. If she could survive Dick Yates, she could overcome a nobody like Trina Lee without any trouble. She was born for this type of challenge, and she wasn't about to give in before it started. Her confidence swelled.

"I've totally got this."

Chapter Five

Trina ran her hand along the piping on the passenger seat of Ellison's Maserati. She'd ridden in it once before, but she hadn't taken the time to appreciate the detail in the leatherwork. The car was a piece of art, there was no doubt about that, but what entranced her was how soft the leather was. She couldn't stop touching it.

"You okay?" Ellison gave her a quick glance before turning at the stoplight.

She nodded. "Yeah. Maybe I'm a little nervous." She regretted her words as soon as she spoke them. She hadn't meant to be so honest.

"Oh?" Ellison accelerated as she switched lanes, and the engine purred, almost as if happy to be tested.

"I don't like that we have to go to their office. Why can't they come to ours? Ours is so much better." Trina crossed her arms like a petulant child. She knew she was being ridiculous.

"Have you ever been to Whitaker's office?" Ellison asked with a knowing smile.

"No. But I'm sure ours is better." Trina slouched a little in her seat.

Ellison laughed. "I'm sure you're right. I haven't been to his new location. Truthfully, I want to see what type of operation he's running over there. There's a selfishness to this decision. But it's important we play nice and take turns hosting these meetings, too."

Trina didn't have any intention of playing nice with Whitaker or Kendall. "How many times are we getting together as a group?"

Ellison gave her a half shrug. "I'd say once or twice more until the sales are complete. Today we're just going to finalize the ground rules and set up a timeline—it's more of a formality, really, since Whitaker and I worked out most of this stuff already. But you should be involved. I'm the one that pushed for this meeting. I'll probably have a few conference calls with Whitaker throughout the process, but we shouldn't have to be in too close quarters, too often. If that's what you're worried about."

"I'm not worried about anything." Trina knew that was in complete contrast to her previous admission of being nervous, but she wasn't going to dwell on it. She looked at her boss and asked the question she'd been obsessing about since the night of the awards ceremony. "Why are you doing anything with Whitaker? We can sell the Harborside alone. I can do it, Ellison."

"Because we needed him to close the deal," Ellison replied, a look of annoyance on her face.

"What do you mean?" Trina asked.

"I wasn't entirely truthful the other night." Ellison ran her hand through her hair as she spoke. "Langley hadn't finalized his choice. I knew we were close, and I had a feeling we could win the position, but I knew if we teamed with Whitaker, we'd be guaranteed the contract."

"Why, though? We outsell Sharkney over and over again. He's second best," Trina said.

"But he's got the *best* on his staff." Ellison added air quotes.

"Ugh," Trina retorted.

"Agreed," Ellison said. "But Kendall Yates is a force to be reckoned with, and Langley is a good ol' boy who likes to play good ol' boy games. He's a misogynist, and Whitaker had a slight edge because of his genitalia. Not the talent at his agency. And I'm more than sure the Yates name would have helped Langley justify passing over us." Trina saw Ellison grip the steering wheel harder as she sighed. "I got the feeling after my call with Langley before the awards that he might flip on me. So I raised the stakes. After Kendall won, I made a few calls and made it impossible for him to turn down my pitch—we'd work with Whitaker, and the best and second-best realty offices in Boston would represent his project. And since we're splitting the profits, we guarantee success for both of our offices."

"I can't believe you'd be willing to give up some of your profit. Especially to him." Trina hated that Ellison made that decision, even if she was going to directly benefit from it. Somehow it felt like Ellison was lowering her standards. She didn't like thinking that way.

"Compromise is what makes a deal work, Trina. I'd rather lose a little profit to secure the contract of a lifetime. This will change the lives of my agents. All of them, not just you. Langley deals with lots of international clientele, and this is a gateway to a slew of new opportunities, in addition to the chance to further foster a relationship with an innovative developer. As much as Langley is a wealthy old white guy, he's a wealthy old white guy with an excellent design firm at his fingertips and lots of bold ideas. He's changing the landscape of the Seaport District one old run-down building at a time," Ellison said. "Compromise makes the deal work because both sides benefit."

"Fine. But I still don't like it." Trina knew she was being stubborn, but she didn't care.

"But that's not the only reason I did it," Ellison said.

"I mean, it sounds like plenty of reason to me." Trina liked money as much as she liked the rush of closing a deal. She knew that the Harborside had the possibility of bringing about her highest payday to date.

"I did it because you are the best Realtor I've ever worked with, and you deserved that stupid tchotchke more than anyone. And I know you can outsell the pants off Kendall. I bet my profit margin on it. Because you will sell more units than she will, and even though Sharkney might make a little in the process, you'll make a lot. And I can't wait to see what you can do when the cards are stacked in your favor for once." Ellison briefly touched Trina's hand before pulling back. "The playing field is level for once, Trina. Nothing is going to stand in your way. It's you and Kendall and no one else. And you've got an entire office rooting for you and supporting you," Ellison said as she parked the car at their destination. She turned to Trina and added, "All you have to do is accept the challenge."

Trina looked at the woman who had so much confidence in her and had to stifle the urge to cry. She couldn't remember another time she had felt so unconditionally championed. She wouldn't fail. She couldn't. Not with Ellison Gamble putting her neck out for her. This was a bet she was going to win. For the stupid tchotchke, for the unofficial title, and for the sweet taste of revenge for all the times someone else got ahead without working as hard as she had. Or without having to sacrifice as much as she did.

Trina extended her hand toward Ellison. "Let's crush that bitch."

"I'm glad you're on board." Ellison laughed as she took Trina's hand.

"It sounds like I'd be a fool not to be," Trina replied candidly.

Ellison looked up at the building before them and said, "Whitaker certainly knows how to make a statement."

Trina surveyed the very European, very stark looking building.

The white facade with modern accents and oversized windows was unlike the redbrick buildings surrounding it. It certainly stood out, but not in a way that Trina found appealing.

"It's not my cup of tea, I'll say that." Trina noticed the signage was clean, almost sterile. The flat silver letters on the white building face looked elegant, if also slightly understated. Trina wasn't a fan of anything overly modern. She liked art and even architecture with modern accents, but this building left her cold.

"He's in the process of rebranding himself," Ellison said as she exited the car, resuming her conversation when Trina joined her on the sidewalk. "This new office is the home base to his new brand operation. He's trying to appeal more to the international rental crowd. It's fast money, though not always long term. But it's an *angle*, I suppose. Mostly I think he's trying to reinvigorate his business."

"You mean, since you left and became more successful." Trina gave Ellison a nudge with her elbow.

"Exactly." Ellison's smile was blinding. Trina loved that Ellison never shied away from a compliment. She just took them in stride and made no apologies. She owned her successes, a trait Trina shared. She suspected that was one of the reasons she and Ellison got along so well. And why she blindly followed when Ellison led. Like right now.

"Okay, so we go in and hash out the details and get to work." Trina held open the door for Ellison. "Anything I need to know?"

Ellison walked past her and waved to Whitaker as he greeted them from across the sterile metal and glass filled room beyond the marble lined reception desk. She lowered her voice to answer Trina and said through a smile, "Regardless of how polite everyone will be, this is warfare. Don't let them catch you off guard. They will be looking for weaknesses. And you, Trina, are anything but weak."

"Noted and thank you," Trina said as she accepted Whitaker's handshake. Game on.

Chapter Six

K endall had just ended a call when she heard Whitaker greet Ellison and Trina. Her corner office was just off the main conference area, so though she could hear them because her office door was open, she couldn't see them. And that was fine by her, she was glad to have an extra moment or two to herself. She had spent some time this morning going over logistics with Whitaker in between client calls, and though she was more than prepared, she knew that talking about the "contest" versus sitting across from her competition was something else entirely. She wasn't scared of Trina or anything, but she knew this wasn't going to be a walk in the park either. Trina was number two for a reason. But it was up to Kendall to make sure she stayed that way.

She thought back to her interaction with Whitaker today, and though it was cordial, she knew their relationship was still rocky. She had been none too pleased about his commitment to Ellison the night of the awards ceremony, particularly since she was a pawn in that decision. And though she'd dug her heels in and told him to fuck off about her even being involved, part of her didn't want to seem insecure or cave to Trina, either. Because that wasn't the case. She just didn't like people making decisions on her behalf. Like her father had done for her entire life.

And even though Dick Yates was an arrogant, physically and emotionally abusive, narcissistic monster, he was a slick businessman and he certainly had not raised a fool for a daughter. So, when she realized she had an opportunity to leverage her talents to grind down Whitaker's profit margin and increase her own, she jumped at it. And because Whitaker seemed more hell-bent on crushing Ellison than paying attention to his bottom line, she took him for more dollars than he had sense to realize. Because if Kendall was anything, it was an ace negotiator. And a damn good actress, since Whitaker really thought she was offended and hurt, when in reality, she was just annoyed by another privileged, older man trying to run her life. She appreciated how quickly he expressed his remorse, even if it was rooted in getting her to agree to his little game. It meant he was culpable, at least in some ways, which could prove very useful in her future working with him. Whitaker had opened a lot of doors for her, that point could not be ignored, but after this project, Kendall was confident she could open all those doors on her own. And then her position with Whitaker and in the Boston luxury real-estate market would be hers to dictate. And that was something Kendall was very much looking forward to: being in charge of her own destiny, fully.

"So, you have the only other corner office in the joint, huh? You fancy, girl," Trina said from her doorway, startling her.

Kendall surveyed the woman before speaking. Trina was wearing a loose-fitting white blouse with a high waisted, tight-fitted dress pant that was the color of blood. Bright, red blood. It occurred to Kendall that this was the second time she'd seen Trina in red, and it was a color that when paired with her dark black hair was very flattering. Annoyingly.

"What? You don't?" Kendall said as she rose from her desk. She momentarily wondered how long Trina had been standing there, watching her. She'd been lost in her thoughts, which was a dangerous place to be these days.

She raised an eyebrow at Trina. "I would guess a good, solid number two like you would have a nice cushy, corner office with a window. Maybe even a view of the parking lot if Ellison was feeling generous."

"Don't worry about my view, honey." Trina gave her a small smile as she maintained eye contact. "I can see clearly, no obstructions, only dollar signs and unearned partiality."

Kendall didn't let on how much that little shot hurt, even if it did. No weakness was to be shown to this woman, ever. She closed the open file folder on her desk with a laugh. "You've always got something to say, don't you?"

"It's a gift." Trina shrugged in response as she entered Kendall's office without an invitation. Kendall watched her walk around, seeming to take in the room before she paused in front of the filing cabinet near her desk. "You were on the phone when I got here, talking to Daddy?"

Kendall felt her mouth twitch, but Trina appeared to be too focused on the contents on the top of the filing cabinet to notice. And Kendall was grateful for that. And thrilled to see her unwelcomed guest's attention was locked on her Realtor of the Year award. Kendall had made sure to wipe it clean of fingerprints earlier, just in case. She was glad she'd done that now.

"Not so chatty all of the sudden, are you? See something over there that caught your eye? Or just your tongue?" Kendall stepped toward Trina and the award just to see what would happen if she threatened a bite with all these bark barbs they were trading.

To her surprise Trina didn't flinch or move back. On the contrary, she actually stepped into Kendall's space, causing Kendall to halt her movements.

"Not a single thing of interest here." Trina's manicured red nails briefly tapped the cabinet's surface before skimming the award. Her voice was low and her expression calm when she added, "Nothing earned, anyway."

Kendall felt that familiar wave of anger rise, like the first time she'd engaged with Trina. She was being baited and even though she knew it, she still couldn't seem to dial back her emotions. This was her turf, *her office*. She was supposed to be in a position of power today. Every day. Who did this woman think she was?

"Now who's at a loss for words?" Trina leaned in and Kendall reflexively leaned back, something she instantly regretted as Trina's smile broadened. "And just so you know, your lack of rebuttal just means you and I both know you're exactly the fraud I think you are."

"Trina." Ellison's voice caused Trina's unwavering stare to waver. Which Kendall appreciated since she was about to unleash hell on this woman and wasn't above hair pulling or violence, in this moment. "The meeting's next door. We should get started."

"Sure thing." Trina gave Kendall a quick once-over before turning and heading out of the room, her long dark ponytail moving almost as quickly as she did.

Kendall waited until she was alone in her office to growl and curse under her breath. That woman was insufferable. And every fiber of her being wanted to crush Trina into showing her a little respect. But people like Trina didn't bend easily like that. Kendall knew for her to get the satisfaction she truly wanted, she'd have to humiliate her. Humiliation would look as good on Trina as those skin-tight pants, Kendall thought.

She reached out and touched the award Trina had toyed with. She was proud of this and what it meant, and what it could do for her. And she knew that pride was justified. Because she had fucking earned this, no matter what Trina had to say.

"I embarrassed you once, I'll do it again."

"All right, thanks again for coming to our space, ladies." Whitaker addressed Ellison and Trina with a fakeness that made Kendall want to vomit, but she managed to keep it together. "Ellison and I spoke about some ground rules, but we wanted to go over them as a group to ensure the guidelines were clear."

"And to make sure that all parties involved were on the same page and had the opportunity to weigh in," Ellison added as she cast a look at Whitaker. Clearly, she didn't approve of his approach. Ellison was obviously a more polished people-person. Kendall would bet that some of that was because she was a woman. "I want to make sure Trina and Kendall give full approval to what we worked out, Whitaker."

"Right, right. Of course." Whitaker dismissed her as he handed out copies of the rules, formatted on his company's letterhead in bulleted format.

Kendall surveyed the sheet with only a modicum of attention. They had discussed this earlier, so she knew what it said. The meeting was mostly a formality from what she understood, and the sooner it was over, the sooner she wouldn't have to sit across from Trina and look at her smug face.

Trina looked up at her in that moment and winked at her. It was almost as if she could read her thoughts. Kendall held her gaze, unwilling to falter again, until Whitaker spoke.

"The construction of the building will be complete in about four months. That's the projected timeline for the competition. There are twelve units left to sell that Langley hasn't already found a buyer for. He's working with us to finalize the rest of the sales but has reserved the right to sell off any of the apartments through his contacts if the opportunity arises. If that comes about, he will apply the sale to the agent that currently has less sales compared to the other."

"So, when Kendall is losing," Trina said as she looked across the table, "and Langley's old college friend needs a weekend apartment, he'll give her the sale? Because she's in last place?" Trina drummed her fingers on the paper in front of her. "That sounds like a handout."

"It's funny that you think I'll be the one needing the handout," Kendall replied, leaning back in her chair.

"I just think it's a little weird that in the 'rules' you and Whitaker mapped out an escape plan for failure that would directly benefit you," she replied. That woman had such nerve.

Ellison cleared her throat. "That is one of Langley's stipulations, and it's non-negotiable, if he finds a buyer through his network, they get the apartment over someone else. The credit for the sale goes to the losing competitor, but the commission would be divided between both the Sharkney and Gamble's offices. So, on the cash end, it's a draw."

Kendall wasn't thrilled with this rule, largely because it left some part of the sales contest to chance. Which meant that she would have to outsell Trina by at least two units to keep a comfortable lead. She knew she could, she'd just have to hustle.

"I don't like it." Trina sat forward and shook her head. "If the commission gets split, then it shouldn't count at all. You want to make the loser file the paperwork and do the grunt work, fine. But it shouldn't count toward the overall sales tally. Let our work represent itself. No handouts or hand-ups."

"Already trying to change the rules? Is it because you're worried?" Kendall agreed with Trina's argument, but she wouldn't give the satisfaction of letting her know that.

"All I'm saying is that Langley has lots of friends. And I'm sure your father is in that pool." Trina placed her forearms on the table, leaning toward Kendall again. "Who's to say Daddykins doesn't lob you a softball sale under the guise of a Langley prospect to even the score?"

"What kind of daddy issues do you have that you keep bringing up mine?" Kendall snapped.

"Whitaker," Ellison said. "What do you think?"

"I agree with Trina. I'm willing to amend that rule if you are." Kendall watched as his eyes darted between hers and Trina's.

"I'm fine with it," Ellison said with a wave of her hand. "Particularly since the final decision of who wins comes down to the amount of sales revenue that was generated, not the number of units sold. If anything, it simplifies the process."

Whitaker nodded. "I'll make the adjustment on my end."

"Let's move this along a bit," Ellison said. "Like Whitaker said, there are twelve units for sale; there's a mix of end suites and middle apartments, as well as two penthouses, and one commercial unit downstairs facing the back of the building. The commercial unit will be a rental, but Langley wants a long-term contract in that space, one year minimum."

Kendall nodded, this made sense. The commercial space was an unexpected bonus for a few reasons. Depending on what moved in there, it would be an asset to her sales pitch. If it was a coffee shop, she could push the fresh-brewed-coffee-in-your-own-backyard approach. Same thing if it was something else desirable like a small grocery market or café. On the flip side, if it was something that caused a community disturbance, like that apartment building in the North End she was trying to sell that had a dog groomer on the main level, that could be a deterrent. She heard constant complaints about allergies and dogs barking throughout the day. It was murder trying to sell those units because of it. Of course, she'd just started pitching the sales to dog lovers and the like, which helped, but it was still a hard property to move.

The long story short of it was this: whatever that commercial space became would either help or hinder her sales mission. So, in Kendall's opinion, it was best to tackle that first and help dictate the narrative. She didn't want another Pups N' Suds disaster, no matter how long a lease they agreed to.

"Okay, now down to the nitty-gritty," Whitaker rubbed his hands together in excitement. "The winner will be determined by the money she made at the end of the competition like Ellison said: sales revenue is the number we care about. We'll figure that out by contractual agreement. Once the apartment is under agreement and contracted, it's considered sold, even if it's not physically sold by the end of the four months since we all know that process can be longer or shorter depending on the type of sale whether cash, estate-based, or mortgage financed. So, a contract is a sale for either Trina or Kendall, unless it falls through before the end of the competition, at which point anyone can try to sell it."

"Kendall or Trina must be the closers on the deal. Each of you will have support in your offices, but the final sale must be done by you, not a member of your team," Ellison added.

"Right." Whitaker agreed. "That's about it. Unless either of you has something to add?"

"I do," Trina said. Because of course she did.

"Oh?" Whitaker looked put out even though he'd opened the floor to discussion.

"I think it should be noted that no personal sales can count, i.e., neither one of us can purchase a unit to win," Trina said.

"Why? Are you in the market for a new place?" Kendall asked incredulously. "Is that even something you can afford?" As soon as the words left her mouth, she regretted them. That was the kind of classist thing her father would say, not her. What had come over her today?

Trina slow blinked before replying to her. "Don't worry about the numbers in my bank account. Even though I wasn't born with a silver spoon in my mouth and a home for every season, like your pretty little self, I've done well for myself. On my own, I might add," she said, and Kendall felt small, again.

"I'm sorry, that came out wrong." Kendall knew she'd crossed the line and as prideful as she was, she wasn't outrightly cruel. And that had been cruel. "I—"

"I think that came out exactly as you intended it to," Trina said before she directed her attention to Whitaker and Ellison. "No personal sales. No inherited family fortunes tipping the sales' scale. And if someone"—she glanced briefly back at Kendall—"doesn't follow that rule, I vote for immediate disqualification. Regardless of the amount sold. You cheat, you lose."

Kendall gritted her teeth. Trina had effectively called her an heiress, an opportunist, and a cheater in not so many words throughout this entire meeting. But she hadn't exactly acted in the best manner herself. And she regretted that. "Agreed. You cheat, you lose. No personal assets to win the competition. That's fair."

Trina seemed almost amazed that Kendall agreed with her.

"Sounds good to me," Whitaker replied.

"It's a great amendment, I agree," Ellison said. Kendall didn't miss the way she looked at Trina as she spoke. It was almost as if she was proud of her. Kendall couldn't remember the last time anyone cast such a prideful glance at her, especially not someone that was in a position of power or employment above her. Not Whitaker, and never her father. Not that she needed to make anyone proud, that is. She was plenty proud of herself. That was all that mattered.

"Excellent." Whitaker cheered. "Let the games begin."

As Trina and Ellison were starting to leave, Kendall called out, "Trina, wait. Can we talk?"

Trina paused. "About what?"

Kendall watched as Ellison guided Whitaker away, leaving the two of them alone in the conference room. She walked toward Trina's side of the table, she wanted to clear the air.

"I'm sorry about what I said—"

Trina turned to leave, and Kendall reached out to stop her. Trina's head snapped toward her when she touched her elbow, causing Kendall to pull her hand back.

"Your hands are as frosty as your disposition. You can keep them to yourself," Trina said, her voice devoid of emotion.

"Look," Kendall said, running her hand through her hair in embarrassment. "We don't have to be friends, but we don't have to be nasty to each other. I was wrong when I said that before, I'm sorry."

"You might regret what you said, but I don't regret what I said. You are who you are, Kendall: spoiled, elitist, classist, and out of touch," Trina replied. "The sooner you accept that, the faster we can all move on."

Kendall had never been shot down that fast, or that severe, ever. She realized in that moment that she was in for the fight of her career. Shit.

Chapter Seven

Trina's phone buzzed on the desk in front of her. It was her brother, Calvin. She knew her nephew's first birthday was coming up, so she just assumed it was an update about the where and when and advice on ways to avoid their mother. Calvin knew she and her mom weren't on the best of terms, and to his credit, he did a pretty great job of helping Trina navigate that during family parties. Mainly, she was sure, because Calvin and his wife were the only ones throwing all these parties. So these uncomfortable familial interactions were all their doing. If their three kids weren't so cute and precocious, Trina might be annoyed by them. But she loved her older brother, and her sister-in-law, and especially his kids. She wasn't sure she wanted kids, but if she did, she'd want them to be just like Dexter, Hannah, and baby Henry. They were great kids, and she had her brother to thank for that. He was a good dad. And a good brother, even if he did keep having kids and parties that forced her to see all her relatives.

She thought about the dozens of judgmental eyes she'd be subjected to and cringed. That wasn't an exaggeration—there would be upwards of fifty people at her nephew's first birthday party because the Lees didn't do any party on a small scale. Nope. There were aunts, uncles, cousins, grandparents, old family friends, anyone who might need to know how wonderful the doctor son and his lovely family were doing. Which was fine, because Trina liked her brother and his family, but it was hard being a single non-white-collar postgrad degree holding daughter in an Asian family. Forget about being a *gay* non-white-collar postgrad degree holding daughter in an Asian family. That beyond complicated things. But nothing was as frustrating to her mother as her commission-based job. That took the cake. Even over the gay thing, which her mother was fine with, she supposed. Her mother didn't seem to mind her being gay as long as she was successful and brought positive representation to her family name. Which was not achieved by selling real estate. Somehow in her mother's mind, property was a dirty business. Her mother once likened her real estate career to prostitution. That was a fun night.

"Trina, you got a second?" Jax Pearson, her favorite junior agent, leaned into her doorway and rapped on the frame as they asked.

"For you, Jax, always." Trina was glad of the reprieve from her own thoughts. She waved them in. "How are you?"

"Good." Jax's smile quickly turned into a frown. "Nope, I'm lying. I'm nervous as hell."

Trina nodded—she got that. "Come in, close the door." She stood from her desk and waved Jax to the couch nearby. "Sit. Talk."

Jax adjusted their suit and skinny tie, fumbling with the blazer button before popping it open. Jax slipped their hands into their pockets and started to pace. "Like, we've been planning this for so long, and all of a sudden it's just a few weeks away and I'm starting to freak out."

Trina reached for Jax's hand and pulled them down to the couch next to her. "Listen. You don't have to invite your folks. You know you've got an army by your side. We've got you, no matter what happens. You know that, right?"

"I know." Jax exhaled and leaned forward, resting their elbows on their knees. "It's just, family is tough."

"Oh, I know." She squeezed Jax's knee and replied, "You know what it's like being the only daughter in a Vietnamese-Chinese family and being a lesbian on top of that?"

"Nope. Not a clue." Jax laughed. "Do you know what it's like to be trans and living in a new city away from your family about to get the top surgery you've been saving for your whole life only to realize you should probably tell your family about it?"

"Nope. Can't say I know what that's like," Trina answered. "But I can tell you that you don't have to involve them if you don't want to, and it's your body and your decision because it's your damn life. Not theirs. If I might speak bluntly on the matter."

"Please do." Jax gave her a shaky smile.

"Jax. You're an amazing person. With a great heart and a beautiful soul, and if your parents and sister aren't ready to accept that, then screw them." Trina motioned toward Jax's suit. "Plus, you look fucking killer in a slim-fitting suit, one that will feel all that much better when you aren't strapping down parts of your anatomy that you don't need and didn't want in the first place. Right?"

"Right." Jax puffed out their chest and laughed. "It'll be an adjustment, though."

"Meh," Trina replied. "You'll be fine."

Jax sat there for a moment, silent. Their voice was timid when they asked, "You don't think I should tell them then?"

Trina turned to face them more fully. "That's not my decision to make. They know you legally changed your name. They know you're doing well here and have a new life that is better representative of who you've always felt you were, right? Whether they accept that or not, it's a fact. So you don't have to tell them anything if you don't want to. It's not a requirement to fulfill or anything. You don't have to subject yourself to possible rejection if you don't want to. But if you need to tell them, for closure, then maybe you should. Just make sure you're not doing it for validation. Because you might not get that from them."

When Jax frowned at that statement, Trina was quick to add, "But you'll get it from us. We love you just as you are. You don't need to be anyone other than yourself to us. That's the truth. Tell them if you want to or need to. Then close that chapter and start the next one."

"Yup. You're still the best at pep talks. Crown retained," Jax replied.

Trina made a raise-the-roof motion with her hands and pretended to hear cheering. "I'd hate to let my loyal subjects down. Your queen adores you!" she called out to no one.

"Are you talking to your imaginary village folk again?" Lauren asked as she walked into Trina's office without knocking.

"At least they respect me for the icon I am," Trina replied.

"At least," Lauren teased.

Trina looked back at Jax and said, "It's all going to work out, whatever you decide."

"What are we talking about? This seems serious." Lauren paused her ribbing and turned her attention to them both.

"Top surgery and transphobia, aka family matters." Jax's expression wasn't as heavy as the topic. They seemed in better spirits.

"Woof." Lauren recoiled and shook her head. "Fuck 'em."

"That's what I said," Trina added, "though much more eloquently."

"Well, that's why you are you and I am me." Lauren paused. "Did I say that right?"

Trina stood up from the couch and pulled Jax with her. "I'm not even going to humor that. I assume you barged into our heart-to-heart for a reason?" She was being playful. She loved Lauren's lack of boundaries.

"Rude. Those convos are always to include the kooky best friend," Lauren replied, feigning hurt.

"Aye-aye, Captain." Jax saluted her.

"Good talk," Lauren replied. "Okay, peeps, it's meeting time. Ellison is ready to reveal this insane plan. So scurry-scurry."

Jax was out the door before them both, and Trina had to laugh. Jax made sure the office ran clean, an invaluable asset to all the agents there. If anything needed to be done, Jax would find a way to get it done. Beyond that, Jax was brilliant with tech stuff. They'd saved Trina's ass on more than one occasion. No one navigated social media as well as Jax. No one.

Trina had been anxiously anticipating this meeting since they'd left Sharkney's office yesterday. Ellison told her on their ride back to the office together that she had to finalize some things before informing the rest of the office, and she asked for Trina's discretion until she was ready to make the details of the contest known. But that was the last time they'd talked because once they got back to the office, Ellison had disappeared behind her office door, emerging only to take meetings with the lawyers. The whole thing felt like some big secret about to be unveiled. Even to Trina. And considering Ellison had called every agent and member of support staff in to attend this meeting, it appeared that was exactly the case.

Ellison was standing at the front of the conference room, her hip resting against the long dark wooden table. This was Trina's favorite conference room—it had the best natural light, and there was plenty of room around the table to pace. Which was something Trina did when she needed to think or when she was on the phone about to close a deal. She was a pacer. She had found that pacing had helped her solve a lot of problems in her life.

"Okay, have a seat. We have a lot to cover, and we need to get a jump on this before Whitaker does." Ellison motioned for everyone to sit. At the mere mention of his name, Trina scowled. She disliked him almost as much as Kendall. There was something slimy about him, but she couldn't quite put a finger on just what it was. And Kendall, well, Kendall was just an awful mess of privilege and self-perceived grandeur.

"I've asked you all to come in today because we're taking on a new venture, and it's all hands on deck," Ellison started. "As some of you might have heard, we are undertaking a temporary partnership with Sharkney Realty—"

Someone booed, and the room laughed.

Ellison smiled before continuing, "Starting today, Trina and her team, and this whole office, will be working to sell units in the new Harborside condo complex. The plan is to get as many units under agreement as possible between now and the projected completion date of the building, which is about four months from now. We will work in tandem with Sharkney Realty, but we will not share any intel. We are simply both representing a seller on a large-scale, luxury new construction. And we're competing with them."

Ellison motioned toward Jax. "Jax will be handing out some paperwork with the details of the building, the number of units available, the comps in the area for similar condos. This information is for your eyes only and will answer most of your questions. What I need from you all is to support Trina and her team. She's lead on these sales. Any information or leads you might have on possible buyers goes directly to Trina. Under the competition rules, Trina has to be the closer on all the deals, but team support and intel gathering is allowed within the office."

Jax walked around the table handing out full-color laminated portfolios.

Ellison continued, "Our office will coordinate with Sharkney, so we can stay on top of our respective positions in the sales race and not show a unit if it's no longer available. Also, our two offices have produced parallel marketing materials that demonstrate the collaboration, while maintaining our individuality. You'll see an example in those portfolios."

There was a mass shuffling, and Trina was pleased at how focused and intense everyone seemed to be. She wasn't sure how much the rest of the office would be involved or how supportive they'd be. She knew damn well that there were some jealous agents around that wouldn't take too kindly to Ellison effectively giving Trina all the commission opportunities for the Harborside. But if any of those people were in this room, they were hiding their feelings well.

"Does anyone have any questions?" Ellison asked, and a half dozen hands went up.

As Ellison answered them, Trina waited patiently, taking mental notes. Ellison had told her that they would speak privately afterward, so she didn't bother asking the million questions she wanted answers to in front of the whole group. Especially since some of those questions were of a more private nature.

After ten or so minutes, Ellison dismissed the group. "Lauren, Jax, and Trina, hang back."

The three of them looked at each other like they were in trouble. Trina had expected to meet, but why were the others there?

Ellison closed the conference room door and sat down across from them. She folded her hands on the table and looked each of them in the eye. "Okay, now that the formalities are over, you wanna get those questions off your chest?"

Lauren raised her hand first.

"Lauren?" Ellison asked with a grin.

"Is this for real? Because Sharkney is an ass." Lauren frowned.

Ellison replied, "I am in full agreement with you, Lauren. But yes, this is for real."

Jax raised their hand next.

Ellison rubbed her forehead. "You don't have to raise your hands, guys."

"Sorry." Jax leaned forward. "What do you need me for?"

"It's not me that needs you, it's Trina." Ellison motioned to Trina and she swallowed.

"I always need Jax. Jax is invaluable," Trina said.

Jax gave her a shy smile as Ellison said, "Exactly. Jax, you are officially Trina's eyes and ears in the office. There is going to be a lot of running around over the next few months, and we're going to need extra help on all fronts: paperwork, social media pushes, deadline monitoring, and overall client organization. I want you to live and breathe Harborside and all things Trina over the next few weeks. I'll delegate some of your regular daily tasks and projects elsewhere for the time being. This is the best way for you to get experience with sales and also see the complexity of the behind the scenes."

"On it." Jax clapped. "I can't wait."

"And what about Lauren?" Trina asked.

"Yeah, what about Lauren?" Lauren asked in response.

"Lauren, you are going to double-check Jax's management of Trina's deals. In addition to your own client load, I want you to pair up with Trina on her current active listings and offer support when she needs it. I want another veteran agent on the existing clients, and that's where you come in," Ellison said.

Trina had a handful of houses and condos that were listed but hadn't sold. They needed follow-up and promotion. Lauren and Jax would help her stay on top of her contacts and clients, so no one felt neglected while she focused on crushing Kendall. Ellison had this all mapped out, it appeared. She was glad someone had.

"Coolio. I'm in." Lauren shook Jax's hand, and they did some weird little shimmy. Trina wondered when they got a secret handshake.

"Can Trina and I have the room, please?" Ellison's dismissal was polite. Ellison was always polite. And mostly formal. That suited her, though. Trina couldn't imagine what Ellison was like relaxed and out of work mode. The thought amused her.

"Something funny?" Ellison walked to Trina's side of the table and sat next to her, turning her chair to face her.

"Nothing, really. I was just thinking about how different you are with us than Whitaker was with Kendall the other night and at the meeting yesterday. You treat us like equals but keep a healthy professional distance. I was wondering what you were like outside of work." Trina was honest. She found that being honest was the right choice most of the time. Especially with Ellison.

"Ha." Ellison leaned back in her chair. "I'm always working. This is just how I am all the time. There is no off the clock in this life."

Trina knew that behind that sarcasm, there was truth. She knew it because it was true for her own life, as well. This type of work took up evenings and weekends. It bowled through holidays and vacations. Work like this was time sensitive, high risk and high reward, and cutthroat. An agent caught sleeping on a sale would be out in the cold, and since these deals were bank-breakers, no one could afford to miss a sale. They wouldn't survive in the business if they did.

"It's not a job for everyone, that's for sure." Trina thought of her empty bed at home and the single wineglass by the sink. She never entertained guests for the night. Her trysts were hours long, not days or weeks. That's how it had been for a long time. She didn't foresee that changing anytime soon.

"I just wanted to get a few minutes with you to make sure you're all in on this," Ellison said, her voice soft. "This will be all consuming, Trina. A day and night battle for four long months. Are you sure you want to move forward, now that you've had a chance to think about it? I know I pushed you, because I really believe you're capable of being successful, but this is your chance to bow out if you want to."

Trina wasn't expecting that. "No. Never. I'm in this, all in. This is the opportunity of a lifetime. And screw Kendall and that slimeball Sharkney. I'm in."

Ellison smiled. "Good. We'll do everything to make sure you have what you need to be successful. This is as much an investment in you as it is in the office. We're all rooting for you."

"Thanks." Trina believed that. She'd felt it in the room before her colleagues were dismissed. It was a damn good feeling.

Chapter Eight

Kendall's mind had been racing all morning. She felt like she had a million little loose ends getting tangled in her brain. She was looking forward to this showing with the architect, because she hoped it would ground her a bit and give her a solid foundation to start working from. She needed something tangible that she could have and hold—she needed to be in the space that she was supposed to sell. It was also the day she would start kicking Trina's ass all over Boston. And she was *so* looking forward to that.

After the office meeting with Trina and Ellison earlier in the week to finalize the project, she'd been working hard in her office with the team Whitaker was forcing upon her. It wasn't that she didn't like teamwork. She just didn't like teams. Or anyone less qualified than herself being responsible for anything to do with her clients or her business. Because who could do a better job than her? No one. She just didn't like incompetence, okay? Or maybe it was that she had major trust issues. People had let her down before, so she'd grown used to doing things alone. People always managed to let you down, it seemed. And she was done trying to pick up the pieces someone else broke. That was one of the vows she made to herself when she moved to Boston. She wouldn't rely on anyone to help her achieve her goals or let anyone get in the way. Because by and large, people sucked. This seemed to trickle over to her personal life, as well. Not that she had time for one. But Margo mentioning that at coffee had reminded her that it'd been a long time since she'd ventured into any sort of dating relationship. Not that she needed any distractions right now. And a relationship, sexual or otherwise, would certainly be a distraction. She was fine being alone. She quite liked it, actually.

She pulled her car up to the designated parking area near the construction zone, and a foreman met her with a kind smile. He directed her toward the building's main entrance where Zander Alter, one of Langley's architects and design firm representatives, handed her a hard hat.

"Sorry. It's probably going to mess up your hair, but while we walk through active construction zones, you'll need it on." Zander's hazel eyes were framed by deep smile lines. She knew of his reputation and his vast years of experience, but she was impressed to see how young he appeared. The wrinkling around his eyes was the only sign of age on his handsome, clean-shaven face. But what really struck her was how soft-spoken he was, almost timid. That wasn't a typical character trait in the luxury design business—grandiose and flamboyant personalities were more common.

"No worries." She accepted the hat and pointed to her low bun. "I came prepared for headgear."

He laughed and led her to an elevator, pointing out debris obstacles and kicking a rug out of the way of the elevator door. "It's a mess down here, but we'll be seeing two of the more finished apartments upstairs today, a middle apartment and an end unit. We should have more of each type available to show you over the next couple of weeks, though the design plans are nearly identical, so that's up to you. The penthouse will be last, of course. A lot of that design will be left open for buyer customization, assuming we sell it before we finish, that is."

"Great." Kendall took note of the elevator they were in. Though the walls were covered with protective fabric during construction, she could tell that it was spacious and very modern. An electronic panel with touch screen capabilities displayed the numbers of the floors as well as the weather forecast for the next few days. Along the bottom was a NASDAQ ticker. She motioned toward the screen interface. "This is neat."

Zander blushed. "That was my idea. Everything is so tech driven these days, so it was silly to me to have a regular elevator without the bells and whistles. I know that some people will be turned off by that, but Charles is hoping to attract a younger crowd to this building. We want to ensure people are excited." He shrugged. "But an elevator panel can be changed pretty easily. We'll see what kind of clients you bring, I guess."

The elevator doors opened to the eighth floor and he walked them toward the end of the hall. "We're going to check out one of the middle apartments first today, and then a corner apartment on a higher floor. Both have water views. I was just talking about some of the building's unique attributes with your colleague when I got the message that you were here. So I'll backtrack a bit."

Kendall stopped walking. "My colleague?"

Zander held open the door to the apartment. "Yeah. Ms.—"

"It's about time you decided to show up." The soft, low timbre of Trina's voice was unmistakable. A voice that, even when insulting you, had an appealing quality to it. Another annoying trait, Kendall thought. That feeling quadrupled when Trina came into view looking like she'd stepped off the page of a fashion magazine. Her long dark hair cascaded over the shoulders of her double-breasted gray herringbone coat, and a splash of her bright blue pointed-toe pumps was visible under the straight-leg black trousers. Kendall was impressed by the bold shoe choice—it worked. Not that she'd extend that compliment, ever, but still. She could appreciate good taste when she saw it.

"I'm not late," Kendall replied. "And I'm also not supposed to be meeting you here."

Trina's arched eyebrow and red lipstick smirk made Kendall scowl.

"Well, since I walked out of Monday's meeting without saying good-bye, I figured I'd make it up to you in person."

"Delightful." Kendall had mixed feelings about that meeting. Though it had been very productive, she hadn't behaved the way she would have liked. And she'd been harboring those feelings for a few days. But the flash of joy that crossed Trina's face just now when Kendall failed to mask her disappointment at discovering that Trina was already getting a tour of the space made her a feel a little more justified for her actions on Monday. Marginally. That didn't change that this, however, was not how she'd planned today to go. The less time she spent in Trina's presence, the better.

"Uh, okay then." Zander cleared his throat as he tapped his fingers on the white quartz countertop of the kitchen island. "So, I was just telling Ms. Lee—"

"Trina," Trina supplied as she stepped closer to the kitchen island.

"Sorry. Trina." Zander adjusted his hard hat. "As I was telling Trina, there are some interesting nuances to this unit and all the units along this side of the building."

"Oh?" Kendall tried to ignore how close Trina was standing. "I'd love to hear them."

Zander opened the binder in front of him and pulled out a few face sheets. He pointed to some numbers and graphs and rattled off some information about physics and the glass-to-concrete ratio of the building, and it would all be fascinating to someone, she was sure, but for her, well, it was as boring as the flat gray floor beneath their feet.

As soon as there was a long enough pause for her to interject without interrupting, Kendall asked about the floor. "This is subfloor, right? Is the plan to tile or put wood down?"

"Dark gray slate tile. There will be large rectangles in the common space, smaller ones in the bedroom. Unless the owner wants to switch that up. But the show apartments will have slate. There are some pieces over there for you to see." He motioned toward the other side of the kitchen island near the empty living room space.

Kendall walked toward it, looking for a reason to distance herself from Trina, who, surprisingly, wasn't saying much at the moment. She got the distinct feeling that she was being watched, though. Like Trina was observing her. The feeling was unnerving. She wasn't used to being scrutinized.

The kitchen and living room shared an open concept layout, with floor to ceiling glass windows facing the Boston Harbor water view in front of them. The kitchen was mostly finished with crisp white subway tiles as a backsplash and a marbled white countertop on the island. The cabinets were also white, with small silver pulls on the doors. The appliances were missing, but the spaces were marked with tape identifying where they would go.

She turned toward the windows and allowed herself a moment to appreciate the view. It was a clear day in Boston today, the sun high in the sky and boats coming in and out of the harbor. This was what people would be paying for. The convenience of a concierge and valet was great, and the below ground parking reserved for every unit would be wonderful for the snowy Boston winters, but the view was the selling point, and this view was unbeatable.

"How many bedrooms are in this apartment?" she asked without turning around.

"One. One full and one half bath as well," Trina answered her.

She turned and gave Trina a look.

"What? Zander's on a call. I'm trying to be helpful." The look on Trina's face was anything but helpful. It was almost coy, like she was teasing Kendall.

Kendall looked over Trina's shoulder to see that Zander was indeed on a call, his back to them as he spoke quietly into the phone. She'd been so lost in her thoughts she hadn't noticed him speaking at all. "That's very helpful, thank you."

Trina winked at her. "The rooms are through there. The master closet is impressive."

Kendall hated that Trina had already been through the whole apartment. Or that she was even here at all. "Thanks." She tried not to make her reply sound curt, but she failed.

"Anytime." Trina's smile was mocking. Kendall loathed her.

Kendall followed the short hallway toward the master bedroom. The room was large enough to accommodate a king-sized bed with bedside tables on either side, but not much more than that. Kendall imagined this was one of the less expensive apartments for sale. Maybe it would be better suited for someone who wanted a pied-à-terre in the city. Or someone who wanted to use it as a rental—she could see that being a profitable option.

The bathroom was much like the kitchen, clean and sterile, white and inoffensive. A large soaker tub was in the corner, and the double sinks under the wall length mirror to the left made this an inviting space for a couple. Trina was right about the master closet. There wasn't enough room for a dresser in the bedroom, but the closet made up for that. Custom fit shelves and racks lined the well-lit walk-in, and the finishes were again white with brushed silver. Smaller dark gray slate tiles made up the floor of the bedroom and the closet, which was fine, if somewhat—

"Bland, right?" Trina asked from the bedroom doorway. "That's what you're thinking, isn't it? The floor is fine it's just…uninspired."

She surveyed the way Trina leaned against the door, almost uninterested. She had this way about her of taking up a lot of space without physically taking up any at all. Those heels made her eye-level with Kendall today, and dark brown eyes looked back at her expectantly. "I was thinking that, actually."

"The finishes are nice, nothing too flashy. But there's a bleakness to the apartment. Like it lacks life," Trina said.

"It's empty and unfinished." Kendall didn't want to make small talk with Trina. Even if she had been thinking the same thing.

Trina added, "The only thing that will change will be the staging— pops of color will have to be added to bring warmth to this space. But the view can't save the coldness of it." Trina stood and crossed her arms, rubbing her hands up and down her sleeves like she was cold. "You know, like how you are being right now. Downright frosty."

"I am not." Kendall's knee-jerk reply convinced no one, herself included.

"Okay." Trina looked amused. She pulled out her phone from one of the front pockets of her jacket and asked, "How do you like your coffee, Ice Queen?"

Kendall just glared at her.

"Tall, decaf, flat white, no foam?" Trina guessed. "Or are you one of those basic kinds that are all in on the flavored house brews?"

When Kendall didn't reply, Trina shivered. "It's getting colder by the minute. I'll tell Zander you're ready to move on. Maybe the next apartment will be a little warmer."

Kendall growled in annoyance, taking two deep breaths before she exited the room. Trina was well under her skin, and she could tell that Trina was plenty aware of that fact. Why was she here today, anyway?

Trina loved how irritated Kendall looked. She'd pressed Zander to find out when Kendall would be here because she knew he'd tell her without any hesitance. She'd worked with Zander once before, on another sale a few months ago. He was brilliant but shy. When she found out he was one of the new designers Langley had contracted, she was ecstatic. Zander was open to discussion and suggestion—at least he had been on that other project. That was going to be vital when it came to selling these condos. If she could get his ear on some things, she knew she could help her sales.

She scrolled through her apps and placed a coffee order. She recalled that Zander liked his black, extra strong, and burning hot. She added two of those giant boxes of coffee in her cart and checked the box for all the extras: cups, sugars, the works. She'd completed the order by the time she was back in the kitchen.

"Is the upstairs ready for us now?" she asked Zander, who was waiting patiently by the kitchen island.

He spoke into the radio he had at his hip and nodded. "Yup, but it's an active work zone, so you'll have to wear that once we get up there."

Trina frowned at the hard hat next to her Birkin bag on the kitchen counter. She loathed hats, but head injuries weren't high on her list, either. She reached into her pocket and pulled out a hair tie, pulling her long hair into a low pony. "As you wish," she said as she put the ill-fitting hat on.

"Rules are rules," Zander said with a shrug. "They mess up my hair, too."

Trina pretended to squint. "Not a gray in sight, Zander. Are you seeing Lara on Newbury yet? Or are you just not aging?"

"Oh, I'm aging plenty." Zander ran his hand through his thick hair. "Lara is a genius. Thanks for the referral."

"You know each other?" Kendall asked as she emerged from the bedroom, and Trina thought she looked slightly less annoyed. She would fix that.

"We've worked together before, yes," Trina answered, being careful to add a sweetness to her voice.

"That's nice." Kendall's lips were in a tight line. Trina loved how much she was affecting her today.

She decided to dial it up just a bit, to see how much Kendall would engage. "If you're ready, Zander said we can move on to a corner unit now. Unless you have more questions, that is. Or if you need a little more time to really soak it all in. No rush, I'm not meeting with my first client here until another hour or so from now."

Kendall looked dumbfounded. "You're already bringing someone by?"

"You aren't? Time's a-wasting, Yates." Trina picked up her Birkin and looped her arm with Zander's, guiding him toward the door. "So we're ready then, I guess?"

She didn't bother looking over her shoulder, but she could feel the rage radiating off Kendall like heat from the sun. It was a pleasant feeling.

The tenth floor was loud. Zander had warned them on the short elevator trip that they were finishing the hallways up here today. But he'd completely undersold the deafening thumping noises and dust they had to walk through to get to the corner unit.

Trina hurried through the door, dusting off her shoulders and taking off her protective headgear the minute the door was closed. The noise ceased almost entirely.

"Is this unit soundproof?" she asked as she made her way over to the spec sheet Zander must have left on the counter. She perused it as she waited for his reply.

"Not entirely, but we did add extra insulation to the doors and windows of the corner suites to offset the breeze off the water that comes with it," Zander said.

Trina looked at the space and smiled. This was more like it. The kitchen was more welcoming, the backsplash was still made of white subway tile, but these tiles had subtle blues in them, and there were accent tiles that looked like cracked glass to give the backsplash texture. The countertops were also white like downstairs, but these were much more lushly marbled, and the cabinets here were different colors—the uppers a classic white, but the bottom cabinets a deep gray-black that extended into the base of the large island that had seating for five. The appliances were in and polished, and the six-burner stovetop to her left glowed under the light of the vented hood. The double oven could cook a feast for a dozen, and the refrigerator door panel matched the surrounding cabinets, adding to the elegance of the kitchen setup. Trina most appreciated the upgraded cabinet hardware, which was a glistening brushed nickel with ergonomically fitted handles and pulls, unlike the standard ones in the last apartment. This was an expensive and luxurious kitchen. And one that almost justified the steep price tag on the spec sheet in front of her. Almost.

Kendall asked Zander a few questions, and Trina listened while she took in the fully staged living space. The living room was light and airy, the corner affording two full walls of glass with a door leading out to a private balcony. The walls that weren't glass were painted white, but unlike the empty space downstairs, this condo was staged. A massive TV hung on the wall across from the beautiful though slightly uncomfortable looking gray couch. And though the floor tiles were the familiar dark slate, the patterned arrangement was fresh, and plush rugs warmed the coldness of the floor. Trina was looking at the light fixtures, taking particular note of the chandelier over the medium-sized dining table, when Kendall's voice caught her attention.

"How much can the client customize this space? I mean, besides materials and the like. Could they, for instance, get panoramic doors leading out onto that balcony? Or would that impact the structural integrity of that wall?" Kendall touched the glass separating the living space from the outdoor porch area.

That was a brilliant question. The only access to the porch was through a single, average looking glass door off the living room. A set of panoramic doors would make a seamless transition from indoor to outdoor living, effectively removing any separation between the spaces. The upgrade would improve the space exponentially. Trina was impressed by Kendall's eye for design.

Zander considered her question before answering. "To answer the first part of your question, a buyer can change just about anything and everything. The sooner they get on board, the less renovation needs to be done to make it perfect for them. We're open to any and all suggestions. Whatever makes everyone happy." He stared at the glass wall for a moment before adding, "Panoramic doors are a feature we have planned for the penthouses, but I hadn't considered it here. They would be more expensive, but the framework of the building wouldn't be impacted at all. And the installation would be easy. That's a thought. I'll mention it to Charles."

Kendall looked pleased. "Thanks for clarifying."

Trina studied her for a minute. She'd watched her move around the space downstairs, but she seemed a little different up here. She was more confident, almost as if she had found her groove. That both intrigued and worried Trina. She was doing her damnedest to make sure Kendall didn't feel overly confident. She wanted to keep her on her heels, so to speak. It would be a hell of a lot easier to knock her down that way.

A loud knock at the apartment door drew her attention. Zander hurried over to it, thanking someone before he walked down the long corridor back to the kitchen and living room space. He was holding the answer to Trina's dilemma. She smiled.

"Thanks, Trina." Zander held up a coffee cup with his name on it and gave her an appreciative nod. "The guys thank you, too. That was super nice of you, to buy them all coffee."

Trina gave him a playful smile. "The faster they work, the faster I can sell these units off. It's the least I can do."

She walked to the kitchen island and picked up the coffee with her name on it, easing Kendall's out of the cardboard carrier, too. She turned to find Kendall watching her. She added a little extra hip sway on her way over to her, just for good measure.

"You didn't give me an answer before, so I guessed." She handed the drink to Kendall as she added, "I hope you like it."

Kendall's hesitance in taking the cup gave Trina more glee than it should have. She could tell she had Kendall on the defensive again. Just like that, she had taken control of the situation back, and she fucking loved it.

"What is it?" Kendall examined the cup, spinning it in her hands, as if waiting to find an answer written on the surface.

"Frozen hot chocolate." Trina gave Kendall her best megawatt smile.

Kendall gave her a look. "Are you still going on about this ice queen business?"

"That depends." Trina tapped her coffee cup to Kendall's icy drink in a mock toast. "Are you admitting that your frigid nature joined you on these apartment tours today?"

Kendall raised an eyebrow. "Do you think you can bully me into caving to you before we even get started? Because you can't."

Trina raised her free hand in protest. "Who says I'm bullying anyone? I bought you a drink, to be cordial—"

"To mock me and further promote your narrative that I'm cold," Kendall replied, crossing her arms.

"I don't need to try to make that a thing, it's a fact," Trina pointed out. "And I already told you—I've gotten started. You're behind. My client will be here any minute."

Kendall scoffed. "Assuming you even have a client, you mean. You need to work on your mind games, Trina. This isn't going to work."

Trina cocked her head and appreciated the sincerity of Kendall's retort. She meant every word. Trina felt emboldened by it. "Stick around long enough, and you two can meet. I'd love to see the look on your face when I close a sale right in front of you. In fact, please do stay—I could use that motivation."

Kendall shook her head with a snort.

Trina sighed. "Suit yourself. I'm going to go check out the bedrooms to make sure my client will be as wowed as I know they will. Enjoy your drink—it's great. I promise."

She made her way back down the long corridor toward the entryway, buzzing with renewed energy as she checked out the half bath in the hallway and the smaller second bedroom with en suite bathroom. She had a feeling that teasing Kendall would work, especially after how she'd responded to her at the meeting Monday, but she didn't know just how well until today. The passive bitch-on-heels approach had been a tried-and-true tactic with every other overly friendly blond Realtor she'd crossed paths with. No one wanted to be considered standoffish or unapproachable in this business—it was bad for sales. And Kendall probably wasn't either of those things, since she'd clearly been successful over the past year, whether with or without Daddy's help. Regardless, Trina had hit her mark, again. And she was living for it.

She stepped into the master bedroom suite and cheered. This was perfect. Unlike downstairs, this king-sized bed was oriented on the best wall to see the multi-million-dollar harbor view. And the suite-style space allowed for plenty of extra furniture and maneuverability. A plush looking chaise longue at the foot of the bed by the glass wall, facing the view, added just the right amount of hominess to sell this room. That is, if the view alone didn't.

Trina walked into the master bedroom closet and immediately pictured how she'd lay out her vast heel collection. Designer jackets over there, she envisioned. And her handbags on the shelves under the lights, there and there. This closet was to die for. She had serious closet envy now.

When she emerged from the closet, she found Kendall over by the chaise, snapping pictures of the room on her phone. Trina struck a pose along the closet doorframe, cradling her coffee like a shiny trophy.

"My best angle is from the left," Trina said playfully.

Kendall lowered her phone with a laugh. "Imperfect, are we? I can't believe you'd admit to having a bad angle...seems below your level of narcissism."

"Oh, I never said I had a bad angle. I just said my best was from the left. You know, for future reference," Trina replied.

"Do people actually like you?" Kendall seemed mystified. "So far you are living up to every bad thing I ever heard about it."

"Ooh, I love that you've been looking into me and gathering all that intel," Trina said as she shimmied in place. "All those tongues with my name on it. You're making me blush, girl. Go on. Tell me more."

Kendall looked like she didn't know what to say in response.

Trina gave her the out. "I'll be over here in the bathroom checking out the tile job if you think of a comeback."

She walked past Kendall into the master bath and sipped her coffee as she surveyed herself in the full-length mirror next to the soaker tub. She looked fabulous today. She'd have to send Talia a thank you for the recommendation—this coat was gorgeous. Just the right kind of garment for stirring up some shit, looking divine while doing it.

"All right," Kendall said from the doorway behind her. "I'll bite. Tell me about this likely fictional client of yours. What makes you so sure you're going to get the sale on the spot? Besides your previously discussed bloated ego, I mean."

Trina sat at the edge of the tub and crossed her legs, keeping a watchful eye on Kendall as she spoke. "The client is a DJ friend of mine. We've been on the hunt for a place just like this for a while now. And since they opened that enormous casino just across the water there"—she motioned past Kendall's shoulder to the water view behind her—"living in this building would shave Shay's commute to work down from an hour and a half in bumper-to-bumper traffic to fifteen minutes by water taxi. And when you are paid for your time, every minute counts."

"Your DJ friend moonlights as a croupier? And you think they can afford this place?" Kendall asked, an edge to her voice.

"There you go with that judgmental, classist shit again." Trina walked past her into the bedroom, pausing before heading back into the hallway. "My DJ friend is the house entertainment for the casino and three of the surrounding nightclubs in the area, one of which is within walking distance from here. The near-soundproof quality of the space and the option of your recommended panoramic porch doors will sign that sales contract for me. Thanks for the suggestion—Shay's gonna love it."

"Shay's gonna love what?" Shay entered the bathroom with open arms.

Trina stepped into them and squeezed her old friend tightly. "This place. You're gonna love this place. And you're early. I would have gotten you something to drink." She frowned when they broke apart.

"It's too early for vodka. And no coffee—I need to squeeze in a nap before tonight's gig." Shay gave her that half grin that used to make her heat up in all the wrong places. Or the right places, at the time. That was ancient history, though, and they were just friends now. Shay had been a departure from Trina's usual type, but it had been a wild and fun ride while it lasted. Which was something Trina had a feeling she could rekindle if she wanted to. Shay was fluid like that.

Shay motioned behind her. "Who's your friend?"

"Kendall Yates." Kendall introduced herself, extending her hand and shaking Shay's in greeting. "I'm glad to see you're a real person."

Shay gave Trina a confused look. "Did I miss something?"

Trina gave Kendall a once-over. "Nope. Not a thing."

"*Okay,*" Shay replied, drawing the word out. "I definitely missed something."

"Trina says you're the resident DJ over at the new casino. Encore, right? That's pretty impressive," Kendall replied.

Trina didn't like that she was engaging with Shay. That wasn't part of the plan.

"Thanks," Shay replied. "It's a fun gig. You should come see me sometime. I spin most nights—"

"And that's enough chatting up the enemy." Trina pulled Shay's arm toward the living room. "Let me show you around."

"It's nice to meet a friend of Trina's. Even nicer to know she has some," Kendall called out as they walked away.

Shay stopped short, turning on the spot. "Damn. She's got your number, T. You notch that bedpost and move on, or what?"

"Excuse me?" Kendall looked scandalized.

Trina pressed her palm to her forehead. Shay wasn't one to mince words. "We're just a couple of friendly rivals, that's all."

"So not a *couple*-couple then." That famous half grin reappeared. Shay was such a lady-killer. And with her tall, lean build and easygoing nature, she had no trouble bedding anyone who walked. Trina tried not to let her mind wander to whether Kendall needed a good lay to lighten up, but she went there, momentarily at least. Kendall *was* her physical type, after all, even if her personality left much to be desired. A part of her was curious whether Kendall had someone waiting for her at home.

Kendall laughed. "You're kidding."

"I've been known to from time to time. But no, I'm not." Shay shrugged. "Your loss, though. Trina is a knockout in bed—"

"Shay," Trina hissed. "Totally not okay."

"What? It's true." Shay made the sign of the cross. "It's practically gospel."

"Remember that oversharing thing we talked about? This is totally one of those times." Trina would have been mortified if Kendall didn't look a little bit embarrassed. She decided to savor the moment. "You'll have to excuse my friend. Shay has no filter."

"Job hazard, I guess. All that boom-boom beat and all those beautiful ladies fawning over me means small talk isn't my thing." Shay was joking, but Trina was sure the humor was lost on Kendall. Shay then did the very Shay thing of flirting because Kendall had a pulse and that's what Shay did. "Maybe we should get a drink together. Get to know each other a little better, dance a bit. Make some mistakes. Laugh about them in the morning and then make them again. I promise, I'm a good time. Trina can attest to that."

Kendall appeared to be blushing. "I appreciate the offer, but my plate's pretty full right now. Thanks, though."

"No worries." Shay let the rejection roll off her back like she did everything else. She was easy-breezy that way—nothing really fazed her. Trina envied that about her. Shay turned her attention back to Trina as she stage-whispered, "She's super cute. Maybe I'll buy this place from *her*."

"Keep it in your pants, Casanova. Let me show you how an amazing set of panoramic porch doors is gonna blow your mind." Trina gave a quick glance over her shoulder toward Kendall for good measure. "See you later, Yates."

The curt nod from Kendall told her that she'd won this round. But the intense look that accompanied it told Trina that she was in for a challenge next time. *Bring it on.*

Chapter Nine

Kendall dropped the iced drink into the trash by the elevator, glad to have it out of her hands. She'd been too polite to throw it in Trina's face, even if her instinct told her to. Instead she'd left it on the kitchen counter, but Zander had innocently run it out to her here, thinking she'd forgotten it. He was sweet and obviously brilliant, but clearly also obtuse if he thought she'd ever accept any olive branch, faux or otherwise, from Trina.

That woman was something else. The nerve, the brashness, the arrogance… "Bitch," Kendall said to no one as the elevator closed, locking her inside with her thoughts. She couldn't think of a more colorful word for Trina than that. And that astonished her, because she had a lot of colorful language to draw upon. But that one seemed to fit, so she went with it.

As she exited the elevator and greeted the contractor downstairs, she thought about what had happened upstairs. Today had been a revelation of sorts. She'd finally gotten to see the spaces she was supposed to sell, *and* she had a chance to see Trina in action. Well, not in sales action, but she saw how she engaged with Zander and with the other workers. She saw her easy confidence and annoying cockiness, both at play during different times today. And she saw how seamlessly Trina moved from antagonizing her to being sweet with Zander and Shay.

Trina Lee was more complex than Kendall had initially realized. And her observations about the spaces were spot on. Clearly, Trina knew a thing or two about luxury real estate and design. And she was quick on her feet, witty, and sarcastic, while also managing to be a little cutting at the same time. Trina had a way with words that Kendall hadn't been expecting. She'd managed to wind Kendall up and down enough that Kendall felt dizzy. Kendall wasn't used to being made to feel like she was off-center. But Trina had managed that with ease today, making her feel just a little less sure of herself.

"That won't happen again," Kendall said as she slid into the driver's seat in her car, closing the door and buckling her seat belt before checking her calendar. She had a few client meetings later at other properties and was due back to the office to complete some paperwork before then. She found herself looking forward to the drive to her office. She needed the time to think.

As she pulled onto the highway, she let herself admit that the idea of Trina closing a deal today enraged her. She didn't like starting off behind. Granted, she had already gotten the ball rolling on the commercial space deal with Cyclebar, thanks in large part to Margo's comment at their coffee date the other day, but still, a sale was a sale and every one counted.

She dialed by voice command, and within a few rings, she was connected to Clyde at her office. Clyde. What kind of name was that around here? She couldn't wrap her head around it.

"Hey, Kendall. What's up?" Clyde's pleasing baritone filled her car.

"I want you to organize a list of all the available units at the Harborside—I want to know their location in the building and their stats. I'd like it ready by the time I get back after my appointments this afternoon." No time to waste.

"Absolutely. I'll get right on it," Clyde replied.

"Great." Kendall disconnected the call but after a few moments she called back.

"Yes?" Clyde asked.

"Thanks. I wanted to say thanks." Kendall hated how forced that felt to say.

"Sure thing. See you later," Clyde replied before hanging up.

Kendall sighed, annoyed at herself. She needed to be better about that. She needed to be more polite and less demanding. She was the first to admit she wasn't very comfortable or experienced with the ins and outs of teamwork and trusting people on the business front. She didn't think she was rude, exactly, but she knew she could be short with people. Another nasty trait she'd picked up from her father. Except she didn't carry that character flaw into her personal relationships like he did. Only her professional ones, it seemed. She had no trouble being kind and caring and patient with her friends or lovers. Just with her colleagues or her rivals.

Friends and lovers, she thought. As if she had either of those. Besides Margo, Kendall could count on one hand the people she would call friends. And none of them were local or had even talked to her in years. That was on her, she knew that. She'd pulled back and left, not them. But that's how it had to be for her to be free. For her to feel like she could breathe for the first time in her entire life. She had to leave everything and everyone behind to save herself. And she would do it again in a second if she had to—she knew that. Which was why she could also count on one hand how many lovers she'd had in the last few years, in the years following her breakup with Collette. She didn't like feeling tied down. She didn't like feeling vulnerable or exposed. She knew that pain, she knew how easily it could be exploited, and she wasn't about to take on that burden again.

As she drove, she thought back to Trina and Shay. Shay had that effortless, liquid sex vibe about her. She straddled the androgynous line, with a defined jawline and careless shag haircut. But it fit her. Her understated leather jacket and jeans paired nicely with her sparkling white sneakers, but her thirty-thousand-dollar Bell & Ross watch made a clear statement. She might seem like an attractive but forgettable disc spinner at first glance, but she had the pennies to prove her worth. And the confidence to push the envelope with her flirtation. Shay hadn't hesitated at all to ask Kendall out. It was as if she was used to every person on the planet finding her attractive. Like rejection was no big deal.

Kendall, on the other hand, didn't like rejection. And she couldn't imagine putting herself out there so cavalierly. What a life that must be to live, she thought. One where people tripped over themselves at the thought of you finding them attractive. She mulled that over. She *had* had that life in the past, though. Maybe that was why Shay's forwardness had irked her. She was used to getting her way in her past life. She was used to women dropping to their knees in front of her. She loved it then, though she questioned their motives now. She knew damn well that her path had been paved in gold from birth, and reject it though she might now, she wouldn't be where she was today without the Yates legacy doing the heavy lifting.

That's why Trina got under her skin so easily and so damn deeply. Because she'd called out all the times Kendall had benefited from her legacy, and she'd been right. Not that Kendall would admit that to Trina, but it was true, at least parts of it. The truth was, she was a product of her father and his successes. And try as she might to get out from under his shadow, she knew she couldn't, not really, not until he was dead and forgotten. If that day ever came.

But with the jail sentence, it was clear that her father's shady business dealings had finally caught up with him. One of the reasons she left Connecticut was to get away from him and the shame he'd brought to the Yates name. She knew all those doors that opened for her because of her name and lineage would slam shut. And she wanted to be far away from that when it happened. And she had been. She'd earned her own way here in Boston—she'd had a new start. For the first time in a long time, it seemed like her destiny was her own, and that was a wonderful feeling.

As she eased into her parking spot at work, she thought about the other reason she'd left her home. Her father's volatile temper and manipulative emotional abuse had staggered her accomplishments and her life, like fragmented pieces of a broken glass that could never be repaired. But when his meddlesome, domineering ways also led to the end of her engagement to Collette, she finally was able to admit to herself the cycle was never going to end. It had taken *that* for her to realize just how much he had interfered in her happiness. He had ruined a huge part of her, including the best and most loving relationship she had ever known, and it didn't seem like she would be able to fix those parts. That's why she ran when Collette left. She needed to live in her broken places to see how bad things had gotten, to try to start over. To try to be someone she wasn't, even if the person she once was had been afforded every advantage. The fact that his conviction happened shortly after the breakup was just sort of lucky. She was already leaving, but with the sentencing, no one questioned why.

Her mind wandered back to Trina as she shut off her car.

As much as she disliked that woman, a part of her was intrigued by her. Maybe more so now that she knew she'd dated, or at least slept with, another woman. Was Trina gay? Did she label herself? Kendall thought about how Trina looked today, stunning in that jacket and heels. How Kendall's breath had caught when Trina playfully posed by the closet door. Kendall had snapped a picture of her then, almost out of reflex. She knew she'd look at it again later. The lighting had been perfect, and Trina had looked infuriatingly beautiful while mocking her. And something about that turned her on a little. She had no problem admitting that Trina was gorgeous, but she'd never tell Trina that.

Because she was both beautiful and infuriating. They canceled each other out, Kendall told herself. They had to.

She shook her head, trying to free herself of Trina's image. She needed to focus on something else, anything else. She went through her mental Rolodex of clients who might have interest in the Harborside. A few came to mind right away, but if she wanted to be competitive, she knew she'd have to start fishing, and that was something that made her a little uncomfortable. She wasn't used to this side of the business. She'd had success finding what a client wanted, matching them to their dream home. But she had limited experience finding a client to match a house. That took a little more thinking. She would be selling an idea, sales at the literal ground level. So she had to polish her acting skills and make sure her pitch was airtight. Then she'd have to find a market to shop it to. Country clubs? That boutique gym and spa on Newbury Street? Maybe she could brainstorm with some of the other agents at the office—she was sure one of them must have a client who would want to see the best new thing in town. Which of course would mean she'd have to trust their judgment. Something she was working on. She seemed to be working on a lot lately.

CHAPTER TEN

Trina pulled a glass out of the cabinet and did a tiny victory dance on the way over to the kitchen island where her preferred bottle of cabernet sauvignon was patiently waiting. This was her favorite celebratory vino, the wine that got her through every sale or professional victory, every amazing first date or incredible roll in the hay. This was the wine she rewarded herself with when she was going to have a quiet moment home alone, when she could savor the wonderfulness of the day or night she was reflecting on. This was her soak in a hot bathtub with lots of girlie-scented candles and fragrances and get buzzed on wine. Tonight was one of those nights. And this glass of wine was so, so earned.

She poured a generous serving and pulled the silk robe a little tighter over her naked chest. The weather was still wet and cold—spring in Boston could be chilling. She was eager for the warmth of the summer, her favorite season. And though the temperature in her apartment was plenty high, she knew she wouldn't feel completely warm until she was luxuriating in that ridiculously overpriced soaker tub she had installed when she moved in four years ago. Or when she finished this glass of wine. Deliciously warm, completely content. Paradise awaited her.

She picked up a slice of brie and a grape from the wooden cutting board next to her glass—this would suffice for dinner tonight. As she swirled the contents of her glass, aerating the wine, she thought about today. Shay had loved the apartment and wanted to start the paperwork immediately. Trina had known she would be impressed, and though she'd hoped for that outcome, sometimes Shay was slow to pull the trigger. But not this time. This time Shay jumped in with both feet, and that made Trina burst with pride. She'd found the right match for her friend and managed to secure a sale against Kendall, while also being able to sort of rub it in Kendall's face.

She took a sip of her wine and sighed happily. This was heaven. She was sure this was what winning tasted like, if winning had a taste. And though she was celebrating a victory, she knew she'd taken a risk today.

It had been bold to schedule a showing with Shay when Kendall might be around, but she wanted to put Kendall on edge a bit. She wanted her to feel pressured, because she had seen angry, annoyed Kendall at the gala, and Trina knew she was more than capable of handling that version of her. The villain version of her. She'd had plenty of experience handling villains and cutting them down piece by piece. She was all about vigilante justice, usually. You know, within reason. Mostly. Villains she could handle. If Kendall stayed a villain, everything would work out perfectly.

But Trina wasn't so sure Kendall was a villain, at least not entirely. She'd seemed to have real remorse after her crack about Trina's personal wealth at the meeting the other day, and though Trina shot down her apology, she could admit that Kendall seemed ashamed of her words. That was one of the reasons she watched her so closely today—she wanted to get a better idea of who Kendall really was. She'd watched her mannerisms and the way she carried herself as she spoke with Zander. Kendall was very attractive, which Trina found bothersome, but she was also poised. And not in an I'm-better-than-you kind of way, like she had expected. More like a quiet confidence, like Kendall knew what she was capable of. Because when Trina had gone out of her way to push Kendall out of her comfort zone, she saw that poise falter. She saw Kendall appear human, nearly insecure, if only for a moment. But she'd seen it.

And Trina couldn't shake that image. She'd almost felt bad for antagonizing her. Almost. Because try as she might to be a coldhearted badass, which she totally was, she was also kind of a softy. Or a cactus, like Lauren would say. She could be prickly upon first meeting, but Trina knew that her soft center won out most times. That was true with all her professional relationships turned friendships—with Lauren and Jax and, to some extent, even Ellison. She and Ellison had a pretty close bond, and she was protective of that.

Trina took another slow sip of her wine and thought about Kendall's remark about being astounded she had friends at all. That had unexpectedly wounded her. Kendall had just been shooting her mouth off, but she'd felt herself armor in response, and her knee-jerk reaction was to cuss Kendall out. Which was and wasn't out of character for her. She wasn't one to be pushed around, but she wasn't someone who lashed out without warrant, either. Maybe it was Shay flirting with Kendall, which was fucking ridiculous, or maybe it was the look of surprise on Kendall's face when Shay revealed that she and Trina had had an intimate relationship. Trina wasn't sure. She wasn't sure if the friendship snipe, the flirtation by Shay, or the look of embarrassed surprise on Kendall's face after the revelation of at least some part of Trina's sexuality had set her off, but that whole exchange left a bad taste in her mouth. And any generosity of spirit she might have felt in response to Kendall's momentary insecurity from earlier evaporated. Because Kendall had attacked her ability to be a friend. And that was one thing she was damn good at. Well, besides being a kickass Realtor.

She looked at her now empty glass and frowned. She hadn't even made it into the bathtub yet.

"I'm gonna need more wine," she said as she refilled her glass.

Her cell rang on the counter next to her. Lauren was calling.

"Hey you, what's new?" Trina smiled into the receiver, glad to have her friend on the line.

"Oh, nothing much, just calling to say I heard about Shay, and you're a fucking rock star, Rock Star. That's all." Lauren cheered.

Trina bowed to no one. "Why, thank you. I'm celebrating as we speak."

"Cab sav and a hot bath? Takeout or something homemade tonight?" Lauren knew her so well.

"Cheese plate. Extra grapes. Some strawberries and this delightful fig spread from Savenor's Market that I forgot I had in the pantry." Trina made a mental note to clean that thing out. She was sure it was loaded with expired *everything*. She didn't often cook for herself, preferring takeout or salads. But she liked having things around to cook, if the spirit moved her. It just usually didn't. She was mostly alone at night, and her nights were often late ones. Realty work had a way of bleeding into all hours. And since she was practically always working on the weekends, it wasn't like she had big meal prep days.

"Ooh, save me some fig stuff. When are we having a girls' night?" Lauren was typing on the other end of the line. The rhythmic sound was lulling Trina into a trance. She needed to get into that tub before this wine got entirely to her head.

"Maybe next week? It all depends on how this weekend goes. I have a few client appointments at the Harborside lined up. But I could totally use a couch veg sesh."

Lauren and Jax had been working overtime this week helping her organize her client files and set up prospective buyer appointments. She owed them both a huge debt of gratitude. If she ended up winning this thing, she planned to spoil them both stupid.

"I'm in. You name the time, I'll bring the wine and, hmm, pizza? I'm kinda really feeling pizza right now. Like a shrimp scampi pizza. God, doesn't that sound delicious?" Lauren rambled as the typing continued.

"Sure, whatever you want. Just make sure it has extra garlic— you know how I like it." Trina finished a strawberry and picked up the cutting board and wineglass as she headed toward her master bath. She cradled the phone against her shoulder as she asked, "What are you doing right now?"

The sound of typing slowed. Lauren sounded embarrassed. "Honestly? I'm deep diving into a rabbit hole on social media."

"About what?" Trina wasn't sure she wanted to know. Lauren was known to go all investigative reporter on shit.

"You don't want to know." Trina could now hear the click of a mouse in the background.

"Well now I have to know, Lau." Trina huffed.

"I'm looking up Kendall."

Trina stopped short and almost lost a grape to the floor in the process. "What?"

"You're mad," Lauren said.

"I'm not." Trina wasn't—well, maybe she was. Why was Lauren looking up Kendall?

"You are. I know that tone. Don't be mad," Lauren said. Trina didn't think she could ever be mad at Lauren, so it was sort of a moot point.

She looked at her wineglass. "I'm going to need more wine for this." She moved back to the counter, set down the food, and uncorked the bottle again. "Spill."

"Well, I talked to Jax, who'd talked to Shay, who'd mentioned that she'd casually asked Kendall out and—"

"Whoa. Slow down. Jax and Shay were talking? And Shay said what?" Trina was lost.

"Yeah. Shay called the office to set up a meeting with her lawyers, and she and Jax got to talking, and long story short, Shay volunteered to DJ Jax's top-surgery fundraiser. Isn't that cool?"

"Aw, she did? That's awesome." Trina meant that. She wanted great things for Jax. She knew that Shay's involvement would draw a packed house. Every penny would help.

"I know, right? Shay's the shit. Anyway, not the point." Lauren shook her head. "The point is Shay was all *I kinda asked Kendall out, because she's hot*, and everyone had a laugh except me because I was all *Whoa, she's the enemy, but also what did she say?* and then I realized I didn't know anything about her, so now you're all caught up. I'm home alone, not on a date or getting laid, researching the enemy on social media, because Shay thinks she saw Kendall check her out. So now I have to know if she's a little gay or not. That's the truth. I'm a stalker."

"You're a mess," Trina pointed out.

"I am," Lauren conceded, "but I'm your mess. And I found some stuff, if you're interested."

"I'm listening." Trina's phone buzzed, and she pulled it away from her ear to see who was calling. The concierge downstairs. She'd call them back—this was too good to interrupt.

"Okay, so don't get mad—"

"Lauren, if you start with that, then I probably am going to be mad," Trina said.

"Right, that's why I'm prefacing it with temper your temper, Trina," Lauren replied.

"Why am I going to be mad?" Trina played along for information's sake.

Lauren hesitated. "Well, I didn't find a whole hell of a lot at first because it looks like Kendall just deleted her whole social media history and started fresh when she moved to Boston, but there was a bunch of stuff on her family and her father specifically that was kinda juicy—"

"Like what?" Trina was intrigued.

"There's some legal thing going on with him now, civil suits or something. And there's this juicy bit about how his longtime business partner died doing the nasty with his secretary, and that once he died, Dickie boy got caught in the midst of all his realty shenanigans because no one was covering up his tracks anymore," Lauren said.

"We knew that's why he was in jail, right? What does this have to do with Kendall? Her father's a crook, and somehow Kendall is, too? Is that what you're getting at? The rotten, cheating apple doesn't fall far from the infested tree?" Trina asked. Okay, maybe she was more than annoyed that Shay had asked Kendall out. And then told people she knew about it.

"Maybe? I don't know. I wasn't that interested in Big Daddy Yates. I was more interested in the pretty brunette in all the pictures with Kendall and her father that were dated before Kendall suddenly disappeared from social." Lauren sounded excited now.

"You lost me again." Trina finished the last slice of brie and retrieved the rest from the fridge, slicing it into small, snack-size slivers. "Are we not talking about her father and the dead guy with the secretary?"

"No. We've moved on to the hot brunette lesbian girlfriend Kendall had for two years before she fled Connecticut like her pants were on fire and took up residency as a thorn in our sides. That's what we're talking about." Lauren sounded downright gleeful.

"Shut the front door." Trina's cell buzzed again. She was sure it was the concierge again, so she ignored it. "You skipped a few steps there. What are you talking about? What brunette?"

Lauren gave an exasperated huff. "Okay, so this is the part where you're gonna be mad. You know my friend Claire, from my softball league?"

"Yeah?" Trina had met her once or twice, but they hadn't spent any considerable amount of time together. She seemed nice, though, and funny. Super sarcastic. She did PR work, if Trina recalled correctly, and she had a bunch of older brothers. "Isn't she the one who dates that tech genius, with the place a few blocks behind our work?"

"Shelly White, yeah." Lauren continued, "Anyway, I couldn't find out who this mystery girl was, so I might have called Claire and asked her girlfriend to do some facial recognition nerdy internet stuff that's way over my head and see what she could find out, and whammo. The mystery brunette is Collette Newsome."

"You asked one of *Forbes* magazine's most innovative tech leaders to look into some pretty brunette who shared a few photos with Kendall? Seriously?" This was extreme, even for Lauren.

"When you say it like that, I sound crazy," Lauren scoffed.

"I mean, am I wrong?" Trina felt like she should track down Claire and Shelly and apologize on behalf of Lauren, who clearly needed a hobby.

"Earth to Trina," Lauren said, her voice raised slightly, "you're missing the big picture."

"And that is what exactly? You've given me a lot of information to take in, some of which makes you seem a little unstable," Trina replied.

"You're the worst." Lauren sounded annoyed. "I'm calling Jax."

"No"—Trina held her hand up reflexively, as if that could stop Lauren through the cell signal—"I'm sorry. Tell me more."

"Kendall and Collette weren't just girlfriends. They were engaged. And then, suddenly they weren't, and Kendall deleted all her social media and is now here in Boston." Lauren was talking so fast Trina had to strain to keep up.

"Okay. So she can't hold down a relationship, so what? It's not like you and I are fighting girlfriends off with sticks or anything." Trina would be lying if she said the girlfriend-fiancée thing didn't intrigue her, though. That was an interesting tidbit Lauren had uncovered.

"Well, I mean, we don't know why they broke up or anything but…" Lauren teased.

"But what?" Trina's phone buzzed again. "Sorry, the desk downstairs keeps calling me."

"Oh, I dropped off those shoes you left at my place earlier. I forgot to mention that," Lauren said as the typing sounds resumed.

"Oh, cool. Hang on." Trina clicked over and said, "You can just send them up. I'm expecting them." She didn't wait for a reply before clicking back to Lauren. "You were saying…"

"We don't know why they broke up, but Collette was a member of the Yates sales team. She was a colleague of Kendall's, and she disappeared from all pictures and mentions about the same time Kendall did. Something happened, Trina. I just know it," Lauren stated matter-of-factly.

"Like, she's dead?" Trina added, skeptically. It was decided— Lauren had finally gone off the rails.

"Oh no. She's not dead," Lauren replied. "Well, she could be, I guess."

"She's what?" Trina nearly choked on a grape.

"But that's unlikely because she's scheduled to be in Boston in the fall to give some seminar on sales or something. Which would be hard to do if she was dead." Lauren's voice cut out. "Crap. My mom is calling in. I've blown her off twice this week already. Catch you up tomorrow at work?"

"Sure." Trina felt like her head was swimming, which upon inspection of the now empty second glass of wine, didn't seem all that surprising.

"'Kay, love you, bye." Lauren disconnected before she had a chance to reply.

A knock at her unit door further distracted her from the bath destination. Which seemed like it might not happen now. She pulled her robe closed and crossed her arms. The silk offered her little modesty.

She pulled open the door expecting to see Gary there with her favorite yellow heels that had taken up residence at Lauren's after their last girls' night. And the heels were there, but not Gary. No. Holding her shoes was… "Calvin?" Trina stood there in the doorway, stunned to see her brother looking slightly disheveled, holding her shoes with a bashful expression on his face.

"Hey, sis." He ran his hand through his hair. "Can I come in? I come bearing footwear." He held her shoes up with a small grin.

"Yeah, of course. Come on." She stepped out of the way, and that's when she noticed that Calvin had something else with him besides the shoes—a suitcase. "Cal, what's with the suitcase?"

"Do you have anything to drink?" Calvin handed her the shoes and left his suitcase by the hallway as he moved to the counter and took a slice of brie off the cutting board. "Ooh, you're drinking the good stuff tonight." He grabbed a clean goblet from the cabinet and poured himself a glass, which he quickly drained, much to Trina's horror. "That's a fancy robe. Do you have company or something? I'd say I would come back, but I don't know where else to go so…"

"No, I don't." Trina grabbed a throw blanket off the back of the couch and wrapped it around herself, feeling a little naked in her robe in front of her brother. She put her hand over the brim of her brother's glass as he went to refill it. "Stop chugging my hundred-dollar-a-bottle wine—it's insulting."

"Okay. Got tequila?"

Trina glanced over at her bar. She did. But she couldn't remember the last time she'd seen her brother have anything stronger than wine.

He was already examining her liquor selection by the time she got her question out. "What are you doing here, Cal? I mean, I'm always thrilled to see you, but what did you mean that you don't know where else to go?"

"Lisa doesn't know I'm here. I'm supposed to be at a conference out of town this week. But I needed to get away. I needed to try to find what I lost." Calvin looked over his shoulder at her, his eyes wet with tears as he spoke. "You know, maybe I've had enough tonight. I'm just going to crash in the guest bedroom for the night—is that okay?"

Calvin didn't wait for an answer. He walked past her, pausing only to kiss her on the cheek as he rolled his suitcase in the direction of her guest room.

"Cal, I think we need to talk." Trina tried to hide the worry in her voice. What was happening?

"Maybe tomorrow." Calvin looked tired. Her happy, cheerful, super-dad brother looked beat. And beat down. "I need to sleep. Thanks for the warm bed, Trina."

She watched him disappear behind the guest room door without another word. She surveyed her kitchen. Two empty glasses sat on the counter, a forgotten cheese board accompanied them, and a bottle of tequila was perched dangerously close to the edge of the bar top.

She pushed back the tequila and placed the glasses in the sink, cleaning up the cheese board as she went. She was no longer hungry or thirsty. And that bath was definitely not happening tonight. Because her big brother was in her guest room looking like he'd lost his whole life. And she had no explanation as to what the hell was going on.

Her phone buzzed on the counter. It was Lauren.

Here's the intel from before. Mom is still talking. Kill me. ;)

Then Trina's text thread filled with links to photos on Facebook, Instagram, Twitter, LinkedIn, and a bunch of other sites. Some featured this Collette person, some were articles about the Yates family real estate empire and Dick's fall from grace, but what caught Trina's attention was the series of engagement photos of Kendall and Collette. They looked so happy and in love. There was one of them kissing that looked downright, well, hot. Trina wondered what happened between them. They looked so perfect together. Was Kendall a villain here, too? Was she the reason it ended?

She poured herself a glass of water and shut off the kitchen light, pausing in front of the guest room door to see if she could hear her brother. The room was dark, no light shone from under the door, and it was peep-quiet in there. He must be asleep.

And as she made her way to her bedroom, the night having taken a very different direction than it had begun, she felt a little less excited about the day and a lot more confused as to what would happen next.

CHAPTER ELEVEN

Kendall looked at the spreadsheet on the screen before her and sighed. She only had a couple of her own clients who might be interested in the Harborside on this list, because the fact was, she spent most of her time moving people into large suburban properties. The rest of the list was made up of prospects recommended by some of the other agents in her office. She'd have to cold-call some of these people, but she'd do her damn research before putting her neck out there, please and thank you. This type of real estate work was her least favorite, where she had to sell a property. She much preferred shopping to meet her clients' needs.

Still, the Harborside offered a unique opportunity. That part of the Seaport was booming—dozens of restaurants were within walking distance of the apartment building, and a Trader Joe's just popped up four blocks away. You could live an entirely pedestrian existence and not miss a beat, especially since all those restaurants had award-winning cocktail lists, and two had clubs attached. And then there was that newly opened casino just a short water taxi ride away. This location had just about everything available at your fingertips. Kendall knew it would sell—that's why she agreed to this foolish bet to begin with—but time was her concern. The right buyers were out there, but she didn't have the luxury of taking her time to find them. If she wanted to beat Trina, which she fucking did, then she'd have to move fast. Especially if Trina had closed the deal with Shay the other day. She was a step ahead, and Kendall couldn't stomach that.

She opened a browser window. She'd have to do a quick Google search to vet some of the names on this list. She'd look up net worth and job titles, she'd search for bankruptcy histories or failed business deals that might have made headlines. In luxury real estate, you never wanted to meet someone blindly. Research was key, even though there were sometimes visible clues. Trina's friend Shay was the perfect example. If you weren't paying attention to the details, like the glittering diamond-covered watch or Gucci sneakers, you might miss a sales opportunity. But she preferred to dig, so she wouldn't have to go by appearances. That was something else she'd learned from her father: everyone lies, but the internet is forever. That's one of the reasons she scrubbed her past as best she could, but she was no fool. She knew parts of her were forever frozen in time, out there to be seen and weaponized against her.

After a few searches turned up nothing of real interest about the first two names on the list, she turned her attention to something more interesting: Trina. She hadn't spent much time researching her because she hadn't been on her radar. But she was more than on her radar now. In fact, now Trina was wearing a bright red target. She should find out more about the competition, even if only to find out a way to get under Trina's skin like she seemed to have no trouble getting under hers.

Trina's name brought up dozens of pages and links. There were accolade articles and useless titles like *Salesperson of the Quarter* and other hokey plastic trophy awards that all Realtors knew were more for morale than signs of professional standing. Still, Kendall couldn't believe how many *things* she found linked to Trina. She stumbled upon an article in which Trina was named one of the top thirty under thirty in Boston. The article was a fluff piece, short and sweet, but the picture of Trina was a showstopper. She looked powerful and provocative, while still managing to be professional and somehow also sexy. Red looked great on her. Kendall found herself wondering if that was Trina's favorite color.

She added *LGBT* to her next search and found a treasure trove of information. Trina seemed to chair, cochair, or financially contribute to every LGBTQ committee or subcommittee even tangentially related to real estate and community development. She was like the hot gay poster woman for Boston-area real estate.

Kendall scanned a photo from some local health center's annual gala. Ellison was standing with Trina, who was next to that woman who was with Trina on the balcony the night they'd met, Lauren Calloway. Another person was there as well, a younger, more androgynous looking person named Jax Pearson. The caption stated that all four of them worked for Gamble and Associates. Was everyone at that office gay?

She allowed herself a few more moments to drift online,

loading Trina's public Twitter and Instagram feeds, but they were just professional pages, full of decorating tips to spruce up a house to sell, and showcasing listings available. About a third of the way down the page, Kendall recognized a photograph showing one of the Harborview apartment interiors. The angle of the shot was beautiful, and the lighting was perfect. It looked like a professional photo, but Trina had paired it with a selfie, obviously taken at the same time, in that to-die-for master closet. Kendall even knew when it was taken—she recognized the designer coat.

She reached across her desk for her cellphone and had no difficulty finding the picture she'd snapped of Trina by that closet door. The pictures on her phone were mostly work related, with an occasional shot of a menu. But not people. Trina, in that jacket with those vibrant blue shoes, would have been a welcome change from all those architectural shots, had she been any other woman. Kendall examined the candid she'd taken. Trina's shots were much nicer, cleaner. But this impromptu picture captured a moment that Kendall hadn't been able to forget. She'd been simultaneously irritated and intrigued by Trina in that master bedroom. She'd let her guard down for a moment, and her impression was that Trina had noticed and lunged. The coffee tease had been almost flirtatious. Like Trina was enjoying herself. It was only after the fact that Kendall was able to appreciate Trina's smoothness. She wasn't sure what to make of Trina. Particularly since she kept staring at her lips in this picture and wondering what they tasted like. Which was fucking counterproductive, right now.

"Focus on the task at hand, Kendall," she scolded herself as she placed the phone down. Her eyes lingered on Trina's picture until the screen lock kicked in and the phone went black again. "You're not going to sell anything staring at your competition." And ogling her.

She tapped her fingers on the desk as she thumbed through the notes she'd taken after that initial walk-through. A few words stood out to her: *rental property*. That's it. She'd start there.

She picked up her phone and dialed Clyde's line.

"Hi, Kendall. What's up?" Clyde said.

"Hi. Can you do me a favor? And please feel free to hand this off to someone else if you're busy." Kendall was trying to be more gracious and grateful. Clyde was supposed to be her point person in the office for this project, but she could at least try to be nice while giving orders. She was learning, anyway.

"Sure, fire away," Clyde replied.

"Can you get me a list of all the luxury property rental companies that operate in the area? Those catering to both local and international clientele." She paused before adding, "Basically, anyone who rents to people with lots of cash who are looking for short- or long-term stays in a bustling new area."

"Okay, I'll start with rental companies, but do you want me to look into other realty offices as well? Lots of Realtors work the rental angle. I know a few people who might have some leads." Clyde's suggestion was a good one. And his offer to go beyond her request was more than kind.

"Absolutely. That's a great idea. Let's start with the companies that deal exclusively with rentals, and then get me a list of a few realty offices that do as well. This is good. Thanks, Clyde." Kendall felt energized. This was a good starting place. She could feel it.

"No worries. I'll get right on this." Clyde disconnected, and for the first time since she was forced to start relying on other people, she felt reassured. Clyde's brainstorming with her might just kick-start her sales search. Maybe giving people the benefit of the doubt and working as a team wasn't such a bad idea after all.

She looked back at the list from before, feeling a renewed confidence in her colleague's suggestions. "Okay, you can do this. Be charming, be sweet, sweep them off their feet. And get them to open their wallets," Kendall said to herself as she cracked her knuckles and fired up the search engine again. "Let's see what secrets you all are keeping."

❖

Trina watched as Jax stood at the other side of the conference table and fiddled with something on one of the three enormous whiteboards that Lauren had brought in.

"Care to share what's happening in that amazing brain of yours, Jax? Because I'm totally in the dark here," Trina teased, but she was grateful for the distraction. Calvin didn't answer when she knocked on the guest room door this morning, and she didn't have time to wait around. She texted him that they should get dinner together later to talk, but she hadn't heard back. She was feeling unsettled about the whole thing, and this was exactly the kind of diversion she needed.

"Right." Jax looked at Lauren. "Are we ready?"

"Ready, Freddy." Lauren gave them a thumbs-up, then leaned

toward Trina to ask, "Don't these whiteboards feel like we're doing super-secret spy shit? I mean, I feel like Q in a Bond film."

"Wouldn't a high tech approach be more like Bond? This is literally a whiteboard. With markers," Trina pointed out.

"Color markers with meanings and purposes." Lauren rolled her eyes. "I knew my whiteboard would be lost on you. It's a place for brainstorming, Trina."

"And doodling, it seems." Jax frowned at the angry devil caricature Trina had drawn in the corner when Jax and Lauren were muttering to each other earlier.

"That's not a doodle—that's a portrait of Kendall," Trina corrected. "I'm keeping my enemies close."

Lauren's eyes widened. "Trina, that means she can see the board." She leaped out of her chair and erased the figure.

"Hey," Trina protested, "she wasn't real, Lau. Though I'll accept your compliment that my drawing was such an impressive likeness."

"Your drawing was crap." Lauren waved the marker at Trina and shook her head. "The whiteboard is sacred. Only Jax or I can write on it. Stop fooling around."

Trina held up her hands in surrender. "Fine, fine. Can we start now? I have phone calls to make." *I'm worried about Calvin.*

Jax cleared their throat and motioned for Lauren to resume her position next to Trina. "So, I agree with Trina wholeheartedly that there's a more efficient digital way to do this, but I have to say the tangible action of holding a marker and crossing things out is kinda fun."

"Told you," Lauren said, a smug expression on her face.

"I'll humor you both." Trina leaned her elbows on the conference table. "What are all these columns and numbers?"

Jax stood a little taller, looking proud. They pointed to the first whiteboard. This one had the projected end date for the contest and a grid map of the Harborside. Each square section was labeled with a letter and a number. The lines were perfectly straight and clean—it was kind of amazing. "These are the apartments available for sale. You are denoted with a red marker and the letter *T*—Kendall is blue and has a *K*. When either of you makes a sale, we'll mark the apartment with the appropriate designation. This will help us get a visual sense of what apartments are left, and also who's ahead in the sales race."

Trina smiled at the red *T* on the apartment she'd shown Shay. That was a nice start.

"Both offices have agreed to report all contracts by the end of day," Jax added, "so the information will be up to date. Which is awesome." Then Jax pointed to the whiteboard in the middle. "Okay, this whiteboard is the numbers board. This is where we track sales numbers, as well as both projected and final costs. Ellison wants to do a little data analysis during this project. So we'll be collecting some side numbers as well, for that part."

Trina nodded. That seemed legit. "And that board?"

Jax gave her a broad smile. "That's your hit list. Individual people, corporations, country club managers, biotech firms new to the area, and property management companies—all the people and entities this office has intel on who might be interested in the Harborside. Each category will have subcategories, and like I mentioned before, we'll collect data as we go to give us a clearer final picture."

Trina stood and walked over to the hit list. She leaned against the conference table and cocked her head as she reread the list again. "Some of these were my ideas, but what about the others?"

Jax looked bashful. "Well, you said you thought a younger, more modern clientele might be a good fit for the Harborside. So I took it upon myself to investigate some of the new tech start-ups in the area. They seem to have liquid cash, with lots of young executives living in big houses in the suburbs with growing families, while looking for ease of living. I bet if we built a rapport with a few of them, we could find someone interested in a Seaport-based condo offering an easy commute during the workweek. Part-time city living."

That was a smart angle, and Trina liked it. "Nice. And the country club thing?"

Lauren spoke from behind her. "That was my idea. I'm working with our PR folks to fine-tune a pitch about the Harborside. I know Langley's team has the basics down, but I think we can improve upon it. I think you should set up a few in-house presentations at the clubs just outside the city. There's gotta be a few empty nesters looking to downsize or for an apartment in town, like Jax was saying. Maybe they have a favorite grandkid who needs a pretentious gift? Who knows? I think it's worth a shot, even if it just builds your client portfolio for the future."

As funny and kooky as Lauren could be from time to time, Trina knew that brain of hers worked nonstop and in such a different way from her own that she'd learned to ride the Lauren-wave when it came her way. Lauren's brilliance wasn't always crystal clear from the start, but that's what was so amazing about her—she'd knock your socks off if you stuck around to see her work her magic. Trina wasn't about to stop believing in Lauren now. If Lauren said it was a viable angle, then it was a viable angle. She'd try anything to win.

"I'm down. Who doesn't like a little sales role-play?" she replied.

Lauren made a show of fake shivering. "That was creepy, even for you. No. Leave it up to me to write the script. You just look hot and be charming, on script, until after the presentations."

"I like it when you're bossy." Trina gave her a suggestive wink.

"Ladies." Jax drew their attention back to the hit list. "Is there anything else we should add? I want to start divvying up these categories today."

Trina stared at the list for another moment. "What about concierge branches of the local hospitals? And colleges or universities? There are plenty of international prospects we could meet through those avenues. I went to school with about a dozen kids from Europe and Asia whose parents paid for their college in cash and put them up in luxury condos while they lived here." Trina tapped her chin as she thought out loud. "I once dated a girl from Saudi Arabia who lived in her parents' condo in the Four Seasons for her entire sophomore year. She was a wild one. I wonder what she's up to these days?"

"Ooh, was she the screamer?" Lauren asked.

"Aren't they all, eventually?" Trina shot a sly smile to her bestie.

Lauren shook her head. "You are something else."

The squeaking noise of Jax's marker on the board interrupted their silly banter. "I updated the list. We'll keep making changes as we go," Jax said as they examined their handwriting.

"How are we monitoring the boards? Like, what if they get erased by accident?" Trina could see someone leaning against one of them and totally screwing up the system.

"I take photos of them daily, and all of this information is actually in databases. This is just for us to see the big picture all at once," Jax replied.

"Traitor," Lauren said, her brow furrowed.

"What? We're using your method and mine—it's a winning combination." Jax tried to convince her.

"I like it. All of it." Trina stood up and looked at her two closest work friends. "I know you're busting your asses to make this work. I really appreciate it. We're going to wipe the floor with Kendall and Sharkney. I have no doubt about that."

Lauren stood and put her hand out in front of her. "Are we doing a *Yay, team!* here? Because I feel like we could and totally should."

Jax stepped toward them, extending their hand toward Lauren's. "I'm in."

Trina shook her head and placed her hand on top of theirs. "Why do I feel like this has something to do with that secret handshake you two do? Is this some nerd initiation thing? Am I being initiated?"

"Yup." Lauren beamed as she raised her hand, tossing it up in the air with Jax's and Trina's by default. "Go, team."

Chapter Twelve

C al!" Trina called as she stepped through her apartment door, juggling her purse and the grocery bag she'd overfilled. Gary had offered to have someone carry it up, but she only had one bag, so she figured she could manage. But as the bag ripped and the three-pound bag of clementines landed on her foot, she began to rethink that decision. "Ouch."

Calvin came running from the direction of the kitchen, wearing her apron. "I'll take that." He scooped up the broken bag and grabbed the runaway fruit before hustling back to the kitchen. "Dinner's almost ready. Go wash up and hurry back."

Trina laughed. "I'm not one of your kids, Cal."

Calvin winced. "Sorry, force of habit. But you should wash your hands and get changed—we're having pasta and red sauce, and it'll definitely ruin that blouse."

Trina looked down at her white shirt and nodded. "You are wiser than you look—I'll give you that."

"Well, since everyone says you look just like me, then that must be a compliment to you as well," Calvin replied as he stirred a pot on the stovetop.

"I'm so much more attractive than you." Trina slipped off her heels and headed toward her room to get changed when she noticed the goblet he was cradling as he cooked. "Are you drinking my wine again?"

"I made you dinner," Calvin reasoned as he raised a half-full glass of red, her favorite red, no doubt. "I'll pour you some."

"Oh, all's forgiven then," she replied sarcastically.

"Dinner's in five," he called back just as she closed her bedroom door.

Trina had to admit that whatever he was making smelled wonderful. Though she couldn't imagine what he'd made it with, since she hadn't done her weekly grocery order yet. She'd stopped at the Asian market up the street to pick up some of her brother's favorite snack foods, since she didn't keep anything like that around, and since she knew her pantry and fridge were bare. She was hoping she could bribe him with his favorite treats to get him to open up to her about why he was lying to his family and sleeping in her guest room. But if he was drinking the good shit, maybe she wouldn't need the treats to get her answers. Maybe the booze would do the work for her. He did seem in a pretty great mood, after all.

She unzipped her skirt and slipped the blouse over her head, tossing both in the dry cleaning pile by her dresser. She went into her en suite bathroom and freshened up, then pulled on her favorite sweatshirt and yoga pants. The sound of Calvin happily singing along to a Taylor Swift song made her breathe a sigh of relief. The wine was working, or he was feeling better than he had been last night. She knew she couldn't push him. As agreeable as Calvin was to just about everything, he didn't like to be cornered. She figured no one did, really. She knew she tended to get nasty and lash out when she felt cornered. Her brother was capable of the same, though she hadn't seen it since they were young children. He was a much calmer person than she was and had pretty much always been that way. That was one of the reasons why they'd remained so close. They complemented each other nicely.

"Perfect timing," Calvin said as he placed the oversized pasta dish on the island in front of one of the barstools. He gave her an exaggerated bow as he placed a wineglass next to the dish. "And your wine, madame."

"Thanks." Trina sat on the barstool and breathed in the hearty marinara smell. "This looks amazing."

"I hope you think it tastes as good as it looks." He sat next to her with an identical looking plate. "I've been experimenting with Bolognese the last few months. I love Italian food. We never had enough of it growing up."

Trina sipped her glass and laughed. "Gee, I wonder why?"

Calvin gave her a toothy grin. "Do you remember, when you were little, how you thought all meatballs came from a bag?"

"Oh no. Don't bring that up." She would rather not relive that moment.

"You came home so mad from that girl's house in fourth grade—what was her name again?" he asked.

"Francesca Toloni." Trina would never forget the embarrassment of that day. She and Francesca has walked in on Francesca's mother and grandmother making meatballs in the kitchen, and Trina had been dumbfounded. It had never occurred to her that you *made* meatballs, and that they didn't just come from a store-bought freezer bag.

"You came in yelling at Mom and Dad in every language we'd ever learned—English, Vietnamese, Chinese. And I feel like maybe a little Spanish from Señora Warnock's after-school program, too." Calvin was laughing so hard he was wiping tears away. "You kept saying something about looking like a fool and being a bad American over and over again. I mean, aren't meatballs Italian, not American? I never sorted that part out."

"Laugh all you want, but that was easily one of the most embarrassing moments of my childhood. I was already different from the other kids. The fact that I didn't know where meatballs came from was just the icing on the cake." Trina could laugh about it now, but at the time, she'd been mortified. And she shouldn't have been since there was plenty about her culture that her peers didn't understand, but when you were trying to fit in and you were so different from everyone else, the little things were the things that mattered. To her credit, Francesca never mocked her in public, only when they were alone together. But that was probably because she liked Trina, like, *liked* her. Which was something Trina discovered when they were both in their teens. One night, after sneaking a few sips of Francesca's grandmother's grappa, an emboldened Francesca gave Trina her first same-sex kiss. Francesca brought a lot of firsts to Trina's life after that point, but it all started with meatballs.

Calvin finished his glass of wine with a chuckle. "Mom was so mad that you were so mad. We didn't have meatballs again for months after that. And she made those from scratch from that point on."

"Which was a marked improvement from the bagged version, so you have me to thank," Trina said between bites. Her mother *had* been mad. So mad. That was one of the things her mother did well—get angry and stay angry. For as much as her mother embraced American culture, she rebelled against some of it, too. Trina had offended her with her comments when she came home that night, something that adult Trina could see. But nine-year-old Trina was too busy being embarrassed and worried about her social standing to think it might offend her uncool, overbearing, and strict mother so much that she took meatballs out of their diet for nearly a year.

"You know, the crazy thing is that you'd think I would have naturally made the correlation that meatballs were handmade because everything food related in our life was handmade. It's not like there was an abundance of Asian cuisine restaurants or even grocers when we were growing up. Mom and Grandma were constantly cooking and freezing batches of this and that for later. I don't know why I thought Italian food, or any food, would be different."

"Meh. We get in our heads about stuff—it's what we Lees do. We can't see what's right in front of us. It's our Achilles' heel." Calvin sighed and the sigh was like a ten-thousand-pound weight between them.

"We're not talking about meatballs anymore, I assume." Trina pushed aside the rest of her plate. Calvin had majorly overserved her. She was beyond full.

Calvin looked at her and shook his head. "I think I hate my life, Trina."

"What?" Trina asked as that broken version of her brother from last night reappeared.

Calvin stood and began clearing their plates. He covered the remainder of Trina's abandoned dish in plastic wrap and placed it in the fridge for later, and then he moved toward the dishes that lined the sink's edge.

"Cal." She placed a hand on his forearm. "The dishes can wait."

He fidgeted on the spot, uncomfortable. "I needed a break."

"I don't understand. Come back and sit. Talk." Trina sat at the island and motioned for him to join her, but instead, he paced. Because that was the other thing Lees did, pace.

"I love Lisa. I do. She's the love of my life and I can't imagine my life without her," Calvin started, "and I love my kids. I really do. And as much as having kids is difficult a lot of the time, they bring so much more *life* into your, er, life. You know?" He ran his hand through his hair, causing it to stand up in short, spiky black points. "It's just, have you ever woken up one day and felt like you were drowning? Like you'd done everything you were supposed to do but you still felt unfulfilled and with too much responsibility to remember how to breathe?"

Trina had felt that way. More than once. But her responsibilities were largely based in work, rather than family. She remembered feeling that way last year when nothing she did seemed to be enough for her mother or her family. She'd lost her love of real estate and for much of anything. That's when that unexpected article about Boston's 30 Under 30 helped kick-start her again. That article had fueled her incredible sales year. She'd forced a reinvigoration that was record-breaking by most estimations, but only because she suddenly had an image to uphold. And that had been enough, until a few weeks ago. Because even with all her sacrifices, she still hadn't been awarded the top prize she so badly wanted for herself. Kendall took home that title and that award. Another slight against how hard Trina had to work for everything. So though it wasn't the same thing her brother was describing, she'd been there in her own way, too. "Yeah, Cal. I have."

Calvin stopped pacing. He smiled at her as he said, "I hate being a dentist."

"You what?" Trina thought she'd missed a transition there.

"I never wanted to be a doctor of any kind. Mom wanted me to be a doctor. I wanted to be an artist, a poet, a busker—anything that wasn't sterile and clinical and *a doctor*. But Mom would never have allowed it. The firstborn and only son was going to be a—"

"Doctor, a lawyer, or a pharmacist," Trina supplied.

"Right." Calvin made one last lap before he sank down next to her. "I woke up a few months ago and realized I hated my life. Except I realized it wasn't my whole life I hated, just my job. But I built my entire life around that job. The practice is booming, I'm booked up to my eyeballs in client appointments and Lisa wants to send all the kids to private school."

"Have you told Lisa—"

"And Henry's party, oh God, don't get me started on that epic affair. Mom has Lisa convinced that every person in this country with the last name Lee needs to be invited and also put up for the night at some nearby B and B, on our dime. The head count for this party is over a hundred and fifty people. For a one-year-old! And you know what happens at the Zhua Zhou…"

Trina did know. It was Chinese tradition to have an enormous celebration on a child's first birthday. On the Zhua Zhou, it was customary to place a series of objects in front of the baby and let them choose one of them. These objects were supposed to predict a child's career and personality traits. Almost like a crystal ball to their future selves. Though it was weighted heavily toward tradition and a celebration of the child's life, she knew that part of it was also to guide the parents on how to provide enlightened education to enable their child's future successes. Which Trina always took to mean that this was the opportunity for the parents to force their will on the child's future prospects. She knew Calvin felt the same way.

"Have you and Lisa decided on what you'll place in front of Henry?" She was almost afraid to ask.

"I don't want to do it," Calvin replied.

"Oh, damn." He wasn't messing around. "You want to pull the plug on the birthday as a whole? Or just the Zhua Zhou? Because Mom is going to freak out regardless."

Calvin dropped his head. "I know. So is Lisa."

"So no birthday or…?"

"No controlling anyone's life. No making decisions or predictions about anyone's life. No influencing the type of education they have to help them get to the goals you want for them." Calvin was exasperated. "I don't want my kids to wake up someday and hate their life like I do."

"Wait." Trina cocked her head to the side. "Are you saying you think that because you picked up a stethoscope at your Zhua Zhou, you hate your life now?" Trina hadn't been born yet, but she'd heard stories about how Calvin had practically lunged after the medical equipment. That story was one she'd heard often—both her parents were so proud of their young prodigy.

"Yes." Calvin paused. "No. But yes, sort of."

Trina gave him a moment to elaborate.

"Mom and Dad pushed me into science. They forced me to do summer school classes in mathematics and biology. I was groomed to go into a life of medicine, and all Mom ever does is say that I knew I was destined for that as a child, because I picked up that fucking stethoscope." Calvin barked. "Did anyone ever think I picked it up because it was shiny or because it was the biggest thing on the table? Or maybe it was just the closest thing to me? Why does everything have to be fucking prophetic?"

"Cal, this is some deep shit you're dealing with." Trina rarely heard her brother curse. She wasn't mocking him, but was he really blaming his feelings of failure on a stethoscope?

"The point is"—Calvin shot her a look—"I'm tired of walking

the line that was drawn for me before I knew what a line was. I'm done being perfect. I want out. I want to be like you."

Well, hold on, did he just insult her? "Feel free to walk that bit back and try that again. You're staying in my house while on the lam, I might add. Insulting me will get your ass evicted, right quick," Trina said.

"What I mean is that I don't want to be burdened by anyone's expectations anymore. I want to be more like you, living free and in the moment," Calvin reassured her. "You never cared what Mom or Dad thought. You just went to the beat of your own drum. And I never appreciated that. I never saw how freeing that mentality was. You're living your best life, Trina. And I'm so envious of that."

Trina scoffed. Calvin had no idea how many times she'd beaten herself up about not living up to the bar he had set. He had no idea how much she'd fought against the unrealistic standards he'd unintentionally set for her by being the perfect first child. She would never be the golden child that her brother was, and here he was, condemning the title and wishing to be more like her, a failure in their mother's eyes.

The irony was almost too much to handle. But just as she was about to serve him the fiery retort he deserved, she stopped and swallowed it instead. Because the look on his face was too sincere, too honest, too vulnerable. His problems were his own and assigning whatever blame he chose to, to whomever or whatever, was his decision. But she had no right to make this about her. And she wouldn't. Because her big brother, the golden boy, was broken in front of her, and she knew what she needed to do in that moment, and being honest with him about how his choices had trickled down to hurt her wasn't on the table for tonight.

"Okay." Trina took a breath. "So you're not going to be a dentist anymore, and Henry isn't going to be forced into pharmaceutical sales—"

"Or dentistry. Or surgery. Unless he wants to be," Calvin replied.

"Right. So what now?"

"I have no idea." Calvin looked like he might cry.

"When are you supposed to be back from this conference you're not attending at the moment?" Trina had to help him sort this shit out, because it was stressing her out and because she needed her big brother back.

"A week from yesterday," he said.

"Fine. We can work with that." Trina tried to give him an emotional boost. "We have six days to figure out how to fix your mess of a life. No problem. Easy as pie. It'll be a walk in the park."

Calvin looked as skeptical as she felt.

"We'll figure it out. I promise." Trina wasn't so sure she'd be able to come through on that promise, but right now, it had to be enough for them both.

Chapter Thirteen

Kendall ducked into the Starbucks near Margo's Cyclebar to grab a coffee since her next client meeting was close by. She didn't have time for a class today, but she was planning to meet Margo at the Harborside in the next few days to show her the commercial space and have a cocktail and dinner night on the town. She needed the break from all the chaos this Harborside project had brought into her life. And she just missed her friend. She seemed only to be working lately, and it was making her cranky.

The line was longer than she would have liked, but it was moving quickly, so she checked her phone to load the pay app when she noticed a text from Clyde telling her that her next appointment for the day had rescheduled. Well, it looked like she had more time on her hands than she'd originally thought.

"A grande caramel macchiato, please, with skim milk." Trina's unmistakable voice sounded from three people in front of her.

Intrigued, Kendall leaned over to try to see her but was distracted when the guy in front of her dropped his mile-long handwritten order list. Oh, hell no. She might have had a cancellation and more time than she had anticipated, but she didn't have *that* much time.

She slipped out of line and stepped behind Trina as the woman behind her was distractedly examining the granola bar selection.

"Anything else?" the barista asked.

"Grande iced French vanilla house blend, skim milk, two sugars," Kendall supplied, and Trina whipped around to look at her. "What? You offered before, and since you struck out with your guess, I figured I'd give you a chance to make amends for it."

Trina looked amused, giving her a small smile before turning back to the barista. "And that, please. Oh, and two cake pops."

"Cake pops?" Kendall asked as Trina tapped her card on the reader and moved toward the pickup counter.

"Mm-hmm. Always cake pops," Trina replied matter-of-factly. She looked great today, again. She had on a flowy mid-length pleated black skirt with ridiculously high red heels and another gorgeous coat, this time a tan trench coat that was open in the front revealing a professional yet sexy neckline that Kendall's height advantage made seem maybe more sexy than it was. Not that she was complaining.

"Good to know," Kendall replied, distracted. Why did Trina have to be so fucking good-looking? She hadn't been able to stop looking at that picture she'd taken of Trina since their run-in at the Harborside. Maybe it was because now she knew Trina and Shay had been bedroom partners. That revelation piqued her interest. But what was it about this woman that drew her in so much? She'd bedded plenty of beautiful women. She could be around them, no problem, and yet Trina made her feel so many things no one else did—anger, excitement, intrigue, and now, very clearly, also lust. She was all over the map with her.

"Why? Do you plan on surprising me with cake pops sometime?" Trina asked, her mood seemingly playful. Kendall hoped it stayed that way. She was feeling a little flirty herself today.

"Under the right circumstance, I probably would," Kendall replied.

"Oh, and what kind of circumstance would that be?" Trina asked as a barista called out their order. She handed Kendall her coffee and waited for her reply.

"Friendly ones," Kendall said as she raised her cup in acknowledgment. "Thank you for this."

"You're welcome," Trina replied as she moved over to the stand with napkins and stirrers. She handed Kendall a napkin. "I'm shocked you think I'm capable of being friendly."

"Why's that?" Kendall asked, holding the napkin because Trina gave it to her, not because she needed it.

"Well, you were astounded I even had friends," Trina said with a smile.

Kendall got the impression Trina might be flirting with her. That excited her. "Maybe that was a little harsh of me," Kendall admitted. She wasn't looking for a fight. If anything, this was the longest exchange she'd had with Trina that hadn't resulted in insults. It was refreshing. "I apologize for suggesting that you aren't friend material. That was wrong of me."

"Thank you." Trina seemed genuinely appreciative of her statement. She was glad, because she meant it.

"I think, and I could be totally wrong here, but I think that maybe, *we* could actually find a way to be friends by the end of this," Kendall said, not knowing what had come over her today. Was it the two potential contracts she was about to close on at the Harborside? Was that what was making her feel so emboldened and sociable today? Or was it that trench coat and those warm brown eyes that were looking back at her with such curiosity now? Maybe it was both.

Trina seemed to consider this, a mirthful expression on her bright red lips. "I have a feeling we're a lot alike in many ways."

"Which could explain why it's so easy for us to, uh, antagonize one another," Kendall said.

Trina gave her an innocent slow blink. "You think I antagonize you?"

Kendall leaned on the napkin counter and faced her more fully. "You don't?"

Trina arched an eyebrow as she sipped her coffee. Her bright red lipstick left a mark on the plastic lid. There was something alluring about that.

"No retorts? Honestly, I look forward to our exchanges. There's something so, I don't know, exciting about waiting to hear what your opinion is on all matters," Kendall admitted. She hated being Trina's target, but there was a tiny part of her that enjoyed the verbal sparring. She'd never met anyone quite like her. She was intrigued by her. And attracted to her, even if she tried to ignore that part.

Trina gave her a full smile, the first really free smile she'd gotten from her, maybe ever. "Kendall Yates, are you admitting that you like it when I take you down a peg or two?"

"I never said that," Kendall corrected. "I merely said that I don't hate running into you like I used to."

"Ah, the truth comes out." Trina smiled into her coffee as she took another sip. "You hated when I showed up unannounced. That's a revelation, since you did such a good job of hiding that."

"I definitely did not," Kendall said, embarrassed.

"No, but I was being polite," Trina replied.

"And friendly," Kendall noted.

"I *am* capable of it," Trina said, and Kendall felt like maybe they were making a little progress here.

She decided to push the envelope a bit, because she wasn't ready for this banter to end just yet. "Do you have somewhere to be right now?" Kendall asked without thinking.

"I always have somewhere to be," Trina said as she surveyed her curiously. "Why do you ask?"

"My meeting just canceled. And I, thankfully, got to skip the line because of you"—she motioned to the guy she was previously behind who was still at the register sorting out his order—"and I plan to enjoy this delightful coffee that you bought me, but I'd like to do it with you. If you're free."

Trina gave her a once-over before answering her. It was almost as if she was sizing her up, but a part of Kendall hoped it was because she was checking her out. "Sure."

"Great," Kendall replied, feeling a mix of nervousness and excitement. What was coming over her? "It's nice out—care to sit outside for a bit?"

"Sounds good. I could use a little vitamin D," Trina said, following her as she led them to the small table and chairs outside of the Starbucks entrance. She sat across from Trina, facing her, as Trina settled into the chair looking out at the parking lot before them.

Trina took a long sip of her drink and closed her eyes, leaning back into the chair as the sun shone on her face. She looked peaceful and content. Kendall couldn't remember the last time she'd just basked in the beauty of the moment the way Trina appeared to be doing. She really needed to work less and live more like Margo kept telling her.

"You're staring," Trina said without opening her eyes.

"*Staring* feels like a negative word. Like a stalkery word. I'm merely sitting across from you, appreciating your ability to soak up the sun," Kendall said, and Trina smiled in response. She wondered if Trina's lips felt as soft as they looked.

"If you don't find tiny moments to forget the stress of the world, you'll go crazy," Trina said as she opened her eyes and looked at Kendall. "Sometimes I get lost in my responsibilities. But sometimes, someone invites you to share a coffee, and you take them up on it."

"Even if you're the one buying?" Kendall asked, glad to be sharing this moment with her.

"Even then." Trina turned to face her, resting her coffee on the table between them.

After a few moments of quiet, Kendall asked what had been on her mind for days. "So, you and Shay, huh?"

Trina, who had been wiping the condensation off her cup, paused at that question. She looked up at Kendall with those big brown eyes and Kendall wanted to lean forward to see them better.

"It was a long time ago," Trina said, before asking, "Are you jealous?"

"Of Shay." Kendall's filter had clearly left the fucking building. What was in this coffee?

"Hmm," Trina hummed, giving her a half smile, and her mouth looked delicious.

"Does that surprise you?" She watched Trina's lips because she could.

"No, I'm the total package," Trina joked before adding, "but maybe I'm just stunned you're admitting it."

"I'm sure there's lots about me that would surprise you," Kendall replied. There was lots about her that was surprising herself at the moment. Like how she was openly flirting with her competition and enjoying it.

"You're flirting with me," Trina said with a raised eyebrow as she sipped her coffee.

"Does that bother you?" Kendall asked. She didn't see any point in denying it.

"No," Trina replied as she cradled her cup in her hands. "What made you ask me for coffee just now?"

"I don't know," Kendall admitted. "You were here, and I was here, and there was coffee, and I guess I just wanted to talk to you a bit, without fighting with you."

Trina watched her without saying anything.

Kendall fidgeted in her seat. "I also…" She paused. "I wanted to apologize again for what I said to you in my office."

"I'm over it," Trina replied, but Kendall wasn't.

"It was rude. And out of character for me. And I'm sorry. Truly." She reached across the table to touch Trina's hand in hopes of conveying her sincerity. When Trina didn't pull away like before, she continued, "I didn't mean it. And the part that makes me so upset about having said it is that that's exactly the type of thing my monster father would say, and I can't handle knowing that I'm even capable of that. So again, I am so, so sorry."

Trina fluttered her fingers against Kendall's as she asked, "You and your father don't get along?"

"That's an understatement," Kendall said, enjoying their contact.

Trina looked up from their hands, and Kendall saw empathy in her eyes. "Families are complicated."

"They are." Kendall nodded. Talking about her father these days made her feel vulnerable. She stroked along the back of Trina's fingers, appreciating the softness of her skin. She found the action soothing.

Trina turned her palm over and pulled Kendall's hand into hers. "I accept your apology."

"Thank you." Kendall was grateful. And glad to be holding Trina's hand, which fit perfectly into hers. "And thank you for the coffee."

Trina used her free hand to open the little pastry bag that sat on the table between them. She pulled out a cake pop and handed it to Kendall.

"For me?" Kendall took it, smiling.

"I'm a good sharer," Trina said as she took a bite of hers, all the while keeping their hands joined. Kendall was aware of how nice that felt.

"There's so much to learn about you," she replied.

"I'm a total conundrum, I know," Trina said as she finished her treat, pulling the empty stick to wipe along her plump lower lip, drawing Kendall's eyes back to that delectable looking mouth again. Trina squeezed her hand before releasing it. "I have a meeting across town, and I have to go, but this was nice."

"Yeah, it was." Kendall grabbed her own cup just to occupy her now empty hand. She already missed Trina's touch.

Trina stood, placing her hand on Kendall's shoulder as she started to walk past.

"Just so you know, I wasn't wrong about your coffee order before—flavored, house blend," Trina said, as she briefly massaged Kendall's shoulder before toying with her hair.

"I guess I'm just—what did you call it?—basic," Kendall said, looking up at her.

"Basic isn't a bad thing, I suppose." Trina looked down at her with a smile. Her fingers grazed Kendall's cheek as they left her hair, and Kendall felt her body heat up. "Have a good day, Kendall."

"You, too."

And as she watched Trina walk away and climb into her car, she decided she already was.

CHAPTER FOURTEEN

Kendall smiled when Zander mentioned that Trina would be by the building later. She was looking forward to seeing her again after their impromptu coffee interaction. She couldn't simply drum up a reason to see her, but if they happened to run into each other at the Harborside, that would be fine by her.

Since Trina's office had notified Whitaker that Shay's purchase of the unit was official, Kendall had been working overtime to make at least one competing sale. And though she hadn't closed a deal as of yet, she'd already had those two incredible meetings with different rental firms that were interested in centrally located apartments. She hoped those would develop into something more concrete, but the real victory here was that she'd secured the rental of the commercial property on the first floor, rear of the building. A Cyclebar franchise was going in, and she had Margo to thank for that.

Kendall's goal today was to see how far along the penthouses were coming. She had a few showings later in the week for the other spaces, but the penthouses were the units she was most interested in. Even though they were tracking progress unit by unit, the winner would be determined by highest net sales, and there was no better way to achieve that than to sell a penthouse. Or two.

She exited the elevator to meet Zander and adjusted her hard hat for about the dozenth time. She hadn't thought out her hairstyle today, and the tight bun she had in place didn't allow for the hard hat to sit squarely on her head.

Zander met her at the elevator on the top floor. "The two penthouses are roughly the same size, but this one"—he pointed toward their left—"has a little more square footage indoors, but less patio space. The other one has more outdoor space, with a smidge less indoor footage. It's negligible, and both are plenty expansive, but they're a little different."

"Can I see them both?" Kendall needed to get an idea of just how different the spaces would be before she could find the perfect buyers.

"Er, yes?" Zander didn't seem so sure. "One is much more finished than the other, so we can check that out, but you'll have to bear with me as I walk you through the blueprints for the other. It'll take more imagination."

"I've got plenty of that, not a problem." Kendall was confident that she'd be able to navigate the plans without any difficulty. She'd spent her life in real estate, after all.

"Okay then, let's see what's behind door number one." Zander opened the unit door and Kendall's jaw hit the floor.

The entryway wasn't anything overly special—rather, it *was* incredibly impressive, but not as impressive as what was beyond it. This unit was on the left side of the building facing the city side of the harbor's edge. The Harborside, once complete, could be the tallest building on the water's edge, and this view, from this height, was absolutely astounding.

"It's breathtaking, right?" Zander's smile was comically large. "Those panoramic doors went in earlier today, they don't open yet, but if you want to see the balcony, I can take you out one of the makeshift side doors."

Kendall nodded. She certainly wanted to see the outside. But she should probably see the inside first. She looked left and right and could see the skeleton of what she presumed would be the kitchen. The massive open-concept layout had what appeared to be plans for two islands. What she assumed would be the living room area was filled with construction materials, but even though it was crowded with pallets of tiles wrapped in plastic and endless pieces of wood flooring materials, she could tell that this room was an impressive size. She could envision elegant dinner parties that flowed from the double islands into what would surely be a lush living space. This area alone was easily as big as the entire kitchen and living room of one of the corner suites she had seen earlier. Like the one Trina had sold to Shay.

Trina. Her daydreaming halted. Zander had told her she would be by later but hadn't specified when. Though she was hoping to run into her here, she didn't want it to be when she was viewing this space for the first time. Zander said today was the earliest anyone could see the space, which meant Trina hadn't seen it yet. She wanted this edge—she wanted the early bird advantage. She had a competition to win, after all, and she'd sort out her physical attraction issues later.

"Tell me everything you have planned, Zander." Kendall wanted the information from the source himself. She wanted to see his vision as he did, and the best way for that to happen was if he told her the story directly. "Spare no details. And let's for sure see that other penthouse. I'll keep an open mind."

❖

The sun was setting when Trina pulled up to the Harborside. And though it wasn't raining, there was a nasty wind today, the kind that chilled you to the bone. Trina hurried through the doors, eager to get out of the elements.

Trina knew that Zander was too busy to keep her up to date on the building's comings and goings, but she also knew from past experience that the security desk would be a hub of information. So she did what she always did: made friends with all the right people.

Victor was the new daytime guy at the temporary concierge check-in. But Victor was the real deal—he was slated to be one of the full-time concierges when the Harborside was up and running. Victor was an important person in Trina's life now. It was up to her to make sure he knew that.

"Hey, Victor," she said as she walked in.

"How are you, Ms. Lee?" Victor was all business—polite, but all business nonetheless.

"Victor, we went over this," Trina said as she approached his desk. "Trina is fine."

"Sorry, ma'am." Victor shifted in his chair. "How are you, Trina?"

"I'm good," she said. "How are things around here?"

"Coming along nicely, I'm told. They finished the parking garage downstairs, so they're painting it now. Today's been a busy day for deliveries, too. Lots of flooring and slate coming in. The service entrance has been a revolving door." Victor seemed to be loosening up a bit. That's exactly what Trina wanted.

"Lots of visitors today?" Trina fished, but she already knew that Kendall was on-site. That was why she was here. She'd called over to Victor twice today to get a feel for the property and see who was on the list of approved visitors for the day. She'd mentioned to him that she was planning on bringing a client by and wanted to make sure that Zander would be on-site, so she could introduce them. That wasn't entirely true. She had wanted to see Zander and the penthouse progress, but she wanted to make sure that overlapped with when Kendall was around. The truth was that Jax had stumbled upon a rental agency that was already in talks with Kendall about purchasing a unit for long- and short-term rentals here at the Harborside. The rental angle was one of the avenues Trina had intended to pursue, but if the admin at the rental agency was to be trusted, Kendall had effectively sealed the deal, and it was a matter of paperwork now.

"Ms. Yates is up there now with Mr. Alter doing a penthouse walk-through. One of Mr. Alter's design people was here earlier. But other than that, just workers," he replied.

"Did Kendall come alone?" Trina asked nonchalantly. This was what she really cared about. Kendall's admission that she was jealous of Shay and her obvious flirtation over coffee had been on Trina's mind constantly over the last week. Particularly the way she'd caught Kendall staring at her mouth. She'd seen another side of Kendall she hadn't been expecting, and their playful, flirtatious banter had come easily. Part of her wanted to see if that was a fluke.

"Yes. Just her today," Victor said as the phone rang beside him. He held up a hand to her as he answered it.

Trina took the opportunity to look around and try to get some intel on Victor. She knew from past conversations that he had two little boys, ages six and eight. And she knew that Victor was planning a big Caribbean holiday with his wife, sans kids, just before the full building opening as a sort of last hurrah. But outside of that, she didn't know much.

As Victor spoke into the receiver, he shuffled some papers on his desk. That's when she noticed the Red Sox game schedule taped to the back of the call log sheet. He must be a Sox fan.

"Sorry about that," Victor said as he disconnected, "someone closed the delivery door and I had to put out a quick fire."

"Do you have to check on that?" Trina asked to make conversation.

"No, they worked it out." Victor nodded toward the coffee in Trina's hand. "Is that for me?"

"Oh! I totally forgot." Trina handed it over to him. She had been so focused on information-gathering that she had forgotten about the drink altogether. "It was so warm in my hands that I completely spaced."

Victor took it with a broad smile. "Thanks so much for this. I was starting to drag."

"Sorry I held it captive for so long," Trina said. "And now that I know how you like it, I'll bring some by whenever I can."

"Thanks," Victor replied.

Trina liked when people remembered little things about her, like the way she took her coffee or tea. That was how she approached everyone she met—she learned a little bit about them to make them feel important, because *she* liked feeling that way. So she rarely missed a birthday or overlooked a significant anniversary or a hobby that interested someone. That attention to detail had served her time and time again in this business, and in life.

She pointed toward the baseball schedule. "So, are you a big Red Sox fan?"

Victor blushed as he shuffled the sheet to the back of the pile. "Yeah. My boys love baseball. I used to go to all the games with my dad when I was younger. I try to take them to as many home games as possible, but it's hard."

"Hard because it's hard to get tickets or hard because it's expensive?" Trina knew that Fenway Park was one of the most expensive ballparks to attend as a family. Her brother talked about it all the time since her oldest nephew got into T-ball and wanted to go to every game. Trina had been to a few games, but baseball wasn't really her thing. She'd gone mostly for the people watching.

"Both," Victor said as he shook his head. "I'm on two different wait lists for nosebleed seats for the upcoming Yankees–Sox series. Hopefully one of them will pan out."

"Does your wife go, too?" Trina asked as someone walked in behind her.

"She likes to be a part of the memories and support the boys' interests. But she thinks baseball is too slow and boring. I think that's only because she doesn't understand the rules of the game," Victor replied.

Trina could relate. She knew next to nothing about baseball. And she was more than fine with that.

"Excuse me, Ms. Lee," Victor said as he stood to address the woman who had entered behind her. "Can I help you, miss?"

The attractive brunette smiled, and Trina noticed her bright blue eyes. "I was supposed to meet a Realtor friend out back at the new commercial space, but it's locked. I know she has a meeting upstairs sometime, and I was wondering if I could just hang out here and wait for her. It's freezing outside," she said with a full body shiver.

"Uh…" Victor was noncommittal. "I don't have you on the list."

She was meeting a Realtor friend, huh? Trina saw the opportunity and went for it. "Hi, I'm Trina. You must be a friend of Kendall's."

The woman surveyed her cautiously. "Yes."

"It's all settled then," Trina said as she turned back to Victor. "I'll vouch for her. And I'll give her a tour of the commercial space while Kendall finishes up with Zander. That way no one will be inconvenienced."

Victor didn't seem thrilled with this idea, but Trina wanted to get some one-on-one time with this friend of Kendall's. She'd have to push a little harder.

She tried again. "Say, I have a friend that works over at Fenway. Let me see if I can pull some strings and get you bumped to the top of that ticket wait list. It's no guarantee, but I'll try my best."

Victor's eyes lit up. "Oh, wow, thanks."

Trina motioned for the visitor log before looking back at Kendall's friend. "We'll have Ms.…?"

"Channing. Margo Channing," Margo replied. Preempting the question on the tip of Trina's tongue, Margo added, "And before you ask, yes, my mother is a Bette Davis fan."

Trina looked back at Victor. "We'll have Ms. Channing sign the log, and I'll take her out back. Sound good?" Trina waved Margo forward, hoping to distract Victor enough into letting her sign in. She knew there were strict rules about who could enter or leave the building. She was surprised Kendall hadn't thought ahead to put Margo on the list.

Margo scribbled her name down and Trina gave her a wink. Trina's plan to run into Kendall today had been well choreographed, but meeting Margo in the lobby was a pleasant surprise. She decided to go with it.

"I'll come with you to unlock it." Victor stood from this post and ushered them through a back entrance to the commercial space that kept them inside the building.

"That wind is intense today," Trina said as a low howl rumbled through the corridor that led to a service entrance at the back of the building.

"It's even worse being out in it," Margo said, sweeping her hair behind her ear. "I must look like a tumbleweed."

"Not at all," Trina assured her. Quite the contrary, Trina thought she looked great. She was very pretty, and she was dressed like she had plans later that night. "I love your jacket, by the way."

"Thanks," Margo replied.

"We're here," Victor said as he opened what Trina guessed to be one of the rear doors of the commercial unit. "You can come back this way when you're done. You'll avoid the weather that way. I'll lock this door when you're back."

"Thanks, Victor." Trina touched his shoulder as he walked by. "You're a lifesaver."

Victor gave her a brief nod before he headed back toward the hallway.

"I really didn't expect him to let me stay, and I never would have predicted that he'd let you sign me in," Margo said with a laugh.

"Same, girl. Same." Trina was usually plenty confident in herself, but Victor was kind of a wild card. She was glad her gamble had paid off.

Trina led the way in and Margo exhaled audibly.

"Oh, wow."

The space was cavernous and dark, still in the skeleton stages, really. But one entire wall was all glass and faced the harbor. Now that the sun had set, the cityscape across the nearly black water glowed with nightlife and activity. The Boston Harbor Hotel looked majestic lit up, and the arch and dome that were so famous illuminated the walkway between the buildings like a guiding light. For a commercial space, this view was incredible, even at ground level.

"Damn," Margo said. "I might need to get transferred to this location when it's all done."

Trina used her phone's flashlight to find a light switch on the wall nearby. She flicked the switch and brightened the space, at the expense of some of the glow from across the harbor.

"Oh?" she asked. Trina's office had been informed that Kendall had scored the commercial rental space with a contract to Cyclebar. But it was a rental, not a sale. And though it would count toward the total, Trina wasn't exceptionally worried about it. She was, however, curious as to how Kendall had been able to move it so quickly. It seemed maybe Margo was the answer to that one.

"I'm an instructor at the Cyclebar location in Chestnut Hill,"

Margo said as she walked along the window view. "But this space is going to be incredible when it's done. So maybe I ought to exercise some of that seniority."

"Is that how you know Kendall?" Trina was curious about Margo and how she knew Kendall. Her mind momentarily wondered if she and Kendall were more than just friends. And she cursed Lauren for planting the *Kendall was in a gay engagement* seed in her head, because that intrigued her, too. Well, that and how their impromptu coffee date went the other day.

Margo nodded. "She took one of my classes a few months after she moved here, and we totally hit it off."

"Hit it off?" Trina pressed again. Now she had to know if they were more than friends. She felt a little jealous.

Margo turned to face her as she replied, "Yeah. She's super easy to talk to and vent to. I think we spend most of our time together gossiping about work, though I fill a good amount of that time complaining about Mr. Right Now, if you know what I mean."

Well that answered that question. "Oh, for sure. Relationships are impossible these days."

"Exactly." Margo sighed. There was a moment of quiet before Margo asked, "How long do you think it will take them to finish this space?"

"Cyclebar is probably negotiating that directly with Langley. But I'd imagine they'd want to have it up and running by the time the building is completed, if possible. That would certainly help sales."

"That makes sense." Margo leaned against the folding table that was near the middle of the room and checked her phone. After scrolling her screen for a moment, she looked up at Trina and said, "You know, you're different than I expected you to be."

"You had expectations of me? We only just met, Margo. And I put myself on the hook for a favor to Victor to save you from the unruly New England spring weather. That seems rude," Trina teased.

"Ha-ha. I'm sure you'll figure out the Victor thing just fine. And no one asked you to step up to be the knight in shining armor or anything," Margo sassed her right back. Trina liked this woman.

"I'd rather be a queen than a knight, but I'll accept your reluctant gratitude," Trina replied playfully.

Margo bowed. "Thank you, Your Eminence."

"Even better, and you're welcome." Trina leaned against the

table next to her. "So, more about these expectations. What were you expecting?"

Margo surveyed her before she said, "I guess I expected you to be less friendly, or I don't know, I guess I thought you'd be a b—"

"Bitch?" Trina supplied. "That's what your friend called me the first night we met."

"After you verbally attacked her, I'm told," Margo replied. Trina liked that she didn't mince words. That was refreshing.

"Eh, maybe. I suppose it's all a matter of perspective," Trina said. "Well, I'm glad to not meet your expectations then. I'm not so bad, I promise."

Margo gave her a small smile but said nothing. Almost as if she was still reserving her opinion on the matter.

"Kendall already met one of my friends, and now I've met one of hers." Trina paused. "Care to share some juicy gossip about her with me?"

"Not particularly," Margo replied, her tone light. She clearly wasn't offended by the gentle needling—that was good. Trina hadn't meant to offend, and she was half joking in her request. Half.

"Fair enough," Trina said.

"I will tell you this, though." Margo turned to face her. "She's very competitive. Like one of the most competitive people I've ever met. You should see her in class—her performance is unparalleled most days, almost superhuman. It's like even the prospect of a competition drives her. And you seem nicer than I expected, so I feel kinda bad that she's going to beat you."

"I appreciate your candor, but I respectfully disagree," Trina replied.

Margo raised an eyebrow as she said, "You seem awfully sure of yourself."

"I am." Trina didn't feel the need to elaborate. She wasn't here to make enemies. Sure, it annoyed the hell out of her that Margo just assumed Kendall would steamroll her, but that's what friends should say. She'd expect nothing less from Lauren. Well, more expletives, for sure, but not doubt.

Margo gave her a broad smile. "I like you."

"I like you, too," Trina admitted. "And I really do love that jacket—where did you get it?" She didn't get any bad vibes from Margo. If anything, she thought she was a pretty decent, down-to-earth kind of person. Which made her wonder if her initial perceptions of Kendall had been wrong. The Kendall she had coffee with seemed playful and funny. She was charming and easy to talk to, with no hint of the frostiness of their initial exchanges. If Kendall could be friends with someone like Margo, maybe she wasn't so bad after all.

CHAPTER FIFTEEN

Victor was engrossed in what seemed to be an angry, frustrating phone call with someone when Kendall got off the elevator in the lobby. She handed him her hard hat as she checked her phone for the time. She had two missed calls and a few texts from Margo. Shit. It was later than she'd thought.

Kendall started to dart for the front door when the movement of Victor's arm caught her attention. He held his hand over the receiver, blocking the mouthpiece as he said, "Your friend is out back—I already let her in. You can go through the indoor hallway entrance—" Someone yelling on the muffled phone line drew Victor's attention back to the phone.

Kendall took the interruption as a sign and hustled out back. She'd told Margo she would meet her there to give her a quick tour since Margo was going to be shopping in the area anyway. And since Kendall was meeting Zander, it had felt serendipitous. She had planned to grab drinks with Margo afterward to thank her for helping secure the Cyclebar contract—it was the least she could do. And honestly, she had been itching for a social engagement with her bestie. These past few weeks had been intense, so intense that she'd missed most of Margo's spin classes. But she needed a chance to decompress, and outside of working out—and, well, having sex—the only way Kendall knew how to do that was with good wine and a great friend. And gossip. Lots of gossip.

She hurried through the building along the corridor that Zander had showed her earlier. This pathway would be great for the staff of Cyclebar and for any of the residents who wanted to attend a class. The fact that they'd never have to leave the building was a huge plus, especially with the way New England weather could be unpredictable. And today's howling wind was the perfect example. Zander wouldn't allow her to go onto the unfinished balcony of the second penthouse on their tour because he said the winds were too dangerous. She hadn't argued with him because how could you? It sounded like a tornado up there.

She speed-walked to the employee entrance as she chastised herself for being late. The space was a blank canvas, save for a folding table and some chairs that she'd seen in there earlier. Margo must be bored out of her mind, assuming she'd hadn't left yet.

Kendall reached for the doorknob and cursed under her breath. She'd been in such a rush to get here that she'd forgotten to ask for the key Zander had left at the desk with Victor so she could take Margo here after their meeting. And she just realized she'd forgotten to add Margo to the visitor log, too. Fuck. There'd surely be hell to pay for that. Victor was a stickler.

She mentally crossed her fingers and hoped that Victor left this door unlocked when he let Margo in and was glad when the door opened easily under her touch. But what she wasn't expecting was to find Margo belly laughing with Trina.

"Oh, hey," Margo said with a wave as she wiped a tear from her eye. "I must have gotten the times mixed up, because when I got here, the door was locked."

"Don't worry," Trina interjected. "I was in the lobby chatting with Victor when Margo popped in looking for you. It was an easy schmooze to get him to open up for us," Trina said.

"It was a masterful schmooze—she's underselling it," Margo added.

"Anyway, I hope you aren't mad," Trina said lightheartedly, which would have irritated Kendall if not for their coffee flirtation the other day. She could differentiate playful versus goading Trina now. She hoped.

"No, not at all," Kendall replied. She was more curious than mad. What was Trina telling Margo that had her in stitches? She focused her attention on Margo "You didn't mix up the times—I'm late. Sorry."

Margo dismissed her with a wave. "Listen, the cocktails will be there when we get there. I'm off tonight and it's a cheat day. And you're buying. It's all good," she said. "How was the penthouse tour?"

Trina chimed in, "I hear it's amazing up there. I'm headed there myself now."

"Ugh, I'm jealous," Margo said.

"If you don't have anywhere to be," Trina said, "then come up with me for the tour. You've gotta see how the one percent lives, amirite? Let's play. It'll be fun."

Margo's eyes lit up and Kendall felt cornered.

"As long as it doesn't cut into my cocktail time, that's fine." She was trying to be open-minded. She wasn't sure where she stood with Trina. The coffee meet-up had been harmlessly friendly. If not a little more than friendly. And yet, she was still in a very heated competition with this woman. Then there was the issue of her growing attraction to her. Also, the occasional bitchy snark from the past. Was that still a thing? Or would they be more civil now?

"It'll take, like, five minutes. I won't even do the whole Realtor tour thingy—we'll just go as spectators to the lifestyle of the rich and famous," Trina said as she held out her elbow for Margo to take. "C'mon. It's still in the construction phase—it's a cool thing to experience. I promise not to take up too much time."

Margo squealed and slipped her arm into Trina's as she mouthed *thank you* to Kendall.

Kendall watched in awe as Margo and Trina practically giggled together the entire elevator ride up to the penthouse. It was like they were old friends sharing a schoolgirl crush. She couldn't remember a time when she'd seen Margo so giddy and silly. Or Trina, for that matter.

When the elevator pinged at the penthouse floor, Kendall watched as Trina slipped her arm around Margo's waist and guided her out, laughing and chatting animatedly with her. Kendall stayed a beat behind them, watching the scene before her unfold, because she couldn't believe it. She was glad to see her friend was having a good time, but with Trina? She wasn't sure how she felt about that.

"Oh damn," Margo said as she entered the larger of the two penthouses. She spun on the spot with her arms out à la Julie Andrews in *The Sound of Music* and said, "This is just the foyer, Kendall. The foyer! I could host a Zumba class in here."

Trina, who had started talking to Zander when she arrived, stopped to ask, "Did someone say Zumba?"

Kendall watched in disbelief as her nemesis sashayed back to the foyer and started doing what she presumed were Zumba moves with her bestie. They were so compatible it was almost painful. Would she lose her best friend to Trina's seemingly endless charm?

"You're pretty good at that," Margo said after a few moments of dancing with Trina. "You should come to one of my Cyclebar classes and we can see if that rhythm translates to the pedals."

"Don't tempt me," Trina replied, and Kendall started to wonder if this was such a good idea. She didn't need her professional and personal lives overlapping. Ever. Margo was *her* friend, after all. She might not know where she stood with Trina, but Margo was off-limits.

"Ladies," Kendall said, feeling insecure, "Margo and I do have plans."

"Right, right." Trina held up her hands. "Sorry. I got carried away by the rhythm of the imaginary beat."

"Mm-hmm." Kendall was mildly amused, even if she was pouting a bit.

Trina and Margo wandered the space, peppering questions at Zander as they went, but to her credit, Trina seemed to be keeping this more social than work-based, as she'd promised downstairs. Before Kendall knew it, they were already in the second penthouse, and Zander was showing Margo and Trina some of the blueprints he had explained to Kendall earlier.

This unit was the least developed of the ones she had seen, and instead of using a kitchen island as a workspace, Zander was using a mock table of plywood and some sawhorses. Margo seemed captivated by what he was showing her. She forgot how exciting this part of the process could be.

"She's lovely." Trina had somehow snuck up on Kendall without her noticing.

Kendall examined Trina's face, looking for signs of sarcasm, but she saw none. "She is."

"I can't believe she hangs out with the likes of you." And there it was.

Kendall rolled her eyes.

Trina gave her a sly smile. "I'm kidding. I can be friendly, remember?"

"I do." Kendall remembered how Trina had taken her hand when they talked. There was a gentleness to that action that she appreciated. But that didn't mean that she approved of Trina poaching her friend.

"Be honest, are you a little worried that I'll steal her?" Trina asked.

Yes. "Please"—Kendall gave her a look—"as if that was a possibility."

"I think most things are a possibility," Trina replied with a smile. "Except for you beating me, that is."

"Oh, we're still playing at that, huh?" Kendall was glad to see that though their exchanges were more pleasant so far, Trina was still as competitive as ever. Which she was more than fine with, since she still planned on crushing her.

The pocket of her suit jacket buzzed. She fished out her phone to see a text from her office manager. Both the rental agencies she'd been dealing with had gone to contract on units. Feeling emboldened, she turned the screen toward Trina as she said, "That looks less likely since I just contracted on not one, but two unit sales tonight. *And* I have the commercial contract to boot."

Trina's smile didn't waver as she said, "Congratulations, Kendall. That's quite the accomplishment."

She didn't know what she was expecting, but she wasn't expecting that. Nor was she expecting her phone to start vibrating again with another call, startling her.

The phone flew out of her hand and, try as she might, she juggled it like a game of hot potato before ultimately losing control. But before it smashed into a million pieces on the unfinished concrete beneath their feet, Trina caught it. Kendall breathed a sigh of relief.

Trina's expression was unreadable, but the anger in her voice was unmistakable when she said, "Your daddy's calling. Maybe he wants to congratulate you on the sales as well. Or did he help?" Trina handed her the phone and the name on the screen, *Dick Yates*, caused her to recoil a bit. "I let myself get distracted by the Kendall who invited me to coffee. I forgot about this Kendall." She motioned toward her. "This Kendall gets ahead with help, over and over again. Damn, the news is hot off the press, and he's already on the line. I guess your relationship is less complicated than you led me to believe."

"He didn't…I'm not…" Kendall fumbled as she sent him to voice mail. She'd been afraid of this happening since the moment she'd heard he was released from prison, but man, what fucking timing he had. "It's not—"

"It's okay, Kendall. No worries. You just keep doing you." Trina started to walk away but stopped to add, "I mean, it's all you know, right? Hand up, hand out. Say hi to Pops for me."

That dig hurt. Kendall's grip on the phone was painful. She felt her hand shake with the frustration she was desperately trying to conceal.

Things between her and Trina seemed to be getting almost civil until this. But like the flick of a switch, they appeared to be right back at square one. And her father…What did he want? She felt herself start to unravel.

She needed air, and she needed to be out from under Trina's misdirected judgment. She'd earned those sales. All of the sales that had gotten her to this point were hard-earned, regardless of what Trina thought.

Kendall felt flushed and wanted to cool off. The last thing she wanted was to give Trina any more ammunition against her. She needed to get out of there fast.

Margo was walking around with Zander, across the room, listening intently to whatever he was saying. The temporary balcony door Zander had shown her earlier was just to her left. Kendall could briefly slip out and take a breath of the cool air to calm herself. She'd only need a moment or two. No one would even notice.

She moved toward the door, pushing against it to get outside, but the door didn't budge. She had seen Zander open it briefly earlier, but she didn't remember seeing Zander *unlock* it. Was there a lock? Kendall pushed harder, but nothing happened. Her throat felt tight, and she seemed to be getting hotter by the second. She started to feel dizzy and uncomfortable in her own skin. Why did her clothes feel so tight?

"Hey, are you okay?" She looked up to find that she'd drawn Trina's attention. If she didn't get air now, she might faint.

She threw her body weight into the door and it burst open, but the wind outside was too much for her, and she quickly lost her grip on the doorknob. She spilled out toward the balcony, and the door slammed against the newly installed panoramic glass. The cracking sound would have made her cringe if she wasn't more worried about the speed with which her face was quickly approaching the glass railing of the balcony.

"Kendall!" She heard her name called out and felt someone stop her just shy of smashing her face into the rail.

She fell to her knees and took a deep breath, but the icy cold wind around her caused her lungs to burn when she inhaled. She coughed as someone stroked along her back.

"Hey, hey," Trina said, her face just inches away. "Are you okay?"

Kendall coughed again. She didn't feel okay. She felt like she was coming down from a heart attack and a near death experience, and why was it so windy right now?

"I'm going to need you to say something." Trina's hand was under her chin lifting her head up. Kendall was aware of how warm her touch was, which must mean that she was cooler now, not that she felt better.

Trina's fingers brushed along her forehead, seemingly looking for something. "Did you hit your head? Are you all right?"

"I'm fine." Kendall barely managed the words. She felt overwhelmed by the concern on Trina's face. And maybe it was the lack of oxygen, but she also found herself lost in the deep brown of Trina's eyes and the little flecks of amber in them that she hadn't noticed until now. "I'm okay."

"Oh my God." Margo's voice sounded panicked. Kendall could see her and Zander running toward them through one of the now cracked panoramic doors.

Another brutal gust of wind came, and the door that had been flung open started to slam shut. Bracing herself, Kendall tucked her head toward her chest and leaned as far from the building as possible. But the impact never came. She looked up to see Zander holding the door, straining against the wind. He'd saved her from what certainly would have been a concussion. But he wasn't the only one.

Kendall became aware of the feeling of Trina's arms around her and Trina's body pressed to her side, pushing her forward onto the flat surface of the balcony floor. It seemed that Trina had moved them both to escape the door. She wasn't sure if Zander had gotten there in time, or if Trina had moved them enough to avoid injury, but the whipping wind didn't allow her much time to think.

"Inside," Margo yelled as she pulled her and Trina back from the balcony, as Zander and the out of control door followed.

The door closed with a heavy thud as the wind howled outside. Zander grabbed a piece of loose plywood from nearby and propped the door shut.

"Are you okay?" Margo was all over her now, turning her head this way and that.

"I'm fine, I'm fine." Kendall tried to wiggle out of her grasp. She was trying to see past her. Where had Trina gone so quickly?

"Is everyone all right?" Zander knelt beside her before looking in the direction of where the makeshift counter was. Kendall assumed that's where Trina was—not that Margo would back the fuck up enough for her to see.

"The panoramic glass isn't faring too well," Trina said from across the room. "I hope you can get your money back on that one, Zan."

Kendall groaned. It was her fault the glass was broken.

"You're hurt," Margo said insistently. "That's why you're groaning—you're hurt. We need to get to a hospital."

"What?" Kendall shook her head. She felt a little woozy, but she was sure that was the panic attack and the excitement of nearly falling to her death, not because she was actually hurt. "I'm fine. I told you."

"Then what's with the groaning?" Margo put her hands up in frustration.

"I'm groaning because I'm the reason the glass is broken. Now, will you help me up?" Kendall asked before holding her arms out to Margo.

By the time Kendall was upright and the woozy feeling had faded, Zander had already braced the cracked glass with tape and was moving large pieces of pressed wood in front of it.

"Don't overinflate your sense of importance, Yates." Trina's sarcasm sounded from behind her. "That glass should be able to withstand whatever Boston weather throws at it."

Kendall turned to glare at her, but she froze. Trina's forehead was bleeding. "Trina, you're—"

"She's right. It must have been defective," Zander said while still analyzing the door, completely oblivious to Trina's injury.

"Better to figure that out now than when I'm showing it to a client later." Trina chuckled as she dabbed her head with what looked like a tissue.

Kendall pushed past Margo to get closer to her. Trina was using her cellphone camera to assess the damage, but she was struggling with the angle. Kendall reached out as she said, "Here, let me."

Trina paused. "It's fine, just a scratch."

"Just let me." Kendall took one of the fresh tissues out of Trina's other hand. She pressed the tissue along Trina's hairline while using her other hand to brush back Trina's now windblown hair. "It looks mostly superficial. Did you hit your head?"

"There was a lot happening. I'm not sure." Trina stayed still, and Kendall was grateful for that. She'd never been this close to Trina—well, except for on the balcony—but this was an intentional closeness. Trina was about a head shorter than her, but clearly her height had nothing to do with her strength since she'd stopped Kendall's forward momentum toward the railing.

Kendall used the fingers of her free hand to part the hair on either side of the laceration, and Trina winced. "I'm sorry," Kendall said. "I don't mean to hurt you."

"It's just a little tender," Trina replied. "I'll live, I'm sure."

Kendall pulled back the tissue she'd been holding to Trina's forehead to examine the wound again. She was glad to see that the bleeding had stopped. "I think you're all set."

"Thanks." Trina took the tissue and checked Kendall's handwork with her cellphone camera. Kendall didn't miss the way she checked herself out in the reflection, blowing herself an air kiss as she did. She also didn't miss the way Trina's lips looked so full and plump while she did it. "Well this wasn't a typical day at the office, huh?"

Kendall laughed before getting more serious. "Thank you."

"For what?" Trina asked as she rubbed her shoulder.

"For stopping me from eating the rail out there. You're a hero." Kendall motioned behind them.

"Sure. I was the closest person, after all. Just good timing, I guess." Trina looked uncomfortable. Kendall hadn't seen that side of her before.

Kendall watched her carefully as she added, "You usually have no problem receiving compliments, right? Why then, when I'm being sincere, are you unnerved?"

"When have you complimented me in the past?" Trina asked. "And have you been insincere before? Because that speaks more to your character than mine."

Kendall sighed. "God, you're insufferable."

Trina took a step back as she said, "I'm not the one who tried to pitch myself off a building today because someone mocked my codependence on my father, Drama Queen."

Kendall scoffed, "I did not—"

Trina held up her hand. "I'm kidding. About you intentionally putting yourself in harm's way, that is. Not about your codependence with your father. That's your own shit to unpack."

"He didn't—" Kendall started to reply but stopped herself. Now was not the time to debate anything. "Thank you, again. I really appreciate it."

Trina reached for her purse and gave her a brief nod as she said, "I'm glad you're okay. I'd hate to win this competition because you died on the job. That doesn't seem very gratifying."

"For either of us," Kendall replied.

"Exactly. I want you to be healthy when you lose. It'll make it more rewarding," Trina said as she rubbed her shoulder again.

Kendall reached out to touch her elbow. "Is your arm okay?"

"Probably. I'll have my doctor brother look at it. And since he's currently in my guest room, I might as well put him to work," Trina replied.

"You live with your brother?" Kendall didn't mean for that to come out as judgmental as it sounded.

Trina looked horrified as she replied, "Absolutely not. He's supposed to be attending a conference nearby, but plans changed. So he's crashing on the guest bed."

"That's good of you, to put up with him, I mean. I'm sure that's a challenge as an adult to have someone else in your space." Kendall hadn't shared a space for an extended period of time with anyone since her relationship with Collette had ended. She liked her privacy and alone time. Or she couldn't hold down a relationship. Or both.

"I'd be lying if I said it didn't totally derail my routine a bit, but I'm glad to be there for him. He's a good guy," Trina replied, and Kendall smiled at their similarities. Kendall hated when her routine was disrupted, and it amused her that Trina was the same way.

Kendall could tell she was being genuine. As an only child, she'd often wondered what it would be like to have a sibling.

"I'm really glad to have run into you tonight," Kendall said, realizing she'd had her hand on Trina's elbow the whole time they'd been talking. She gave Trina's elbow a quick squeeze before letting go. "I hope your arm is okay."

Trina gave her a wink. "I'm more concerned about my face, but thank you."

"Your face looks fine," Kendall said, trying to reassure her.

"Oh, girl, I know it's *fine*," Trina replied, "but thanks for the compliment."

Trina was a piece of work. "Well, now you can't say I haven't complimented you, can you?" Kendall pointed out.

"I suppose," Trina said as she turned to go. "Have a good night with Margo. You probably don't deserve her."

"Probably," Kendall replied with a smile. The easy banter from the coffee shop appeared to be back, and she hoped it stayed that way.

"Don't forget to call Daddy back," Trina added, and any remotely positive feelings Kendall had the moment before faded like the expression on her face. For a few blissful moments, she had forgotten about him.

"Well, this was enough excitement for one night. I'm off," Trina announced as she said her good-byes.

Kendall watched as both Zander and Margo flocked to Trina. It never ceased to amaze her how easy Trina made all personal interactions. Margo hugged her and their brief conversation looked sincere. Almost familial. How could someone that so easily put her on edge seem to put everyone else at ease? Trina Lee *was* a goddamned conundrum. And in between insults tonight, she'd also saved her life.

It was decided: Kendall needed a drink.

CHAPTER SIXTEEN

The waiter brought the beef carpaccio to the table, and Kendall exhaled. She hadn't realized how hungry she was until it was time to order. In no time this table would be filled with nearly every appetizer on the menu, but she had no regrets.

"Are we going to talk about earlier? Because it seems to be on your mind." Margo took a sip of her martini and waited.

"You mean at the construction site?" Kendall knew damn well what she meant. She was avoiding talking about it for a reason.

"Oh, so that's how this is going to go?" Margo gave her a look as she signaled to the waiter that she wanted another drink. "That's fine. I'll just eat all this meat and cheese and drink the top-shelf shit on your dime while you brood."

"I'm not brooding," Kendall pouted.

Margo's expression was dubious. "Oh, cool. What are you doing then? Because it seems like brooding, but I'll let you tell me how you're feeling. Since you're obviously feeling something."

Kendall groaned. "You know, it would be easier to brood, if I was brooding, which I'm not, if you weren't so logical and mature about how you process emotions."

Margo placed her hands together and bowed. "I'm doing yoga on my off days from teaching spin class. I'm centered. Get used to it."

After a long pause, Kendall exhaled. "I'm brooding."

Margo nodded and reached across the table to pat her hand. "Ah, sweet progress. Hey there, Acceptance, welcome to the party."

"What were you two laughing about when I got there?" Kendall had been wondering that since the moment she walked in. What had Margo in hysterics? Was Trina that funny? That seemed unlikely to her. But she hadn't expected her to save her life tonight, either.

"Trina was telling me about this time she walked into the wrong apartment with a set of potential buyers, and they interrupted what appeared to be an extramarital affair that coincidentally included the sister of one of the buyers she had with her," Margo said as she shook her head. "Trina said a legit catfight broke out between the sisters, and she ended up in the hallway with the husband, the near-naked boyfriend, and the little chihuahua that lived there, while the sisters warred behind the closed door."

"Damn." Kendall had definitely had her share of awkward client interactions. She'd shown up for more than a handful of open houses where the seller had forgotten the scheduled time, or was indisposed, but she'd never walked in on an actual affair. That was a juicy story for sure. "How did she mix up the apartments?"

"She said the concierge at the desk was new and gave her the wrong apartment keys. But since it was next door to the apartment she thought she was visiting, she was under the impression she had made an error on her end."

"An error? She's imperfect. Who knew?" Kendall hadn't meant for that to slip out. It sounded so jaded.

Margo picked up one of the mozzarella sticks that had just been dropped off. "She's not that bad, you know. She's funny and silly. Very self-deprecating and charming."

Kendall gave her a look. "You're my friend, not hers."

Margo held up her hands in surrender. "No one said I was befriending her. I'm just saying she's friendly and playful. I could see her as someone you could like."

"Someone I could like?" Kendall had thought that maybe that could be true after their coffee exchange, but now she wasn't so sure. "Not likely."

Margo rolled her eyes. "I didn't mean someone *you* could like—I meant someone *one* could like, in general. She seems personable. Like, we were only in the room together a few moments, and I felt comfortable around her. She's a people person. That's obvious."

"You haven't seen the other side of her yet." Kendall thought after her coffee date with Trina that she might be able to get past their history of sparring and sniping. She certainly wasn't innocent in the matter. But Trina had turned on her so quickly when she'd seen the incoming call from her father that her head had spun. Because Trina had a way with words that made her blood boil. Without hesitating, she accused Kendall of nepotism again. And this time hurt more than the others, maybe because she thought they'd turned a corner or had a connection. And this time Trina sounded angry, where in the past she just sounded arrogant.

Just thinking about it now was getting her antsy, like she needed to get up and move. She reached for her cocktail instead, taking a generous sip. "She's got a reputation for being ruthless for a reason."

Margo cocked her head to the side. "Here's a quandary: Is she actually ruthless? Or does she just get the job done?"

"What's the difference?" Kendall knew there was a difference, but she didn't want to give Trina the benefit of the doubt because she was still sore about earlier.

"Hear me out," Margo said between bites of the quesadilla that just arrived. "I'm someone who interacts with all types of people all day long, and I ask them to push themselves beyond their level of comfort all the time. That brings certain fundamental personality traits and flaws to the surface. Most people don't like to be pushed beyond their comfort zone. Would you agree?"

"Sure," Kendall replied. She certainly didn't like being pushed outside of her comfort zone.

"Well, the person I met today, the one I spent only about fifteen minutes with until you walked in, was a person who was resourceful and resilient," Margo said with a shrug. "She might interact with you in a more aggressive or ruthless way, but to me, she seemed resourceful."

Kendall mulled that over for a moment.

"And furthermore," Margo said with a sweeping gesture of her hand, "she's also kind of a hero. A *she*-ro if you will. Because regardless of her feelings about you, assuming they mirror your feelings about her, she still dashed out to that balcony to help you."

Kendall still couldn't wrap her head around what transpired. "It all happened so fast."

Margo put down her drink and leaned forward as she asked, "That's the thing—what *did* happen? All I know is I was talking to Zander about crown molding, and then there was this brutal temperature change and a howling sound like someone had opened a vacuum. Oh, and you and Trina were on the balcony floor."

"I had to get some air—I felt like I was overheating—so I opened the door to step outside for a bit," Kendall said.

"Are you sick?" Margo reached across the table to touch her forehead again.

She brushed her off with a laugh. "No, I was…" Kendall didn't want to admit it.

"You were what?" Margo pressed.

"I was angry." Kendall sighed.

"Angry?" Margo asked. "What were you angry about?"

Kendall thought it seemed ridiculous now, but in the moment, she'd been overwhelmed by anger. "I got news that I'd closed both those rental deals that we were talking about earlier."

"That's awesome, congrats!" Margo said.

"Thanks," Kendall replied.

Margo wiped marinara sauce off her mouth as she asked, "So why were you mad then?"

Kendall tried to explain it. "Trina and I were trading insults, mainly that she thought you were too good a person to be my friend, and I told her about the rentals to be spiteful because she threatened to steal you from me, and I was feeling momentarily insecure, but then my father called, and she saw and insinuated that he helped me get the deals, and then my throat felt tight and my body felt like it was too hot, and I needed some air."

"Whoa, your dad called?" Margo's eyes were comically large.

"Yeah." Kendall chewed the inside of her lip. She felt anxious talking about him. That phone call brought so many feelings to the surface for her.

"What did he want?" she asked.

"I didn't take the call." Kendall had no intention of talking to him, ever. She assumed it had something to do with him being out of prison now and wanting something from her. Or just to terrorize her. That was absolutely a possibility. "Anyway, he called, and Trina saw, and she accused me of trading on his name, again, and then it's like my hands were shaking, and I felt sweaty and ragey and I needed to get out of the room fast. So I opened the door to the balcony, and you saw what happened next."

Margo looked concerned. "That sounds like a panic attack, not just anger."

Kendall had no recollection of ever experiencing one of those. "You think so?"

Margo nodded. "Sure, I used to get them all the time before my swim meets in high school. It's one of the reasons I gave up swimming and competition in general. The pressure was too much for me."

Kendall finished her drink before saying, "Maybe you're right."

"I usually am," Margo added with a small smile.

"Now you sound like *her*." Kendall groaned.

"She thinks I'm too good for you?" Margo asked with a sly smile.

"That's the part you're choosing to focus on?" Kendall asked in disbelief.

"No," Margo dismissed her, "of course not." Margo seemed to reconsider this. "Maybe I'm just flattered she thought I was a good person, and I got momentarily distracted. I mean, she's hot and successful and charming, did I mention that?" Margo asked.

"More than once now, yes," Kendall replied with a huff.

Margo cleared her throat. "I'm going to say something, and I want you to hear me out."

"This sounds like a setup." Kendall gave her a wary glance.

"I think you do like her. At least deep down, and I think that because of that, when she teases you and insults you, it makes you more mad than it normally would if she was just some bitch you had to crush," Margo said matter-of-factly.

"She *is* just some"—Kendall paused, choosing her words carefully—"*one* I have to crush. She's an obstacle to my goal. That hasn't changed."

"Call her a bitch," Margo challenged.

"Why?" Kendall asked. This seemed stupid.

"Because I know you can't. Not at least without regretting it afterward," Margo said, crossing her arms. "You like her, and though you two might trade insults, I think she likes you, too."

Kendall thought about the connection she felt to Trina at Starbucks. She thought about the easy flirtation and the gentleness of Trina's fingers on her shoulder and cheek. "Why do you say that?"

"The balcony thing was all kind of a blur until we got you both back inside, but I can tell you what I saw, and what I saw was someone bracing you after your fall, and then there was face touching with affection and concern," Margo said.

"Where did you see affection in there? I'll admit she did seem concerned, but that's all." Kendall made no attempt to deny her gratefulness to Trina tonight. She had been concerned, and Kendall appreciated that.

"In the designated kitchen area," Margo answered. "And I was talking about you."

"Me what?"

"*You* were touching her face with affection and concern," Margo replied. "It was so obvious. You two had, like, a moment. Like, at one point I thought you were going to kiss her."

"That's ridiculous," Kendall replied almost out of reflex. But Margo's words felt suddenly heavy. She recalled noticing the beautiful, deep brown of Trina's eyes on the balcony and feeling the comfort of her weight against her. And in the kitchen, she'd noticed the softness of Trina's hair as she examined her wound, and how her skin matched that softness. And those lips, she couldn't help notice the fullness of Trina's lips when she spoke. Kendall had noticed all those things, even if she'd tried to ignore them.

"All I'm saying is from where I was, it looked like you two were having a friendly, borderline-intimate conversation. Like with laughter and winking and smiles. And you put a hand on her arm, affectionately, and she didn't shrug you off."

"I'm going to need another drink," Kendall said as she looked up to find the waiter.

"That's not a denial." Margo cheered as she grabbed another mozzarella stick from the seemingly ever-forming pile of food on the table.

"If you say so," Kendall replied, because she didn't have an answer to that. Margo was right—something had changed over coffee and then again after the near catastrophe tonight, even though Trina still irritated the hell out of her. Trina had gone above and beyond tonight to ensure Kendall's safety, and that made Kendall feel all sorts of things, one of which was certainly confused.

❖

"Ouch." Trina winced as her brother pushed along the edge of the cut.

"Sorry," he said. "I just want to make sure it's closed."

"By forcing it to open?" she asked as she accepted the wineglass Lauren gave her.

"I still can't believe you didn't just let her fly off the balcony," Lauren said with a head shake. "That was your chance."

Trina laughed, because she knew Lauren was kidding. Lauren wouldn't even give a dirty look to a fly, let alone wish death upon one. She didn't have a malicious bone in her whole body. That's one of the reasons Trina loved her—she was seemingly unjaded by life. It was refreshing.

"Your forehead is going to be fine. It'll be tender for a few days, but you won't scar or anything," he said.

"Whew. That's a relief." Trina reached for a slice of pizza and winced again, this time because her arm throbbed.

"That shoulder, on the other hand," her brother said with a frown, "no pun intended, is a little bruised. And I'm no physical therapist or orthopod, but my guess is with rest, you'll be fine in a few days. Probably."

Trina gave him a look. "Of all the times for you to be a useless kind of doctor…"

Calvin smiled as he said, "But hey, your teeth still look great. Don't forget to floss. Let's keep that gingivitis on its heels."

"See? Useless," Trina said but she was glad he'd looked at her. That damn shoulder ached more by the hour. "I need more wine."

"On it," Lauren said as she appeared with the bottle. Trina was glad she was here—she'd missed hanging with her bestie. Trina had found herself dialing Lauren before she was even out of the parking garage at the Harborside. She wanted to see her friend, to dish a bit. Because tonight had been a lot, and she needed to talk about it.

Calvin's phone rang and he looked at it, his face the picture of anxiety.

"Is that Lisa again? You should just tell her, Cal," Trina encouraged. "Tell her, and give her a few days to get ready for you to return."

Calvin didn't seem so sure.

"Trust me, give her time to process your midlife crisis before you walk into the same room and announce that you're having a midlife crisis. Do it in phases. It'll be less traumatic for both of you," Trina said with confidence. She knew her brother was about to embark on a possibly life-changing conversation, but she also knew that her sister-in-law was levelheaded and in love with her brother, and that she deserved some time to process what her brother had clearly been warring with for months.

"Okay," Calvin said with a sigh. He took a plate from the counter and piled three large pieces of pizza onto it. "Thanks for dinner."

"Go get 'em, Cal," Lauren said with a supportive cheer. Trina laughed. Lauren was the best. They watched in silence as he walked into the guest room and closed the door.

"He's dead," Lauren said.

Trina nodded. "Oh yeah."

"Who would have thought, your perfect brother with his perfect life would be the first one to crack and fall into crisis," Lauren said with a frown. "It's never the ones you think, is it?"

"I don't know. I suppose it's hard being perfect all the time," she replied. Her heart hurt for her brother. She knew he was going through a lot, and though in some ways it felt like he was fed with a silver spoon most of his life, he was still her brother, and she could see how troubled this whole thing made him. "He's not like me, Lauren. He's not built for insecurity and failure."

"Oh, and you are?" Lauren asked skeptically. "You called me over tonight because Kendall locked down both those rental deals, and you're bummed out."

Trina pouted. "I called you over because we both nearly careened off a balcony, and I'm injured."

"Liar." Lauren tugged Trina by her good arm toward the couch.

Trina settled onto the plush sofa with a sigh. "Fine," she admitted. "I'm bummed out."

"I know," Lauren said as she gave her hand a squeeze. Lauren settled next to her, tucking her feet beneath her as she turned to face her. "I was expecting to hear from you. Jax called me to warn me."

Trina figured Jax might have reached out to Lauren, too. The only reason Trina had been able to maintain her composure tonight when Kendall started gloating about her sales was because she'd had the heads-up early on. Jax had gotten word through their connections with admins at the rental offices that both of the deals were effectively done. And Jax had called her with that information while she was in the lobby, before she'd run into Margo. She'd had time to armor herself, fully expecting Kendall to bring it up. What she didn't expect was how much of a lead she'd have on the information. Or how much, even with preparation, Kendall's gloating would bother her. She hated losing. Hated it. And losing to Kendall wasn't an option.

"Her dad called her while she was bragging about the sales," Trina said, remembering the flash of anger she'd felt when she'd seen his name. She had no doubt he'd helped her achieve her goals up to this point. Whether actively or passively, she knew with her heart that Kendall Yates had succeeded in life because of her family and her father's power. But Kendall's reaction to his phone call planted seeds of doubt about his involvement in these deals. Kendall had looked freaked out.

"You think he helped her?" Lauren asked as she removed the mushrooms off the slice she was eating with surgical precision.

"I don't know. Probably," Trina said as she took the discarded mushrooms off Lauren's plate and ate them. "You know," she pointed out, "I got you a cheese pizza specifically to avoid this situation."

Lauren frowned as she said, "Your brother took the rest of the cheese with him into the guest room."

"He's the worst."

"No, Kendall is." Lauren bumped her elbow. Lauren chewed happily by her side before she asked, "So, what happened on the balcony?"

Trina had replayed the events of tonight on the ride back to her apartment. Something changed with that phone call from Dick Yates. She saw Kendall's walls crumble, like she was unnerved. But she'd been too angry about Kendall's gloating to care and had wandered off, until she heard Kendall struggling with the balcony door. That's when she saw the pale, ghost white of Kendall's face. "Kendall was fine until I called her out on being a fraud when her father called. Then something, like, broke in her, and she looked pale and sweaty, like she was having a panic attack."

Trina had seen Jax struggle with panic attacks. She and Lauren had both gotten accustomed to Jax's triggers and warning signs. Kendall had some of those signs tonight: paleness, sweat on her brow, labored breathing. Trina knew something was wrong well before the wind took that door from Kendall's hand. "It all happened so fast. It was like a blur. Kendall was pulling on the temporary door, and then she was falling out of sight."

Trina had watched Kendall struggle with the door and had stepped toward her to help—not that she was sure why, but she had. Then, suddenly, the door was open, and Kendall was falling, and Trina just reacted. She grabbed Kendall's arm in an attempt to stop her descent but ended up falling down with her in the process. She'd found herself pressed to Kendall, bracing her, and that's when she noticed how fast Kendall's heart was beating. And when she'd assessed her for injury, she noticed the coolness of her skin and the fading beads of perspiration. Kendall had looked dazed, like she wasn't fully aware of what was going on, but then something changed. Trina had been worried she hadn't done enough, and that Kendall *had* hit her head, because suddenly Kendall started looking at her, like, *really* looking at her. It was the kind of look that Trina would have considered almost intimate if the circumstances had been different. That feeling made her uncomfortable, and as soon as they were both safely inside, Trina put as much space between them as possible.

"I can't imagine what that would have looked like. It sounds scary." Lauren passed her plate of abandoned mushrooms to Trina to finish. "I don't know that I would have dove out after her."

Trina finished the veggies and placed the plate on the coffee table in front of them. "I didn't give it a lot of thought. It was sort of just happening."

"Well, it was certainly brave," Lauren added.

Trina wasn't so sure about that. "I think I feel a little responsible."

"What?" Lauren asked. "Why?"

"I don't know. I had really been antagonizing her, and, like, then the call came in, and…"

"And what?" Lauren asked.

"And maybe I should lay off her a bit." Trina couldn't believe the words coming out of her mouth.

Lauren looked as gobsmacked as Trina felt. "Your brother is a garbage doctor. You clearly have a concussion."

Trina laughed and her shoulder hurt. "Ouch," she said. "Shut up."

"Why else would you feel the need to give Kendall a break?" Lauren asked.

"We had coffee the other day, and she was, I don't know, sweet. And flirtatious, and charming," Trina blurted out.

"You did what?" Lauren was looking at her like she'd said that in another language. But she was pretty sure she'd used English.

"I was at Starbucks and she jumped the line and stepped behind me and added her coffee order to mine," Trina recalled. "And then she asked me to stick around for coffee for a bit."

"And you're just telling me this now?" Lauren looked offended.

Trina scrunched her nose. "Sorry. It's been a weird week."

"What else happened?" Lauren asked.

Trina bit her bottom lip. "Uh, there was some banter, and maybe Kendall alluded to being jealous that Shay and I had a relationship in the past."

"Because Shay is hot? I totally get that." Lauren fanned herself.

"No, ass. Because I'm hot, and she was jealous that Shay got a piece," Trina replied.

Lauren gaped. "She said that?"

"Yup," Trina replied. "And she also apologized for being a classist asshole in her office, and maybe we held hands for a minute or two."

"Held hands?" Lauren smiled, and Trina wished she hadn't mentioned that last part.

"Kind of, sort of." Trina sighed. "Okay, there was hand-holding. A bit."

"Wow." Lauren said before asking, "Why?"

"I don't know. It seemed appropriate at the time. Look." Trina paused. "All I know is that it felt totally normal, and I thought we were maybe moving onto a different playing field, but then she was gloating and her dad called and I forgot about all the niceties. Until she almost died. Then they came rushing back." Trina recalled the intense look Kendall had in the kitchen that mirrored the one she had on the balcony. Trina remembered being dazzled by the sparkle of Kendall's green eyes as she caressed her brow and scrutinized her head wound. Kendall was beautiful, after all, even if she was supposed to be her archnemesis. And Trina had been feeling a little shaken about what had transpired, try as she might to hide it. Kendall's concern was appreciated, and her touch, much like the other day, was electrifying. And Trina wasn't sure if that was the endorphins, or if it was just because Kendall was touching her face and holding her arm while thanking her for being there tonight. But the genuineness of the exchange, the ease of the small talk that followed, and those eyes all made Trina need space. Because *that* Kendall, the one in the kitchen, *that* Kendall was like coffee shop Kendall, the one Trina could see herself liking more than just casually. And Trina needed her to be anything but that for her to be able to win this bet.

"You like her," Lauren said, and Trina wasn't ready for that kind of declaration yet, but the desire to kiss Kendall in the kitchen while she cradled her face was certainly there.

"Honestly, I don't know what I like right now. This wine, this pizza, your company: yes. Kendall Yates? Maybe. I don't know. The jury is still out," she said. "But the fact is, regardless of what happened tonight or at the coffee shop, I still need to win this competition."

Lauren nodded. "Okay, we'll shelve the *Kendall is hot and you want to kiss her* thing because you're totally right. We need to talk strategy now that she's in the lead."

Trina hadn't forgotten that part. "How do we beat her?"

"I'm way ahead of you," Lauren said with a mischievous grin as she pulled a file out of the purse on the floor next to them. "I brought by some brainstorming ideas Jax and I were running through today. Remember Mrs. Clarke?"

"The recent widow of that stock-market mogul and the wool heiress who loves to play competitive bridge and wears too much jewelry all the time? Of course, she's my role model." Trina felt like Amelia Clarke was doing it right—she was at all the major social events in the city, she dabbled in philanthropy, she loved animals, and Trina had suspicions after their last exchange that she might also be interested in women. "What about her?"

"She's playing in a bridge tournament at The Country Club this Friday. And my sources tell me that she's looking for a fancy city apartment not far from the casino to continue her reign as Boston's Bridge Queen," Lauren said.

"Well, damn." Trina was feeling better by the moment. "Let's give her a call then."

CHAPTER SEVENTEEN

K endall took a deep breath and exhaled. She didn't want to do this, and she certainly wasn't in the mood to schmooze today. Especially not following the news that Trina had contracted another corner unit over the past few days. Whatever lead she once had was quickly slipping away.

She turned off her car and sat in the driver's seat, brooding for a minute. The past week had been a blur. Ever since her run-in with Trina at the Harborside, she'd been a little off. Sure, she'd finalized those rental sales and things were going well with the Cyclebar contract, but she felt like she was spinning her wheels on ideas to move the other units. All her calls had resulted in dead ends. And now she was going to do a face-to-face with someone she had never met, and she loathed the idea of being shot down in person. Because she hated failure, and though this wasn't guaranteed to end in failure, she wasn't confident it wouldn't.

Clyde had recommended she reach out to a few of the area country clubs to see if she could advertise there. It wasn't a bad idea, but she'd never ventured into this realm before, so her meeting with the marketing director today felt like a job interview. She didn't usually shy away from advertising her skills and promoting herself, but this made her uneasy for a few reasons and they all had to do with her father.

Her father had made a habit of touring the country club scene in his early days of building his real estate empire. He'd rubbed elbows with all the right people and made most of the connections he later used to expand his business. Lots of politicians and wealthy small business owners liked those clubs, largely, Kendall assumed, because membership made them feel superior to those who couldn't afford the annual dues. Kendall knew most of her father's business deals and political canoodling was done on the golf course or at the private poker tables at most of the Connecticut clubs. In Kendall's mind, these sorts of places allowed people to brag about all their wealth and laugh about all their privilege while managing to make social connections to ensure they'd always be one step ahead of the average person. All in all, Kendall thought country clubs were gross, just like her father.

Dick Yates had called her three times since that night at the Harborside, and he'd even ventured to leave two messages. The first one was requesting her ear to talk, but the second one, a few days later, was demanding. Kendall could hear the seething rage in her father's voice over voice mail, and it had made her shiver. He was angry that she was avoiding his request to speak with her, which made her want to talk to him even less.

That angry voice mail had rattled her. She wasn't used to being on the defensive these days. Well, except of course when Trina put her there. But that was a different kind of defensive than what her father made her feel. Trina made her feel curious. Almost excited. Like she *wanted* to verbally spar with her, sometimes. She liked that Trina was smart and witty. And she couldn't stop thinking about their coffee date and the night on the balcony. She'd found herself wanting to call Trina, to check on her head and arm. She wondered how she was feeling and if she might run into her at the Harborside again soon. She wanted to.

"Okay, Kendall," she said aloud. "You can do this. Go in, make a good impression, sell some properties." *And see Trina again.*

❖

Marcia Hardwick had a captivating personality. She was effervescent and cheerful without being annoying. She certainly looked the part of a country club marketing director. Her chin-length blond hair was perfectly coifed, and her large diamond stud earrings glistened as brightly as her perfectly fake teeth. Her pale blue eyes twinkled when she spoke, and the hue of her cardigan matched her pencil skirt almost effortlessly. She was perfectly perfect for this job, and Kendall found herself nodding along to everything she had to say. Kendall would estimate that she was in her sixties, though she didn't look it. Her forehead didn't move as much as her grandiose expressions called for, so Kendall figured she'd had some work done, but tastefully so.

"Now if you're ready, I'd love to give you a brief tour. I think in addition to finding our club a welcoming place for your marketing purposes, you'll find it a wonderful place to socialize. We are taking new memberships," Marcia said as she led her out of the beautiful, light-filled office facing one of the many golf courses on site.

"Oh, that's good to know," Kendall replied to be polite. She had no intention of joining, but she figured it wouldn't hurt to perpetuate the facade.

"Normally we limit outside marketing to only certain days and times during the month, but I'm sure we can figure something out. The Harborside is an exciting addition to the Seaport, and a few of our members have been talking about it," Marcia said as she showed Kendall one of three dining areas in the main building.

"Well, that's great to hear," Kendall replied as she skimmed over the daily menu for the main dining hall posted by the host desk at the entrance. They were serving halibut today. That sounded good.

"We have a big bridge tournament about to end, so this dining room will fill up shortly. We do take walk-ins but prefer reservations. There are two smaller dining areas, one at the ninth hole and one in the clubhouse by the gym and sauna. That one tends to offer lighter fare and healthier options," Marcia said as she flashed a devilish smile. "The main dining room has the best lobster mac and cheese on the planet, but it's not light on the butter or the cream."

"That's why it tastes so good, right?" Kendall replied. "The bad stuff always tastes the best."

Marcia patted her nonexistent belly as she said, "Oh, don't I know it. I must be careful around here. The food is just too good."

Kendall would bet that Marcia was probably the same size she was in high school, but she didn't argue the point.

"You don't have that problem, I can see—you're in amazing shape." Marcia laid on the flattery.

"Thank you," Kendall replied.

"What do you do to keep so fit?" Marcia asked.

"I do a lot of indoor cycling these days, but I was a tennis player in my youth." Kendall had been inside many clubs like this one, when she was too young to realize that her father was taking her along as a prop, not as a bonding activity. When she got older, she noticed that her tennis matches tended to draw the attention of a lot of the men at the club. She stopped playing after a while because of it.

"Well, we have a beautiful fitness area, and we do offer a multitude of exercise classes. I think you'll find the selection to be appealing. Let's look at the clubhouse and spa area. I'll give you a quick tour of the women's locker room facilities, too, so you can get an idea if the club would be a good place for you—you know, outside of visiting us to bring us knowledge of the real estate opportunities in the city." Marcia seamlessly moved from promotion to advertising without missing a beat. She was smooth.

"I'd like that," Kendall said as she watched a few golf carts of men and women cruise by beyond the enormous glass wall facing the golf course. The weather had been beautiful today. She imagined it was primo golfing weather, if that was your thing. She'd never taken to golfing, too slow and boring. She'd much preferred tennis or racquetball when she was younger, but she enjoyed the self-competition indoor cycling had brought to her. She worked well alone, even when just working out. People let you down, after all.

After a short golf cart ride and a few pit stops where Marcia showed her the grounds and the most popular meeting places on the property, they finally reached the clubhouse.

"And this is our spa area. We have a sauna and a steam room off the pool entrance, and just through those doors"—she pointed beyond them—"are the massage area and facial zone. We have an esthetician who comes in on Tuesdays and Fridays for skin treatments, and we have a mani-pedi woman—Mondays and Wednesdays year-round but she's here with a team daily, Monday through Saturday, during our busier summer months."

Marcia looked up at the clock on the wall above them and paused. "Oh, it's later than I thought. I have to get back to the main building for a meeting, but please, show yourself around and enjoy the grounds. If you decide to try that mac and cheese, let them know you're a guest of mine. I'll leave some information about our membership opportunities for you at the main concierge desk so you can grab it when you sign out today."

"Thank you, I'd like that. And thanks again for taking the time to meet with me today," Kendall said.

"Of course! Anytime, just call me. But hopefully I'll be seeing you around on a more social basis soon," Marcia said as she shook her hand. "I think you'll like it here."

"I'll read over the information, thanks," Kendall replied. "And I'll be in touch to set up that real estate talk."

"Perfect. It was great meeting you—enjoy the rest of your day."

As Kendall waved good-bye to Marcia, she heard a familiar voice behind her.

"Oh, Bertie, you're not kidding anyone. I saw you kick that ball on the eighth hole. I'm just too classy to call you out on it," Trina said to an older woman wearing a bright white visor.

"Nothing gets past you, huh?" Bertie laughed, her gravelly voice indicative of years of smoking. "What's the plan for the rest of your day, sweetie?"

"I'm meeting Amelia after the bridge tournament, but I'll probably stay around for drinks afterward. You in?" Trina adjusted her long ponytail. She was wearing a tight-fitting long-sleeve pale pink golf shirt with a bright pink plaid skirt that matched her knee-high golf socks. She looked like cotton candy, positively edible.

"I've got a canasta game at Suzy's later. She'll want to talk about how great her lawyer son is, no doubt. I'll entertain her mindless frothing because she makes the best gin fizz this side of Route 9," Bertie said as she took off her visor, revealing a partially flattened curly mop.

"We all have our strengths," Trina replied, still not noticing Kendall.

"Have fun with Clarkie," Bertie said with a snort. "Just don't call her that—she hates it."

"Duly noted, bye, Bertie." Trina gave her a wave as she opened a nearby locker.

Kendall leaned against the wall behind her, watching for a moment before she finally spoke. "I didn't know you were a member here."

Trina jumped. She spun on the spot, her hand at her chest. The startled look on her face faded, and that familiar taunting smile appeared as she replied, "I didn't know you were a stalker."

"I'm not." Kendall pretended to examine her manicure. "I'm here on business."

"So am I." Trina crossed her arms over her chest, and Kendall noticed the swell of her breasts under the tight fabric of her shirt.

"Then you're not a member? Because it sure seemed that way." Kendall nodded in the direction Bertie disappeared. "Seems like you have a regular golf partner."

Trina uncrossed her arms and took a seemingly casual step toward her. "Not a member, just using a guest pass. The weather was too good to pass up swinging the clubs today."

Kendall gave her a once-over again. "A golfer, huh? That seems like too slow an activity for you. I never pegged you as a golfer."

"I play for leisure and business, not for exercise. And you've never pegged me, but I'm glad to know you think about it," Trina replied, and Kendall felt herself blush.

"That's not what I meant, I—" Kendall sputtered. Trina looked like she was enjoying herself.

Kendall tried to step back as Trina stepped into her space, but the wall behind her made her stop short. The smirk on Trina's face indicated that she noticed.

"And since we're on the topic, I'm not sure why you're under the false impression that I would be the one being pegged and not doing the pegging." Trina's face was inches from hers, and Kendall squirmed on the spot. Not just from the closeness—well, maybe the closeness was a factor because Trina looked delectable in that golfing outfit. But what Trina was saying made Kendall, well, hot. "You just keep underestimating me, and maybe you shouldn't."

At this close range Kendall could smell the faint scent of sunblock on Trina's face and something sweet, like perfume with just the hint of sweat. It was pleasant. It reminded her of summer. She licked her lips and Trina smiled.

"As much fun as this is"—Trina stepped back, and Kendall started to exhale—"I have to shower before I meet my client. So if you'll excuse me, I'll be getting naked at that locker in a moment and rinsing off around the corner."

Kendall's attempt at a controlled exhale failed, and she coughed. Trina's statement almost sounded like an invitation. "Good luck with that." Kendall was amazed she'd managed to choke out a reply.

Trina didn't hesitate in her response. "I don't need luck. I'm pretty adept at getting wet and lathering myself, but thank you for the well wishes."

Kendall had to laugh—she'd practically fallen into that one. "With your meeting, good luck with your meeting. I should have clarified."

"Thanks," Trina said as she pulled her shirt up and off, exposing a matching light pink sports bra. Kendall did her best not to stare at the lithe, beautiful body that had been silhouetted by the now missing shirt, but it was a fruitless battle. Trina was as attractive nearly naked as she was fully dressed.

Kendall averted her eyes when Trina continued to strip in front of her, something that she had a feeling was slower and more intentional than it would have been had Kendall not been there.

Kendall's suit jacket pocket vibrated, and she jumped at the

sensation. She placed her hand against the outside of the pocket to still
the phone, but her jolting motion must have drawn Trina's attention.

"No phones in here, Kendall. It's against club policy," Trina said,
and Kendall hazarded a glance in her direction.

Trina was wrapped in a soft, luxurious looking towel with The
Country Club's logo on it. She closed her locker and stepped back into
Kendall's space. Kendall was frozen on the spot, though the desire to
reach out and trace her fingers along Trina's naked shoulder was almost
unignorable.

"Who's calling this time, I wonder?" Trina asked as she looked
up at her with a mischievous expression. Kendall felt herself shudder
when Trina reached into her pocket and withdrew her phone.

Kendall glanced down at the phone's screen but allowed herself
the opportunity to appreciate Trina's cleavage. Being taller than Trina
certainly had its benefits.

"Margo," Trina said with a smile. She held the phone out for
Kendall to take.

"Oh, you're not just going to answer it?" Kendall was joking. She
could feel the heat emanating off Trina's body against her own, and
though she probably should have left a long time ago, she didn't feel
the need to move out of this spot. Or this proximity.

Trina raised an eyebrow in her direction before sliding her thumb
against the glass face of Kendall's phone, answering the call. She
brought the phone to her ear but kept those gorgeous brown eyes locked
on Kendall's. Kendall let herself get lost in them while Trina talked.

"Hey, Margo. It's Trina." Trina spoke softly into the phone, and
Kendall could have sworn she'd stepped even closer to her. Kendall was
only barely aware of what Trina was saying because she was captivated
by the pink gloss on Trina's lips and the way those lips moved as she
formed words. What the words were, Kendall found that she didn't
care.

"Mm-hmm, I'll tell her. Thanks, Margo. Have a good day."
Trina disconnected the call and slipped Kendall's phone back into her
pocket. She pressed her palm against the fabric, and Kendall reflexively
grabbed her wrist.

"What did she have to say?" Kendall asked as she stroked her
thumb along the inside of Trina's wrist.

Trina didn't pull back from her touch. Instead, to Kendall's libido's
delight, she reached out with her other hand to pull at the bottom hem

of her suit jacket, lightly grazing the front of her thigh in the process. Kendall's clit throbbed with want.

"She said to have you call her later, when you weren't busy," Trina replied, not breaking eye contact.

"Am I busy?" Kendall pulled Trina by the wrist, bringing their chests together.

"Do you want to be?" Trina asked as she licked her lips and Kendall needed to taste them.

"Yes," Kendall answered honestly. She wanted to be busy with Trina's lips on her mouth and her fingers on her body, exploring and pleasuring her. She wanted to taste the smell of summer on her skin and feel that tongue against hers.

Trina moaned in response and pressed her hand against Kendall's thigh.

Kendall tightened her grip on Trina's wrist, pulling her arm around her waist and lowering her head until their lips were only millimeters apart. As she leaned in to close the distance, the sound of a small group of gabbing ladies entering their area of the locker room caused her to pull back. In a flash, Trina's hands were off her body, and the space between them felt cavernous.

Trina adjusted the towel around herself as she smiled and greeted the women. Kendall noted that she seemed familiar with a few of them. Once the group finally dispersed, Kendall found herself frustrated and a little out of breath. She looked to Trina to gauge her reaction to what had almost happened and found Trina chewing her bottom lip in the most adorably sexy way.

Kendall briefly glanced left and right to make sure they were alone before she made the first move this time, stepping closer to Trina. "That was awfully rude of those women," she said.

"To walk through the ladies' locker room?" Trina asked, sounding amused.

"Obviously," Kendall replied. She brushed a hair off Trina's forehead and remembered the wound from the other night. She danced her fingers along the area as she sought it out. "How's your head?"

"*Fine*," Trina parroted from the other day, and Kendall laughed.

She traced along Trina's face to her jaw, turning her head to the side to get a better view of her neck and shoulder. Kendall wanted to kiss along the column of her neck. She trailed her fingers along the soft skin before her, and Trina shuddered under her touch. That's when

Kendall noticed the faint bruise on her shoulder. She pressed the tissue just to the left of it, not wanting to hurt Trina.

"Is this sore?" she asked, genuinely concerned.

Trina closed her eyes as she replied, "A little, but that feels nice."

Kendall massaged the area a bit, resting her free hand on Trina's hip to stabilize her. Trina's eyes opened when Kendall massaged along her hip as well.

"I think maybe we got caught up in the moment back there," Trina said, and Kendall paused her movements.

"Just then?" Kendall asked as she squeezed Trina's hip once more, holding her close while sliding her other hand down from Trina's shoulder to her hand.

Trina caught her hand and entwined their fingers. "Maybe now, too."

Kendall pulled Trina against her again, this time clutching the fabric at Trina's hip to try to keep herself from moving too fast. Because she wanted to move fast. And she wanted this towel out of the way.

"What are you thinking right now?" Trina asked as she leaned forward and brushed her lips against the edge of Kendall's.

Kendall sighed, turning her head to catch those lips, but Trina pulled back a bit.

"Tell me," Trina implored, her dark eyes almost taunting.

"That I want to kiss you," Kendall whispered as she leaned toward her again. "And that I'd like to take this towel off you."

"In that order?"

"Yes," Kendall replied. She wanted very much for both of those things to happen, the order of which didn't *really* matter, but tasting those pink lips was high on her priority list.

"So kiss me," Trina said, her lips pouty and full.

Kendall didn't hesitate to close the distance between them, and she wasn't disappointed when she did. Trina's lips were as warm and as soft as they looked, and when Trina dropped her hand in favor of cupping Kendall's jaw, pulling her mouth closer, Kendall all but died on the spot. Because like everything else Kendall had seen or observed of Trina, she kissed like she owned the room, like she owned the moment, and she certainly owned Kendall's mouth. The feeling was more than electric—it was almost spiritual.

Trina's touch on her jaw was insistent but gentle, and when her tongue slid past Kendall's lips, Kendall's sex tightened with anticipation and pleasure. Kendall let her free hand wander, caressing Trina's side, toying with the top of the towel while she still clutched the fabric at Trina's hip. At some point Kendall's suit jacket must have come open because Trina's warm hand at her low back was pulling her forward and slipping beneath the waist of her pants in a wonderful massaging motion.

Kendall leaned into Trina walking her back with each kiss and gasp for breath until Trina was back against the lockers where their flirtation had begun. Kendall moaned when Trina bucked under her touch as she clawed at the towel covering Trina's breasts.

Trina gasped into her open mouth, clutching at Kendall's upper back beneath her jacket as Kendall worked the knot loose that was holding the towel in place. Trina pulled Kendall against her, pinning her to the lockers, and she let out a low purr when Kendall dared to kiss away from her mouth to lick along her neck. Trina's hand was in her hair, and Kendall's hips thrust forward as Trina scratched at her scalp. The involuntary movement elicited a pleased hum from Trina, and Kendall would have done that again and again if that reaction was guaranteed except Trina shifted from beneath her.

Trina guided Kendall's lips back to her mouth, giving her a searing kiss before slowing Kendall down, deepening the kiss and dragging out the sensuality of it. Kendall ached for more, for faster, for harder, for less towel and more skin, but Trina shook her head and laughed against her lips as the kiss slowed to a more casual exchange than the heated make out that made Kendall almost light-headed.

"That's some mouth on you, Kendall Yates," Trina said as she licked across Kendall's lips before placing chaste, teasing kisses along the edge of her mouth. "And though this has certainly been the highlight of my day, I do have a client meeting, and we are in the middle of a locker room, and maybe we should take a rain check on this." Trina pressed her lips against Kendall's as she guided Kendall's hand away from the juncture of her hip and thigh. Kendall sighed against her mouth, not from disappointment, but from surprise. She had no idea her hand had wandered that much. She'd been so caught up in the kissing that she'd lost track of where her hands were.

"A rain check?" Kendall asked, hopeful. She rested her hand against the locker beside Trina's head to keep from touching her. The coolness of the metal was a sharp contrast to the soft, pliable warmth of Trina's skin. She much preferred touching Trina.

"If you kiss me like that again, you'd better do more than just massage my hip." Trina cupped Kendall's face and pulled her lips down to kiss her again. "I've got other places I want you to rub."

"Fuck," Kendall said as Trina released her hold on her face.

"If you're lucky," Trina said as she pressed one last chaste kiss to her lips, nipping Kendall's bottom lip playfully. "I hate to leave you yearning and feeling unfulfilled and all, but I've got to get cleaned up before this meeting."

"Who says I'm feeling unfulfilled?" Kendall kissed her again, not ready to be done yet.

Trina boldly reached out and slipped beneath the lapels of her jacket, grazing her fingers over one of Kendall's erect nipples. Kendall groaned at the contact. The sensation was electrifying.

"Your body is telling me all kinds of things," Trina said as she pulled her hand back. "The least of which is that we probably have unfinished business."

The sound of a locker opening and closing a few rows over made Kendall startle and step back. Trina was right—this wasn't the time or the place. If only she could communicate that to her throbbing clit.

Trina gave her a flirtatious smile, and Kendall wanted to move back into her space, but Trina stepped into hers first. Kendall wrapped her arms loosely around her body, savoring the feeling of Trina's shape in her hands, as Trina got up on tiptoe to whisper in her ear, "I'll think of you in the shower."

Kendall closed her eyes at the sensation of Trina's lips on her earlobe. Kendall's lower abdomen tightened almost painfully at Trina's words.

"You can keep the towel as a parting gift. There's plenty more. Bye, Kendall. Thanks for the kiss," Trina said with a quick kiss to Kendall's cheek before she slipped out of Kendall's grasp and walked away, naked and perfect, leaving Kendall with a handful of fabric and a mind full of dirty, dirty thoughts.

CHAPTER EIGHTEEN

Trina wasn't sure how long she had been staring off into the distance, but if the amused looks on her colleagues' faces were any indication, it had been longer than she thought.

"Are you with us today, Trina?" Lauren teased. "Or are you still daydreaming about kissing the tall blonde with the emerald eyes?"

Trina shot her a look. "I told you that in confidence."

Jax gave her a sheepish smile and said, "If it makes you feel any better, I'm pretty good at keeping confidences, even if they weren't shared with me directly. Your secret is safe with me—I promise."

"Evidently it isn't with Lauren." Trina gave her best side-eye to her friend, but they both knew she was full of shit. She wasn't mad at Lauren for telling Jax. She was mad at herself for kissing the enemy. And liking it so damn much.

"So, have you two talked about the locker room lip-lock yet? Or are we all supposed to pretend it didn't happen?" Lauren asked. "Because I don't think I can do that. It's too juicy to ignore."

"Lauren," Trina whined.

"What?" Lauren asked as she raised her hands in frustration. "I can't remember the last time you called me with a kiss-and-tell—let alone one that happened in the middle of the afternoon while you were courting a potential client—in a women's locker room with your primary competition, which you referred to as one of the best kisses of your life. Did I leave out any details?"

Jax said, "Well, you left out some of those details when you told me, but I feel like I'm all caught up now."

Trina groaned and dropped her head into her hands as she squeaked out, "I'm an idiot."

Lauren plopped next to her and patted her back as she said, reassuringly, "You're not an idiot. You're just sexually frustrated and wildly attracted to your archnemesis. Really the issue here is that you probably need to have an orgas—"

"With Kendall?" Trina asked, whipping her head up so fast she got dizzy.

"Wow, obsessed much?" Lauren said with a laugh. "I was going to say have an orgasm by yourself—that is, you probably should let off a little steam more often, so you aren't a vibrating fucking rabbit of unfulfilled sexual desires—but *your* mind went to Kendall, so the cat's out of the bag."

Trina felt her jaw drop. "Well, damn."

Lauren said, "I don't know why you're shocked. Kendall *is* your type. And the sexual tension between you two has been insufferable."

"Liar," Trina replied.

Lauren gave her a look. "Seriously? You two are like a lit match and dry wood."

"There hasn't been any sexual tension," she denied.

"Look, I'm going to break this down real easy for you, because I love you and I need you to pull your head out of your ass long enough to accept the facts so we can sort out how to deal with them," Lauren said. "You two are absolutely vibrating together. You get under Kendall's skin as easy as you breathe, and I've seen the devilish look you get in your eyes when you two are trading insults. It's like some twisted game. And you should probably see a therapist about that."

Trina huffed in response.

"Furthermore," Lauren continued, "it drives you crazy that she's ahead in the competition, and ahead in life or title or height or whatever inspires your rage at any given moment—"

"Like how she's had everything handed to her, and her father's connections have paved her entire way," Trina supplied.

"Yes, perfect example. Let's use that," Lauren replied. "It boils your blood that someone who you perceive to be unworthy of advancement and success is both advancing and successful, particularly against you—"

"Hey—"

Lauren held up her hand. "Let me finish."

Trina begrudgingly nodded.

"Kendall is successful and is an immediate and legitimate threat and rival, and that bothers you no end because…why?" Lauren asked.

"Because she didn't earn it," Trina replied matter-of-factly.

"That's what you assume, anyway," Lauren said.

"Whose side are you on ?" Trina asked, not seeing the point.

"Yours," Lauren said. "I'm on your side. The side that knows Kendall is a formidable foe, and beautiful, and your type, and smart, and savvy, and super-hot in a pantsuit, and though she might have achieved her advancements with help, she absolutely walks the walk. So the past is the past, and the fact is right now, she is here, in your face, and just as competitive and shrewd-minded at business as you are. And that is the biggest turn-on you've ever had for as long as I've known you. You like smart, sassy, confident, boss bitch women, who own an outfit, own a room, and own all the good and the bad that comes with it. And Kendall, from what I can tell and from what you've told me about her, is all that and perfect teeth as well." Lauren mimed a mic drop.

Jax clapped. "Wow."

Trina just gaped at her. Shit. She was totally right.

"So in summary," Lauren said with a grandiose hand gesture, "you think she's hot because she is. And she's a badass independent woman, just like you. As friends or enemies or whatever, you two will always spark."

"Like a lit match and dry wood," Trina repeated as she shook her head.

"A lethal combination," Lauren said with a shrug. "Or a recipe for really hot sex. It could go either way."

Jax made an exploding motion with their hands and Trina swallowed hard.

Trina frowned, unsure of how she felt about all this open sharing and emotions talk. But she couldn't stop herself, either. "That's how the kiss felt—it felt electric. Like a charge. And I felt drawn to her, even though I knew it was a bad idea. I had plenty of opportunities to stop, and I didn't."

Lauren nodded. "And why would you?"

"Because she's the enemy," Trina said, though she was having a hard time believing her own words. Sure, Kendall was her rival, but she was second-guessing the enemy part. But only on the basis of how amazing Kendall's mouth felt against hers and how desperately she'd wanted Kendall to pin her to the locker and have her way with her, so she was probably a little biased. Like she was hoping for goodness or humanity or whatever if it came with mind-numbing orgasms, which, by Lauren's deduction, was almost certain.

"Sure. Your attraction to her and the fact that she's the enemy can both be true. It's not one or the other. Those realities can coexist in this world," Lauren said, and Trina wondered if she'd been meditating again. Because this was extra deep.

"Fine." Trina sighed. "I think she's hot and capable and incredibly sexy when she volleys insults with me, and I particularly love it when I see her get rattled, especially when I step into her personal space."

Trina thought about their meetings at Kendall's office and in the penthouse and again in the locker room. She'd intentionally stepped into Kendall's space to take away her sense of stability and superiority. She'd been doing it for years. Whenever someone used their size, their power and connections, or their physical position in the room to intimidate or invalidate Trina, she stepped toward them. She'd found that nine times out of ten, they backed up. It didn't matter that she was smaller, or slighter, or less powerful—she took up space, *their* space, and it unnerved people. And it worked on Kendall like a charm, until the country club moment, when Kendall stepped into *her* space and kissed her like no one had ever kissed her before. And in that moment, Trina knew that she'd lost that edge. She couldn't play the space card anymore. Because Kendall had been in *her* space, and they'd nearly humped as a result. In fact, Trina was confident that if she'd had less self-control and hadn't had a meeting, they would have done a lot more than just humped. She'd fantasized about how many ways that would happen since it nearly did, and that was doing nothing to help her win this competition.

"Okay, so the facts are on the table and you've been enlightened." Lauren brought the conversation back full circle. "Now we have to figure out how we're going to deal with these facts."

"Right," Trina said as she inhaled a deep breath. "What do I do?"

"About what?" Lauren asked, looking confused.

"About being attracted to someone I'm supposed to hate," Trina said as she motioned for Lauren to catch up.

"Oh, nothing. You can't do anything about that," Lauren said as if the writing was on the wall.

"I'm lost," Trina said, feeling overwhelmed.

"Can I?" Jax, who had just finished adding Trina's newly contracted unit to the whiteboard, spoke for the first time in a long time.

"Please do." Lauren motioned for them to go on.

Jax stood then sat back down. They said, "You can't unthink Kendall is sexy. She just is. But that doesn't mean you have to jeopardize this competition because of it. You just need to figure out what you want, what you're comfortable with, and what your boundaries are."

"You're both assuming this is more than a one-time thing, right? Because that's the vibe I'm picking up," Trina said. She wasn't so sure it was something to worry about. She could admit they shared a fantastic, lusty, consenting dynamic, and it could be just that. Admitting to her attraction was the first step, and Lauren had basically dressed her down over that today, so that was done. She was attracted to Kendall. Fact. And she liked kissing Kendall. That was also a fact. That didn't mean she couldn't still beat her ass at this competition. She might even enjoy that victory more now.

"She's not even listening. We lost her," Trina heard Lauren say.

"What?" she asked, dumbly.

Jax sighed. "You got it bad, girl. Just accept it."

"Yeah, maybe just try not to sleep with her until after you win," Lauren rationalized. "Maybe consider the kiss as a way of you getting something out of your system, and it won't be an issue moving forward. Like, maybe you'll just be able to be in a room with her and not be wondering what it would feel like to have her touching or kissing some part of your body."

Trina felt her eyes widen at that comment.

Jax and Lauren burst out laughing.

"Exactly. Not a chance in hell of that happening." Lauren patted her on the back again. "You're so screwed."

At that, Trina laughed, too. Because she so, so was.

"Okay, are we done mocking me now? We have business to attend to." Trina was eager to change the topic.

"I suppose." Lauren exhaled dramatically.

Jax spoke next. "I've been overhauling and updating your social media presence over the last few weeks to try to generate some interest in younger tech-savvy buyers, like we discussed. So far, it's been working. You have two appointments later this week. One is with a hotshot bioengineering supervisor looking for a place closer to work, and the other is a recent divorcee looking for a rebound place."

"Awesome," Trina said, pleased to hear that Jax's approach was working.

Jax handed her some paperwork. "The details are in there, but I cc'd you on a few emails as well. I'll make sure we have full profiles before your meetings."

"Thank you," Trina replied. She was grateful for Jax's initiative.

Having her colleagues help during this competition had been invaluable to her, for so many reasons. Because they were more than just coworkers to her—they were family.

"Speaking of potential buyers," Lauren chimed in, "how did it go with Amelia Clarke? Or do you remember anything from the afternoon besides the kissing?"

Trina rolled her eyes before she said, "It went really well. She's interested in seeing one of the penthouses this week."

"Nice!" Jax exclaimed and they all laughed.

"That would be a damn game changer," Lauren said.

"I know," Trina replied. That had been on her mind since their meeting. Selling a penthouse would elevate her to a comfortable lead. And if these two appointments Jax set up gained any traction, she'd be soaring. "I'm trying not to get my hopes up too high."

Lauren smiled. "Just lay on the flirt. You said you thought Clarke might be into women, right? Use all that pent-up sexual tension from your Kendall encounter to motivate you. Consider Kendall the practice and Clarke the game day."

Trina didn't bother to mention that she'd relieved some of that tension in the shower at the club after she'd separated from Kendall. She'd had to—there was no way she could have focused through a meeting otherwise. And she was glad she did, because Amelia had been friendlier than usual over drinks. Though she was flattered, as beautiful and enigmatic as Amelia was, she wasn't her type. Trina sighed. Kendall was.

Jax got a call and excused themselves.

"Hey, are you doing okay?" Lauren asked once they were alone, her expression patient and loving.

Trina nodded but didn't feel okay. She felt anxious. "It's been a long week."

Lauren stood up from her chair and leaned against the conference table, opening her arms. "Come here, bring it in."

Trina leaped out of her seat and snuggled into her best friend's embrace. She'd been missing this kind of contact, this affection. They really needed a girls' night soon.

Lauren kissed the side of her head and rubbed her back. "How's Calvin?"

Trina's brother had reemerged an hour or so after his phone call to his wife the night they had all been having pizza, but Lauren had already left. According to Calvin, the call had gone well enough, but he knew he had some explaining to do and restitution to make. Trina was glad he made the decision to head home the next day, but a part of her was sad to see him leave. She liked the sound and comfort of having someone around all the time. She'd lived alone for so long she'd forgotten how nice it was to hear someone tinkering around in the kitchen or singing off-key. She missed being in a relationship with someone, and having her brother in her space reminded her of that.

"He's okay," Trina said. "Lisa has him sleeping on the couch, but that seems to be ending. She's going out with her friends tonight, so he's bringing the kids by for dinner to make sure the house stays clean until her return. I'm looking forward to it." Calvin had been catching her up almost daily. She enjoyed the new reconnection with her brother, even if it came about because he was struggling with his own identity. She'd be there for him, like she always had been. She knew he'd do the same for her.

"He's a good guy," Lauren said, her embrace remaining constant. It was so, so nice. "He'll figure it all out."

"I know," Trina replied.

"You will, too," Lauren said, and Trina knew she was talking about Kendall.

Trina sighed again, not so sure about that.

"When are you seeing Kendall again?" Lauren asked, but not in a prying or accusatory way. Just in a best friend kind of way. Trina hugged her tighter.

Trina buried her head in Lauren's shoulder as she whined, "In about an hour."

Lauren pulled back as she asked, "Seriously?"

"Seriously," Trina said. "She and Whitaker are coming by for a quick meeting to discuss something Langley changed regarding the marketing or whatever. I think it's because Kendall got an opening to pitch the property at The Country Club, and they're updating the marketing materials."

"Damn," Lauren said. "They have to do that in person?"

Trina picked at the edge of the paper in front of her as she replied, "I guess since we went to their office once, this is their turn to stop by and socialize or whatever. I'm sort of dreading it."

"Because of the kissing?" Lauren asked.

Trina nodded. "It'll be the first time I've seen her since."

Lauren rubbed up and down her arms for a moment before sitting next to her at the conference table's edge. "What do you want to happen?"

"Truthfully?" Trina asked.

"Always," Lauren replied.

"I'm not sure," Trina admitted. "On the one hand, I'd like to pretend it didn't happen, but on the other hand…I really, really liked it. Like, maybe too much. And a part of me is curious to see how today goes—like, maybe it was a one-off. Maybe the circumstances at the club were just perfect for that to happen, and seeing her today might not affect me at all."

"Do you really believe that?" Lauren asked.

"No," Trina said, honestly. "I've been physically attracted to her since the beginning. I've just been ignoring it. But now that I know she can kiss like that…"

Lauren nodded in understanding. "Look, you can't predict the future. Nor should you try. I had this nutty Aunt Carole who was really into tigers and tiger paraphernalia, and she was convinced she was psychic, and long story short, she wasn't and was nearly mauled to death by one of her illegal pets. You and I can't predict the future, and neither could Aunt Carole, or she wouldn't have attended that all-you-can-eat wing festival before feeding her tigers, so we all just have to take whatever life throws at us."

Trina shook her head. Lauren could be so normal and so kooky at the same time. "I love you. Do you know that?"

"I do. And I love you, too," Lauren said as she gave her another hug. "Listen, whatever happens, I'll support you. But I'll also remind you if you're making bad decisions. Because that's my job, too."

"Fair enough," Trina replied, glad to have someone who had her back.

"So, just between us squirrel friends," Lauren said with a nudge, "how good a kisser was she?"

"*So* good," Trina replied, because that was the truth, and she knew she was in trouble.

❖

Kendall had intentionally arrived at Gamble and Associates early. She wanted to beat Whitaker there because she was hoping to get some time with Trina to see where things stood between them. Not that she expected anything to have changed, really. But there had been some serious making out and maybe things might be different now. Part of her hoped they would be, but that was because she regretted not asking to join Trina in that shower. Not that Trina had extended the invitation, but Kendall got the feeling that if she had asked, Trina wouldn't have turned her down. And she had wanted to ask. So very badly.

There was a voice in her head that kept telling her to be careful, though. She didn't entirely trust that this wasn't another way for Trina to get in her head, which she most certainly was. She'd gotten the signals that Trina had enjoyed herself, and they did discuss a rain check, which was promising. But could this just be part of a long con? Could Trina be trying to distract her in order to beat her? Kendall wasn't so sure. She wasn't exactly the paranoid type, but Trina had a way of surprising her. She couldn't count anything out, least of all Trina.

But she couldn't stop thinking about that kiss, either. And how badly she wanted that kiss to happen again, and more.

She checked the time on her phone. If she wanted to get Trina alone, it was now or never.

Gamble and Associates' office was light and bright, airy and welcoming. There was a mix of modern and classic New England charm that made it feel more like a home than an office. It was masterful design—Kendall had to admit that. And such a stark contrast to her office, which had a coldness to it, especially when the sun went down. She hated being in the conference area at night—it felt so sterile. She did the best she could to bring some warmth into her personal office, but this place blew that out of the water.

She was greeted by a handsome young guy named Evan at the front desk who led her back toward Trina's corner office and right into Shay, who was emerging from Trina's office.

"Kendall," Shay said with a carefree smile. "This is a very pleasant surprise."

"Hi." Kendall tried to conceal her shock. "How are you?"

"I'm good. Better now," Shay said, and Kendall swore her blue eyes sparkled. "You're looking lovely today. What's good?"

Shay was flirting again. Kendall would have been flattered if she wasn't a little annoyed that her window to talk to Trina before the meeting was closing.

"You're early," Trina supplied, appearing at Shay's shoulder.

Kendall wanted to ask if she was annoyed, but Trina's expression told her she wasn't. She looked almost pleased.

"What can I say? I was eager to see your office and judge your personal style," Kendall replied.

Trina raised a perfectly shaped eyebrow as she said, "Have I ever given you the impression that I somehow lacked style? Because we both know that's not true."

Kendall didn't disagree. Still, she took the opportunity to appreciate Trina's outfit today. What Kendall had begun to consider as Trina's signature bold red was present in the form of a tight pencil skirt that added a pop of color to Trina's sheer black blouse. Kendall noticed the double panel of material over Trina's chest, giving the impression of opacity and modesty, though the plunging neckline kept the sexiness of the outfit front and center. Kendall deeply approved of this outfit, particularly the slit in the skirt, which exposed a good amount of Trina's left thigh.

"Shay!" someone called out behind her. "It's great to see you."

Kendall was only barely aware of the conversation Shay started to have with someone else when she noticed Trina had dipped her head to make eye contact with her.

"My eyes are up here, Yates," Trina said, her volume just loud enough for Kendall—and Kendall alone—to hear.

Kendall matched it as she replied, "I was distracted by your slit. I'd ask for you to forgive me, but I'm not sorry about it."

"This skirt is a favorite of mine," Trina said as her lips curved into a small smile, and Kendall was sure that Trina had caught her double entendre. Trina's blood-red lipstick was begging to be smeared by Kendall's mouth, and she would be more than happy to oblige. "I'm glad you like it."

"That might be an understatement," Kendall replied. "I have to admit, though this isn't you in a towel, it's a close second to one of my favorite looks of yours."

Trina leaned against the doorframe of her office, looking fabulously seductive as she asked, "Have you been keeping tabs on all the looks I turn? Or just the ones where I show a little skin?"

"So far they've all been quite memorable," Kendall recalled. "The herringbone coat with the blue shoes at the Harborside, the trench coat ensemble at the coffee shop, the cotton-candy dream at the club…" She paused. "I wasn't entirely honest before, though. You in a towel wasn't my favorite look—I have another."

"Do tell," Trina replied.

Kendall hazarded a step toward her to whisper, "I think I liked you out of the towel, walking away, best of all. I just wish you'd been walking toward me and not away from me."

Trina swallowed before licking her lips. Kendall was captivated by her, waiting impatiently for her reply. Would she flirt? Would she back down? Would she tell Kendall to fuck off? She knew she was being more than forward, and though she probably should care, she didn't. She wanted Trina to know where she stood after that kiss, and where she stood was impatiently waiting and wanting more.

Trina's hand flitted at her waist before reaching out toward Kendall, but as Kendall anxiously anticipated her contact, the feeling of Shay gently touching her elbow startled her.

"Oh, I'm sorry. I didn't mean to spook you," Shay said when Kendall turned to face her.

Kendall brushed it off. "I was distracted, but that's on me. What's up?"

Shay gave her a half smile that Kendall was sure most women fell head over heels for and asked, "Do you have plans for Friday?"

"Plans?" Kendall asked to stall. Was Shay really about to ask her out? This wasn't the most ideal timing, since she was working hard to get Trina into her bed.

"Yeah, there's a fundraiser and—"

"Oh, I'm not sure Kendall would be interested in that," Trina interrupted.

Kendall turned to look at her and noticed that Trina looked uncomfortable. She wanted to know why.

"Tell me more," Kendall replied, not missing the way Trina's expression changed to one of annoyance. Kendall hoped this wouldn't blow up in her face.

"Jax here"—Shay pointed to an attractive younger Gamble and Associates employee who Kendall recognized from those photos she saw of Trina online at the LGBTQ gala from years past—"is having a fundraiser to raise some cash for their top surgery, and I'm DJing. You should come. Let me buy you a few drinks, and we can dance. Have a good time for a good cause," Shay said, ever the charmer.

Kendall watched as Jax looked at Trina, seemingly concerned. Trina's face remained unreadable, though Kendall would bet that she was masking the annoyance she'd shown before. Jax seemed worried, Trina seemed annoyed, and Kendall was curious.

"Hey, Jax. It's nice to meet you," Kendall said, extending her hand. "I'd be honored to do my part and help out if I can."

Jax looked flabbergasted as they shook hands. "Thank you."

Kendall redirected her attention toward Shay as she said, "Thanks for the invite. I'd love to go."

"Great." Shay's smile broadened, and Kendall was struck by how truly alluring Shay was. There were a lot of beautiful people in this friend group, she mused. "I'll get your number from that business card I grabbed at the Harborside, so I'll shoot you a text with some of the details."

"Thanks," Kendall said. "I'll see you Friday."

"Excellent," Shay replied, and Kendall watched as Shay and Jax headed toward the exit. She didn't miss the way Jax looked over their shoulder at Trina, almost as if doing a visual check-in with Mom. That amused her.

"In my office, now." Trina's flirtatious tone from before was gone. But Kendall would be lying if she said this authoritative command didn't make her a little wet.

"Am I being called in to see the principal?" Kendall asked.

Trina stepped back to let her by before closing the door behind them. "You are something else."

"Something good or something bad?" Kendall asked as she looked around Trina's office, taking it all in. The office was massive, the view was gorgeous, and there wasn't a parking lot in sight.

"I suppose that is yet to be determined." Trina leaned against her desk, her arms crossed over her chest. "Why are you going to the fundraiser?"

"Because I was invited," Kendall replied. She saw the framed article about Trina's top thirty under thirty accolade. That picture of Trina was Kendall's favorite.

"Well, consider yourself uninvited then," Trina said.

Kendall turned to face her. "Oh? And you have that authority?"

Trina replied, "I'm hosting it. So yes."

Kendall was impressed by that. "This was your idea? As in you're the party planner du jour? You wear many hats, don't you?"

"I take care of my people, and I love to throw a party. That's how Shay got involved. I want this to be a success for Jax. No hiccups, no problems, just smooth sailing so they get the life they deserve," Trina replied, her passion palpable.

"And why would my attendance be disruptive?" Kendall failed to see the connection. "Because that seems to be what you're implying."

Trina huffed. "I have no problem going toe-to-toe with you,

Kendall. I can take your insults in stride and give as good as I get, but I don't want any trouble for Jax. They have enough on their plate without being uncomfortable that my rival is there on their big night, possibly causing trouble."

Kendall was offended. "You don't think I can play nice?"

"I'm not sure, can you?" Trina asked, her arms still crossed, her posture defensive. Trina was serious about this. Her body language alone was deafening.

"I played plenty nice at The Country Club, didn't I?" Kendall replied. She didn't want to extinguish what was happening between them. She'd come here with a clear objective, and pissing Trina off was not it.

"That's different," Trina said, as she uncrossed her arms. "I can take care of myself—I told you that. What happens between you and me doesn't carry over to the people that I love in my life. I can separate those worlds. But not if you step into my safety bubble and fuck with my people."

Kendall put her hands up in surrender as she said, "I have no intention of fucking with your people. I promise. I was being polite and accepting an invitation to something that I think is important and has value. Plus, we both know I have Yates money to bleed, so, let me."

That did it. Trina's expression cracked, and her walls started to come down. "Did you just use *my* rich bitch attack on yourself to win this argument?"

"Were we in an argument?" Kendall risked a step toward Trina. "Because I thought we were role-playing a little—you know, you tell me what I can and can't do, and I tell you I'm not interested in being ordered around unless it's in the bedroom. You know, like that."

Trina sucked in a breath, and Kendall was glad the temperature of the room was heating back up again. She stoked the fire some more as she said, "I came here early to see you and talk to you about how I can't stop thinking about that kiss at the club. But if me going to that fundraiser is going to get you all hot and bothered, and not in the way I was hoping to get you hot and bothered, then I won't go."

She stepped into Trina's space and leaned forward, whispering into her ear, "I'll just leave a big, fat check on your desk, and you can tell Jax it was an anonymous donation. But I'll be sorry to miss seeing what you decide to wear. Because I have a feeling that's probably worth the money all by itself."

Kendall started to lean back, but Trina's hand grasped her hip, pulling her close. Trina surveyed her closely, seeming to take her all in before she said anything.

"Be generous and on your best behavior, and maybe you'll get that rain check we discussed," Trina said as she placed a kiss next to Kendall's mouth.

"Deal." Kendall turned her head and caught Trina's lips before she could pull away. She kissed her slow and teasingly, tugging her plump bottom lip between her teeth and licking the flesh. Trina moaned into her mouth, and Kendall felt Trina's hands on her low back, pulling her forward.

Kendall knew she could get Trina up onto this desk without any trouble, and she would have, if a knock at the door didn't stop her.

"They'll go away," Trina said, as if reading her mind.

Kendall nodded, not caring if that was true or not, because one of Trina's hands had left her low back and was palming at her breast through her shirt. That and Trina's hot mouth on hers were all she could focus on right now. Until Trina's thumb dragged over her erect nipple, getting all her attention. Kendall shuddered. This felt so good. She didn't want it to stop. "Trina," she said on an exhaled breath.

Trina rolled the flesh between her fingertips while deepening their kiss, and Kendall saw stars. She wrapped her arms around Trina to stabilize herself, pressing her back against the desk, when a louder, more aggressive knock came from the door. This one was followed by an insistent hiss.

"Trina," the voice said, "make good decisions. This is a bad decision. Open the door. It's time for your meeting."

Trina broke the kiss and dropped her head back with a frustrated sigh. "Ugh. The meeting, I totally forgot."

Kendall had also, but she was less concerned about that than she was about the long column of Trina's neck that was now exposed. She brought her lips to the warm skin, and Trina's fingers wove into her hair, holding her close as she kissed along Trina's neck.

"You need to stop that, or we're both going to miss this meeting," Trina said, though Kendall was acutely aware that Trina's grip in her hair was keeping her doing exactly what she intended to continue doing.

"Let's just tell them we decided to meet together, one-on-one, and that we'll send them the minutes of our meeting," Kendall said between kissing and licking Trina's neck.

"And what will the minutes say, exactly?" Trina breathed out as Kendall made her way back to Trina's lips.

"Oh, something like we had a heated oral debate," Kendall said before she kissed Trina hard, dragging her tongue along Trina's as she felt Trina's hips buck against hers. "And that a conclusion wasn't reached, but there was definite promise for an incredible outcome upon future meetings."

Trina's desk phone rang, and she pulled back from the kiss with an exasperated gasp. "Future meetings? As in plural?"

"Yes, we have much unfinished business to attend to," Kendall said as she leaned back in, but Trina's fingers on her lips stopped her.

Trina answered the call. "Mm-hmm, yes, I'm aware. I'll be out shortly. Thanks for the thorough follow-up."

Kendall heard cursing over the line, but Trina hung up before she could decipher who it was.

Trina sighed and rested her forehead against Kendall's. "Let's reschedule this discussion for another time when both of our bosses aren't in the conference room waiting for us."

Kendall nuzzled her nose against Trina's before nodding. "Maybe coming here early was a bad idea."

Trina pulled back quickly, and she was out of Kendall's embrace so fast that Kendall almost fell forward. She hadn't realized how much of her weight she'd been resting on Trina until Trina was suddenly absent.

"You're having second thoughts about seducing me in my office then?" Trina asked, and Kendall noted the edge to her voice.

"Not at all." Kendall reached for her, but Trina stepped back. "That's not what I meant."

Trina gave her a skeptical laugh and Kendall could tell she was treading water.

She tried again. "What I meant was that maybe it was a bad idea coming early today because now I certainly won't be paying attention to anything we discuss in the meeting, since my mind will be entirely on you and those lips and"—she reached out and grabbed Trina's hand, pulling her close, then ran her hand along the exposed skin at the front of Trina's thigh—"this slit. That's what I meant."

Trina appraised her before giving her a subtle nod, acquiescing. Kendall gave her one last chaste kiss and squeezed her hand.

"You're probably going to need to reapply your lipstick," Kendall said as she stepped out of Trina's personal space. She needed to cool down, and that wasn't going to happen if she was still in kissing distance of Trina.

"And you'll probably want to wipe your mouth," Trina said as she handed her a tissue from her desk. "I need a second—I'll meet you out there."

Kendall finished wiping her mouth and checked her reflection with her cell phone to make sure she was red lipstick free. She walked to the door, her hand still on the doorknob when Trina called out behind her. "I'm glad you came early."

"Me, too," she said, turning briefly to give Trina one last glance before she walked out into the cooler air of the main office, and right into the sights of an annoyed looking Lauren Calloway.

BET AGAINST ME   • 173 •

CHAPTER NINETEEN

"I didn't see a closed-door meeting between you and Kendall on your schedule today," Lauren said coolly on their walk to the main conference room. Ellison had recommended she be in attendance to help keep track of the meeting's specifics, which Trina had originally thought was a good idea, but that was before all the kiss-shaming Lauren was doing right now.

Trina glanced at her, careful to keep her expression neutral. "It was sort of an impromptu meeting of the minds."

"Is that all that met in that office? Your minds? And not your mouths?" Lauren replied.

It was clear she wasn't going to give up that easily. Trina had been impressed by the number of hushed profanities Lauren had gotten out after she'd called Trina's office line. Trina had counted no less than eleven in the short trip the receiver made from her ear to the cradle, and those were only the ones she could hear.

"It was a comprehensive meeting. There were many levels of discussion and expression involved," Trina said through a smile as she entered the conference area to find Kendall, Ellison, and Whitaker looking over some paperwork on the table.

"I bet," Lauren said. "Did one of those levels involve expressing yourself through a wardrobe malfunction? Because the top button of your blouse is undone."

Trina's hand flew to her chest, only to find there wasn't any button out of place.

Lauren snickered next to her. "Busted."

Whitaker stood when he noticed her and greeted both her and Lauren with that smarmy smile of his and that overly aggressive handshake that Trina hated. She really loathed this man.

"It's wonderful to see you again, Trina." He was such a phony.

"From what Ellison was just telling me, you've been very busy with the Harborside project. Kudos to you."

"Thanks," Trina said.

"Ellison said you just got a call from someone looking to visit the penthouse space," Kendall said. Up to this point Trina had been successful in avoiding looking at Kendall, but now that became inescapable. "That's a big win." Kendall looked amazing with the setting sun shining behind her. Her blond hair glowed with the burning light, giving her an almost angelic look, at odds with the woman with all the naughty words and even naughtier tongue who she'd tangled with in her office. But now, Kendall looked the picture of innocence and composure. Trina had a deep appreciation for Kendall's versatility. She hoped that translated to the bedroom as well.

"Thank you," Trina said with a gracious nod as she sat across from Kendall at the table. "I hope it amounts to something more than a causal walk-through." She hadn't bothered to mention to Kendall that Amelia Clark had been blown away by their meeting at the club. Nor did she plan to mention it. Because whatever was going on between them had little to do with the competition. Trina didn't intend to share more than was necessary, and she certainly didn't have any intention of taking her foot off the gas. Kissing and fondling and whatever else might or might not happen were separate from the task at hand. They had to be. She wasn't about to lose a bet that would prove she was the best Realtor around. Or make her a fortune that most Realtors only dreamed of. No, Trina was in it to win, and no amount of gorgeous blond bombshell with that sexy mouth was going to sidetrack her from that mission. But that didn't mean she wasn't above sampling the fruits offered to her. And so far, the fruits were very, very sweet.

"Thank you for agreeing to come by today," Ellison said. "I just wanted to touch base on a few details that Langley sent along. It seems that he'd like to change things up a bit."

Trina didn't like the sound of that, and if the expression on Kendall's face was any indication, she didn't either.

"Oh?" Kendall said, and Trina tried not to stare. Kendall was wearing another signature suit, tailored perfectly. This one was dark blue with tiny pinstripes, so tiny Trina might have overlooked them had she not been up close and with her hand palming Kendall's breast. She tried to shake off the memory to focus, but that seemed impossible because Kendall chose that moment to play with the lapels of her jacket, exposing the silk camisole beneath it, and Trina knew how soft that fucking shirt was because it had been in her hand minutes ago.

"Yes," Ellison continued. "It appears as though Langley has been doing his own marketing unbeknownst to us, and he'd like you both to take some of his prospective buyers for walk-throughs."

Trina figured she should speak, not just gape. "So we're supposed to play tour guide to people we have no opportunity to vet or research in any way? What if they're just dead ends and time sucks? We're Realtors, not babysitters."

Whitaker said, "That was one of his stipulations, that he would be able to introduce any buyer to the mix that he'd like. I think it's a great idea. Think of the pool of prospects we'll be exposed to."

Whitaker had a way of talking like he had dollar signs in his eyes. Trina noticed his use of *we*, like he was going to do any of the bitch work. Sure, this could amount to a sale, or it could be a giant distraction. And she had plenty of those.

Kendall leaned forward, placing her forearms on the table as she spoke. "I can see both sides, Trina's and Whitaker's, but I'd like to know a little more. What are his expectations? Are we just going to get a list with a bunch of names on it? Or are these people actually viable prospects? Because I'm with Trina on that one—I don't have time to flip through a Rolodex of people who aren't legit."

"Look at you two, getting along so well." Lauren had been quiet up until then. Trina wished she'd stayed that way.

"I think you'll find that I'm generally agreeable to most things," Kendall said in response. Trina didn't miss the way Kendall's gaze lingered on her before flicking back to Lauren. "A good point is a good point. And I don't intend to lose traction by distractions."

"You have traction to lose?" Trina replied. She couldn't help herself. Mainly because she felt like that distraction comment was partially directed toward her, and sure, she agreed with that sentiment, but she didn't need it verbalized in front of her boss and best friend, one of whom knew she was making out with Kendall just moments before. Because that was just embarrassing. And Trina had no intention of being embarrassed. Ever.

"Well, now that you brought it up," Kendall said with a sweet smile that Trina interpreted to mean a mic drop was coming, "I was planning on updating your office today that I'd contracted another middle unit this morning."

"Seems like you've had a busy day," Trina replied, knowing full well that meant that Kendall had regained the lead.

"There have been definite pluses to today, yes," Kendall replied, unblinking.

Trina broke eye contact first. She addressed her question to Ellison. "So Langley wants to spice things up, fine. Any new information we need to take in?"

"One more thing," Ellison said with a sigh. "He wants to jump into a new project and take Zander with him. But since the complexities of the Harborside require Zander's full attention, Langley wants to finish the building early."

"How early?" Kendall asked.

"A month," Whitaker said, and he looked gleeful. "That makes things all the more exciting, doesn't it?"

Trina wanted to slap that grin off his face. More exciting? That made an already tall order nearly impossible. "You're kidding."

"We're not." Ellison's frown told her everything she needed to know. Had Ellison been given a heads-up on this information, Trina was confident she would have warned her this was coming. But Ellison looked as disappointed as Trina felt. A month's less time to sell the remaining units? That exponentially increased the challenge.

"Well, we'd better get back to work then," Kendall said, sliding her chair back. "Are we done here?"

"Just about. We have a few small marketing details to go over, more changes and input from Langley, but they're minor details," Ellison said. Trina was getting the feeling that Langley was more of a control freak than she'd thought. Maybe this was why Ellison had been so careful to juggle so many moving pieces to secure this contract. She made a mental note to inquire about that later.

By the time the meeting was over and the information packets were distributed to them, the sky was dark. Somehow this day had completely gotten away from Trina.

Whitaker was hovering by the conference room door, chatting with Kendall, who had mostly been quiet for the rest of the meeting. They both had. Trina was still processing what had happened in her office and the new information Ellison had presented to them. She'd need to meet with Lauren and Jax about Kendall's newly contracted unit and the change in the length of the competition. Not to mention the stack of faceless names that Langley had distributed to them both.

She wanted to get a jump on that list before Kendall, but she'd need help. Speaking of help, where the hell had Lauren wandered off to anyway?

Kendall seemed to notice that she was itching to get out of the room, since she moved aside just enough for Trina to squeeze by. But as Trina nearly escaped the room without incident, she felt Kendall's fingertips at her low back. It was just a passing touch, but the subtle contact made her shiver.

Both Lauren and Jax were waiting outside the conference room door, one looking bored, the other looking anxious. They both started talking at once.

"What happened with the—?" Jax asked.

"Is Ellison serious about this timeline—?" Lauren started.

Trina held up her hands, overwhelmed by the questions. "Let's meet in the conference room in five."

Jax nodded and headed off in that direction, but Lauren lingered. Trina had been hoping to have a moment to talk to Kendall alone before she left, but it seemed that Lauren had other plans.

"I'll be right with you," Trina said, trying to convince Lauren to disappear for a few seconds.

"Got somewhere else to be?" Lauren's question was borderline accusatory.

Trina gave her a look.

"Fine. But I'm telling Jax that you hooked up with her in your office while I wait," Lauren threatened.

"You wouldn't," Trina said, knowing full well that Lauren totally would.

"The longer you make me wait, the more dramatic and creative I'm going to get with the details. Come to think of it, I'm pretty sure I heard moaning through that door."

"You're evil," Trina replied.

Lauren blew her a kiss as she pointed to her nonexistent watch. "Tick-tock."

Trina headed toward her office, keeping an eye out for Kendall on the way, but she didn't see her. Ellison was on the phone at Evan's desk dictating something to him, and she could see Whitaker walking toward the employee parking lot out back, but she didn't see Kendall anywhere. And she found herself alarmed at how disappointed that made her.

She exhaled as she walked through her office door only to find Kendall standing by the window behind her desk chair.

"That's quite the exhale," Kendall said. "Something on your mind?"

Trina recovered from her initial shock enough to reply. "Truthfully?"

"I'd like that, yes," Kendall said, her voice soft and inviting.

"I was looking for you, and I thought I'd missed you." Trina wasn't sure why she was being so honest. But it felt right, so she was going with it.

Kendall gave her a genuine smile. She seemed pleased by this information.

"We didn't get to talk much before."

"Because of all the arguing and kissing, you mean," Kendall said.

Trina put her hand on her hip and cocked her head to the side as she asked, "Was there arguing? Or was I just being clear about my boundaries and what I was comfortable with?"

"You mean that you were clear regarding your boundaries that involve *other* people in your life. What was it you said? Something about the people you love? Right?" Kendall recalled. "You didn't say much about what your boundaries were. I'd like to hear about those."

Trina thought about what Kendall had just said. She supposed she hadn't been clear about her boundaries because she wasn't quite sure where those boundaries stood at the moment. Particularly the kissing and touching the enemy boundaries. Those seemed blurred.

Not wanting to seem too desperate, Trina bounced the question back to Kendall. "What boundaries are you talking about, exactly?"

Kendall gave her a knowing smile as she motioned between the two of them and said, "These boundaries. The ones between us. What are those, for you? I'd like to know, so I can respect them or disregard them, as necessary."

"Are you that comfortable with the idea of disregarding my boundaries?" Trina asked, amused.

"Well, that depends," Kendall replied, moving toward the front of Trina's desk and closing the space between them. "Are those boundaries material? Because I have no problem breaching your material boundaries if, say, we're kissing and you're pulling at my hair and holding me close and"—Kendall stepped right in front of her, her hand flitting at Trina's hip—"this incredible skirt is in the way of where

I need to be. So I'd test your comfort level by pressing my palm against you, warming you up to the idea of giving me what I want."

"Which is?" Trina asked, stifling the moan that threatened to bubble up as Kendall's grip on her hip shifted inward slightly.

"Disregarding those material boundaries and getting you out of those clothes and underneath me." Kendall's voice was thick with lust, and Trina wanted out of her skirt, now.

"That's rather forward," Trina said as she guided Kendall's hand off the apex of her thigh and onto her rib cage. "Do you struggle with boundaries?"

"Not at all. I just want to know what you like and how you like it. Because if we have any more one-on-ones like we did earlier, I'm never going to make it to that rain check. It's best to be prepared," Kendall said as she massaged the flesh millimeters below her breast. Kendall's other hand cupped her ass just so, and Trina arched her back into the pressure. Kendall's hands were warm and strong, and Trina felt herself leaning more and more into her touch.

Kendall pressed a kiss to Trina's lips softly before she spoke into them. "Do you like me this forward? Can I kiss you when I want to? What are the limits to the things I can do to and with you? Tell me, so I know if you like this. Because I like this, and I want to be on the same page as you."

"Yes, I like this," Trina managed to squeak out before Kendall's lips descended on hers again, giving her a deeper, wetter kiss than a moment ago.

"Good." Kendall kissed her once more before pulling back. She dropped her hand from Trina's ribs to her hip, giving her a brief squeeze before putting some space between them again. "Because I feel like we can have a lot of fun together."

"With certain boundaries," Trina heard herself say, and she wondered who was controlling her mouth.

"Such as?" Kendall asked, keeping a respectable distance. Trina appreciated that.

"This can't interfere with work." Trina hadn't thought any further than that.

"Excellent," Kendall agreed. "And no strings attached—we keep it light. No baggage."

Trina smiled at what Kendall seemed to be implying. "You think I have baggage?"

Kendall shook her head as she replied, "Not necessarily, but I've seen some of your Birkin collection, so you clearly do have some baggage."

"Designer baggage shouldn't count," Trina proposed. "Those are life necessities, after all."

"Is that so?" Kendall asked, teasing.

"It is," Trina replied.

"All right." Kendall paused before asking, "Anything else?"

Trina thought for a moment, but she was drawing a blank. "For now, I suppose that's it."

"So to be continued and adjusted as needed?" Kendall asked, seemingly agreeable.

"I'm good with that if you are," Trina said. This was starting to feel more like a business deal by the second. She hoped that didn't extinguish the heat she felt between them.

"More than good," Kendall said, and Trina wanted to be closer to her, because she felt like there would be more touching and kissing if she was closer.

"As much as I'd like to continue hashing out our kissing rules, I do have to meet with my team before my brother comes over for dinner," Trina said, as she moved toward her door.

"The guest room brother?" Kendall asked following her out.

"Yes, he's resumed his normal residence now. Thankfully," Trina replied. "Do you have any siblings?"

"Nope," Kendall said before giving her a wink. "They stopped at perfection."

Trina stopped short to give her a skeptical look. "You're kidding me with that line."

Kendall shrugged. "It's true."

"If that's true, then I'm the reason there's only two in my family. You're looking at the baby," Trina said.

"The baby," Kendall joked. "This explains so much about you."

"Same for you—the spoiled only-child heir. What a privileged role to be born into. The horror." Trina replied in jest where in the past she would have had an edge. Her impressions of Kendall were changing, but she wasn't sure what to expect of her.

"I'm glad to see that insults aren't off the table with our new agreement," Kendall said with a smile. "I think I'd miss them if they were."

"I'll keep you on your toes, Yates," Trina replied. "You can count on that."

Kendall laughed. She reached out to give Trina's hand a quick squeeze before saying good-bye. "I hope you'll keep me on my back, too. See you around, *baby*."

Trina watched her walk away because she could, but when she looked up, she saw both Jax and Lauren hanging out of the conference room door, watching.

"Busted," Lauren said, and Trina had to agree. She so was.

CHAPTER TWENTY

K endall deleted yet another empty voice mail.

She'd been working hard over the past few days to chip through the list Langley had issued and also manage her own client prospects for the Harborside, when her father started calling daily: no one talking, just silence and then a click. She was positive they were intentionally left contentless. He was screwing with her.

She paced her apartment to get out some of the nervous energy she felt was bubbling up. Her emotions were all over the place.

On what was probably her fiftieth lap through her place, she finally slowed down and took a deep breath. *Focus, Kendall. You can do this, one step at a time, one day at a time. You'll be fine.* She hazarded a glance in the mirror. She looked a little worse for the wear but knew that a shower and fresh makeup would make her feel whole again. Tonight would be a nice escape from the drama because tonight had nothing to do with her. She could be a spectator and a participant in something that was good and kind and right in a world that often felt very dark and wrong. This fundraiser for Trina's friend Jax couldn't come at a better time. And she'd get to see Trina again.

Trina had been on her mind constantly. Had she made a mistake, kissing her in her office? Had she made a mistake, agreeing to no-strings-attached physical intimacy? Was this a really stupid thing to be doing when she was competing to unofficially defend her title of Realtor of the Year and for a giant wad of cash? She was pretty sure all those answers were *Yes, this was a bad decision*, and yet she still had butterflies in her stomach at the prospect of seeing Trina tonight. Because Trina excited her and turned her on in ways she couldn't remember anyone having done. Not even Collette, not ever. And she could use more excitement in her life—well, in the romance department anyway. And especially in the bedroom. Something she was sure Trina would bring. And that made her tremble with want and excitement. Trina was the perfect distraction from those phone calls, and Kendall had no intention of missing out.

❖

The night was clear and cool, not warm enough to go without a jacket, but Kendall didn't care. She'd drop her coat at the coat check and leave that and all her worries behind her.

There was a short line to get into The Mirage, the hottest, trendiest bar in town, which was a good sign—that meant good things for Jax. The sign on the door indicated it was a private event tonight. It seemed as though Trina had rented the whole place. Kendall waited her turn and checked in with the bouncer by the door before depositing her coat at the check counter.

She'd never been in the bar, but she'd heard people raving about it, and she'd checked it out on social media. And from what she could tell, the reviews had been spot-on. The bar had an incredible flow—to the right of the door were restrooms, the coat check, and an ATM. To the left was where all the action was. The bar stretched well over forty feet along the far wall with mirrors behind glass shelves filled with every mixer and spirit you could imagine. The underlighting on the shelves gave each bottle its own showcasing moment, and there were multiple beer taps along the gleaming black marble-topped bar. The bar was crowded, but not in an obnoxious way, and four bartenders were hustling with drink orders. This place was jamming with activity.

Kendall could see multiple waitresses circulating between the tall cocktail tables that were speckled throughout the space across from the bar. In the back of the room, Kendall could see a small stage that appeared to have been erected for the event, in front of an open area that looked like a makeshift dance floor but which, Kendall knew from photos, was usually filled with plush sofas and armchairs. The entire space had tall ceilings with exposed wooden beams framed by thick metal support brackets, with a combination of recessed lights and long pendants that accented the modern industrial yet historic charm of the space. This was one of the most unique combinations of new and old Kendall had ever seen, and as a Realtor, she appreciated the owner's eye for detail. They had style, she'd give them that. She could totally see this bar being a fun place for cocktails and apps after work. Or for a first date. She had an idea of someone she'd like to take on a date.

"You made it," Shay said, appearing at her side.

"I did," Kendall replied. This wasn't who she had in mind, but she did invite her after all. "Thanks for the invite."

"Of course, it's gonna be a great time," Shay said. She was wearing a similar outfit to the first time Kendall had met her: designer shoes and fancy watch with a soft-looking, slim-fitted long-sleeve hooded shirt under a leather jacket. Her black skinny jeans revealed that narrow-hipped androgynous frame that Kendall certainly appreciated. And charm—Shay wore that like an accessory, too. She was oozing with charm.

"I have to go mix some music in a bit—the emcee is going to kick things off in a few—but I'll make sure to swing out a few times to see how you're doing. Or"—Shay flashed a flirtatious smile—"you can always join me in the DJ booth. I can teach you how to spin."

"I'd like that," Kendall said. She'd never had that experience, and she was all about experiencing new things tonight. Preferably with a certain rival Realtor. Where was Trina anyway?

"'Kay, I'll see you in a bit," Shay said as she leaned in and kissed Kendall's cheek.

"You two look friendly," Lauren said to her right, after Shay walked away.

"It's nice to see you, too," Kendall supplied. She didn't want any trouble with Trina's colleague.

Lauren gave her a once-over. She maintained a stern look for a moment before an easy smile broke across her face. "Try as I might to be a bitch to you, I can't be. It's not in my nature. Plus, that dress is fucking banging, so I have to give props where props are due."

Kendall laughed. This dress had been in her closet for a long time, waiting for a special event. She had been excited to wear it here tonight. "Thank you."

"That being said," Lauren replied, her smile faltering a bit, "Trina is still my best friend, and I'm a scrappy girl, so I wouldn't mess with her."

"I have no intention of messing with anyone, I assure you," Kendall said.

Lauren looked up at the stage, and Kendall's gaze followed. Shay waved at her and gave her a wink from behind her turntable setup.

"We're just friendly, I promise," Kendall blurted out, not sure why she felt the need to elaborate.

"You and Shay or you and Trina?" Lauren challenged.

"Shay. There is no me and Shay," Kendall replied. And as for the Trina thing, she wasn't sure what they would call that, it was still in its infancy after all. She wasn't even positive it would go anywhere, but she was hopeful it would go *somewhere*.

"What are we being so serious about? This is a party," Trina said from behind Lauren's shoulder. Kendall would have usually had a witty retort for her, but Trina had rendered her speechless with that strapless black minidress and those candy-apple-red Louboutins.

She held up two glasses of champagne and Lauren took one.

"Nothing serious at all," Kendall replied, forcing herself to make eye contact with Trina. She motioned toward the other glass. "Is that for me?"

"It can be," Trina said. Kendall took her arched eyebrow to indicate that she'd noticed Kendall's gawking. "Truthfully, I wasn't sure what you liked to drink. Assuming you drink. Are you a drinker?"

Lauren chuckled into her glass. "First dates are so weird."

Trina shot her a look. "I'll end you."

"You could try," Lauren replied, before getting distracted. "Oh, I think that might be Jax's sister. Take this." She handed the glass back to Trina. "I want to buy her a drink and be empty-handed when I do."

"Why?" Trina asked. Kendall was wondering the same thing.

"Because then it looks like I haven't already been drinking for forty minutes anxiously anticipating her arrival," Lauren said as if it was clear as day. "Duh."

"Okay, you lost me. But that's fine, go. I'll be over in a bit," Trina said as she shooed her friend away.

"She's—" Kendall started.

"My best friend, so tread lightly," Trina replied, offering her the untouched glass. "Interested?"

"In you? Yes, definitely," Kendall replied as she accepted the drink. She made sure to let her fingers linger on Trina's for as long as possible before separating.

Trina held her newly adopted glass up in a toast as she said, "Then I'd say you have great taste."

"And I bet you taste great," Kendall said as they clinked glasses.

Trina paused before taking her sip. After a moment and a very slow swallow, in Kendall's opinion, she motioned for Kendall to lean in.

Kendall obliged, and Trina nipped at her earlobe, dancing her tongue around the diamond stud Kendall was wearing as she whispered, "Remember our deal—be generous and on your best behavior, and I'll make sure you're rewarded for it."

Kendall shivered at the feeling of Trina's tongue on her flesh and the promise of so much more coming from her mouth. She reached out, cradling Trina's side before sliding her hand along the fabric of Trina's dress to pull her close. She wasn't sure how she would last through the night if the teasing started this intensely.

She turned her head to face her, keeping Trina's lips only inches from hers as she said, "If you leave with me now, I'll make sure the check is signed but blank."

Trina reached up, caressing her face before dragging two deliberate fingers along her breastbone and between the low plunging neckline of her dress, then over the fabric until flattening her palm against Kendall's navel.

Kendall's clit ached as Trina's hand moved infinitesimally lower, only to stop as she said, "Few things in this world get me hotter than money, but you in this dress, and imagining what you look like out of this dress, are a close second and third."

Kendall guided Trina's hand lower as she replied, "Then let's not waste any more time."

Trina moaned, dropping her head to Kendall's shoulder before placing a wet kiss to the skin next to her mouth.

Kendall closed her eyes at the anticipation of Trina's hand nearing her sex when Trina stopped her progress, to the ultimate frustration of her clit. She groaned as she blinked her eyes open to find Trina watching her with a wicked grin.

Trina stepped back, but not before barely grazing Kendall's front and making her shudder. Her eyes were dark as she said, "I'm going to do the most amazing things to your body later tonight, so enjoy the party, but stay sober. Because I don't want you to forget any touch, kiss, or lick. Do we have an understanding?"

Kendall was practically a puddle at this point. She nodded as she replied, "Absolutely."

"Good." Trina gave her a cutesy grin as she motioned toward the forgotten glass in Kendall's hand and said, "Enjoy your drink. Just remember to stay hydrated."

"Oh, don't worry," Kendall answered honestly. "I'm plenty wet."

Trina's eyes dropped briefly to her crotch before she replied, "All the more reason to keep you that way, then."

Kendall had to refrain from panting as Trina walked away. She was vibrating with tension and anticipation and lust, and she could not wait for this night to begin.

Chapter Twenty-one

The music was perfect, the pacing of the night had been lightning fast, and people were having a good time. This fundraiser had gone off without a hitch, and Trina could not be prouder. But she knew most of the success of tonight was due to the friends and colleagues she'd reached out to for help. Without them, she'd be nowhere. She was proud that she'd managed to coordinate all the best people to help make Jax's night a raging success.

One of those people, Mira Donahue, owner of The Mirage, was looking at her this very moment. Trina headed toward her station at the end of the bar and slid into an empty seat.

"Can I get you a drink, Hostess with the Mostest?" Mira asked. She and Trina had become friends a few years ago when Trina had been looking for a location to host a realty-related meet and greet. They'd hit it off immediately, and Trina considered Mira to be one of her favorite people: easy to get along with, incredibly intelligent, and the best intoxicologist she had ever met.

"I prefer Hostess with the *Hotness*, but I accept your version," Trina said. "Just a water, please."

"You're drinking for free tonight, as was our agreed upon perk for booking the space, and you want water?" Mira asked as she pushed a full ice-cold glass toward Trina. Trina had promised to add the cost of any drink she consumed to her donation, and she meant to make good on that. Mira hadn't argued in the least—she was the best.

"I have something to do after, and I want to make sure I'm plenty alert," Trina replied.

"Something? Or someone?" Mira asked as she leaned against the bar. "Because I've seen how you and that hot blonde have been getting on all night, and I would bet the afterparty is with her."

Trina would dismiss it had anyone else said that, but not Mira. Mira didn't miss a thing. She had this incredible ability to be aware of all things at all times. Trina had assumed it was from years of working in the service industry—she was sure Mira always had to have her wits about her—but in the few times they'd hung out outside of The Mirage, Mira had been that way, too. Her attention to detail was unparalleled, something that was clearly reflected in the design and success of this place. Mira took time to adapt to whatever the world threw at her. And her ability to read people was no different.

"I hope so," Trina said looking out toward the dance floor. Kendall was up on the DJ stand with Shay, and the two of them were laughing as Shay showed her something. Trina felt a twinge of jealousy because she knew what was happening. Shay was notorious for inviting the women she liked into her booth and showing them the ropes. It was a parlor trick that got women out of their underwear every time. And she got it, because it had worked on her, too.

"Well, she's been watching you since the moment she walked in, so my money would be on you getting laid tonight for sure," Mira replied.

"We'll see," Trina said as she sipped her water. Mira went to attend to another guest and left Trina with her thoughts. She wondered if anyone else had noticed her and Kendall's flirtation throughout the night. She'd done her best to keep it superficial and causal. Ellison was there, after all, and the last thing she wanted to do was draw attention to whatever was happening between them to her boss, of all people. She found herself feeling a little ashamed, actually. Like she was worried if Ellison found out, she'd think less of her. And since nothing had really happened with Kendall, up to this point anyway, she didn't feel the need to advertise it, least of all to Ellison, who had put all her chips on Trina beating Kendall. Which Trina hoped would also happen. She just hoped winning the bet and bedding her weren't mutually exclusive.

As if on cue, Ellison stepped up to the bar, ordering a glass of water as well. She turned to Trina with a congratulatory expression. "You pulled it off—tonight is a major success."

"Thanks," Trina said. Compliments from Ellison always made her feel like a champion. And though things had gone off swimmingly so far, there had been one hiccup that she couldn't shake. "I'm so glad Jax's sister showed up, but I have to admit, I felt for Jax when they realized their parents declined the invitation." That was an understatement. When Jax's sister Sarah showed up alone, Jax seemed pretty hurt.

And Lauren got pretty sweary. And Trina wanted to drive to Middle of Nowhere, Bumfuck, USA, to beat Jax's parents' asses, but since Sarah was there, she knew Jax felt some support. So that helped a little.

"Families can be tough," Ellison said and something in her voice told Trina that she knew that firsthand.

"Yeah." Trina thought about her family dynamics and her own feelings of rejection and inferiority. She almost exclusively felt those pressures from her family, her mother, in particular. That kind of shit wore you down. Calvin's midlife crisis was the perfect example of that. "We'll be the family Jax needs."

"You already are," Ellison replied, and Trina knew she was right.

Ellison leaned against the bar top, facing Trina as she changed the subject to the one on everyone's mind tonight and asked, "Do we have a final total yet?"

"Lauren's in charge of the tally—she's in Mira's back room adding up the checks and cash now. The credit card amounts auto-totaled, so they should be easy," Trina replied. Besides being an outside-of-the-box thinker, Lauren was also an absolute numbers wiz, like a total phenom. One of Trina's favorite things was to randomly call out a seemingly impossible equation and time how quickly Lauren got the answer. She never ceased to be amazed by that woman and couldn't imagine her life without her.

"I overheard numerous guests pay their bar tabs and then round up the total to add extra to Jax's fundraiser. Linking the two payment options was genius," Ellison said.

"I can't take any credit for that," Trina replied. "That was all Lauren's and Mira's idea. Lauren was the one who came up with the extra tipping idea, but Mira was the one that made the card receivers do double duty. It all worked out."

"Of course it did," Ellison said. "Because you were the mastermind behind organizing the team. And that's when you work best, in a team. You find people who complement you and make everyone successful because of it. You know when to compromise and when to stand your ground, Trina. That's an invaluable skill to have."

"I probably learned a little of that from you," Trina replied. That was true. She'd never had a boss quite like Ellison. There were certainly times that she entertained going out on her own, but she loved her colleagues and teammates. She wasn't the type to be solitary—she knew that. Well, except in the dating department. But maybe that was changing.

She risked a glance to the stage to see Kendall when Ellison replied, "Maybe, maybe not. When are you meeting with Amelia Clarke again?"

Kendall was leaning close to Shay, who appeared to be talking in her ear. Kendall laughed. Trina wondered what they were talking about.

"Uh," she replied distractedly, "Monday afternoon, I believe."

Ellison stood up from the bar and peered over her shoulder as she said, "I was shocked to see her here tonight."

Trina was already looking in that direction, so it wasn't like she could play coy. She answered with the truth. "Shay ran into her at our office meeting the other day and invited her. Whatever pads Jax's pocket, right?"

Ellison seemed to consider this for a moment before asking, "Does it make you uncomfortable?"

Trina watched Shay put her arm around Kendall's waist as they spoke. That made Trina uncomfortable. She wasn't uncomfortable with Kendall being here, per se, but only because they'd discussed it first. But this, this Shay touching her thing, certainly did make her uncomfortable.

"We talked about it. I told her if she was going to be an ass, she couldn't come. She agreed to play nice and write a fat check. So I'm okay with it, then," Trina said as she continued to watch them on the stage standing close and looking cozy. She was aware of just how hypocritical she was in that moment. Saying one thing, while feeling rage things. It was a complicated headspace to be in.

"Ever the negotiator." Ellison patted her arm. "You're a good friend to Jax."

As Trina envisioned strangling Jax's idol Shay, she didn't feel like such a good friend. "Thanks."

"Ladies, the numbers are in." Lauren was clutching a zippered leather bank bag to her chest with an enormous smile.

"And?" Trina couldn't wait to hear the outcome.

"We got it all, and then some. This will cover Jax's surgery, recovery needs, professional *and* personal wardrobe update, and probably a trip to Tahiti with a bevy of ladies," Lauren joked. "People were beyond generous. Jax is gonna freak."

Ellison cheered and Trina felt elated. This was everything she had hoped for and more.

Ellison excused herself to chat with someone on the other side of the bar, and Lauren stepped into Trina's space, her mouth in a smirk as she said quietly, "Kendall's donation was five figures."

Trina's jaw dropped. "You're kidding me."

Lauren shook her head. "Nope. And she left a note to have one of us circle back to her if our goal wasn't reached." Lauren gave Trina a once-over. "You got a million-dollar pussy there, huh, girl?"

"That would be seven figures," Trina pointed out. "But she hasn't had the pleasure yet, so five is a fair starting point."

"Whatever," Lauren said with a laugh. "You said pay up and she certainly did. I'm not saying you should spend the night on your knees or anything, but maybe you should."

"I won't be the one kneeling." Trina nudged her. "But I got the message. Let's present Jax with the total and shut this party down. I have places to be."

She looked up to the stage to check on Kendall and wished she could retract everything she'd just said. Because Kendall was onstage, kissing Shay.

CHAPTER TWENTY-TWO

The kiss was unexpected. Because of the volume of the music, Kendall and Shay had been close for the past twenty minutes or so, speaking into each other's ears, because they had to. This wasn't like the conversation on the dance floor at the beginning of the night with Trina. This wasn't intimate with the promise of more. This proximity was purely logistical. Until Shay kissed her, and then it was a big mistake.

Kendall stepped back from the kiss, her face no doubt displaying the surprise she felt because Shay looked confused.

"Sorry, I thought—" Shay started.

Kendall held up her hand, stepping back farther. "No, maybe I wasn't clear. I like you and think you're great and would certainly hang out with you more in a social setting, but as flattered as I am, I'm kind of seeing someone. I think."

"You think?" Shay asked, her easy smile back again.

This woman rebounded like no other—it was incredible. Kendall would probably have been offended by that if her mind hadn't started going into panic mode. Had anyone seen the kiss? What if Trina…? "Yes, although that might be in jeopardy now," Kendall said as she searched for any sign of Trina in the crowd. "I have to go. Thanks for a fun night. Sorry if I gave you any mixed signals."

"I'm not sure that you did," Shay said with a shrug. "Anyway, good luck with that person you might be seeing. Hopefully I'll be seeing you around more often."

Kendall was off the stage as fast as possible, but she found herself blocked by the crowded dance floor. The emcee had emerged, and Shay had cut the music as announcements were being made and people were cheering. It sounded like they'd reached their money goal tonight, but

Kendall couldn't care less. She needed to find Trina and explain what just happened, because surely someone there saw the kiss. She weaved and dodged the bar patrons, all the while searching for Trina. But she kept coming up short. Trina was nowhere to be found.

She picked up her pace, heading toward the main bar area. That's when she nearly ran right into Lauren and found all the answers she was looking for. Etched on Lauren's face was the undeniable look of dissatisfaction. Kendall's hopes fell.

"It's not what it looked like," she hurried out. "She kissed me, not the other way around."

Lauren raised an eyebrow but infuriatingly said nothing.

"She saw, right?" Kendall asked, already knowing the answer as she palmed her forehead out of frustration. "I promise you, I didn't—"

"She's by the coat check, and there's a car waiting out front," Lauren said after a pause. "You probably have about two minutes to fix this before she's gone."

"Thank you," Kendall breathed out, squeezing Lauren's hand as she raced toward the coat check.

She put aside appropriate social maneuvering to get there just in time to see Trina pulling on her coat. Her own coat was toward the front, and she grabbed it, slipping it on as she tossed the attendant the first bill she could get her hands on, which happened to be a hundred. Kendall didn't give it a second thought—she had a woman to stop.

"Trina, wait." She barely had her arm in the sleeve of her jacket when Trina's hand reached for the exit door.

If Trina had heard her, she didn't show it. Kendall had to run to catch her before she got into the car outside. Why was the exit so fucking crowded right now?

By the time she did catch up to her, Trina appeared to be eyeing the line of waiting cars, trying to identify which one was hers. Kendall knew she had mere moments.

"Please." Kendall lightly touched Trina's elbow as she tried again. "Wait."

Trina turned to look at her, and Kendall's heart sank. She looked disappointed. Not angry, just sad. Kendall would so have preferred angry. But sad, well, that was a look she decided in that moment that she never wanted to see again on Trina's face.

"It's fine, Kendall," Trina said. "No strings attached, right? That was your stipulation, and I agreed to it. You're free to kiss anyone you wish."

"Good," Kendall said as she turned Trina by her elbow to face her fully. "Because the only person I want to kiss is you."

Kendall didn't give Trina the chance to reply. She cupped her face and kissed her as fully and as passionately as she could. She tried to convey through her lips how badly she wanted this, how much this moment was the memory she wanted for tonight. And though at first Trina let the kiss be one-sided, soon Kendall felt her warm up, a smile on her lips as they parted for Kendall to deepen the kiss. And she did. She ignored the honking horns and the cheering people around them, and she lost herself in the feeling of Trina's lips against hers.

Trina pulled back with a gasp, and Kendall chased after her lips.

"Easy, Tiger. Message received," Trina said, looking flushed. Kendall hoped it was from the kissing and not from embarrassment, as it appeared they had drawn a crowd. Trina looked over Kendall's shoulder and dropped her head to Kendall's chest. "Maybe we should take this, uh, conversation someplace more private."

"Your place or mine?" Kendall asked as she ran her hand through Trina's hair, fighting every urge she had to kiss her again. Which felt more impossible by the second because Trina's lips were the perfect plump red right now.

"The Uber is booked for mine, so..." Trina replied, her hand along Kendall's waist, under the open jacket Kendall hadn't had time to close.

Kendall was desperate to feel that hand on her skin, with no fabric getting in the way. She was sure she'd agree to anything Trina asked as long as she promised to touch her the way she ached for her to.

"Lead the way," Kendall said, her body thrumming with excitement and anticipation.

Gratefully, Trina didn't live far from The Mirage. Before Kendall knew it, she was stepping off the elevator of the fancy apartment building onto Trina's floor. Kendall wasn't sure how Trina had maneuvered the key into the lock, since her lips had been busy along Trina's neck since the lobby. She paused her adorations long enough to step into the apartment after Trina and take a quick look around.

Trina's place was stunning. She had an amazing view through the balcony to the left, and the open concept living room and kitchen gleamed with high-end appliances and accessories. The white marble countertops looked pristine, and the island was enormous. Kendall looked back toward the living room for any surface to deposit Trina on and was drawn to the large, comfy looking gray sofa with chaise. That would do quite nicely for what she had in mind.

"Shoes off." Trina had dropped her jacket and was pulling off Kendall's as she spoke against her lips. "But know that I really like your choice in shoes tonight."

"Thank you." Kendall gladly obliged, and Trina walked her backward until she bumped into the back of the sofa. Her hands left Trina's body to stabilize against the surface behind her, and Trina stepped so close to her that their hips touched. Kendall went to reach for her, but Trina pressed her hand back to the sofa back. She mirrored the position with her other hand, pinning Kendall's palms to the plush fabric.

"I have wanted to get you all to myself for longer than I'd like to admit," Trina said between breathless kisses. It occurred to Kendall that she didn't need to bend to reach Trina's mouth, and she broke the kiss to see why.

"You're still wearing shoes." Kendall's observation was briefly silenced by Trina's lips.

"It's my house," Trina said as she nipped at her bottom lip, making Kendall's lower stomach clench. "But it's more that I could use the height advantage."

Kendall's laugh faded quickly as Trina's hands settled on her breasts. She pressed against Kendall, making her arch back in response, before she massaged and kneaded the flesh. Kendall moaned, and Trina's lips found hers again. Trina dragged both her hands down Kendall's sides, grinding their hips together as she owned every clothed inch of Kendall's body, stopping just short of where Kendall desperately wanted her.

"You're killing me," Kendall breathed out and Trina nuzzled her nose.

"Good," Trina replied. Trina kissed her way to Kendall's ear and commanded, "Turn around, but keep those hands on the couch."

Kendall pulled back, watching Trina for a moment. She was so, so beautiful and confident, and sexy with her hair slightly tousled from their kissing. Her lipstick was a little smudged, but the rest of her makeup was flawless. Kendall hadn't noticed earlier the intricate detail Trina had used when applying her eye shadow. Standing this close, she could see four or five shades, blended to perfection on Trina's lids. The color combination brought out those gold flecks in Trina's eyes that Kendall had noticed on that fateful night on the balcony. She had the most gorgeous eyes.

"You're watching me," Trina pointed out. "You're supposed to be turning around."

Kendall moved her hands for the first time since Trina pressed them down. She caressed Trina's jaw and held her face, bringing their lips together softly as she said, "I was just appreciating how fucking magnificent you are."

Trina exhaled against her lips, and Kendall wanted to find a way to get closer to her. Trina entertained her desire to kiss for a little longer before she said again, "Turn for me. Hands on the couch."

Kendall nodded and did as she was told. One of Trina's hands combed through her hair, gently scratching at her scalp, as the other slowly traced down the skin of her back, between her shoulder blades to the top of her dress. Trina unzipped the zipper slowly and painstakingly until the dress pooled at Kendall's feet. Kendall's bra followed to its place on the floor, and Trina pressed a delicate kiss over her spine.

Trina's hands explored her back, rubbing and massaging until her hands settled at her hips. She stepped up behind Kendall, pressing her hips against Kendall's ass as she raked her short nails down Kendall's back.

Kendall shivered in response, her hands clenching the luxurious fabric under her palms. Her hands twitched as she fought the urge to reach behind her and bring Trina's body closer. She wanted to feel Trina's weight on top of her, even if that meant she had to stay in this incredibly sexy but vulnerable position.

Trina teased her a few moments longer before gripping her hips and turning her on the spot.

"You are beautiful," Trina said, her hands reaching out to caress the underside of one of Kendall's exposed breasts. Her other hand toyed with the top of Kendall's panties, which had been rendered useless earlier in the night on the dance floor with Trina. She was eager to get out of them, but Trina seemed to be in no rush.

Kendall traced her fingers along Trina's collarbone, until she located the side zipper of Trina's minidress. She kissed her as she worked the zipper down, her hand greedily caressing Trina's exposed side until the dress was out of the way. Trina broke away from her mouth long enough to step out of the dress and kick it aside, all the while keeping those too high heels on. Kendall appraised her and groaned. Trina's dress didn't allow for a bra, so two tiny pasties stood between her and the nipples she so desperately wanted to suck on, but those were quickly forgotten when her gaze traveled lower, across Trina's flat abdomen to her naked and delicious looking sex.

"No panties," Kendall noted, thrilled.

"Does this offend you?" Trina looped her arms around Kendall's waist in a sweet embrace.

"Standing is offending me," Kendall said as she stepped closer, bringing her clothed sex to Trina's naked one. Trina purred at the sensation, and Kendall wanted her hands and mouth there. Kendall looked beyond Trina's shoulder toward the rest of her apartment. "Give me a quick tour, specifically to the master bedroom, please. In fact, skip the audio part of the tour unless it's you moaning. I'm really more interested in the visible and the tangible parts," she said. Emboldened by Trina's hands gripping her ass, she slipped her hand between them and teased across Trina's wet lips.

Trina whimpered, and her grip on Kendall's ass became almost painful. "The couch is so much closer," Trina said, spreading her legs for Kendall.

Kendall dipped lower, dragging up and down, teasing more and more. Trina's head was resting on her shoulder again, the same position as earlier, but this time, Kendall could feel Trina's want in her hand. And it was a wonderful feeling.

Kendall kissed Trina's temple as she toyed with her slick, heated flesh and said, "I'm going to need someplace to really spread you out." She punctuated her words by gliding through Trina's wetness. "I'm not interested in being confined to a less than ideal space, when I can get all of you all over me. If that's all right with you, that is."

"It is," Trina panted out as Kendall found her clit and grazed over it. "But I'm not so sure I'll make it if you keep that up."

Kendall lingered for a second longer before pulling her hand back. "Well, we can't have that."

Trina let out a frustrated whine as she gripped Kendall's hand and practically dragged her to the back of the unit.

"Guest bedroom, guest bath, laundry area, office," Trina rattled off between stolen kisses along the way. She stopped short at the last door at the end of the hall and finally kicked off her heels. "No shoes in the bedroom. Bedrooms are for sex and sleep. Not shoes. That's the rule."

Kendall gave her a brief nod as she replied, "I have no intention of sleeping."

"Neither do I," Trina said as she opened the door and pulled Kendall through it.

The king-sized bed on the far wall was magnificent. The silk sheets and soft looking down comforter looked like heaven. A heaven that was missing this gorgeous specimen holding her hand, that was.

Trina brought her to bed, tossing back the covers and throwing pillows as she crawled into it. Kendall climbed over her, pausing just short of lying on top of her for Trina to pull off her panties. Now that they were both naked, Kendall seized the opportunity to stare at her and take in the sight before her. She'd always thought Trina was stunning, but there was something about the way her raven hair spread over the stark white sheets that hypnotized her. And those red lips, she had to have them. She kissed Trina as she dragged her thumb over one of Trina's nipples, only to find the barrier was still in place.

She pulled back from the kiss and raised an eyebrow as she said, "These have to come off."

Trina winced and covered her eyes with her forearm as she said, "I know."

"Want me to?" Kendall had every intention of removing them, but she knew where Trina's trepidation came from. This was a sensitive area to remove adhesive from, even the easy-peel kind. Especially after a night of foreplay and fondling, which they seemed deeply immersed in.

"No, yes. Ugh, have mercy." Trina bit her bottom lip and remained hidden under her arm.

"I promise to lick it better if it's sore," Kendall said.

Trina bucked her hips in response, and Kendall decided they'd waited long enough. She leaned forward, licking the edge of the pasty as she eased the border away from Trina's skin. With each millimeter of movement, she lapped the area, loosening the hold and soothing the flesh, like she'd promised. Soon she had both pasties removed, and Trina's nipples were erect and swollen, begging to be sucked on.

Kendall closed her lips around one bud and Trina's hands found her hair again. She felt Trina grind up against her as she sucked and licked the sensitive tissue, and she slid her hand between them, stroking the heated flesh of Trina's core, and Trina started to pant again. Kendall moved to her other breast and dipped deeper, caressing her opening before dragging up to her clit and back again, slow and deliberate. Trina cursed and clawed at her scalp, her legs spreading for Kendall with each stroke and rub, and Kendall felt her start to tremble.

She kissed up her chest to her mouth, silencing a deep moan as she slipped into Trina fully, easing two firm fingers in the tight heat that enveloped her. She flexed her fingertips to glide along Trina's ridged inner walls, and Trina cried out.

"Jesus, fuck, Kendall." Trina's words were short and sharp like her breathing. Kendall toyed with her nipple while she continued to stroke and thrust in and out of Trina at a pace that was so slow, Kendall was afraid she'd lose her rhythm. But the slower she pressed and glided and fucked Trina, the louder Trina got. Until Trina finally begged, "More. Faster, deeper, more. Make me come."

Kendall's body clenched and shook at the command, her rhythm and pace increasing with each gasp and sigh Trina exhaled. It didn't take long for Trina to come undone by her touch, and the sounds of pleasure and the rushing heat that accompanied that orgasm nearly pushed Kendall over the edge as well.

Trina's body pulsed beneath her, and Kendall eased her down with gentle kisses along her jaw and neck. She kept her fingers inside Trina until she felt her walls relax, the spasming slowing. She dragged her thumb over Trina's clit, and Trina bucked against her hand, crying out again.

"Too much?" Kendall asked as she moved to Trina's hip, holding her close.

"Just a little," Trina said as she dropped her head back on the pillow, trying to catch her breath. "I might be broken."

Kendall frowned as she said, "I hope not. I'm not done with you yet."

Trina laughed and looked up at her with a lazy, sated grin. "We're just getting started, lover. Don't you worry. I just need a minute to recharge."

"Just a minute, though, right?" Kendall asked as she became painfully aware of her own aching cunt. She shifted to relieve some of the pressure, and Trina noticed.

"Oh, baby," Trina said, pushing Kendall onto her back and climbing on top of her. "I'm not about to make you suffer. This is exactly the kind of respite my clit needs. My mouth on yours should recharge me plenty fine."

Kendall's mouth dropped open in understanding as Trina leaned down and teased her nipples before moving lower. "I won't last long if you do that," Kendall warned as Trina licked a zigzag down from her navel toward her sex.

"We have all night," Trina said, looking up at her once more, her nose nudging Kendall's clit and sending shock waves through her body. "Tell me. How many licks will it take to make you pop?"

"Not many." Kendall barely got the words out before Trina proved her right. And it was the most wonderful right she had ever been.

CHAPTER TWENTY-THREE

Trina gasped, sure that she would suffocate from sexual exhaustion and pleasure if Kendall didn't stop doing that thing with her tongue that had already given her three mind-bending orgasms since last night.

She clutched at the confident hand that pressed on her thigh, keeping her legs apart, as she succumbed yet again to Kendall's talents.

She collapsed back on the bed, her body so stimulated it was almost numb. The only thing she could feel with great certainty was the delicate way Kendall had intertwined their fingers on her leg. She pulled Kendall up to her but kept the contact, because it felt nice to hold hands post sex.

Kendall lay on her side facing her, her long blond hair a sexy looking, gorgeous mess around her face and tickling Trina's shoulder. Trina rolled to face her, easing into the position gingerly as she was still coming down and sensitive.

Kendall smiled at her, a knowing, teasing smile that Trina would have scoffed at had she any energy left to do anything other than gaze at the emerald eyes across from her.

"What are you thinking?" Kendall asked as she brought their joined hands to her mouth and kissed along Trina's knuckles. It felt heavenly.

"Mostly that I can't feel my legs," Trina replied honestly, and Kendall laughed. "I mean, it's like I know they're there, but I wouldn't trust them to attempt a full stand just yet."

"That sounds pretty serious. You should rest," Kendall said as she pulled Trina onto her chest and lay flat on her back.

Trina snuggled close, pulling the comforter over their bodies as she melted into Kendall's arms. She was so warm and soft, yet strong in all the right places. Trina knew if she stayed like this, she'd doze off. She was tempted to. It felt too good to move.

"This is so nice," Trina let slip without meaning to. She immediately felt embarrassed at the overshare.

"This *is* nice," Kendall replied in kind as she tightened her grip around Trina's shoulders. "I don't think I expected you to be a cuddler."

"Really?" Trina looked up at her.

"Really," Kendall replied. "I mean, I didn't really give it much thought. Well, that's not entirely true. I thought about fucking you a lot, but I didn't think about what would happen afterward."

"A lot, huh?" Trina asked, pleased with this information.

Kendall looked embarrassed. "Wait, you didn't?"

Trina kissed her because she could. "I didn't say that. I was just curious about the frequency of these sex daydreams you were having about me."

"They weren't all daydreams," Kendall replied. "Some were night dreams. Some were shower dreams. And I'd prefer to call them *scenarios*, not dreams. Because scenarios have a better chance of coming to fruition than dreams."

"You just said coming," Trina pointed out.

Kendall rolled her eyes as she said, "So not the point."

"You're right," Trina agreed. "The point is you've been thinking, dreaming, and or planning to bed me for quite some time, and now that you have, what did you think? Did I live up to your expectations?"

"Oh, please," Kendall replied. "There was no way I could have ever anticipated how incredible that was going to be. Any of it."

"All of it," Trina said as she kissed her again. "It was all incredible."

"It really was," Kendall said as she looked at her. Something about her tone intrigued Trina.

"Why do you sound surprised by that?" Trina asked. She'd had no doubt a night with Kendall would be memorable. Why had Kendall felt differently?

"Because this is *nice*," Kendall said as she motioned between them. "This postcoital snuggle, pillow talk thing. It's nice. So on top of great sex, I'm also just happy to be cuddling you in bed. Which isn't something I usually do."

Trina considered this a moment. She was a cuddler, through and through. She would snuggle for warmth or affection or boredom. She was super physical in all things that she did—she was a hugger, a passionate kisser, a dedicated lover, and a fucking snuggle connoisseur. She thought about her past relationships, friendships and romantic ones, and there was a constant that occurred to her. She liked feeling secure and protected when she was being vulnerable with someone, which, she supposed, was now. What would make you feel more vulnerable than sleeping with the enemy?

"You're very good at it." Trina burrowed deeper under the covers as she caressed Kendall's naked side. "Why fight it?"

Kendall kissed her forehead and sighed. "I don't fight it. I just don't do it."

"Why?" Trina asked. She genuinely wanted to get to know Kendall better. And what Kendall was saying was in direct conflict with what she was doing.

"I suppose the opportunity doesn't arrive that often," Kendall replied.

"That's…kind of sad."

Kendall shifted into a stretch, and Trina worried she might have scared her away. She wasn't ready to give this up just yet.

"Tell me what's different this time," Trina pressed, hoping to get Kendall to open up and stay a little longer.

Kendall looked at her, and she wanted to kiss her again, but she waited, because she also really wanted to hear what Kendall had to say.

Kendall seemed to be lost in thought, and Trina felt bad for pressuring her. "I'm sorry, I didn't mean to—" Trina started.

"I was engaged," Kendall blurted out, and Trina propped herself up on her elbow to get a better look at her.

She waited for Kendall to elaborate. She already knew about the engagement thanks to Lauren's deep dive into the dark web, but she'd nearly forgotten about it. And she wasn't sure how it in any way related to them cuddling after sex.

Kendall rubbed her forehead, but her brow remained creased. "It wasn't recent or anything—that's not what I meant. Actually, I have no idea why I said anything to begin with."

"Maybe they're on your mind," Trina supplied, truly hoping Kendall was not thinking about her ex while they were in bed together.

"She's not," Kendall said curtly. "I'd be fine with never seeing her again in my life."

Trina wanted to know why, but she didn't push.

After a moment, Kendall's brow relaxed, and she looked at Trina again, this time her expression much softer. "I was engaged, and I thought I'd found the perfect partner in life and so on and so on. But it didn't work out, and I think I harbored a lot of baggage when that happened. So I stopped doing coupley things with women. It was so gradual—I don't think I realized it. Until now."

"When you were suddenly as amazing a cuddler as you were an orgasm giver?" Trina asked, glad to know Kendall's mind wasn't preoccupied by another woman.

"If you keep flattering me, I might never leave," Kendall said, her light, flirty tone back. Trina really liked this side of Kendall. Flirting with her felt like an electric kind of volley. She was instantly turned on by it.

"I'm not exactly throwing you out of bed," she replied. Trina looked down at Kendall and momentarily entertained the idea of dating her. What would that be like? What was Kendall really like?

"I had noticed that," Kendall said as she brushed an errant hair behind Trina's ear.

It was such a casually affectionate gesture that Trina got what Kendall meant before. She hadn't expected Kendall to be anything more than a great lay, but she was soft and kind. Softer and kinder than Trina would have expected.

"Tell me five things about you. Don't think, just say the first five things that come to mind," Trina said.

Kendall paused. "I hate being late. I don't like people who make excuses. I love key lime pie more than anyone else I know. And, evidently, I like cuddling with you after having sex."

"Really great sex," Trina added.

"The best, even," Kendall said as she kissed her.

Trina pulled back from the kiss to say, "That's only four things. What's your fifth thing?"

Kendall frowned. "I think I made a mistake the other day at your office."

"Meaning?" Trina was expecting to hear an anecdote about Kendall, not about what was happening between them.

Kendall's eye contact was suddenly intense. She looked upset and also maybe a little shy? Trina couldn't quite place the emotion on Kendall's face, but something seemed to be bothering her.

"When Shay kissed me last night—"

"Boo, hiss," Trina interjected.

Kendall gave her a look before continuing, "When Shay kissed me last night, I panicked. Not because she offended me or anything, but because I was worried, like, genuinely worried that you would be hurt by it. Because I would have been hurt by it had it been me." Kendall placed her hand on Trina's chest, making little swirls with her fingers on the skin as she spoke. "Then I almost missed you, and when I caught up to you, you said something to me that felt like a gut punch, and I haven't been able to get it out of the back of my mind."

"Even with all the orgasms?" Trina teased.

"Even with those," Kendall said with a smile. "I was wrong the other day to tell you I wanted this to be no strings attached. I don't know why I said that. And if I meant that in the moment, then I was ignoring my own feelings on the matter. Because I'm not a light and frothy kind of person. I don't do casual very well. That's not to say I'm looking for something heavy or, like, matching-tattoo serious or..." Kendall shook her head. "When Shay kissed me, I was worried about hurting you. Because I wanted to be kissing *you*, not anyone else. And I don't think that really follows the no-strings guidelines. Because with that kiss, I felt a very definite string pulling me toward you. And now we're here, and you're naked and beautiful and you make the sexiest noises when you kiss and when you come, and I feel a definite string. Does that make sense?"

"No, it's an absolute circus in your head. You should see someone about that," Trina deadpanned.

Kendall looked stunned. Trina felt bad.

"I'm joking," Trina said, as she climbed on top of Kendall, bringing the comforter up over her head like a hoodie. "You make perfect roundabout sense, and I really prefer this approach to the stringless one."

"You do?" Kendall looked relieved.

"I do," Trina replied. "And to be honest, I don't really like to share."

"You're hard to take seriously with that blanket halo," Kendall noted.

Trina dropped the blanket, shivering slightly at the rush of cold air on her naked skin. She placed her hands on Kendall's breasts and massaged them as she said, "I'm not sure what this means or where this will go, but I'm more than happy to give it a try and see what comes of it. No expectations, no pressure. Just two people who have really awesome sex also trying things like postcoital cuddling and pillow talk."

"And breast play," Kendall added, her breath getting short.

"And so much breast play." Trina leaned forward to connect their lips. She had much more than groping on her immediate agenda, and she didn't plan on waiting any longer.

❖

Kendall was nervous. Coffee with Margo was a regular and usually joyful experience, and this particular coffee date had been on the books for weeks. It was their bi-weekly check in. Never to be missed, only occasionally to be rescheduled. This coffee date was as much for her mental health as it was for maintaining her friendship. And she really needed a mental health check right now. And a friend. Because she was a mess.

"You're earlier than usual," Margo said with open arms. "I thought I might beat you here for a change."

Kendall stepped into her friend's embrace and squeezed her tight as she said, "I had an opening in my schedule." That was true…ish. She had an opening in her schedule because she rearranged some meetings to ensure she'd have extra time at coffee if she needed it. Which she knew she would. She hoped Margo had some flexibility today. They had a lot to discuss.

"I'm happy to see you," Margo said. "I feel like it's been decades."

"Tell me about it," Kendall replied. The feeling was mutual.

"Let me grab some—"

"I already took care of it. I ordered you your usual—is that okay?" Kendall asked, realizing that was sort of rash and selfish. She just really needed to talk and didn't want to waste time waiting in line for coffee.

"Yeah, that's great. Thanks," Margo said as she started to sit across from her. "You okay? You seem kind of jumpy."

"I slept with Trina," Kendall blurted out. She couldn't contain herself any longer.

Margo froze with her mouth open, still somewhere between standing and sitting. "You *what*?"

"Maybe you should sit for this," Kendall said.

"Okay," Margo said as she lowered herself into the seat. She pulled her chair closer and clasped her hands together as she continued, "Back up a bit. What happened exactly?"

"How exact are we talking?" Kendall asked.

Margo shook her head. "I don't need explicit details of the sex yet. Maybe start with how this happened, and we'll work from there."

"Remember how I told you we had coffee?" Kendall asked.

"Yes," Margo said with a look, and Kendall felt bad, because she'd told her about the coffee only as an afterthought over cocktails the night of the balcony incident. And Margo had dressed her down hard for it.

Kendall let out a long breath. "So, we had the coffee thing and then that balcony thing, right? Something changed between us—at least, they did for me. And suddenly, I was seeing Trina in a different light. And then I ran into her at the country club, and she was almost naked, in a towel, and there was bantering and then kissing. So much kissing."

Margo held up a hand to stop her. "Wait, there was kissing before there was sleeping together?"

"That's usually how these things go," Kendall pointed out.

Margo shook her head. "You know what I meant. You kissed her at some point before you slept with her."

"Yes?" Kendall didn't see where this was going.

The server placed their drinks down, but Margo remained silent and didn't reach for hers. Kendall couldn't figure out why she looked so upset.

"What?" Kendall asked.

"I'm just working through my annoyance at you for not telling me that you kissed Trina right after it happened. Because sometime between then and now you managed to fall into bed with her, so one would think that some valuable discussions with your best friend should have happened before that," Margo said as she finally reached for her coffee. "We've talked about this before, Kendall. You don't have to keep secrets from me. I'm in your life for the good and the bad. I've got your back."

Kendall felt like shit. Margo had every right to be annoyed. And she was more than spot-on about Kendall and her ability to share. Kendall had difficulty opening up to people, even to Margo. She had a bad habit of keeping parts of herself hidden—she knew it was a weakness of hers. She dropped her head in shame. "You're right."

"I know I am," Margo replied. "Well, there's no point dwelling on the past, especially when it gets juicier. So what happened?"

Kendall was grateful for the pass. She replied, "Trina's banter had always felt a little flirtatious to me, but I just couldn't put my finger on it because she was also needling me at the same time. But I don't know, maybe I did hit my head that night, because she just seemed different. And I couldn't stop thinking about her. Then I ran into her at the club, and we were in the locker room, and before I realized it, I was flirting with her. Then you called, and she answered and then—"

"This happened the time she answered your phone?" Margo asked, looking scandalized. "Is that why she said you were busy? I was wondering how she got close enough to you to get your phone. That thing is practically attached to you at all times."

"Business hazard," Kendall replied.

"Kissing your professional opponent? Or never being away from your phone?" Margo countered.

"The latter," Kendall replied with a chuckle.

"Well, damn," Margo said. "I feel sort of responsible. I was practically part of the equation."

"Oh, you certainly were. Had you not called, I'm not sure Trina would have reached into my pocket, and there would have been way less touching—"

"And kissing," Margo noted.

"Right."

"So I'm to blame? Or to thank?" Margo asked, seemingly trying to tease out Kendall's feelings on the matter.

"To thank," Kendall said without hesitation. "That kiss started this really wonderful flirtation that led to some really amazing sex. A lot of it actually."

Margo just stared at her. Had she overshared?

"What?" Kendall asked.

"Nothing," Margo said as she slow blinked. "It's just, I don't know, you look a little glowy."

"Glowy?" Kendall repeated.

"Yeah, like, happy," Margo said as she cocked her head to the side, seemingly appraising Kendall in a different way. "You *are* happy. And nervous. Why are you nervous?"

"Because I really, really liked it, and I continue to like it," Kendall said, thinking about the quick make out session she and Trina had managed that morning when they'd coincidentally overlapped tours at the Harborside. Had Kendall not known there were cameras in that parking garage, she would have fucked Trina in the back seat of her car without a second thought. She'd certainly wanted to. And she knew Trina wanted to, since she'd flat-out told her to cancel her afternoon plans and do just that. For a moment, she'd seriously considered it. "Sorry."

"You got lost on me," Margo said. "Where did you go?"

"I hooked up with Trina this morning, and I wandered back there in my mind," Kendall said dropping her head again. "I'm a mess."

Margo let out a low whistle before she said, "We have some work to do. You know what? It's nice out today. Let's take this coffee for a walk. I think walking might help pull you out of that sex fog you're in."

Kendall agreed. Walking sounded nice. "Sounds good."

"I have to say, I'm not really that surprised," Margo said once they were out of the café and walking along the pond across the street.

"Really? Because I was," Kendall admitted.

"Yeah, no. It sort of makes perfect sense. You two are either a good match or mortal enemies. Like two ends of the same battery," Margo said. "It doesn't surprise me that you're attracted to her. She's beautiful. And funny, and charming, and self-deprecating, while also being super confident. I liked her when I met her that night at the soon-to-be new Cyclebar location. She seemed genuine. And she totally saved your life that night, which she could have not done and won this contest easily."

The contest. Kendall had been so wrapped up in her lust for Trina that she'd almost forgotten they were actually competing against each other. And that was the only stipulation they'd both agreed on: whatever they were exploring could not interfere with work. So far, they'd managed to keep the two things apart, except for the kissing in the car earlier. But Kendall wasn't sure if that might change. She hoped not. Though she'd had a successful meeting today with one of the clients on Langley's list. And one the other day. She knew things would heat up again soon, and she knew that Trina had shown that penthouse again this morning. The competition was progressing just as much as her attraction to Trina. And as much as she knew she'd have to address that, she wanted to figure out the Trina issue first.

"After the fundraiser, we had the most incredible night," Kendall said, thinking out loud. "It was the kind of night that I just knew wouldn't be a one-time-thing. I don't think I could have let it. I wanted more. She left me wanting so much more."

"That sounds refreshing," Margo said, her expression kind and supportive, not judgmental. Kendall didn't expect to be judged, but part of her felt like she should feel ashamed, but she didn't know why. She was starting to really like Trina.

"It really is," Kendall replied.

They walked in silence for a few minutes before Kendall looked at Margo and was the most honest she'd been with herself in probably years. "I like her. And I want to see her all the time, but I still want to win the competition. And I'm not sure if those two things can happen at the same time, or if I'm just getting myself excited, but setting myself up to lose one or both of those scenarios. And I'm scared. She excites and scares me."

"I can see that," Margo said. "Can I make an observation?"

"Please do," Kendall said, desperate for guidance.

"This thing between you and Trina, it isn't a scenario. It's your life. And hers. And if you treat it like a business transaction, much like the contest, then you *will* end up feeling unfulfilled afterward. My suggestion is that you really lay everything out for her. Talk about it, so you're both on the same page. Then weathering whatever storm comes will be easier," Margo said, and it sounded so easy.

Kendall walked next to her and thought about what she said. She wanted to call Trina. She wanted to set up a time to see her and talk, not just have sex. But she wanted that, too.

"Can I make another observation?" Margo asked.

"Well, don't stop now," Kendall replied, glad to have the weight of this off her chest.

"In the two or so years I've known you, you've never talked about your feelings this much, or seemed this happy. And I know you're like nervous-happy, but it's still happy. And though you've been carefree and playful since I met you, I don't think until now that I realized *happy* was missing," Margo said. "You deserve *happy*, Kendall."

Kendall's phone rang and she reached for it. Trina's name was on the screen.

"Your happy is calling," Margo said as she peered over her shoulder. "Don't miss out."

Kendall didn't intend to.

CHAPTER TWENTY-FOUR

K endall sat on the park bench outside the soon to be opened Cyclebar at the back of the Harborside. This was her favorite spot to think between client meetings because the bench faced a small, private park for the residents of the surrounding buildings and was only about thirty feet from the harbor's edge. But today, even this million-dollar view couldn't settle her restless brain.

The phone calls hadn't stopped, and the voice mails remained voiceless. The calls seemed almost random, happening now not quite daily, but just often enough to keep her on edge. The unknowns of the situation were keeping her up at night.

"Hello, beautiful." The sound of Trina's voice was a welcome distraction from the restless buzzing of her mind.

"Hi," Kendall said, sliding her sunglasses into her hair to see Trina better. She looked great today, as usual. Her outfit was chic and bordering on impractical, but damn, she looked fine. "That's some sundress."

"You like it?" Trina asked.

"I certainly do," Kendall said, especially appreciating the shortness of it.

"The warmer weather means less fabric and more legs," Trina said as she sat next to her on the bench, crossing her legs and causing the already short dress to ride up more. Kendall traced her thumb along the bottom hem, feeling the smoothness of the fabric.

"Summer is upon us," Kendall said, aware that time was passing more and more each day. "And if this is the sort of regular summer outfit you plan to have in rotation, then I wholly approve."

Trina gave her a flirtatious wink before saying, "I was happy to see you out here. I didn't realize you had meetings on-site today."

"I didn't—well, not really anyway," Kendall said as she continued to play with the bottom of Trina's dress. "I stopped by to make sure the Cyclebar renovations were going well, but then I got sucked in by the view."

"It is gorgeous here," Trina said as she leaned back on the bench beside her. Her gaze was directed out at the water. "I love the water."

"I prefer this view," Kendall said as she appreciated Trina. She'd had enough of the water today. It had offered no respite from her worries. But Trina, on the other hand, in no time at all brought her a peace that she wasn't expecting. Her arrival was a pleasant reprieve, and the calm that came with it was an unexpected bonus. Her attraction to Trina was obvious, but after their night together, Kendall found herself wanting to be around her more, and she didn't think that was solely lust based. Maybe it was because Trina quieted her and made her feel safe. Which seemed ridiculous, since Trina had been an agitator in her world just weeks ago. How quickly that had all changed.

Trina dipped her head to catch Kendall's eye and those brown eyes nearly took her breath away.

"Hey," she said.

"Hey," Kendall replied, leaning in to press a soft kiss to Trina's lips. Kendall felt her stress melt away with that kiss. She cupped Trina's jaw, letting the kiss linger as she caressed Trina's cheek with her thumb. The kiss was sweet and sensual and comforting for Kendall. She wondered how Trina felt about it. After a moment, she pulled back to admit, "I'm glad you're here."

"If you kiss me hello like that every time I unexpectedly show up in your life, then you can expect a lot more unannounced arrivals," Trina said, staying close.

"I wouldn't hate that," Kendall said as she rested her hand on the exposed skin of Trina's thigh. She leaned close, inhaling the smell of Trina's perfume as she nuzzled at Trina's jaw to kiss along her neck. "More of you always sounds like a good thing."

"Oh, baby, if we're going to keep this PG-13 in public, you're going to need to stop that," Trina said between soft pants, though Kendall noted that she didn't push her away.

Kendall sucked on her pulse point for a second longer before pulling back. "You make that very hard."

"Good," Trina replied before pressing a brief kiss to Kendall's lips. "That just means you'll want me more later."

"I always want you," Kendall said, not meaning to be so blunt.

Kissing Trina felt like coming home. And with the amount of uncertainty her father's phone calls had brought her recently, that kiss felt like the stability she needed.

Kendall leaned back in for another kiss, watching Trina lick her lips, when Trina's phone rang, halting her progress. Kendall frowned. "Someone else wants you, too, it seems."

Trina reached for her phone but placated Kendall with a quick kiss first. She sighed when she saw who was calling, silencing her phone and slipping it back into the purse that was next to her on the bench. "It's no one important. Certainly not more important than kissing you under the summer sun."

Kendall shifted on the bench to face her, running her hand through Trina's hair as she admired the strong, intelligent woman sitting beside her. "Oh?"

"Mm-hmm." Trina closed her eyes as Kendall played with her hair. "My mother can wait."

Trina hadn't mentioned her family much except to say that she and her brother got along well, but she freely talked about her niece and nephews. The look of love and pride on her face in those moments was adorable. And since Kendall's family only brought her pain, she was curious about Trina's. "Are you sure? If it's important, I don't want to be the reason you miss it."

Trina opened her eyes as she turned to face her. She put her elbow on the back of the bench and rested her head on her hand while Kendall twirled the ends of her hair between her fingers.

"It's not. I'm sure she's calling to shame me or give me shit about baby Henry's Zhua Zhou. My bet is that she wants her least favorite sister to be put up in my apartment for the weekend so she feels welcome, but not welcome enough to visit more frequently," Trina said. "She's a stress mess over the whole thing."

"What's a Zhua Zhou? Because it sounds important, and now I'm a stress mess about it, too," Kendall said.

Trina laughed that melodious laugh she could never tire of. "In Chinese culture, it's the particularly important first birthday celebration where a baby's destiny is decided when they pick an object that symbolizes a lifelong pursuit or career. Or in our case, it's an elaborate party where the Lees get to show the other Lees, who come from near and far, how much better they are than them," Trina said. "There's some legitimate traditions in there, too, like sharing good wishes and blessings for a fortunate and prosperous existence. But in my experience, my mother turns most of these events into a competition. This is panning out to be more of the same, so I'm avoiding her like the plague that she is," Trina said.

"Do you two talk often?" Kendall asked.

Trina's voice was soft when she replied, "No, we're not that close."

"Why's that?" Kendall asked as she took Trina's free hand and toyed with her fingertips.

"I'm not exactly what they expected, so I think that plays a role in it. But I don't put in a lot of effort either. If you don't like me as I am, then I don't feel the need to prove anything to you," Trina replied, with a slight frown on her face.

Kendall's instinct was to change the subject because Trina seemed like she might get upset, but she wanted to know more about Trina. She wanted to know everything about her. "What do you mean when you say you aren't what they expected?"

"Well, for starters, I'm into women," Trina supplied.

"And I am very grateful for that," Kendall replied.

Trina laughed. "Glad to be of service."

"It's truly exceptional service. I'll fill out a testimonial if you want," Kendall said.

"Please do," Trina replied. "I'm not exactly interviewing other candidates, though, so you can give your comments directly to the source, and they will be heeded accordingly."

"I think you're great in bed," Kendall said. "And I think you're an amazing kisser. And don't tell anyone I said this"—she motioned to the building behind them—"but I think you're a hell of a Realtor, too."

"Your secret is safe with me," Trina said, blowing her a kiss.

She pretended to catch it before returning to her original question. "So what else is there not to like about you? Because I don't see many flaws."

"You're cute," Trina said, avoiding the question.

"And great at oral," Kendall added.

"And that," Trina said before turning serious. "My mother and most of my family are traditionalists. They would rather I was a lawyer or a doctor or married to a nice male lawyer or doctor. The fact that I'm single and in real estate bothers them. I'm selling luxury properties, but my mother thinks I'm selling myself."

Kendall cringed. "Really?"

"Really," Trina said, sounding resigned. "There's no changing her mind, no matter how successful I am. In her mind, my success brings shame to the family. But I'm the only daughter in our little unit, so in a lot of ways, I'm letting her down."

"In her opinion," Kendall supplied. She decided she didn't like Trina's mom.

"My father is less old school and more modern in his approach to things, but he's not in charge when it comes to child-rearing and keeping house. My mother is. That's how those family dynamics work. He and I get along fine, but there isn't any closeness or depth there. Not like how he is with my brother Calvin."

Kendall nodded, taking it all in.

"What about you? Are you close with your family?" Trina asked, and Kendall regretted posing the question to begin with.

"No," she said.

"Just *no*?" Trina pushed. "I gave you a whole spiel, and you give me a monosyllabic *no*?"

Kendall sighed. "I don't like talking about them."

Trina looked hurt. "Is it because I used to call you a spoiled rich kid?"

"Don't you still?" Kendall asked, teasing.

"I mean, I still think it, but I don't say it," Trina said with an easy smile.

Kendall laughed, because even though the conversation was veering toward a topic she disliked discussing, Trina managed to make her feel at ease.

She kissed Trina, nuzzling her nose a bit before replying. She was gathering the courage to be honest with Trina, like Margo had encouraged her to be. Like Trina had been with her. She could do it. She could be honest and vulnerable. She wanted to be vulnerable with Trina, because so far, those instances of vulnerability had been so, so rewarding. And she trusted Trina not to hurt her. She felt safe with her, which never in her wildest dreams of a few months ago would have seemed possible. But now things were different. Kendall was different. And she had Trina to thank for that.

"In the beginning, when we first met, I really disliked you," Kendall said as she leaned back.

Trina's easy smile remained as she said, "The feeling was mutual."

Kendall laughed. "But things are different now."

"I'll say," Trina replied.

Kendall dropped her head, not sure that she could look Trina in the face as she admitted the truth to her. "I disliked you because everything you said about me was true. I was given more opportunities and passes in life than I probably should have gotten, and my family name certainly made things easier for me," she said, looking up to find Trina looking compassionate, not righteous like she could have been. That made her feel better.

"Up until a few years ago, I enjoyed those privileges without remorse. I felt entitled to them, because in my mind, I had suffered enough and deserved them. I was selfish and self-righteous, and in a lot of ways, I know that I still am." She sighed. "The truth is, I don't talk to my family. I haven't seen or spoken to them in years, and I hate my father with a burning passion because he's everything bad you ever thought of me. And there's a part of him in me, which is why all your comments and antagonisms hit me so hard. Because you're right. And you've always been right," Kendall said, feeling overwhelmed by the revelation.

Trina frowned but remained quiet for a moment before she asked, "And when he called that night on the balcony?"

"I freaked. I didn't even know that he had my phone number. It's not like it's impossible to find it or anything, but it'd been over two years since we last spoke," Kendall said, feeling anxious again.

"Why did you stop talking to them?" Trina stilled the nervous movements of Kendall's fingers and held her hand on her lap, caressing her knuckles with her thumb.

"My father is a bad man, and he felt like I was pulling away from his reign of terror after I got engaged, which to be fair, I was. I had every intention to leave his company and start out on my own, and I guess he caught wind of it. So he made my ex-fiancée an offer she couldn't refuse: a leadership position and partial ownership of one of the companies he was expanding on the other side of Connecticut with the stipulation that she had to dump me. It was the kind of dream opportunity that anyone with ambition would jump at since it was a guaranteed success. My father wouldn't let the expansion fail—he's too narcissistic for that—so it would be a life changing promotion. For the ambitious. My ex appeared to be more ambitious than in love with me because she took the offer and left with barely an apology. That was it for me, the last straw. I quit the company and left his control the next day."

Kendall remembered angry crying and rage packing. She'd torn her office apart in her fit to leave and took every file and contact she'd ever made with her. She'd half expected her father to come after her with complaints of theft of company property or whatever, but he didn't. He let her go without much fight, but she'd figured that was because his lawyer and best friend had died around the same time. Maybe her father was in his own stage of mourning and couldn't be bothered with her. Either way, she didn't hesitate to leave. She had considered her departure without immediate retribution to be an amicable divorce from her father and his unruliness. And until recently, it had been.

"And your mother?" Trina asked. She was holding Kendall's hand tightly now.

"She married him and stayed with him even though he's a notorious philanderer and emotional and physical abuser. I offered to take her with me when I left, but she refused. So she can have him. They can rot from the inside together," Kendall said.

She missed parts of her mother but knew that her mother had never been the affectionate, loving type. Her mother and father worked together because they were both selfish, and they each benefited from their union. Kendall knew there was no love between them, and for a long time, she'd had those types of loveless relationships, too. But she thought Collette was different. She'd been wrong.

"Hey," Trina said as she released her hand in favor of lifting her chin, bringing Kendall's gaze up to hers. She brushed away a tear on Kendall's cheek, and Kendall sucked in a sharp breath at the look of empathy on Trina's face, not pity or annoyance, which she thought she might find there. Trina looked at her like her feelings mattered, and Kendall wasn't sure how to process that.

"I don't know your father, but if you tell me he's an asshole, I'm going to believe you. And you know why? Because I misjudged you from the beginning, and I'm learning that maybe I'm not as perfect as I always thought I was either." Trina's playful wink helped to bring levity to the conversation.

Kendall rolled her eyes at that, because of course Trina would think she was perfect. But the more time Kendall spent with her, the more she thought she might be.

"But also, you deserve better than that. You deserve to have a family that loves you and a fiancée who won't dump you for a hand up," Trina said, and Kendall believed her. "That's the one time I don't believe in compromise—you shouldn't have to compromise your happiness for someone else's."

Kendall thought about that. "I don't think I realized you had such a strong opinion about compromise," she said.

Trina nodded. "Sure. When it comes to business, though. Not when it comes to your personal happiness. Ellison taught me a long time ago that compromise is what makes a deal successful. It's how I've honed my business practice. You have to be able to give a little to get a little. And luxury real estate is no different. It's not just a transaction—it's a series of personal relationships that might involve compromise. But that's not a bad thing."

Kendall appreciated that perspective. She could see why Trina was so successful with interpersonal relations. She clearly had a healthy respect for the process and the complex feelings that were involved. "My father would disagree with you. His mentality about compromise has always been the same—compromise means you have to give something up."

"Your father sounds like a fucking jerk," Trina replied.

"He is, but he hides it well, at least initially," Kendall said. "If you met him, you'd think he was charming and friendly, but if he feels even the slightest bit challenged or crossed, he'll snap. He's volatile like that. And violent."

Trina cocked her head to the side, seeming to take this information in. "Lauren mentioned something about your father and jail when we first started working this Harborside project together. I had forgotten, to be honest."

"He's a crook," Kendall said, with disdain. "He should have been in jail longer."

Trina nodded but didn't say anything.

Then something occurred to Kendall. "Did she look me up or something?"

Trina laughed. "Of course she did. She's Lauren."

"What did you find?" Kendall asked, curious.

"That you were engaged to a woman, and that you were a social media ghost for a bit. But that's all," Trina replied.

"You knew about my engagement before—"

"We slept together, and you brought her up while I was naked next to you?" Trina supplied.

Kendall winced. "Not one of my finest moments."

"It's okay—you were adorable about it," Trina said, and Kendall felt better. Marginally.

"When we, before we…" Kendall was struggling to find the words she wanted to say. "You knew about me before I knew about you. And in the beginning, I used to get the impression you were flirting with me and teasing me at the same time. I thought I was just crazy because I was wildly attracted to you and fighting it, but were you—"

"Flirting with you?" Trina asked with a sly smile on her face.

"Yes," Kendall replied.

"Oh, for sure," Trina answered. "Once I knew you were into women, I wasn't about to let my feminine wiles fail me in destroying your ability to focus. I don't lack confidence in that department, as I'm sure you've noticed."

"I've noticed," Kendall said, giving Trina a once-over again. "I notice all the time. And I think about it all the time, too."

"I'm glad to see my diabolical plan to sweep you off your feet is working," Trina joked as she leaned in to tease Kendall with a faint kiss.

"It is," Kendall said as she caught Trina's lips before she pulled away. "Are you busy right now?" she asked, hopeful.

"Define busy," Trina replied, releasing Kendall's hand to rest it on her thigh again. Kendall squeezed briefly before moving her hand a little higher up Trina's thigh.

"I'd like to get you someplace where we can be less PG-13," Kendall said, feeling bare. She was a mix of emotionally drained and sexually charged. She needed Trina. She needed to feel loved and cared for, and desired. "I need to be under you today."

"I'm showing a penthouse later, around sunset. But I can free up a few hours before then. What did you have in mind?" Trina asked between teasing kisses and lip bites. She was driving Kendall crazy.

"Let's get a room with a view," Kendall said, pulling back to look at the nearby Boston Harbor Hotel. "And let's ignore the view entirely."

"Sounds perfect," Trina replied, and Kendall pulled her up into the intimate embrace she was yearning for.

"I'm so glad you found me sitting here today," Kendall whispered into her ear, grateful.

"And I'm so glad you moved to Boston," Trina replied.

As Trina's hand settled in hers and they made their way back to the parking garage, Kendall thought about how happy she was that she made the decision to leave her father and her Connecticut past behind her. She deserved to be happy, and Trina Lee made her happier than she had ever been.

❖

"So, long story short, my father is a monster, and I'm sure he'll drown in the civil suits he's going to face now that he's out of jail. And I'm fine with that," Kendall said in summary, as she poured Trina a glass of wine. "I just wish he'd stop calling me."

They'd had a glorious afternoon together, but there wasn't a whole lot of talking. Now that Trina was back from her showing at the Harborside, they actually had a chance to catch up. It was nice. Well, except for the part where Kendall was filling her in on all the terrible and exhausting things that had been happening with her father. She was glad to know about them, but whew, what a roller coaster.

"This is all so wild," Trina replied as she pulled the sheet up over her naked chest for some modesty—not that they had done anything modest this afternoon, but still, room service would be arriving any minute. "So what happens now?"

"I don't know," Kendall said. "Gratefully, I've been mostly kept out of it."

"Except for the phone calls," Trina pointed out.

"Right." Kendall sighed. "I don't know what he could want. I'm useless to him, and I'm okay with that," Kendall said as she sipped her wine.

"You're not useless to me," Trina said as she pulled Kendall by the lapel of her hotel robe to bring her closer. "I find you very useful."

"Oh? Useful how?" Kendall asked as she placed her glass on the opposite bedside table. She took Trina's once she finished her sip and placed it beside hers.

"Well, for starters, you know how to touch me in all the right ways to make me scream. I, personally, find that very useful," Trina said as Kendall pulled down the modesty sheet and placed her hand on Trina's sternum, pushing her flat against the bed.

"Is that so?" Kendall asked as she leaned over her, and Trina felt her excitement grow with every promising lick of Kendall's tongue on her lips as she spoke.

"Oh, it's very motivating for me, knowing that you can bring me ecstasy with a few well-placed rubs or thrusts. And don't even get me started on that mouth of yours," Trina said as she playfully fanned herself. "It's a miracle we get any talking done at all."

"Talking is overrated," Kendall said as she dragged her thumb over Trina's nipple, causing her to shudder. "I think there are better ways to communicate want than with our mouths."

Kendall's lips closed around Trina's nipple, and Trina felt her tongue flick against the flesh, teasing it. The sensation was making Trina's sex clench with anticipation and want.

"Show me," Trina said between pleased moans.

Kendall sucked harder, the pressure almost painful before she backed off and left wet, languorous kisses along Trina's areola and the top of her breast. Kendall's fingers replaced her mouth as she brought her lips to Trina's pulse point. She worked her way up Trina's neck to settle her lips by Trina's ear.

"My body wants you. She tells me over and over how she needs you. I listen, because she's so loud in her want." Kendall shrugged off the robe, and Trina savored the feeling of Kendall's warm, naked flesh against hers.

Kendall shifted over Trina, straddling her leg, and she lowered herself until Trina could feel her excitement against her thigh. The wetness was almost shocking.

"My body is excited by you, just talking to you. Feeling you. Seeing you. The desire is all-consuming." Kendall's exhale by her ear made her shudder again, this time from arousal.

Kendall ground her hips down, over and over in a slow, purposeful glide along Trina's thigh. The satisfied pants from Kendall's lips turned her on almost as much as the feeling of her arousal on Trina's leg.

"And I'm tight for you," Kendall said as she lifted her hips, guiding the hand that Trina had gripping her hip, encouraging her motion, and placing it between her legs. "Because I know how good you'll fuck me any way I want it. Any way I need it. And I need all of it." Kendall exhaled again as Trina pressed into her. "Yes, like that."

"What else?" Trina asked as she stroked and rubbed inside Kendall, the heat and the pressure around her fingers making her dizzy.

"Oh, and how my lips miss your skin," Kendall said, bringing their lips together as she continued to roll her hips against Trina's hand. "And how they want to taste you while my clit is in your palm. Don't stop. Let me show you how much my body needs you and wants you. Let me show you how wet and tight I get for you."

"And swollen," Trina said against Kendall's lips as she stroked the heated flesh in her hand. Kendall's body was showing her everything she needed and wanted. That was true. And Trina knew, even without Kendall's words, she could read her desire just by touching her. The breathy pants, the pleased whines, those added to the moment, but Trina knew Kendall was already screaming her desire.

Trina increased her pace as she pushed Kendall on her back, climbing over her to claim her, to own her. Kendall said she wanted to come undone underneath her, and she planned to make sure she had a whole night of that.

Trina watched as Kendall closed her eyes, her breathing fast and short as Trina led and teased, drawing every touch out as much as possible.

Kendall whimpered before calling out, and Trina felt her body ignite under her touch. Trina cradled her, kissing her neck as she came down.

Kendall cursed, looking at her with those green eyes that melted her, as she said, "It's never not incredible. Ever."

"Mm, good, baby," Trina said as she kissed the side of her mouth. "And you're right. I don't need you to talk. Your body says everything I need to know, and I love it."

Kendall gave her a bashful smile, and Trina wondered if she said too much. That love word was dangerously close to spilling out. Did she love Kendall? Or did she just really lust after her? She certainly lusted after her. But as Kendall closed her eyes in a happy, sated, relaxed state, Trina's desire to hold her overcame her desire to please her. She wanted to please her, sure, but she wanted to hold her and comfort the woman who'd cried on the bench earlier, the one whose broken family left a broken person. But this creature next to her wasn't broken. She was magnificent and worthy of love and affection and touch. And orgasms. So many of those.

Trina reached for Kendall and wrapped herself around her, ignoring her own thrumming desire in favor of this type of closeness.

Kendall pulled her close and watched her, not speaking for a few long moments. Trina didn't find the intensity of her look to be overwhelming. If anything, she felt flattered by the way Kendall appeared to be taking her all in.

Kendall reached out and touched her face, so gently she was almost not touching her at all. It was like she was afraid Trina might break or something. Her voice was a mere whisper when she said, "You are the best thing to happen to me in a long time, and I know I don't need words to tell you that, because they wouldn't do justice to the way I feel anyway."

Kendall placed Trina's hand over her heart, and Trina smiled at the steady, happy thump below her palm. It was as if Kendall's heart beat only for her. This was a different way Kendall's body was communicating with her. And she loved this just as much as the others.

Chapter Twenty-five

"A re we celebrating tonight?" Lauren asked on the line and Trina adjusted her AirPod to hear her better.

"I have plans with Kendall," Trina said, wincing.

"Seriously?" Lauren sounded mad.

"I know we've been trying to get together more, and I am in no way trying to squash those plans, but I had a dinner date scheduled with Kendall long before Amelia Clarke decided to pull the trigger on that apartment," Trina reasoned.

"A penthouse. Not just any apartment, Trina. Amelia Clarke is buying a penthouse. And that means we need to drink copious amounts of champagne and eat chocolate on your couch in pajamas," Lauren whined.

"It's midweek, and tomorrow is a workday," Trina pointed out.

"When has that stopped us before?" Lauren replied, and she was right. "Fine, be all lovestruck and gooey. But know you owe me when this whole thing is over. I'm thinking a girls' trip someplace tropical."

"What about Jax?" Trina asked, ignoring Lauren's *lovestruck* comment.

"Okay, fine. A girls' and Jax trip. Someplace warm with fruity cocktails," Lauren said, and it sounded like a dream come true.

"I like the sound of that," Trina agreed easily. Lauren and Jax had been busting their asses over the past month since Langley's list had come in. They'd been scheduling and vetting every person who was interested, and to Trina's surprise, most of them were. She'd juggled her own clients, including Amelia Clarke, but most of her recent time had been occupied meeting with Langley's prospects. And she was feeling pretty good about selling another corner unit to one of them. But it had been very, very busy. And trying to get intimate alone time with Kendall that didn't just equate to sex had been challenging. Not that she was complaining about the spontaneous and fantastic sex, but having a meal with her might be nice. Especially since she'd found herself missing Kendall when she wasn't around.

Trina had felt herself getting more attached to Kendall with each tryst, but she felt like they'd reached a pinnacle in their newly budding relationship with that conversation on the bench by the harbor that led to the magical night at the Boston Harbor Hotel. That was the most vulnerable Kendall had ever been with her. In between soft touches and gentle kisses, Kendall shared stories of her life before Boston and of the way her father had tormented her over the years. Once she'd had a better understanding of Kendall's truths and experiences, she felt awful about some of their initial interactions and how often she'd taken easy digs at her because of her family connections. But when she voiced that, Kendall had kissed away her concerns.

There was no way she could have known, and yet she still harbored guilt because deep down she knew that their relationship had changed. This was no longer just an office romance or sexy summer fling. She was starting to get real feelings for Kendall. And if the multiple daily calls and texts were any indication, then she was on Kendall's mind as much as Kendall was on hers.

"I assume you're cooking tonight," Lauren said, knowing her so well.

"I am." Trina picked up a pack of cremini mushrooms and examined them.

Lauren asked, "And what are you making her?"

"Tiger shrimp with oyster sauce and glass noodles," Trina said as she chose an assortment pack that included oyster mushrooms.

"Oh, damn. You're pulling out all the stops," Lauren replied. "Are you making those sticky buns, too?"

"You know it," Trina said.

"I'm drooling, just so you know. You haven't made those in forever. I think I'm jealous," Lauren said.

"Relax, boo. I got you. I'm making a double batch of everything," Trina replied as she checked the contents of her shopping cart. "I'll make your noodles extra spicy. Don't worry."

Lauren squealed. "I love sated and laid Trina. She's so giving and thoughtful."

"Shut up," Trina replied with a laugh. "I'm always thoughtful."

"Okay, fair point," Lauren conceded. "But I'm still saying the prevalence of sticky buns is because she's the best sex you've ever had, and you're bliss baking."

"I can deal with that," Trina replied. Lauren was right. She had been on cloud nine lately. And she knew she had Kendall to thank for that—something she planned to do lots tonight.

"So, not to point out the elephant in the room or anything, but did you plan to talk about the Clarke deal?" Lauren asked, bursting Trina's bliss bubble.

"I don't know. No, I don't think so," Trina replied, worrying her bottom lip a bit. She hadn't planned to say anything, largely because she and Kendall had stuck to that part of their agreement very well. They'd kept work talk out of their personal relationship, unless work interfered with their attempts to get together for an afternoon delight or a cup of coffee and a make out session. Trina was fine with that. They were still invested in a competition after all.

"Well, did you talk about her two contracts from the other day?" Lauren asked.

"Nope. We certainly did not," Trina said. She'd found out earlier in the week that Kendall had contracted two more units, but she hadn't said anything, and Kendall hadn't brought it up. Kendall was ahead, until Clarke contracted, of course. And now Trina had a big lead. She hoped this didn't change things between them, but she wasn't so sure it wouldn't.

"What are you going to do?" Lauren asked.

Trina sighed. "Save my celebrating for you and me time. Tonight I'm going to make dinner and probably have lots of sex, and tomorrow will be another day. Let's get drinks after my last client meeting tomorrow and have a belated celebration. Then have that girls' night you mentioned. And we can pick an island for when this is all over."

"When you win, you mean," Lauren said. "Let's not lose sight of what's most important."

"Right," Trina replied. Because even though the sex was phenomenal, she wasn't about to lose sight of the end goal—winning.

"Have fun tonight," Lauren said. "Love you."

"Love you, too," Trina said as she disconnected. She looked at the contents of her cart and smiled. It had been a long time since she'd made someone a meal like this. It felt nice to plan and prep. She was so looking forward to tonight, and nothing could derail that.

❖

Trina surveyed the kitchen and stovetop: everything was ready to go. The sticky buns were formed and just needed to be heated up, the tiger shrimp were peeled and cleaned and were marinating. The mushrooms were seasoned, and the fresh-cut scallions and baby bok choy were rinsed and prepped. The pot of water was already on the stove for the noodles, leaving her plenty of time to get dressed. This dinner would cook quickly, so she wouldn't start it until Kendall got here for fear of overcooking the shrimp. There was nothing worse than rubbery shrimp.

She took in the open concept living room and dining area to make sure things were perfect. The pillows had been fluffed and chopped, the surfaces cleared of mail and wiped down. The room looked great—not that she expected to spend much time in this area aside from eating. She knew they'd end up in the bedroom, and she was excited about that, but she still wanted the place to look nice. It's been a long time since she'd entertained company with dinner and not just sex. She was a little nervous about it. Like, excited nervous, but nervous all the same. Kendall had a way of doing that to her. The feeling was invigorating. The anticipation she got every time before seeing her was better than foreplay, and so far, the foreplay had been amazing, so that was saying something.

She felt herself getting turned on thinking about Kendall and all the things she wanted to do to her tonight. She pulled at the lapel of her silk robe and closed her eyes as she caressed the skin by her collarbone and upper chest. She'd have to change soon if she wanted to be ready for Kendall. She laughed at the thought. She was already *ready* for Kendall. So ready.

Her cell phone rang, and she smiled when she saw who was calling. "Speak of the devil," she said into the receiver.

"Are we starting the night with name calling or role playing?" Kendall asked.

"Well that depends," Trina said as she looked at the clock on the wall. Kendall wasn't due for another forty-five minutes. "Are you calling to cancel or because you missed me?"

"I always miss you," Kendall replied, and Trina's heart swelled. "And I was calling to tell you I was going to be early, if that's okay with you."

"Early? Excited much?" Trina teased. She was grateful she'd showered and done her makeup already. She just needed to change, so Kendall could come up if she was close.

"You could say that," Kendall replied. That made Trina's clit swell.

"How far away are you?" Trina asked, her desire pooling.

"I'm in your lobby. So a couple dozen floors, a short elevator ride, then just a doorway away," Kendall said, her voice thick with seduction. "Can I come up?"

"I'm not dressed, so you'll have to wait a few minutes when you get here," Trina warned. "But yes, please do."

"Don't get dressed," Kendall said before disconnecting, and Trina shuddered at the implications of the command.

The knock at her door happened sooner than she was expecting. She did a quick hair and makeup check in the mirror in the foyer before she opened the door.

Kendall was waiting, holding a massive bouquet of red and pink flowers and what looked like a bottle of champagne. And though that was a welcome sight, Kendall herself looked great. She was wearing slim-fit dress slacks and heels with a soft-looking flirty top. She had her hair down today, the thick blond waves cascading around her face like a halo. And those eyes sparkled again tonight, bright green and full of sexy flirtation. Kendall looked incredible.

Kendall gave her a once-over as she tugged at the knot holding Trina's robe closed. "I'm glad you heeded my request."

"Was it a request? Because it sounded like a command," Trina replied, catching her breath as Kendall stepped into her space, closing the door behind her.

"Maybe it was a little of both," Kendall said, her lips parted in a small smile. "Come here—I missed your lips."

Trina stepped into Kendall's open arms, and Kendall greeted her with a soft, sensual kiss. The kind of kiss that promised more, in an unhurried way. Trina loved it.

"Let's put this on ice and these in a vase, so I can greet you the way I want to," Kendall said as she licked across her lips, before pulling back. "My hands are too full for me to appreciate that robe. Is it silk?"

Trina took the gifts and turned toward the kitchen, looking back at Kendall as she said, "It is."

"Good," Kendall replied, taking off her shoes. "That means it'll slip off easily."

Trina picked up her pace, eager to be available for whatever Kendall had in mind. She filled a vase with water before depositing the flowers in it, making a mental note to clip the ends later. Kendall washed her hands at the sink as she picked up the champagne and read the label. The Veuve was a nice choice—not too pricey but far from inexpensive. She happened to be a fan of this brand. Kendall had good taste.

"It's cool, but not cold. And I think it should be cold before we open it." Kendall stepped up behind her and looped her arms around her waist. Trina settled into the embrace as Kendall nuzzled the back of her ear.

"Flowers and champagne? You really know how to spoil a girl." Trina turned her head to meet Kendall's lips, but Kendall pulled back teasingly.

"It's not often someone offers to make me dinner." Kendall nuzzled her ear again, dancing her lips along Trina's jaw but avoiding Trina's attempts to kiss her. "Plus, we're celebrating."

"Oh?" Trina asked, not focusing on anything but Kendall's hot mouth on her jaw and the hand that was working on the tie of her robe.

"It's not every day that someone contracts a luxury penthouse sale," Kendall said as she freed the robe tie. Trina inhaled at the rush of cool room air that chilled her skin now that her robe was open.

"I thought we weren't going to talk about work," she said as she closed her eyes to the sensation of Kendall's lips on her earlobe and her hands on her naked stomach.

"I don't plan to do much talking," Kendall said before sucking on her earlobe a bit. "But that doesn't mean I'm not going to acknowledge how exciting that sale is for you."

Kendall flattened her hand on Trina's abdomen, pulling her against her as she slid her other hand down the front of Trina's naked thigh. Trina opened her eyes to watch. She didn't want to miss a thing.

"It is exciting, yes. But maybe not the most exciting part of my day, at least, not anymore," Trina said as she watched Kendall's hand leave her thigh and reach for the champagne.

"Then what is the most exciting part, so far?" Kendall asked as she brought the cool glass bottle close to Trina's upper thigh. She could feel the chill emanating off it.

"This. You," Trina said biting back a hiss as Kendall pressed the bottle against her inner thigh. This bottle was plenty cold, in her opinion. She shuddered in response.

"See? It's cool, but not cold enough," Kendall said as she moved the bottle up, moving dangerously close to Trina's hot, naked sex.

Trina bucked back to avoid the coldness, but Kendall's hips held her in place. She closed her eyes in anticipation when Kendall's lips were at her ear again, asking, "Refrigerator or freezer?"

Trina let out a shaky breath as she felt the bottle move away from her skin. "F-freezer." Trina felt Kendall turn and heard the appliance door open and close but was keenly aware that Kendall kept one hand on her the whole time. A feat that seemed impossible, but Trina didn't question it. Because soon she was being spun on the spot, and she opened her eyes to find Kendall looking at her like she was on the menu for tonight.

"I should show up early every time," Kendall said, speaking directly to Trina's exposed cunt. She pushed Trina's robe open more as she asked, "Are you always naked when you cook?"

"Only when I'm fresh out of the shower and waiting on a hot date," Trina said as she reached out to feel if Kendall's top was as soft as it looked. She grabbed a handful and pulled Kendall to her. The fabric was warm and felt luxurious against her naked chest.

"Lucky me," Kendall said as she finally acquiesced to Trina's attempt at kissing her. Kendall gripped Trina's hips and lifted her up, sitting her on the island that was behind her. "Let's have a little dessert before dinner, okay?"

"Fuck," Trina said between kisses as Kendall spread her legs and stepped between them, her lips on Trina's mouth while one arm hugged her close.

"Hopefully, lots," Kendall said as her free hand returned to teasing the inside of Trina's thigh, stroking and massaging skin with each swipe, moving closer and closer to where Trina ached for her.

After a tauntingly close swipe that made her gasp, Kendall pressed against her, rubbing through her lower lips and teasing her clit while moving through her wetness. Trina moaned into Kendall's mouth as Kendall kissed her with the same attention to detail she was employing at her sex. Trina was so turned on she might come just from the foreplay.

"You're already ready for me. Were you that excited about tonight? Or was it the kissing?" Kendall asked before deepening the kiss and gliding her tongue along Trina's, all too briefly for Trina's liking.

Kendall pressed into her more deliberately, separating her lips and circling her tight opening as she asked, "Or can you tell just how badly I want to be inside you?"

Trina spread her legs farther and reached between, guiding Kendall's fingers inside her with a roll of her hips. The sensation was amplified by the pleased, grateful moan from Kendall's lips against hers.

"Yes," Kendall breathed out, as she moved in and out of her slowly. "I have been dying to feel how tight you are all day."

Trina wrapped her legs around Kendall's waist and scooted forward, so that Kendall bottomed out inside. The depth reached by Kendall's fingers was making her see stars, and she had no intention of slowing the accelerated climb she was on. Not while Kendall held her tight while she continued to kiss her with such a passion that left Trina gasping for breath.

"You feel so good," Trina panted out. "Don't stop."

Kendall spread her fingers a bit, and Trina felt her body accommodate them on the next roll of her hips. The feeling was incredible, so full and so firm. Kendall was hitting every spot she needed her to.

"Kendall," she warned. She was getting close.

"I don't think there's any feeling in the world that feels as good as being inside you," Kendall said against her lips, and Trina came hard and fast in her hand. She might have made it a little longer had Kendall not stroked her desire as much as her pussy. But as Trina rode her orgasm down, slow and drawn out by Kendall's loving, affectionate touch, she started to realize that it wasn't just Kendall's touch that she lusted after. Or the orgasms she gave her so skillfully. It was her affection, too. Her mouth on her ear, her lips on her skin, the way she said all the right things to make Trina come again and again. Trina didn't just *like* sex with Kendall—she loved it. And a part of her was worried that she might be falling in love with Kendall, too. Especially if she kept saying stuff like that.

"I so missed you today," Kendall said as she slid out of her, kissing her face and cheek.

And saying stuff like *that*, Trina thought. "Why today in particular?" she asked as she snuggled into Kendall's embrace. Kendall's shirt felt like the softest, warmest blanket she'd ever touched. The glorious texture against her skin was making her nipples hard. and that sent tiny sparks down to her already overstimulated sex.

"Long day, not enough of you." Kendall nuzzled her nose as she hugged her. "So many of my days don't have enough of you in them." More perfectness—Trina was dying a little.

"That seems like a crime. I'm pretty fun," Trina said, as she tried to insert a little humor to lessen the other feelings Kendall was stirring up.

"You're *so* fun." Kendall kissed her softly. "And I am *so* hungry. Please tell me this food is going to be as good as the ingredients look."

"It will. I promise you'll love the way it tastes," Trina said in full confidence. This meal was a home run.

"As much as I love the way you taste?" Kendall asked, glancing down between them and Trina had to bite the inside of her cheek to calm her libido down.

"No promises. But I tell you what," Trina said as she cupped Kendall's jaw, bringing her gaze back up to her face. "We'll have some dinner, and then I'll let you have some more, for…what did you call it? Dessert? And you can tell me which one satisfies you more."

"That is a plan I can get behind," Kendall said with a playful nip to Trina's bottom lip.

"Oh, I hope you do more than just get behind me. This was a wonderful and unexpected start to the evening, but I hope there's more in our future," Trina said as she reached out and stroked the crotch of Kendall's dress slacks, pleased to hear Kendall moan in response.

"Maybe we should skip dinner," Kendall said in a breathy exhale, her eyes closed as Trina rubbed across the apex of her hips again. "I'll survive a skipped meal if you're the dessert."

"And if I'm the dessert, then what's this?" Trina asked as she maneuvered her hand under the waistband of Kendall's slacks and into the too tight space of the fabric against Kendall's pussy. She was pleased by the heat and wetness she found there.

Kendall shifted her weight, spreading her legs and leaning back to give Trina more space as she flicked the button open on her slacks, before placing her hands on the counter on either side of Trina's hips. Her eyes were dark as she looked at Trina with her mouth open. In short, fast breaths she said, "Anything you want it to be. An appetizer. The whole fucking meal. Anything."

Trina loved how much Kendall desired her. She loved feeling how turned on Kendall was by pleasuring her. She wanted to reciprocate that for her and show her how much she looked forward to their time together. Trina rubbed up and down over the flimsy fabric of Kendall's panties before she moved them to the side and pressed directly against her wetness. The feeling was almost as delightful as the sounds Kendall was making in her ear. The desperate, heated pants of pleasure and excitement. This was the soundtrack that Trina never grew tired of. She wanted more of it, louder and in stereo.

She found Kendall's clit and teased it, moving against it and away as she read Kendall's body's reactions and movements, calculating the force and pressure she should apply and deny to get Kendall more and more excited. She took a page from Kendall's book and licked at the shell of her ear as she said, "I think about fucking you and being fucked by you all day, every day, and I have for longer than I'd like to admit." She placed her forefingers on either side of Kendall's clit and gently squeezed as she added, "But especially since I saw you snap that picture of me during our first tour of the apartments together."

Kendall cried out at the sensation and her hips bucked into Trina's hands as Trina moved away again, teasing but not relenting. Kendall kissed her, keeping their lips close as she asked, "You saw that?"

"Mm-hmm." Trina hummed as she dipped lower, gathering Kendall's wetness before continuing her slow, deliberate stroking. She knew Kendall wouldn't last much longer by the way her breathing and hip movements had picked up.

She rubbed her clit again, this time directly and with more force as she asked, "Did you masturbate to that image of me? I hope you did. I let myself envision what that would look like. I let myself imagine the sexy sounds you would make as you came thinking of me. Sounds like these," Trina said as she increased her pace, and Kendall started to crumple against her, her breathy, melodious noises and exhales telling Trina she had Kendall at the edge. "Did you finish hard and fast, baby? Or was it slow and drawn out?"

"Hard and fast," Kendall admitted, and Trina rewarded her honesty with a blistering kiss.

"Come like that for me now and I promise to make the next one achingly slow and endlessly frustrating. We can drag it out all night. I have so many things I want to do to you," Trina said as she pleasured Kendall more, and Kendall climaxed against her fingers with a muted moan, the sound lost in a kiss Kendall placed against Trina's neck.

As she caught her breath, Kendall rested her head on Trina's shoulder, leaning in to her. Trina kissed the side of her head as she slowed her ministrations before looping her arms around Kendall and pulling her close as she stroked her back and cradled her head. This feeling was almost as good as the orgasms, Trina thought. She loved Kendall's weight against her, her fatigued and sated body in Trina's hands, such a delicate balance of affection and protection. She wrapped her legs around Kendall and pulled her closer still, eliminating any space between them. Kendall replied in kind, her arms tightly encircled around Trina's waist. This was the most complete hug Trina had ever experienced with anyone. And it felt incredible.

She hoped it would never stop, and Kendall seemed to be in no hurry to pull away from her. After forever, but still not long enough, Kendall pulled back.

Trina brushed the hair out of her face as Kendall smiled shyly.

"So, you saw me take the picture, huh?" Kendall asked.

"Sort of, it was more of an educated guess. I saw you taking pictures that day, and though I wasn't sure you got one of me, suggesting that you did felt like a worthwhile gamble," Trina said as she rubbed her thumb over Kendall's kiss-plump bottom lip.

"I think taking this bet was the smartest decision I ever made," Kendall said, and Trina knew she was talking about their working relationship that had now spurred a very legitimate sexual relationship.

"Me, too," she said as she wondered if a romantic relationship that evolved to more would be in the cards for them. Could she maintain this passion and attraction after the contest had ended? Or was competition driving some of this attraction she felt? She wasn't so sure. Because in moments like this, work and beating Kendall were the last things in her mind. Pleasing her, on the other hand, was front and center. And in some ways, that made Trina a little nervous. Was she losing her edge because Kendall was incredible in bed? Or had she been without human affection and this type of intense, compatible sexual attraction in so long that she was ignoring red flags? Trina decided in that moment that if this was the feeling that came with ignoring red flags, she was fine with it. Because for the first time in a long time, Trina felt loved and cared for and lusted after and protected. She felt safe in Kendall's embrace. She had no problem being vulnerable with Kendall, and that was the biggest revelation of all—Kendall made her want to be vulnerable. Something that had never happened this quickly in a relationship before.

Kendall sighed, but Trina could tell it was a happy sigh. And that made her heart flutter. "Ready for dinner?" she asked as Kendall pulled back from their embrace.

"Absolutely," Kendall said. She looked down and added, "You might want to put on clothes, though. I mean, I could watch you cook naked all day, but I feel like you might get cold. And then I'd want to warm you up, and then we'd end up doing all that again, and we'd get nowhere. Which I'd also be fine with, but you seem to have gone to some trouble with this meal prep and it'd be a shame to waste it all."

Trina laughed as she pulled her robe back on and closed it as Kendall helped her off the counter.

"You're so thoughtful," she teased.

"Mostly I'm hungry. And I'm not going anywhere until you throw me out, so I think we'll have time to revisit our, uh, welcome greeting after dinner," she said with a wink.

"Good," Trina said as she went to the stove to start warming the ingredients. In no time the smell of fresh garlic, scallions, mushrooms, and bok choy cooking filled the space.

When Trina passed Kendall to deposit the glass noodles in the pot, Kendall's hand settled on her naked thigh. "You're still barely dressed. The food smells great, but you are distractingly beautiful and hardly clothed. Still. You're making this a challenge," Kendall said as she kissed her neck.

"I'll toss on some clothes—you pop the champagne," Trina said, after she let herself appreciate the attention Kendall paid to her pulse point. She shifted out of Kendall's grasp to head toward the bedroom as she added, "The glasses are to the left of the sink, on the top shelf."

"Maybe don't bother with underwear, though," Kendall called out.

Before Trina could reply, someone rang her doorbell.

She stopped her progress toward the bedroom and turned.

"Are you expecting someone else?" Kendall asked, holding up three flutes instead of two.

"No, absolutely not," Trina said. "I'm not interested in sharing you."

"You should tell that to whoever is behind door number one," Kendall said as she opened the champagne bottle with a satisfying *pop*.

Trina tightened the robe around her chest and marched to the door, ready to tell whoever dared to interrupt her date night to fuck off. She had to get up on tiptoe to look through the peephole, and to her surprise, her brother and her nephews were on the other side. And Calvin looked panicked.

"Cal," she said, opening the door. "What's wrong?"

"Lisa is at a Girl Scout sleepover with Hannah, and Dexter took a softball to the face at his game and I can't get his nose to stop bleeding, so I have to take him in to get it cauterized," Calvin said, exasperated.

"Oh, buddy," Trina said as she looked at Dexter and frowned. "You okay?"

"I'm fine." His response was mumbled, largely, she would bet, due to the massive wad of tissues he had stuffed up his right nostril. "We won the game," he said with an obstructed smile.

"Well, then it was all worth it, huh?" she asked as she ruffled his hair.

Calvin pushed past her, juggling baby Henry and two large bags, one of which Trina recognized as Henry's diaper bag, but the other, she had no idea about.

"Anyway, Henry has a cold and I don't want to take him to the hospital if I don't have to because who knows how long we'll be there. So I need you to watch him for a bit. I brought his diaper bag and his Pack 'n Play, and—" Calvin stopped. "You have company."

"I do," Trina said, glancing over her shoulder to find an amused looking Kendall leaning against her counter, holding two full champagne flutes.

"And you're making dinner...Tiger shrimp? You're making tiger shrimp?" Calvin looked scandalized. "This is a date. Crap. Okay, um, I should have taken the hint when you didn't answer your phone."

"But you didn't and now you're here," Trina said, knowing he would only ask for her help if he was desperate, and the bright red cheeks on Henry's tired looking face told her he was. Henry looked rocked, and Calvin looked overwhelmed.

Calvin shrugged. "You're en route to Children's, so I figured it was worth a shot."

"We'll watch him," Kendall supplied from behind her shoulder. Kendall seemed to have abandoned their drinks in favor of proposing a ridiculous plan.

"We will?" Trina asked as she watched Kendall reach for Henry.

"Sure," Kendall replied, smiling as Henry went right to her, snuggling into her chest and closing his eyes with a yawn.

"Great." Calvin exhaled before seeming to realize he didn't know who the attractive blonde holding his son was. "And you are?"

"Kendall, Kendall Yates," she said, extending her hand to him as she cradled Henry with her other one.

"Oh, damn," Calvin said as he shook her hand. "You're *that* Kendall."

"Are there other Kendalls?" Kendall asked Trina, again looking amused. Trina was not as amused.

"Not that she mentioned to me," Calvin said as he looked at Trina and gave her a once-over. "Silk robe, fancy dinner, champagne, archnemesis, and archnemesis's lipstick on your earlobe. That's some date."

Trina reflexively grabbed her right ear, and Kendall laughed beside her. "Shut up. Go. We'll watch him."

"Thanks," Calvin replied, looking relieved. "It was nice to meet you, Kendall. Oh, I'm Calvin, by the way, her favorite brother."

"My only brother," Trina corrected. "My options are limited in the favorite department."

Calvin laughed. "Thanks again. I'll call you when I'm on my way back here to pick him up. He's got some dinner in the lunch pail and—"

"Cal, go." Trina ushered him and Dexter toward the door. "I know how to keep him alive. He'll be fed, dry, and sleeping when you get back. Just don't forget to come back for him."

"Maybe do, he's cute," Kendall said, and Trina's heart melted a little as she saw how entranced Kendall was with her littlest nephew.

"All right. Thanks again," Calvin said.

"Go," Trina said good-bye but not before kissing Dexter on the head. He must have been scared. She would have been if she was in his shoes.

As she closed the door and turned around to find her girlfriend slow dancing with her baby nephew, the night's interruption seemed less of a burden and more of an opportunity to get to know Kendall better. Or fall more in love with her.

Chapter Twenty-six

Kendall made another loop around the living room, humming softly as she went, making sure baby Henry was snuggled close.

The evening had gone in a hugely different direction than she had anticipated, but she wasn't bothered by it. She'd loved it. Because tonight she'd gotten to see a different side of Trina.

The night had started off with an immediate spark. Their chemistry, once she'd been able to recognize what that was between them, was off the charts as usual. Kendall was in awe at how quickly she and Trina could heat things up. She'd never had a lover who felt as compatible as Trina did. There was just something about the way she moved and talked and kissed and fucked. Trina hypnotized Kendall, like she was under a spell. She loved it. And tonight was no different, except for the slightly sick sleeping baby cradled to her chest. That was unexpected, and yet also lovely.

"You okay? Want to trade?" Trina asked as she dried off her hands at the kitchen sink.

"I'm good. Selfishly, I'm loving this and don't want to give him up," Kendall replied honestly. Trina had fed him and tried to put him down in the Pack 'n Play that Calvin had left for them, but Henry was so congested that he just kept waking up and crying. The only way they could get him to sleep was by holding him upright a bit and bouncing him. They'd taken turns during dinner, but Kendall took over when Trina started to clean up. And she was just as happy, because she could watch and interact with Trina while scoring all the baby snuggles. It was the best of both worlds. Plus, she couldn't remember the last time she'd gotten baby snuggles like this. And Henry was an A-plus snuggler, much like his aunt.

Trina nodded in understanding as she said, "Yeah, he's certainly a lovebug. Hannah was like that when she was little, but Dexter had places to be, things to destroy, no time for cuddles."

"He seemed sweet at the door," Kendall recalled. He also seemed brave, because that could be a traumatizing experience. She probably would have quit softball after an incident like that.

"He's very sweet. And sure of himself. I never worry about Dexter—he'll do fine in the world," Trina said as she hand-dried the last dish from dinner. A dinner so amazing that Kendall wanted to relive it over and over again. Trina was a talented chef, among her other talents, it seemed.

"Where did you learn to cook like that?" Kendall asked. She'd never been much of a homemaker. She had a few things she could whip up, but her repertoire was limited.

"My mother and grandmothers, mostly," Trina replied as she poured them each a glass of water. "I usually order in most nights, but I like cooking. It's just a tricky thing to do for one person. Like, I'm too lazy."

"Or just tired after killing it out in the world all day," Kendall supplied. That's what she told herself about her own lack of cooking inspiration.

"Or that," Trina said as she leaned against the counter looking adorable.

Henry shifted in her arms, but she could tell by the quick jerk of movement that he was fast asleep. She took one last walk around the room before slowly lowering herself to the comfortable looking chaise she'd been eyeing since dinner was over.

She watched Trina now, on tiptoe, attempting to put the last of tonight's dishes away. Kendall allowed herself the opportunity to appreciate the way Trina's yoga pants hugged her ass and the way her loose-fitting off-the-shoulder shirt hiked up as she reached, exposing a little of her toned stomach. Kendall could tell by the lack of panty lines on the yoga pants that Trina had skipped the undergarments like she'd asked. Kendall smiled at that.

"What are you smiling about?" Trina asked as she sat next to her on the couch, so close that Kendall could rest her free hand on Trina's knee.

"I was just thinking about how even in clothes, you look gorgeous," Kendall replied, as Trina passed her a glass of water to sip. She handed it back to Trina to put on the table in front of them and she settled back into the soft chaise with her bundle of snuggles.

"Careful. I can't attack your face like I want to without waking Henry. And if you keep that up, I'm not going to be able to contain myself," Trina replied, taking Kendall's hand into hers as she lounged next to her.

"I'll make it up to you later," Kendall said, leaning as close to her as sleeping Henry would allow. She pressed a sweet kiss to Trina's lips as she vowed, "I promise."

"I'm going to hold you to that. We have unfinished business to attend to," Trina said as she ran her thumb over Kendall's knuckles.

"Really? Because I'm pretty sure you finished just fine," Kendall said, recalling the start of their night with a happy, lazy grin.

"So did you," Trina retorted, her perfect lips parted in the most delightful way as she teased her. "But I think we both know there is more fun to be had."

"I won't argue with that." Kendall could think of a few more things she'd like to do with Trina.

"Unless...I mean, I never asked, but do you have to be somewhere? Things got a little hijacked and I realize if you need to bail, you got a little stuck," Trina said, motioning toward Henry.

"Are you kidding me? This is pretty much my idea of a perfect date night: flirting, kissing, fooling around, a wonderful meal, great champagne with even better company, and endless baby love. I mean, the only thing that would make this night better would be if someone rubbed my feet and told me I'm pretty," Kendall joked.

"Well, when you put it that way," Trina said as she slid off the couch and settled on the floor before Kendall. She reached out and took one of Kendall's feet in her hands, caressing it before massaging it. "I happen to think you are very pretty."

Kendall swooned. Trina's touch felt amazing. Her night was made. "Well, I happen to feel the same way about you, so we're in good company."

They settled into a comfortable silence as Trina worked the sore muscles of her feet with expert precision. The heels she wore to work did a number on her arches, something Trina seemed to notice as she paid extra attention to those spots.

"I know I told you before, but your place is gorgeous. Really, every detail is so spot-on and beautiful," Kendall said, realizing she felt that way about Trina, as well.

"Thanks. To be fair, most of this was done before I moved in. The last owner was a single matchmaker who got hitched and moved to a house in the burbs. She had a real eye for design. I didn't have to change much," Trina replied.

Kendall noticed the splashes of red throughout the mostly white and black space. Trina's place had a nice blend of many different style approaches. The splashes of red tied the styles together nicely.

"I just assumed based on this space and your wardrobe, but maybe I should ask—is red your favorite color?" Kendall asked.

Trina smiled up at her. "It is, but that's just a coincidence."

"What do you mean?" Kendall asked.

"The whole nature or nurture debate. Red in Chinese culture is good luck. It represents strength and prosperity and joy, happiness, stuff like that. It's a celebratory color. I happen to be a fan of it, but some of that, I admit, is probably based in the familiarity of cultural comfort habits," Trina replied with a shrug.

"I think you look incredible in red," Kendall said, as she thought about her favorite picture of Trina, the one from the magazine article. "But I also think you look incredible in nothing, so…"

"You're so smooth. I think I'll keep you."

"Please do," Kendall said. She wondered what Trina meant by that. The more time she spent with her, the more she found herself missing her when she wasn't around. Kendall wondered if Trina felt the same way. She was being honest earlier when she'd said this was her idea of a perfect date night. She couldn't remember another time when she'd laughed so freely or felt so entirely loved. Trina's attention to detail and her little touches throughout the night made Kendall feel special in a way that she hadn't in a long time. Trina made her feel so many things that they overwhelmed her, but the feelings also snuck up on her in a way. And tonight was the perfect example of that. Kendall loved how easily Trina chatted about her niece and nephews and her brother. She'd talked a little more about her family heritage and some of the struggles she'd faced growing up. And even when some topics bordered on deep, every conversation segue still managed to feel normal and natural. There were no awkward pauses or uncomfortable silences. And Kendall loved watching Trina interact with Henry, the way she sang to him in English and Chinese and Vietnamese and tried to teach Kendall those bits of her childhood, too. She loved her nephew, and it was so apparent. Kendall hadn't expected this softer side of Trina, the family side, the loving, selfless side. There were so many layers to this woman she had yet to discover.

But what Kendall most enjoyed was how Trina shared her affection, so earnestly and without seeming to expect anything in return. Kendall found that she wanted to be more loving to her in those moments. She felt drawn to her. She wanted Trina to know she appreciated the freedom and frequency of her touch. This foot massage was no different. She hadn't been fishing, yet Trina had happily obliged. And what she was doing felt heavenly.

"If you keep that up, I might marry you," Kendall said, without thinking.

Trina laughed. "Can you imagine the look on Whitaker's and Ellison's faces?"

"I feel like Ellison would give an awesome wedding gift," Kendall joked.

Trina nodded in agreement. "Oh, totally. She's the best."

The conversation switch toward work should have changed the temperature of the room, but for Kendall it didn't, probably because in Kendall's opinion it had happened so organically. Much like her decision to bring flowers and champagne tonight in celebration of their date, but also of Trina's success. She knew she should probably be mad about Trina's penthouse sale, but she wasn't. She felt happy for her. It was a weird headspace to want good things for Trina but also to want good things for herself. So far, they'd managed to straddle two worlds, but she knew that delicate balance would shift soon. She wondered what would happen to their budding relationship when that happened. Could she keep Trina in her life if Trina lost this bet? Or could Kendall maintain this if she was the one that lost? Could she even lose?

A few months ago, she would have confidently said no, but she had underestimated Trina. And the more time she spent with her, the more she saw just how special and talented Trina was. She had a way with people that was sort of mystifying to Kendall. She put everyone at ease and managed to make them feel special, seemingly with no effort at all. Some of it was small stuff, remembering their birthday or favorite coffee order. But Kendall had taken mental notes, and time and time again, Trina had shown up and celebrated each individual person in a way that was so intentional and so pure, it was easy to see why those closest to her cherished her. The bonds she had with her colleagues and friends were tight. So though Trina had a reputation for being ruthless in the real estate business, Kendall was beginning to see that most of that was negative hype and not fact. Because the woman before her was kind and gentle and thoughtful. Shrewd, intelligent, and bold, also, but not malicious. Trina Lee was as beautiful on the inside as she was on the outside, and Kendall didn't know what to do with that information.

"You may have found my kryptonite." Kendall sighed. "I had no idea I needed this so badly."

"You better be careful, we Chinese-Vietnamese folks know a thing or two about reflexology," Trina said as she pressed her thumb into a particularly tender point on the sole of Kendall's foot that resulted in her wincing before sighing in relief. "I shall make you bend to my every whim with a single touch."

"You already do that to me," Kendall replied, not meaning to be so candid. But once it was out in the air between them, she was glad to have said it. "I would probably do anything you'd ask me to. Your touch is addictive."

"You say that like it's a bad thing," Trina teased.

"It is and it isn't," Kendall replied. "It is because I appear to have less and less willpower around you, but it isn't because I so, so love the way you make me feel."

Trina seemed touched by that comment and Kendall wanted her closer. "Come here, come closer," she said as she reached for Trina, exhaling happily as Trina settled against her side.

She closed her eyes at the combined warmth of Trina and Henry, savoring the grounded feeling of Trina's arm across her waist. This felt so incredibly right to her.

"I'll take him." Calvin's voice startled her. She hadn't realized she'd fallen asleep.

Calvin was standing over her, holding Henry's bags. His expression was kind, but he looked tired. Kendall shifted Henry off her chest and into his arms, careful not to wake him.

Calvin scooped up his son and nodded toward Trina, who slept soundly at her side, curled up next to her on the chaise. "Tell her I said thank you and that I'll call her tomorrow. I have to run—Dex is asleep in the car, and I don't want him to wake up and panic that I'm not there."

"Will do," Kendall said, her voice heavy with sleep.

Calvin got two steps from the couch before he turned back at her, his expression solemn. "Don't hurt her, Kendall. She's my sister, and she deserves the best. And she doesn't make tiger shrimp for just anyone, so if she thinks that you're the worth her time, then you probably are."

"I won't," Kendall said, and she meant that.

"Good night," he said as he left the apartment as whisper-quiet as he'd entered.

Kendall looked at the beautiful creature in her arms and thought about what Calvin said. She had no intention of hurting Trina, but she knew that their path was uncertain. But her feelings about Trina were anything but uncertain. She was falling in love with her and there was nothing she could do about it.

Trina shifted in her arms, looking up at her sleepily as she asked, "Where's Henry?"

"Calvin came and got him," Kendall said as she sat up. "C'mon, baby. Let's go to bed."

Trina yawned and stretched but took Kendall's hand without complaint. And as Kendall pulled back the covers of Trina's bed and crawled in next to her, she had to do everything in her power not to say what was on her mind as she kissed Trina good night. She wasn't ready yet, or at least, she wasn't brave enough to be ready yet. But that was the hardest swallowed *I love you* she had ever tasted.

CHAPTER TWENTY-SEVEN

Trina stared at the whiteboards in front of her, lost in thought. The past few weeks had been a whirlwind. She only knew what day it was because Jax had been so kind as to start texting her morning reminders after she misdated a dozen or so legal documents earlier in the week that resulted in everything having to be reprinted and re-signed. It wasn't that she wasn't paying attention, but a lot had been happening. And gratefully, her team had her back.

After Amelia Clarke contracted the penthouse, things had progressed quickly at the Harborside. Langley's tighter deadline was clearly being felt by the workers and Zander. The apartments were all effectively complete, minus the last penthouse. There had been some measuring error in the ordering of some windows or something. It wasn't really anything she was concerned about since she didn't have anyone interested in the space.

Kendall closed on two more of the midsize units the week of the penthouse deal, and though Trina was ahead in sales, Kendall had contracted more apartments, and with the commercial space rental, they were neck and neck in the competition. Trina really needed to sell one of the remaining two units, but one of them was the monstrous, unfinished penthouse. She was sure the perfect buyer existed for that space, but she just didn't have a clue who that might be.

And try as she might, staring at the whiteboard wasn't revealing any new ideas to her.

"Oh, I didn't know you were in here," Jax said, pausing as they opened the conference room door.

"I'm just hoping and praying that if I stare at this monster long enough, some revelation will occur," Trina said, defeated.

"Any luck with that so far?" Jax asked.

"None, it's been a fruitless staring contest between me and the wall. And I think the wall has won," she said with a sigh.

"I'm glad I found you, actually," Jax said, looking a little nervous. "What's up?"

"Well, you know how I've been going over the social media aspect and keeping up your brand representation with posts and blogs?" Jax asked.

"Yeah, and you've been killing it. I haven't had to worry about a single post in months. You're a champion," Trina said, meaning every word.

"Right. Thanks. Glad to help," Jax said. "But that's not all I've been doing."

Trina paused, evaluating them. Jax was shifting their weight from foot to foot, and wringing their hands. Something was wrong. "Why do I get the feeling you're about to drop a bomb on me?"

"Because I am." Jax frowned. "Kendall contracted the last regular unit today."

"Oh," Trina replied, feeling a pang of disappointment. She wanted to be happy for Kendall, but that meant her lead might be over, and the only way to win was to unload the impossible-to-sell remaining penthouse. She should feel happy for Kendall, and she did, but she also kind of didn't. It was a complicated feeling, much like all feelings associated with Kendall lately.

She was all over the place with Kendall these days. Her attraction to her increased with every exchange they had, but so did her deeper feelings for her. The love ones. Because try as Trina might to ignore them, they were there. And they were getting louder by the moment. Which didn't help their previously healthy competition. Because work was slowly seeping into her happy. Even though she tried to keep them apart, Kendall beating her in this competition would certainly wound her ego. But if she still had her as a bedroom partner? And a lover? A girlfriend, even? Would that outweigh the loss? Or make it worse?

Jax held up their hand. "I ran some numbers, and I've been doing some searching and, well, I think we need to talk."

Trina braced herself. "I'm listening."

Jax let out a heavy sigh as they walked over to the whiteboard wall. Trina watched as Jax added a blue *K* to the last unit on the little blueprint design they had drafted. Then Jax moved to the totals column and notated the amount the unit was contracted to sell for and what Kendall's final sales total would be. Trina was afraid to look at the number. She closed her eyes, trying to calm the anxiety that threatened to settle in her chest.

Jax cleared their throat and Trina hazarded a glance.

"How?" Trina asked as she gaped at the numbers before her. She was still in the lead. Narrowly, barely, but still in the lead. "How is that possible?"

"Well, that's the thing. It shouldn't be," Jax said. "You should be behind, marginally, but you aren't. So I ran the numbers again and again, and I looked at the contract for this unit, and Kendall sold it for under asking."

"What? Why?" Trina asked. That didn't make any sense. These units were priced high but were fair market value. There was no need to undersell a unit—the demand had been there so far. And yes, they were getting close to the accelerated end date, but still, the last corner unit should have gone to a bidding war. Trina had been counting on one. "Why would Langley agree to that?"

"Right. So that's part of the bomb I have to drop," Jax said, looking worried.

"The bomb isn't that Kendall sold the last sellable fucking unit?" Trina asked, incredulous.

"No." Jax sighed.

"Sorry I'm late," Lauren said as she threw open the conference room door. She stopped short when she noticed Trina. "Oh, you're here."

Trina looked between her friends and asked, "Why do I get the feeling that I'm the last to know about something important?"

"Because you are," Ellison said as she walked in, closing the door behind her. "What did I miss?"

"Just the numbers adjustment," Jax said, looking even paler than a minute ago.

"What's going on here?" Trina asked, starting to panic.

"Jax has been doing some data collection throughout the competition, like I asked. Initially, it was truly only that—collection of data and stats as a way for us to tweak our business plan and improve upon future sales with future new builds since the Seaport has been so newly developed lately," Ellison said, her expression serious.

"Okay," Trina said, eyeing Lauren as she moved to sit next to her, when every other seat at the table was wide open. "So?"

"So," Lauren said, taking her hand, "we noticed something about the data."

"You're freaking me out a bit," Trina said, finding little comfort in Lauren's contact.

"When Langley introduced his preferred buyer list to you and Kendall and told us he planned to shorten the deadline, I started to do a little more research on the contracts that came in, because I noticed a trend," Jax replied, still looking sickly.

"Which was what?" Trina asked.

"Kendall was moving units twice as fast as you were. From the same list of potential buyers," Ellison supplied.

"Don't make me say that's because she's a better Realtor," Trina said, not wanting to accept that narrative.

"She's not," Lauren said defiantly. "That's the thing, it's rigged."

"What are you talking about?" Trina asked. Lauren's expression lacked Jax's nervousness—hers was one of anger. "What's going on?"

Ellison said, "Trina, we went back over the list Langley gave us. We thought Whitaker had arbitrarily split the list between the two of you, alternating every other name on the list. But it wasn't done arbitrarily. Jax found a pattern in the list Kendall was given."

Trina waited for one of them to elaborate.

"Dick Yates is the pattern. It turns out that Langley used to be a member at Dick's preferred country club, so we think they might have been friendly," Lauren said, squeezing her hand. "Jax found that most of the names on Kendall's list had a connection to past business dealings with her father. Some more diluted than others, but others, well, others were blatant."

Trina didn't want to believe what they were saying. She could deal with being beaten by Kendall on their own terms, if Kendall had in fact outsold her. She might be miserable to be around for a while, but she would survive. But if everything Kendall told her was a lie *and* she'd been helped, all along, that was something Trina couldn't stomach.

"Then I went back over both of your numbers from last year, and I saw that Kendall closed a deal on the final bank day of the year, which, as you know, is like a Hail Mary," Jax said. "I got the idea to look into that more closely when Lauren forwarded me that information about Dick Yates being convicted of fraud. Anyway, long story short is that Kendall sold that property to the daughter-in-law of one of the people named as a defense witness in his trial."

Trina pulled her hand away from Lauren, feeling betrayed. "You've been looking into Kendall this whole time?"

Lauren shook her head. "No. I haven't. I swear. Once you two shacked—" Lauren paused, looking at Ellison.

"You don't have to censor yourself on my behalf," Ellison dismissed her concern. "I was outside the bar the night of the fundraiser. I saw the kiss."

Trina felt her ears heat up in mortification. Ellison knew about her and Kendall?

"Well, okay," Lauren said, looking guilty. "Right, so, no. I didn't. I promise you I only did that original deep dive that we talked about before you two started, uh, dating."

"She's telling the truth. I just have a bizarre memory for names," Jax said, supporting Lauren. "I dated a girl in high school with the same last name as her Hail Mary sale. I noticed it when I was looking over the data we had been collecting because it was familiar to me. Anyway, the person Kendall sold the final unit to today has the same last name. That's the unit she's selling for under asking price. Evidently, they're related somehow."

Trina had gotten plenty of referrals from family members and sold within families, so that wasn't unusual. But the connection to Dick Yates was. Trina felt like she was going to faint.

"Do you have any solid proof that Kendall knew about these connections?"

Lauren and Jax looked between each other but said nothing.

Ellison replied, "No. We don't. It's only speculation."

"I mean, it feels pretty rock-solid to me," Lauren added, the anger from before present on her face again. "How could this many coincidences align so perfectly? She's cheating, Whitaker is obviously in on it since he helped divide the names on the list, and she's just as crooked as her father. And don't get me started on the Langley connection."

Trina's head was spinning. She needed some air. "I need a minute to wrap my head around this."

Ellison stood, motioning for Lauren and Jax to leave with her. Lauren took Trina's hand once more and squeezed it. Trina reciprocated, glad to have her friend by her side, but also heartbroken.

Ellison closed the door after they left and turned back to face her.

"Listen," she said, her voice soft, almost maternal. "I meant what I said before. We have a whole lot of speculation and not a ton of hard evidence. Otherwise I'd call this whole thing off right now. I'll be honest with you—I'm having Jax and some other people look into it more, but the point of telling you was to make you aware of the situation. So you can protect yourself."

"You mean from Kendall," Trina replied.

Ellison frowned. "I overhead Lauren and Jax talking the other day about you two. I saw the kiss, but I admit, I didn't realize it was serious or that you two might be dating." She sighed. "Clearly, I underestimated things. So yes, Kendall is certainly among the people you should protect yourself from."

"Too late," Trina muttered, feeling lost and a little nauseous.

"I know you have a lot to process, so I'll leave you to it," Ellison said as she gave her a sympathetic look. "But I'll be in my office if you want to talk. We're here for you, Trina. Always."

Ellison closed the door behind her, and Trina felt the walls around her cave in. She didn't hear the door open again, but she felt Lauren's arms around her, holding her as her sobs and the reality of the situation consumed all the air in the room. She was in love with Kendall Yates, and Kendall Yates had been lying to her all along.

CHAPTER TWENTY-EIGHT

Kendall checked her phone before nervously tapping her fingers on the steering wheel.

She had had restless nights the last week, worrying herself over Trina. Things had been getting more and more serious between them, and Kendall was finally ready to admit that she was invested more than she ever anticipated being. She was in love with Trina, and if she didn't tell her, she was going to explode. Which in and of itself would be stressful and make her feel vulnerable.

But something in the last week had changed between them, and she wasn't quite sure what it was. Trina had slowed their text exchange, and when she did respond, her texts were brief. She sent Kendall to voice mail when she called and hadn't been available at all, in any capacity, even for coffee. And Kendall got it, she really did. They were in a sprint to the finish line, and they had a penthouse to sell. But only a penthouse, because Kendall had contracted the last individual unit there was, something that probably wouldn't have happened if she hadn't gotten a referral from an old client of hers, and if she hadn't been able to convince Langley to be flexible on the price. But she knew he wanted to wrap up the Harborside project, so she figured it was worth pursuing, and she'd been right.

Part of her was worried that maybe Trina was avoiding her because the competition had finally come between them. She'd hoped, maybe foolishly, that they could keep their relationship going while the competition raged on. And they seemed to do a good job of it. Kendall went out of her way to make sure she didn't gloat or brag about her sales, because, honestly, she hadn't felt the need to. When they were together, she only wanted to focus on them. Because Trina deserved her entire attention. And anything that happened outside those walls, outside the bedroom, didn't matter. And Kendall had finally allowed herself to admit that.

Now if only she could tell Trina that to her face, maybe she could thaw the frost that had settled between them. Her feelings for Trina hadn't changed—they'd only intensified. But had Trina changed her mind? Kendall worried most about that. She had thought they were on the same page. She had felt like their last few times together had been making love, not just having sex. She had seen the way Trina looked at her, lovingly, deeply, the way you look at someone who means the world to you. She'd felt loved, wholly and entirely, when she was in Trina's presence and in her embrace. But what had changed? What had Kendall done to ruin the best thing that had ever happened to her?

She had to find out, because she couldn't sleep at night knowing that she might have missed her chance to tell Trina she loved her. Because maybe her inability to say it was exactly why Trina pulled away. Trina had always been vulnerable and open with her. She never hid her affections or her feelings. But Kendall had. Because she'd steeled her life around hiding her softest most fragile parts. The same parts that Trina loved so easily. How had she fucked this up?

So she drummed her fingers on her steering wheel and worked up the nerve to find out why Trina was being so distant and if she'd lost her opportunity at happiness. Because the only happiness Kendall could recall in the last two years, the only real happiness she had felt, had been when she was with Trina, or thinking about Trina, or kissing Trina, or waking up next to Trina. Trina was the common denominator in her happiest memories, and she needed to get that back.

The concierge was on the phone as she walked in. He gave her a broad smile and waved her past, which she was grateful for since she hadn't figured out what she would say to anyone, let alone Trina.

Kendall watched the elevator numbers flick by and let out a shaky exhale when the doors opened to Trina's floor. She was nervous, but she didn't know why. They hadn't ended their last time together on bad terms, but she just had a feeling that something was wrong. Trina had never been distant with her, not once they'd started their physical relationship. But that had changed.

She stopped outside of Trina's door and texted her once more. *Are you home?*

No reply. No surprise. She wasn't even sure if Trina was home—she'd found herself in the car driving here before she'd mapped out a plan. She just had this gut feeling that she had to be face-to-face with

Trina and have an organic exchange. Because she was worried if she overthought it, she'd back out. And she had no intention of leaving here tonight without telling Trina how much she meant to her. To tell her how much she had changed since meeting her and how badly she wanted to continue their courtship after the competition ended. She wanted to tell her how little she cared about the competition. She needed to get some of this off her chest because it was making her feel like she was suffocating.

She knocked at the door and held her breath. What did she have to lose?

"That was fast," Trina said as she opened the door, but Kendall watched her happy expression drop off when she saw her. "Kendall."

"Hey," Kendall replied but she got the impression she wasn't who Trina was expecting. "Expecting someone else?"

"Lauren," Trina said, her expression unreadable. "What are you doing here?"

That wasn't the reception Kendall was hoping for.

"I was in the neighborhood," Kendall lied. "And I was hoping we could talk."

"About what?" Trina asked, leaning against her doorframe with her arms crossed over her chest. The posture was defensive, and so was the lack of invitation in.

"Us," Kendall said, feeling like her window was closing. "I meant to tell you something last time we were together, and I didn't. I haven't been able to stop thinking about it. And I miss you," Kendall said, reaching out to touch Trina's hand only to recoil when Trina leaned away from her touch.

"You missed the sex, you mean." Trina's reply had an edge to it. "I guess the dry spell has not been to your liking."

"What?" Kendall *had* missed the sex, but only as an afterthought. She'd missed Trina.

Trina looked at her with indignation. She hated it.

"When were you going to tell me that Langley and your father used to play golf together?" Trina asked.

"I don't know what you're talking about," she replied, feeling blindsided.

"And when did you plan to mention that the last sale you made last year, the one that put you into position for Realtor of the Year, came from one of your father's connections?" Trina asked. "Sometime between lying to my face and making me feel bad for you? Was that the plan?"

"I—"

"Or better yet, when were you going to tell me that every fucking apartment you sold at the Harborside was linked to your father and his business?" Trina asked, her nostrils flaring in anger.

"I earned that last sale of the year on my own, like all the rest of them. I told you that. I thought we were past the baseless accusations stage." Kendall felt her temper flare. She hadn't come here for a fight.

"*Baseless*, that's a rich word choice considering I have mounting evidence a mile long to prove it," Trina said as she rolled her eyes. "I can't believe you turned out to be everything I thought you were."

"What evidence?" Kendall asked as she put her hands up, clearly missing something here. "What is going on? I came here tonight to talk to you and see if we could reconnect because I felt like I'd lost you somehow. And you're coming for me like you want blood."

"I don't want anything from you," Trina said, and Kendall felt like she meant it. "Not blood, sex, pity fundraiser money, none of it. You can keep it all. I'm done."

Trina started to close the door, but Kendall put her hand on it to stop it. "Wait."

Trina looked up at her with tears in her eyes as she asked, "When were you going to tell me that you were using me for sex, and that I was just a means to an end to win a competition that you already had stacked in your favor?"

"Trina, that's not true," Kendall replied, panicking. She had never seen Trina this upset, and she had no idea how it had come to this. She loved her. She would never intentionally hurt or use her.

"Which part? The part about how you cheated and lied to me? Or how you used me?" Trina asked as she straightened up.

"I didn't use you," Kendall answered. She needed Trina to know that. That's why she was here tonight. To tell her how she really felt about her.

"So you did cheat, then?" Trina challenged, using Kendall's own lack of an answer against her.

"I didn't cheat," Kendall replied, her frustration turning to anger again. Where was this coming from? "I didn't lie to you."

Trina wiped away a tear as she laughed, but it was an empty, hollow sound. "You're lying to me right now."

"I'm not." Kendall swore before asking, "Where are you getting all this information?"

"I didn't *get* anything. Nothing was *given* to me, Kendall. I'm sure that's something you can't understand," Trina spit back and every single word cut worse than the last. "The signs were all there: filthy little ant tracks of nepotism sprinkled throughout your sales history. Just go back and look for yourself. Your father's hand was in every single one of them. And I'll give you the benefit of the doubt here and take that look of shock as sincere and not just great acting, by breaking this to you real simply. You have achieved nothing without him. And you might be under the false notion that you have, but it's all a fucking lie. Just like the relationship I thought we had. I'm so mad at myself," Trina said, shaking her head. "I'm so fucking mad at the fool I've been, when I knew who you were from the start, and I ignored it. That's on me. I ignored the blinking red danger lights and the enormous, flapping red flag, and I let you into my life, and into my pants, like a fucking fool," Trina said as she stepped back.

"Trina," Kendall pleaded. "I'm not sure what you're talking about, but I'm sure we can figure it out. I just need you to back up a bit, slow down, let me catch up."

Trina sighed and pressed her palm to her forehead as she asked, "Why are you here?"

To tell you I love you. "To talk to you about us," she said instead, her head still swimming with the accusations Trina had unloaded on her.

"There is no *us*," Trina said as she dropped her hand from her face, and Kendall could see she was serious. "The chance at *us* ended when you lied to me about your past and about this competition."

"I don't know what you're—" Kendall tried, her heart breaking.

"You know, I really felt bad for you. I believed you when you told me about your father, and all the crazy shit that was going on. I believed you. I wanted it to be true because I was falling for you. And that's the biggest con of all. Because I was nothing more than collateral damage to you in this whole thing, huh?" Trina shook her head, not waiting for Kendall to reply. "Just go."

"Trina, wait, please," Kendall pleaded again.

"She asked you to leave." Lauren's voice sounded from behind her. She didn't bother to look.

"Trina," she tried again.

"Just go. The competition ends next week. Then I'll be through with you forever. And that day can't come soon enough." Trina turned and retreated back into her apartment before Kendall could get another word in.

Lauren stepped in front of her and shook her head. "I warned you not to fuck this up."

Kendall said nothing in return, because even though she had no idea what happened, she still felt guilty about it. And as Lauren slammed the door in her face, she realized that her worst nightmare had come to fruition: Trina Lee was over her, and there was no coming back from that.

CHAPTER TWENTY-NINE

Kendall had barely slept the last few nights going over her sales history. She started at the Harborside sales and went backward, and to her horror, Trina was right. Though not every sale had her father's stink on it, some of them did. But more upsetting than even that was Whitaker's connection to her father. She'd called a few old clients to confirm, but they all said the same thing. Whitaker was the bridge between her and her father. He was the one moving pieces for Dick. He'd betrayed her this whole time, and she'd had no idea.

Now that her lawyer had gotten back to her, and she'd started the process of protecting herself and her client connections, she was ready to confront Whitaker and end ties with him, immediately. If she could find him, that was. He hadn't returned her calls or texts, which was unusual considering how late in the day it was now.

She waited outside of Clyde's office for him to end his call.

He looked up at her with a smile. "Hey, Kendall. What's up?"

Kendall did her best to hide her seething rage. She trusted Clyde, mostly, but she didn't want to let on that something was wrong. "Have you seen Whitaker around today?"

"Hmm, I think he had an early cocktail meeting with an out of town friend," Clyde said as he shuffled some papers on his desk. "Yup, says here that he had a meeting with someone with the initials *D. Y.* near the Seaport"—he checked the paper again—"about two hours ago."

Kendall's stomach dropped. She would bet her life *D. Y.* was her father. "Thanks."

"Sure thing," Clyde replied. "Oh, the competition ends tomorrow, right? I hope everything works out for you."

Kendall laughed. She'd long forgotten about the competition.

That didn't matter anymore. The only thing that mattered now was distancing herself from Whitaker and clearing her name with Trina.

Trina. If Whitaker was involved, then her father certainly knew about Trina. Suddenly her anger toward Whitaker turned into fear. If her father had been puppeteering her life from afar, then he'd know about the competition and her primary competitor. And though she wasn't sure why he'd been helping her all along, she knew that he would see Trina as a threat. And he was unpredictable when he felt threatened.

She called Trina, hoping she might pick up, but it rang with no answer. She dialed her number again and again, but every time, it went to voice mail. She tried Trina's office as she raced to her car. She had to talk to her—she had to tell Trina that she was right and that her father was most likely in town. Because she wasn't sure what her father was capable of, and she didn't trust him.

"Hi, you've reached Gamble and Associates, this is Jax speaking, how may I help you?"

"Jax!" Kendall was relieved. "It's Kendall. Is Trina in the office today?"

There was a long pause.

"Jax, look, I know you probably know what's happening, and she was right. She was right all along, and I had no idea, but I can't find Whitaker and I think he might be with my dad. And my dad's a bad guy, Jax. Is she there? I need to talk to her."

Jax sighed. "Look, I heard about how generous you were at the fundraiser, and I'm a super romantic at heart, so I'm going to say this, but I didn't say it, okay? Because she would kill me if I told you anything about her."

"Okay." Kendall's heart was racing. She didn't know what to do or where to go. But the knowledge that her father was in the same city, probably with her duplicitous scoundrel of a boss, was making her feel jumpy.

"She's got a penthouse tour at the Harborside with one of Langley's connections. We're still waiting on the final info, but she's meeting him there shortly." She heard keystrokes in the background, Jax seemed to be on the computer.

"Who is she meeting?" Kendall put the car in drive and bolted in the direction of the Harborside. She'd wait there all night if she had to, but she wasn't going to let Trina go into any apartment tours today without warning her about her father first.

"Richard something," Jax said, before cursing. "Shit. Is that—?"

"You have to stop her from showing that penthouse, Jax. I'm headed there now." She disconnected the call and gripped the steering wheel so hard it hurt. She had to get to the Harborside before it was too late.

CHAPTER THIRTY

Trina wasn't in the mood to meet any new clients, and she especially wasn't in the mood to charm or schmooze anyone. But the competition was set to end tomorrow, and she would be remiss to skip out on a penthouse tour to a prospective buyer. Still, not having enough time for her team to vet this prospect before she met him made her uneasy.

Luckily, Victor was on the concierge desk tonight. She was happy to see the familiar face.

"Ms. Lee," he said with a smile. "I can't thank you enough for those Red Sox–Yankees tickets. My wife and boys are so excited. Me, too, obviously."

"Glad they'll be put to good use," Trina said. She called in a favor to get those tickets and the upgraded VIP package, but she was glad she did. Victor was a stand-up guy, and he'd always been good to her. It was the least she could do for him. "And remember, the boys will get some free swag, and you and your wife will have an open bar ticket for the first seven innings, so don't be late."

"Oh, we'll certainly be early, no worries about that," Victor replied, looking gleeful. "Is there anything I can do to thank you?"

Trina shook her head. "No. We're good, Victor."

He nodded before adding, "Another late night showing, huh?"

"It's the end of the line tomorrow. It's now or never. Plus, the penthouse is gorgeous at night, especially now that it's finished," Trina replied. She reached into her pocket for her cell, but it was missing. Shit. She'd left it in the car. Her head was a mess these days.

She thought about what he'd just asked her. "You know, I haven't met this client before. My team is vetting him now, but it was kind of a last-minute showing scheduled by Langley himself, and I left my cell in the car. Feel free to check in on me while we're up there, in case he turns out to be a creep." She was half kidding. These things usually worked out fine, but she wouldn't call herself very lucky lately, so better safe than sorry.

"You got it," Victor said as he sat up straighter. "I'll take you both up and hang around outside. Julio is on tonight, too. He can cover the desk."

"Great." Trina felt a little better knowing Victor would be around.

"How's the competition going? I haven't seen Ms. Yates around much. She hasn't been by this week at all," Victor said, making small talk.

"Like I said, it ends tomorrow. And I'm fine with that," Trina replied. She had no intention of seeing or talking about Kendall. It'd been a week since Kendall had shown up at her doorstep, and Trina still hadn't been able to shake the memory of Kendall's face. She'd looked shocked when Trina had told her that she knew about her father's influence on the sales outcomes. Her shock had turned to anger, and then more shock and disbelief. But the look of devastation on her face when Trina told her that she had used her and that it was over was the one that haunted her. Had Kendall really been in the dark about all this? That wasn't possible. And yet a very small part of Trina wanted to believe her reaction was sincere. Maybe it was.

"Hi, I'm here to meet Trina Lee," a male voice said from behind her.

Trina waited to see the expression on Victor's face before she turned around. He didn't seem bothered, so she wasn't going to be. "I'm Trina."

"It's nice to meet you," he said. He was tall and handsome. Trina estimated him to be in his mid to late sixties. He was dressed like he had money, and his athletic build implied he golfed more than worked. "I'm Richard."

"Hi, Richard." Trina shook his hand and was struck by a wave of déjà vu. There was something familiar about him. Like they'd met before. "So, I hear you're a personal friend of Mr. Langley's."

"Charles and I used to hang out when we were young and stupid. I'm looking for an investment property, and he's looking to finish off the building, I'm told. I was in town on short notice, so he's doing me a favor. I appreciate you meeting with me," he said. He was charming, in an inoffensive kind of way.

"Well, let's not waste any time. This is a big unit, and you'll want to take your time checking it out," she said. "Shall we?"

"Yes, let's." Richard motioned for her to lead the way. Trina heard a phone buzzing and saw him reach into his pocket. He cast a quick glance at it before silencing it.

"I'll take you up," Victor said as they walked toward the elevator. He radioed for Julio to cover the desk and waited for his reply before pressing the elevator button. He looked at Richard and said, "I'll need you to sign the log when we finish up, and we'll need a copy of your license for identification purposes."

"Sure, sounds good," Richard replied. The elevator started its upward trajectory, and he commented on the spaciousness of it. "This is a fancy elevator."

The soft vibrating hum from his pocket sounded again, but he ignored it, so Trina did, too.

"It's got top-of-the-line technology, plus live streamed news, business, entertainment, weather, and more. The panel has all sorts of options to make your ride more enjoyable." Trina repeated the phrase she'd used for most of the competition. "That being said, it's highly efficient, so hopefully you'll reach your destination before you realize you're bored." And right on cue, the doors opened to the penthouse floor.

Victor took them to the door and let them in, staying in the kitchen as Trina filled Richard in on the specs. The penthouse was gorgeous, and now that it was complete, she could finally see Zander's vision in place. The night was clear and the air warm, but not hot. Tonight was the perfect night to look out over the balcony and down onto the harbor and her favorite views of the city. She weaved through the apartment, ending with the balcony tour, because this was the money shot. This was the multi-million-dollar view and entertaining space.

"So, are you only in Boston for this business venture? Or do you have family here?" Trina always asked about relatives—that's where most of her referrals came from.

"Business for now, but maybe if I like it, I'll stick around." He looked her over and smirked. "I have a daughter in Boston. I'm sure she'll be ecstatic to hear I've decided to make a new home here."

"It's nice to be close to family," Trina replied.

Richard nodded, but said nothing.

"So, the last stop on tonight's tour is the outdoor living space. Here, let me," Trina said as she opened the panoramic doors and slid them into the wall, doubling the living room size and removing the glass separation between the indoor and outdoor spaces. Richard stepped out onto the terrace and walked toward the elaborately staged rooftop patio, taking in the sights. Trina watched him for a moment before looking out at the water. This view brought her so many painful memories. She looked down at her feet and realized she was standing in the spot where Kendall almost went off the balcony. That was the first time she'd felt sparks between them. They'd had chemistry from the start, and though their coffee date kicked things off, that night on the balcony was when Trina had seen a different side of Kendall. She'd felt like something had clicked between them. That night set off a chain of events that led her to this moment.

She looked back out at the dark lapping waves of the harbor below. She could see the park bench where Kendall cried so freely when she shared her life story with her, and to her left, she could see the hotel where she'd loved Kendall so passionately that she had never wanted the night to end. And yet here, at the site of their first physical contact and connection, what should have been pleasant memories were only sad, painful ones. She wanted to be done with this place, so she could put it and Kendall behind her.

"I have to say, this is more impressive than even the pictures do justice. And I know Charles doesn't skimp on marketing," Richard said, looking pleased.

"It's truly a one in a million kind of property," Trina said. "Everything you could ever want or need is in walking distance, and the view is unbeatable. I'm sure you'd have no trouble making a profit on this unit."

"You don't have to convince me—I'm sold," Richard said with his arms opened wide. "This will do nicely. I'll move in immediately, and I'm sure my daughter will be thrilled."

Trina almost didn't believe her ears. "That's great. Do you have any questions?"

"No, I think the stat sheet you gave me will suffice. I'll work with Charles on expediting this. I'd like to get this contracted and purchased as quickly as possible. I intend to buy with cash, so hopefully that isn't an issue for him," Richard replied as his phone rang, and he checked the screen. A wicked grin spread on his face as he silenced it.

"Do you need to get that? I can wait." Trina was being polite. She didn't want to wait, but he was offering to buy the penthouse, so she'd at least be polite. Plus, whoever was calling seemed insistent, since she'd heard the vibrating hum at least a dozen times since the lobby.

"No need. She had her chance, but she blew it. You have my

undivided attention." Something about the way he said that made her uncomfortable.

"Did you say you'd be moving in?"

"Right away."

Trina paused. Something he said had caught her attention. "I thought you said this was an investment property."

"It will be," Richard said, as he followed her into the main area. Trina noticed Victor still hovering in the kitchen, and she smiled at him. "But I'll live here until I find a good income source to rent it to."

"That's the best way to do it, I suppose," Trina replied as she headed toward the kitchen island to retrieve her purse, "and a pretty fabulous compromise, living in the utmost luxury for an extended period until you find a way to make a bigger profit on your investment."

"I like to think of it more as a wise business strategy. I'm not a fan of compromise. I've always felt that compromising meant you had to give something up," he replied, and Trina's blood ran cold.

Trina turned to face him, taking in his appearance more closely.

"What did you say your daughter's name was?" Trina asked, realizing what it was about him that was so familiar. It was his eyes. They were nearly the same shade of green she'd lost herself in so many nights over these past few months.

"I didn't," Richard replied, and Trina noticed his expression change. The friendliness from before was fading. He looked inconvenienced by her question.

"Right, my mistake. I'll have my office send along all the required paperwork," Trina said, eager to get out of there. She stepped toward Victor, not trusting Dick Yates now that she'd experienced what Kendall had warned about. "If you have any further questions, please don't hesitate to call."

"I will," he replied with a sickly sweet smile that made Trina shudder.

"Great, so if you're ready, we'll head out." Trina motioned for the door when Victor's walkie-talkie squeaked, and it made her jump.

"Something making you uneasy, Trina?" Richard asked, and suddenly, everything about him felt like a threat.

"Nope, just a long day," Trina lied. "The coffee must be wearing off."

Richard took a step toward her, his voice low as he said, "I guess I expected you to be more of a presence. The way I hear it, you're quite the Realtor."

Trina raised an eyebrow at him, feeling emboldened. She didn't like being intimidated. "And who told you that? Kendall or Whitaker?"

"Ah, there it is," Richard smiled. "You're bright. You're attractive, and you've got a great style—I'll give you that. I guess I was surprised that Kendall has struggled putting you down. But that's only because you hadn't shown me your teeth yet."

Trina wanted to show him a hell of a lot more than her teeth, but she knew she should tread lightly. Kendall had warned her that he had a temper.

"Why did you ask me to show you the property when you could have just had your pawn file the paperwork for you?" Trina's mouth got the better of her.

"Kendall, you mean?" Richard laughed and the sound disgusted her. "Kendall is useless. She can't do a damn thing without me paving the way for her. She'd probably find a way to screw this up." He surveyed her with curiosity. "I know all about your little bet. She didn't deserve my help because she obviously didn't capitalize on it. She deserves to lose. You're guaranteed to win now, right? Why jeopardize a home run by asking a stupid question?"

She scowled. "Who told you about the bet, I wonder? Must have been Whitaker, right? Langley probably doesn't care. And Kendall hates you, so she's not talking."

That got him. "She hates me, huh? Ungrateful bitch. I'm going to love being back in her life again. Boston is a small city. We'll find all sorts of ways to run into each other now. I can't wait to see the look on her face when we do."

Trina snarled at his thinly veiled threat against Kendall. Victor was speaking into the receiver, seemingly oblivious to the exchange. Trina wanted to kick him to get his attention. When he finally looked up, Richard made the first move.

"I think we're done here," Richard said with a false smile now that Victor was paying attention. He stepped toward her with his hand extended. "I'll expect a call this evening. My lawyers are waiting for the required documents. Let's not dillydally. I have a new life to cultivate here."

Trina squinted at his extended hand and laughed at him. "You're every bit the asshole she said you were. She might have undersold it, actually."

Richard dropped his hand as his expression turned to one of anger.

Trina noticed the darkness in his green eyes looked like a raging storm about the erupt.

"That's awfully bold of you." His reply was laced with fury as he stepped toward her. Trina felt like he was about to bubble over.

"Step away from her," Kendall called out from the door Trina desperately wanted to be exiting from.

Richard looked up at his daughter and his grin was maniacal. "Got tired of me sending you to voice mail, huh? It's rather infuriating, isn't it?"

Seeing that he was distracted, Trina took the opportunity to step back, putting some distance between them. Finally, Victor seemed to pick up on the signals and he stepped forward. But Kendall was charging toward her father faster than any one of them could react, and in what seemed like five steps, she was in his face.

"You son of a bitch," Kendall hissed. "They should have left you to rot in jail."

"Is that any way to talk to your dear father after he's decided to move closer to you to be a family again?" Richard taunted her. "I know you've missed me. I see you still can't succeed, even with my help, not that you would have accepted it had you known. You're such a disappointment. You can't even be spoon-fed properly."

"I'm the disappointment?" Kendall laughed. "You're the moron who got caught, Dad. Good luck trying to salvage your legacy with a criminal record."

Richard scowled and lunged for Kendall, grabbing her arm, and jerking her toward him.

"Kendall!" Trina called out, but Victor stopped her from getting to them. She could feel the hot tears on her face, but she felt helpless to stop them.

"Let go of her." Victor had his hand at his hip as he stepped forward.

Richard glared at Kendall before looking back at Trina. A realization crossed his face, and he released Kendall with a shove, casting her into the kitchen island with a thud.

"You're pathetic," he growled at Kendall. "Another example of shitting where you sleep. Did you learn nothing from Collette? It's no wonder you've struggled to win this competition. You've been distracted by another pretty girl. You're a loser. Without me you'd be nothing, and clearly your time on your own has done nothing to change that."

"Fuck you," Kendall said. The anger on Kendall's face mirrored her father's, but Trina noted that only Kendall's face also revealed pain.

Trina was half aware of Victor on the walkie-talkie when she interjected, "You're a garbage human being, Dick. Did anyone ever tell you that? And you're not as charming as you think, scumbag."

Richard gave her a look, dismissing her with a wave. "Words from a fly mean nothing."

The door to the unit opened and Julio led two police officers from the Boston PD into the penthouse. Victor must have radioed for help when Richard grabbed Kendall, but Trina had been too freaked out to notice.

As the officers approached, Trina found the courage to bite back. "Well, this fly has a lot to say about being a witness to you assaulting your daughter. I'm sure that will go over well since you were just released from jail."

The next series of events passed in a blur with Dick Yates being led out in handcuffs. To her surprise, he didn't put up a fight. In fact, after she'd mentioned the jail thing, he stopped talking altogether. Evidently, he realized he was screwed. Either way, Trina couldn't wait to get out of there.

She gave her statement to the police and was almost to her car in the parking garage with Victor as her escort when Kendall caught up to her.

"Trina, wait," Kendall called out, and Trina stopped, not because she had any real desire to, but maybe because she was still in shock about what had just transpired.

Victor gave her a concerned look, but she smiled at him. "I'm good, this is fine, thanks. I'll be fine from here."

"You sure?" he asked.

"I'm sure." Trina surveyed Kendall briefly. "She won't hurt me."

Victor laughed, not understanding the irony of her comment, since just seeing Kendall hurt her. "All right. Good night, Ms. Lee."

Trina sighed as he walked away, and she turned toward her car, the only one in the garage on this floor. It was ominous and lonely, much like how this whole night felt.

"Trina," Kendall said, and Trina felt so very tired.

"Yes?" She didn't bother to turn. She didn't want to see Kendall's face. She knew she would falter if she did.

"Did he hurt you?" Her voice sounded small.

"No." Not physically anyway, but the Yates family sure seemed to emotionally scar her plenty.

"I'm so sorry, I—" Kendall started but stopped. The garage was so empty everything sounded amplified, so when Kendall stepped closer, the sounds of her nervous breaths coming short and fast were deafening.

"Don't. It's okay," Trina said, wanting nothing more than to be in her car and driving far away from this place and far away from Kendall.

Kendall's fingers found hers, and she allowed them to be intertwined because even though she couldn't bring herself to look at Kendall, there was something comforting about feeling her hand in hers again, even if just for this moment.

Kendall squeezed her hand as she stepped closer again, and this time Trina could feel the heat coming off her body. She closed her eyes at the sensation, and her body shook with want and pain and sadness.

"Kendall," she pleaded. "Just let me go."

Kendall's grip on her hand loosened but her fingers caressed Trina's for a moment as she said, "When I came by your place, before everything fell apart, I came to tell you I loved you. And that I couldn't do anything without thinking about you, and that my heart missed you when you weren't there. I love you, Trina. And there is so much we need to discuss and so much I have to figure out. But that part I know for sure. And I am so, so sorry it took me so long to tell you that."

Trina managed to hold the tears in until Kendall pressed a soft kiss to the side of her head, her fingers finally slipping away.

Trina turned and grabbed Kendall's hand, pulling her back. "You don't get to tell me you love me without looking me in the eye, Kendall. That's not how this works."

Kendall nodded, and Trina was surprised to see that she, too, was crying. Kendall cupped her jaw and held her face as she repeated, "I love you. And I'm so, so sorry. About everything. But not about being in love with you."

Trina closed her eyes and leaned in to Kendall's touch. She took a shaky breath and opened her eyes to find Kendall watching her closely, cradling her face like she was the most precious thing in the world, and Trina ached to be held by her.

But she wasn't ready. She couldn't do that again.

Trina leaned forward and pressed a delicate kiss to Kendall's lips before stepping back. "I can't, Kendall. I'm not, I—" Trina sighed. The look on Kendall's face was breaking her heart all over again. "I need time."

Kendall nodded as she wiped at the tears on her cheeks. "Okay, I understand."

Trina reached out and took Kendall's hand once more before she slipped into her car and drove away crying, with Kendall in her rearview.

CHAPTER THIRTY-ONE

The few weeks following the end of the competition had been full of excitement, but Trina felt numb to most of it.

Whitaker Sharkney was found bruised and battered outside of the restaurant where he'd met Dick Yates. Supposedly they'd argued when he found out Dick wasn't going to help Kendall win the competition but planned to give it to Trina instead, as punishment for Kendall failing him.

Dick Yates was arrested for two counts of assault and was shipped back to Connecticut to await sentencing while on house arrest. His assets were frozen when it became obvious that he was trying to hide money in business investments as a hedge against the bankruptcy the civil suits against him all but promised.

The final penthouse at the Harborside remained unsold, but the competition had ended, and Trina was the winner by a narrow margin. Though it seemed like that outcome was the least important thing that had happened.

Kendall quit Whitaker's firm, and the truth of his connection to her father came to light. The rumor was that when he'd reached out to see if Kendall was related to Dick, they struck up a secret partnership that was mutually beneficial. Dick would get inside information on Kendall's successes, failures, and whereabouts, and Whitaker became a major shareholder in some of Dick's more successful ventures. Trina wasn't so sure those ventures would prosper now that Dick was likely going back to jail, but she gave little thought to Whitaker. She'd never liked him, and now she had a reason to loathe him.

As the full scope of Dick's failed plans became clear, it appeared that he'd planned to use Kendall's successes to reinvigorate his own career and rebrand himself in Boston. Whitaker was supposed to be part of that grand plan as well, but none of it ended up panning out. When Kendall blew him off after his release from prison, he decided to take what he could from her, tipping the competition scales in favor of Trina, while establishing residency in Boston at the same time. In his sick fantasy, Kendall would lose and realize how much she needed him, and he would rule supreme in a new zip code. The guy was fucked in the head.

Trina tried, but she couldn't stop thinking about Kendall and what had transpired between them. Kendall had respected her wishes and gone quiet. The only reason she knew Kendall had left Whitaker's firm was through professional gossip. She heard whispers that she was currently using another firm as a base, but that she was probably looking to go out on her own. Which made sense since that was Kendall's plan all along. Staying with Whitaker was never her endgame.

But, oh, how she missed her. She wondered if she would stay in Boston, or go back to Connecticut now that her father had effectively been neutered. What would keep her here now? A part of Trina wanted Kendall to always be just a short drive away, in case she was ever able to overcome her fear of being hurt again. She wanted to be with Kendall, she just didn't know how. Not after everything that had happened. They felt too broken to be fixed.

"Trina," Ellison said with a knock on her office doorframe.

"Oh, hey," Trina said, realizing that she had been staring off into space, lost in her memories of Kendall.

"Do you have a minute? I need to talk to you about something," Ellison said, and Trina waved her in.

"Sure." Trina sat up straighter, and that's when she noticed the gift in Ellison's arms. "What's that?"

"That's what I want to talk to you about." Ellison perched herself on the couch in Trina's office and motioned for her to join her.

Trina walked around her desk and settled next to her boss, her eyes on the ornately wrapped gift. It was huge, almost too large for Ellison to comfortably hold, and Ellison was tall, tall like Kendall. Trina sighed. Everything reminded her of Kendall.

Ellison placed the gift on the floor and patted Trina's knee. "I want to tell you something, and I realize you might have feelings about what I have to say, and I'm going to listen to them as both your boss and as your friend. So feel free to be as candid as you'd like. There will be no repercussions here."

"That sounds like you're giving me a pass to swear. Why are we suddenly okay with swearing?" Trina asked, intrigued.

"We're not. But we both know if I put a moratorium on swearing around here, Lauren would be forever silent," Ellison said and Trina laughed.

"That's fair," Trina replied, imagining her bestie trying to censor herself and failing miserably.

"Okay, I want you to hear this from me before you hear it from anyone else," Ellison said with a short pause. "Kendall is working with Gamble and Associates temporarily until she figures out her next step."

Trina didn't know what to say to that, but she wasn't sure swearing would make her feel any better.

"She'll never be in the office, she isn't formally coming on as an employee, and you'll never have to see her, ever. We're just going to help her manage the sales she had in flux until she finds a place to land," Ellison added.

"Why?" Trina asked, not because she was offended by Kendall still having a way to earn an income, but more because she didn't understand Ellison's motives.

Ellison gave her a small smile. "So many things have happened in the past few months, and I would be remiss to ignore my part in them. A large part of me feels responsible for how things went down between you two, because I could see the spark at the awards ceremony. I could see that if you two were brought together, not as rivals, but as partners, you would be unstoppable. And the business owner in me saw that as a great asset. Whitaker could never have housed Kendall—he doesn't have it in him to foster and promote success. He's too greedy. I knew it would be a matter of time before she dropped him, and quite honestly, I was hoping she'd join our ranks.

"But then it became apparent that other forces were at work, and suddenly a competition designed to make you successful and open up the door to inviting Kendall to join our team got twisted into something rather ugly. I had no idea that Langley had any connections to Dick Yates, and I certainly didn't know Whitaker was working as a double agent for him. I never would have put you in that position, ever. Because as much as I'm your boss, I also consider you a friend. And that matters to me more than our business relationship," Ellison said, and Trina could tell she meant it. Ellison had never minced words with her. It was one of the reasons she liked working with her so much—she let Trina be who she was and encouraged that. She never stifled her.

"Thank you," Trina said.

Ellison nodded. "From the bottom of my heart, if my decision to take on this challenge with Whitaker negatively impacted your life, then I'm sorry. I never meant for any of this to get out of hand, but I suppose this is a lesson on the best laid plans."

"Yeah, well, thank you for that, too," Trina said. "Can I be candid for a moment?"

"I hope you will be," Ellison replied.

"I'm not mad about the competition. I never was. And I'm glad you took the risk even though it didn't turn out the way I expected it to, because we still won, and because of those sales, I've been able to expand my portfolio and help Lauren and Jax establish a more stable footing of their own. And yeah, maybe I fell in love with Kendall and got my heart stomped on, but that's okay, too. Because maybe I needed to be brought back down to earth a little," Trina said, feeling like a weight was lifted from her shoulders. She had regrets, sure, but taking on this challenge was not one of them. So many wonderful things had come out of this, and she wouldn't trade those for anything.

"Good." Ellison briefly touched her knee again before adding, "Because winning isn't everything. And though I want you to beat everyone and be the best because I already think you are, that's not the point. The point is, we all need each other sometimes, and for Kendall, that time is now. So Kendall is working with us for the time being, but I will make sure she doesn't cross your path, ever. Because you are my first priority, okay?"

"Thanks," Trina said, sitting a little taller. "I appreciate you telling me."

"It's the least I could do," Ellison said as she stood. "Oh, one last thing."

"Yes?" Trina asked, her gaze finding the present on the floor again.

"This is from Kendall. She said it's for Henry's Zhua Zhou. She asked me to bring it to you but wanted me to preface it with this," Ellison reached into her pocket and handed Trina a small note. "Hopefully, that's okay, too."

"Uh, sure, yes. Thanks," Trina replied, anxious to read the note.

"I'll leave you to it," Ellison said before departing.

Trina looked at the envelope in her hand. It was plain white but a heavy stock. She opened it to find Kendall's script on a small note card. She smiled at the message.

This is for Henry: for completing his first year around the sun, for being the second best cuddler I know, and for dancing with me in your apartment, with no music needed. I loved my time with him. Thank you for sharing him with me.
    PS: I miss you.

Trina stood from the couch and looked at the box, wondering what could possibly be inside. It was enormous. She wanted to open it, just to see, but it had been wrapped with such care, she didn't dare. Would she give it to him? Of course. But she was certainly curious about it.

She walked back to her desk with the note in hand. She propped it up against a photo she had of her brother and his family and reread it a dozen times before she reached for her phone and texted Kendall a simple note of her own: *I miss you, too.*

❖

The next day, the flowers started showing up. Throughout the workday, florists from all over dropped off bouquets of red and pink flowers and bursting arrangements of bright colors all addressed to Trina with the same message: *With love, Kendall.*

By the third day, the flowers started showing up at her home, too. These were grander than before, in massive vases that had to be wheeled up on trolleys. These flowers were more intimate—long-stemmed red roses wrapped in elegant ribbons, each one tended to with care. The note with these changed slightly: *Love, Kendall.*

And on the fifth day, after an entire week of three to four deliveries a day between her home and office, the largest arrangement yet arrived at her apartment. It was almost as long as her kitchen counter, an overflowing, multilayered picture of perfection filled with red roses and vibrant pink tulips, complemented with dashes of white and yellow intermixed throughout. The ornate greenery spilled out of the stone base and tickled her marble countertop. Once it was out of the packaging and on full display, it looked like an entire garden had sprouted out of her island. The arrangement was massive and gorgeous and smelled incredible. But the note that came with it was what made her smile the most. Because it said, simply: *I love you. Kendall.*

That was when she finally decided to make the call she'd wanted to make all along.

"Hello?" Kendall's voice sounded hopeful.

"I got your flowers," Trina said.

"Oh," Kendall replied. "They're just a small token of my affection, that's all."

"This is your idea of small, huh?" Trina smiled into the receiver. "Just like Henry's birthday gift?"

"Well, in that instance, I didn't know what to get him, so I bought one of everything in the store that had his recommended age on it." Kendall laughed. "But with regard to your flowers, yeah, that's my idea of small."

"I can't wait to see your idea of grand," Trina replied, meaning that.

"Let me show you," Kendall said, and her voice was full of promise.

"Maybe we should start with dinner first," Trina reasoned as the butterflies in her stomach somersaulted. "If you're interested in that."

"Very." Kendall's response came quickly. "When?"

"Tomorrow?"

"I'll bring the food."

"All right," Trina replied, as nervous excitement took over her body.

"I can't wait," Kendall said and Trina felt the same way.

❖

Trina second-guessed her outfit for the umpteenth time as she checked the mirror in the hall. Kendall was due to arrive here at any moment, and she was so, so nervous. She'd contemplated meeting Kendall out somewhere in public, so they could talk, and there wouldn't be any pressure to do more than that, but when Kendall offered to bring dinner by her place, Trina easily caved. Because the truth was, she wanted to have privacy when she and Kendall talked. And she wanted to be here, where she felt safest and most secure, when that time came. And as the doorbell rang, announcing Kendall's arrival, Trina realized that time was now.

She opened the door to find Kendall standing there with a single long-stemmed red rose. And not just any rose—this was the most perfect rose she had ever seen. The luscious red petals were opened just enough to display all of the seemingly endless layers of velvety soft color. And when held by the woman who held her heart, it was an image Trina hoped to remember forever.

"Is that for me?" she asked as she leaned against the doorframe.

Kendall gave her a flirtatious smile as she said, "Something small to add to your collection."

"Oh, I definitely have a collection these days," Trina said, not moving from the spot. She was enjoying taking in Kendall's appearance. Kendall was dressed in comfortable jeans paired with fashionable high-heeled boots, but she had on that super soft shirt from the last time they'd had dinner here together. Trina remembered the way it felt in her hands and against her naked skin. She wanted to feel those things again. "I've had to gift some of them, just so I could maneuver through my office and apartment."

"And did that make the recipients smile?" Kendall asked, and she looked scrumptious.

"It did," Trina confirmed.

"And did the flowers make you smile when they were delivered?" Kendall asked.

"They did."

"Then it sounds like you got just the right amount, and one more wouldn't hurt," Kendall said as she extended the rose toward Trina. "Can I come in?"

Trina accepted the flower and brought it to her nose as she stepped back, ushering Kendall into her home. The simple ease of it also felt like an invitation back into her heart, and the look on Kendall's face told her she hoped that was the case.

Kendall slipped off her boots and placed the takeout dinner bag on the tiny edge of counter that was not consumed by the island garden. Trina watched as she walked over to the sink and washed her hands before pulling two wineglasses out of the cabinet next to the sink. Trina didn't expect her to remember where everything was, but she did, moving seamlessly between cabinets and drawers with comfortable ease.

Kendall looked back at the island while holding all the plates and utensils and gave Trina a frown. "We might have to eat elsewhere. I'm not sure I could see you over this if I sat across from you."

Trina laughed as she placed her single rose into a tall antique vase her grandmother had given her. "Couch?" she suggested, and Kendall was already en route, setting up the meal.

Trina sat on the couch, by the chaise, watching Kendall fuss over this and that. On Kendall's third pass into the kitchen to grab napkins, Trina reached out and took her hand.

"It's fine," Trina assured her, touched by how nervous Kendall seemed.

Kendall stopped, looking down at their hands. "Are you sure?"

"I'm sure," Trina said, not completely sure if they were talking about the same thing. But it was fine, all of it. Because Kendall was here, looking at her like she was the world, and Trina wanted that more than anything. More than the right number of napkins, or a glass of water to accompany her wine, or even twenty bouquets of flowers. What she wanted was right here, in front of her, looking at her like she was everything. And in that moment, she felt like she was.

"Sit. Eat with me." Trina patted the cushion next to her and Kendall joined her.

"How have you been?" Kendall asked as she served them both.

"Fine." Trina shrugged. That wasn't true. "Not so fine, actually."

"Oh?" Kendall asked. "Why's that?"

Trina twirled her fork in the pad thai and took a bite before answering. "I've been thinking a lot about you and us, and about how things ended. And I need to tell you something."

Kendall's full fork hovered near her mouth. "Okay." She lowered it back to the plate.

"You should eat," Trina said as she nudged her hand. "What I have to say doesn't have an expiration date on it. The freshness of this meal does."

Kendall looked at her warily before taking a too large bite. "Okay. I've eaten. What do you need to tell me?"

Trina laughed and wiped a stray noodle off the edge of Kendall's bottom lip with her thumb. She let her hand linger there, just because she'd missed touching her. "I'm sorry."

"About what?" Kendall's eyes were expressive.

"About not believing you. About casting you out of my life like you didn't have any emotional investment in us. About treating you like you didn't love me as much as I loved you." She motioned toward the greenhouse of flowers around them. "Clearly, I was wrong about that."

"What are you saying?" Kendall looked hopeful.

"I love you, Kendall. Do you know that?" Trina asked.

Kendall exhaled, her eyes filling with tears. And Trina wanted to kiss the bottom lip that trembled, but she felt like Kendall had something to say, so she settled for holding the hands that rested on her knees.

"I hoped so," Kendall replied, her voice soft. "But I would understand if you didn't."

"I do, though, so you don't have to worry," Trina said, rubbing her thumbs across Kendall's knuckles. "That's why I was so hurt. Because I loved you so much. And it felt awful to lose you."

Kendall shook her head. "You didn't lose me. I didn't betray you, Trina. I didn't, I swear. I had no idea about any of it."

"I know." Now it was Trina's turn to sigh. Once the Whitaker connection had been fully revealed, it was clear how he'd manipulated the situation. Kendall ended up being an innocent victim in it all.

"I think about that last night at the penthouse a lot." When she'd gotten to her car that night, her phone was full of texts and voice mails from her friends and Kendall. Each of them warned her that their vetting check showed that Dick Yates might be the client waiting for her. Each message was filled with love and concern for her safety. But Kendall's message broke her heart, because the sobbing and panic was so real. Kendall was worried about her safety, and she kept repeating over and over, *Please pick up, please. You don't know what he is capable of, please, please.* "You tried to warn me, even when I'd shunned you. You still tried to save me."

"You stopped me from launching off a building once. It was the least I could do," Kendall teased, as Trina moved their forgotten plates to the table in front of them.

"Still, you were braver than I was. Because when I felt hurt, I pushed you away. But you didn't abandon me when you thought I might need you." Trina felt like she'd dodged a bullet that night, but when she'd left Kendall in that garage, she'd left a piece of her heart with her. "You showed up. I didn't give you that same courtesy. And for that, I'm sorry."

Kendall let out a heavy exhale and her bottom lip trembled again. "Thank you."

Trina reached for her, caressing her cheek, and Kendall looked at her with eyes wet and heart wide open.

"Come here," she said, cupping her face. "I love you. I'm in love with you, and what I really want is to feel your lips on mine and your arms holding me close while you tell me you love me, over and over, all night long. Is that okay with you?"

Kendall smiled as she leaned in, kissing her lips and pressing her back onto the couch. Kendall shifted them both to spread out on the chaise as she laughed into each kiss until the kissing got to be too much for laughter and unnecessary breaths. And Trina couldn't kiss her enough. She couldn't taste her enough. She couldn't feel her enough. So she broke their kiss and stroked Kendall's face as she admitted, "Nothing is going to feel like enough right now, so maybe we should eat dinner first, so I don't have to think about stopping once I get started."

"I love you," Kendall said, looking down at her. "And I love that idea."

"And I love you," Trina replied with a soft kiss to her lips. "And I hate that idea, but you went to all this trouble, so the least I can do is entertain a little dinner with you—"

"Until dessert," Kendall supplied, her hand finding its way under Trina's loose-fitting shirt.

"Until then." Trina nodded, biting her lip as Kendall's hand slid higher.

"That is, unless you can't wait." Kendall's lips found her earlobe just as her hand palmed her breast over her bra.

Trina moaned, turning her head to catch Kendall's lips. "Oh, I can wait. I just don't know if I want to."

"Really?" Kendall challenged as her hand abandoned Trina's chest in favor of slipping below the waistband of her pants. "Are you sure you can wait?"

Trina's hips bucked up at the sensation of Kendall's fingers toying with her panties. She teased, "You want to bet against me?"

Kendall brought their lips back together in a passionate kiss that took Trina's breath away before saying, "Nope, I learned that lesson a long time ago. I'll never bet against you again."

"Good," Trina said as she halted Kendall's hand from getting to where she wanted it most. "How about a rain check on dinner then?"

"Yes," Kendall said, her eyes dark with the want Trina felt all over her body.

"Then grab some of those roses over there, and let's cover the bed in petals while you show me that dessert first was the right idea," Trina said as she shifted out from under the wonderful pressure of Kendall's body without concern of missing it because she knew she'd feel it again in moments on her king-sized bed.

"Promise me I'll get to taste you when I do," Kendall said, and the vision of Kendall's mouth on her sex made Trina practically run to the bed.

"I wouldn't have it any other way."

About the Author

Fiona Riley was born and raised in New England, where she is a medical professional and part-time professor when she isn't bonding with her laptop over words. She went to college in Boston and never left, starting a small business that takes up all of her free time, much to the dismay of her ever patient and lovely wife. When she pulls herself away from her work, she likes to catch up on the contents of her ever-growing DVR or spend time by the ocean with her favorite people.

Fiona's love for writing started at a young age and blossomed after she was published in a poetry competition at the ripe old age of twelve. She wrote lots of short stories and poetry for many years until it was time for college and a "real job." Fiona found herself with a bachelor's, a doctorate, and a day job, but felt like she had stopped nurturing the one relationship that had always made her feel the most complete: artist, dreamer, writer.

A series of bizarre events afforded her with some unexpected extra time and she found herself reaching for her favorite blue notebook to write, never looking back.

Contact Fiona and check for updates on all her new adventures at:
Twitter: @fionarileyfic
Facebook: Fiona Riley Fiction
Website: http://www.fionarileyfiction.com/
Email: fionarileyfiction@gmail.com

Books Available From Bold Strokes Books

Bet Against Me by Fiona Riley. In the high-stakes luxury real estate market, everything has a price, and as rival Realtors Trina Lee and Kendall Yates find out, that means their hearts and souls, too. (978-1-63555-729-9)

Broken Reign by Sam Ledel. Together on an epic journey in search of a mysterious cure, a princess and a village outcast must overcome life-threatening challenges and their own prejudice if they want to survive. (978-1-63555-739-8)

Just One Taste by CJ Birch. For Lauren, it only took one taste to start trusting in love again. (978-1-63555-772-5)

Lady of Stone by Barbara Ann Wright. Sparks fly as a magical emergency forces a noble embarrassed by her ability to submit to a low-born teacher who resents everything about her. (978-1-63555-607-0)

Last Resort by Angie Williams. Katie and Rhys are about to find out what happens when you meet the girl of your dreams but you aren't looking for a happily ever after. (978-1-63555-774-9)

Longing for You by Jenny Frame. When Debrek housekeeper Katie Brekman is attacked amid a burgeoning vampire-witch war, Alexis Villiers must go against everything her clan believes in to save her. (978-1-63555-658-2)

Money Creek by Anne Laughlin. Clare Lehane is a troubled lawyer from Chicago who tries to make her way in a rural town full of secrets and deceptions. (978-1-63555-795-4)

Passion's Sweet Surrender by Ronica Black. Cam and Blake are unable to deny their passion for each other, but surrendering to love is a whole different matter. (978-1-63555-703-9)

The Holiday Detour by Jane Kolven. It will take everything going wrong to make Dana and Charlie see how right they are for each other. (978-1-63555-720-6)

Too Hot to Ride by Andrews & Austin. World-famous cutting horse champion and industry legend Jane Barrow is knockdown sexy in the way she moves, talks, and rides, and Rae Starr is determined not to get involved with this womanizing gambler. (978-1-63555-776-3)

A Love that Leads to Home by Ronica Black. For Carla Sims and Janice Carpenter, home isn't about location, it's where your heart is. (978-1-63555-675-9)

Blades of Bluegrass by D. Jackson Leigh. A US Army occupational therapist must rehab a bitter veteran who is a ticking political time bomb the military is desperate to disarm. (978-1-63555-637-7)

Hopeless Romantic by Georgia Beers. Can a jaded wedding planner and an optimistic divorce attorney possibly find a future together? (978-1-63555-650-6)

Hopes and Dreams by PJ Trebelhorn. Movie theater manager Riley Warren is forced to face her high school crush and tormentor, wealthy socialite Victoria Thayer, at their twentieth reunion. (978-1-63555-670-4)

In the Cards by Kimberly Cooper Griffin. Daria and Phaedra are about to discover that love finds a way, especially when powers outside their control are at play. (978-1-63555-717-6)

Moon Fever by Ileandra Young. SPEAR agent Danika Karson must clear her werewolf friend of multiple false charges while teaching her vampire girlfriend to resist the blood mania brought on by a full moon. (978-1-63555-603-2)

Serenity by Jesse J. Thoma. For Kit Marsden, there are many things in life she cannot change. Serenity is in the acceptance. (978-1-63555-713-8)

Sylver and Gold by Michelle Larkin. Working feverishly to find a killer before he strikes again, Boston homicide detective Reid Sylver and rookie cop London Gold are blindsided by their chemistry and developing attraction. (978-1-63555-611-7)